PRAISE FO[illegible]S OF CE[illegible]IA TAN

TAKING THE LEAD

"Veteran Tan kicks her Secrets of a Rock Star series off with a sultry start... With a satisfying plot and an engaging cast of characters, the only thing slowing readers down will be their refractory period."

—*Publishers Weekly* (starred review)

"4 stars! An emotional whirlwind romance. Axel is as strong and sexy as readers expect in a rock-star hero without being an overly brooding jerk. The length he goes in order to win over emotionally closed-off Ricki will melt your heart."

—*RT Book Reviews*

SLOW SATISFACTION

"Cecilia Tan has a way to seduce you into her stories... you can't put her books down because she's that great a storyteller."

—RakesofRomance.com

"*Slow Satisfaction* is everything I expected it to be. The perfect closing of the curtains to a story that had a fantastic ending."

—SinfulReads.com

"This couple always finds new and interesting ways to raise the heat index."

—*RT Book Reviews*

SLOW SEDUCTION

"The sex scenes here are once again as hot as they are imaginative."

—*RT Book Reviews*

"5 stars! *Slow Seduction* was a tasty treat to say the least. I cannot wait to get my hands on book three. If you are looking for erotica, stop whatever you are doing and get this book."

—DivasDailyBookblog.wordpress.com

SLOW SURRENDER

"4½ stars! This is the BDSM novel all the other millionaire dom heroes want to star in. Tan takes an overused trope and turns it into a dreamy, erotic fantasy that draws the reader down the rabbit hole along with Karina. The sex scenes are lush and erotic . . . Readers will be clamoring for the next book in the series."

—*RT Book Reviews*

"Move over, EL James. Cecilia Tan's *Slow Surrender* is sinfully sweet and sublimely erotic. As with sipping a superb single-malt scotch served neat, you'll savor the slow burn as it builds to a deliciously unanticipated . . . climax."

—Hope Tarr, award-winning author

"Loved, loved *Slow Surrender* and am waiting on pins and needles for book two... another brilliant outing from Cecilia Tan... her characters are full of life and emotion, and so believable. Definitely a keeper!"

—NightOwlReviews.com

"If you are a fan of the billionaire dom, you should not miss *Slow Surrender*. Cecilia Tan weaves a compelling and red-hot tale that will have readers eager for more."

—RomanceNovelNews.com

Also by Cecilia Tan

Taking the Lead

* * *

Slow Surrender

Slow Seduction

Slow Satisfaction

* * *

Black Feathers

Daron's Guitar Chronicles

The Hot Streak

The Incubus and the Angel

Mind Games

The Poet and the Prophecy

The Prince's Boy

The Siren and the Sword

Telepaths Don't Need Safewords

The Tower and the Tears

The Velderet

White Flames

WILD LICKS

A SECRETS OF A ROCK STAR NOVEL

CECILIA TAN

FOREVER

New York Boston

Forever
Hachette Book Group
1290 Avenue of the Americas
New York, NY 10104
forever-romance.com
twitter.com/foreverromance

Printed in the United States of America

RRD-C

First Edition: August 2016
10 9 8 7 6 5 4 3 2 1

Forever is an imprint of Grand Central Publishing.
The Forever name and logo are trademarks of Hachette Book Group, Inc.

Library of Congress Cataloging-in-Publication Data is available upon request.

ISBN 978-1-4555-3364-0 (trade paperback edition)
ISBN 978-1-4555-3365-7 (ebook edition)

CONTENTS

WILD LICKS

PROLOGUE

GWEN

I took to heart the only piece of advice my father ever gave me: "Never let them see you cry."

Those were the words going through my head as I clutched a wrinkled and folded set of pages, sitting on a bench outside the audition room with a dozen other women. At least three had emerged from the room in tears and I tried to imagine what the director and casting agent must have said to them. Did they insult their clothes? Their weight? Did they rip apart their acting ability? Was it all some kind of a test to see if you could stand the heat?

The director, Miles Redlace, was a notorious asshole. But, you know, Hollywood loves an asshole if he's brilliant. He was the "it" director right now, the hip, hot, edgy winner of two Oscars and half the reason I wanted to be in this film. His detractors said he wasn't "edgy," just liked to curse a lot and insult people working for him.

Honestly, insults might be better than the last audition I went to, where they barely noticed an actor was in front of them. I had never felt so dismissed or humiliated in my life. On top of that, I'd overheard the casting director say he was disappointed in the effort people were putting in. How could he tell how much effort an actor put in if he never looked up from his phone or his crossword puzzle?

I'd taken his words to heart, too, though. For this audition, I'd put fake tattoos on my shoulders and arms, did a temporary red wash through my natural blond, and wore a fake nose ring. I did everything I could to be this character, to become what the producers were hopefully picturing in their minds.

My sister Ricki asked me why I even went to these cattle calls. "Let me put the financing together and we'll create a project for you," she said.

She'd never understand why a "vanity project" wasn't what I wanted, because she couldn't fathom why I didn't want to rely on the family money or name to get my start.

I wanted to prove myself. I wanted to prove that my talent got me the part. I always put in a stage name, though anyone who was paying attention could have recognized me. Except maybe this time. I didn't even recognize myself in the mirror.

The door opened and another woman exited dejectedly. She didn't even look at us on the bench; she just deposited the script in the trash bin as she went straight to the parking lot.

A dozen or so of us were still waiting. Everyone looked fresh out of college, like me, though I heard two of them talking and I thought them older. But everyone wants to look young—even when the role wasn't for an eighteen-year-old punk rock rebel girl in a film with the working title *Wild Child.*

I knew how Hollywood worked. I grew up in the film business and I was a realist. I knew I was doing it the hard way. But I had to do it my way.

"Ginger Hill?" called the PA at the door. It took me a moment to remember that was the stage name I picked.

I hopped to my feet, adrenaline surging. "Right here!"

"Oh, no, wait," the woman said, checking her clipboard. "Marian Foy, you first. Hill, you're next."

I sank back down onto the bench, mortified. Why did I feel that way? It was her mistake, but I wished a hole would open in the ground and swallow me up.

Great. Now you're going to go in there all red-faced and flustered. My heart had sped up and didn't seem like it would slow down anytime soon.

I gripped the folded script more tightly, trying to keep my hands from shaking, thinking, *Is this how a wild child would act? Of course not! She would strut in there like she didn't give a fuck what they thought.* The question was whether I could convincingly project that attitude when inside I was feeling the opposite. A great actor could.

An eternity later—or maybe only an agonizing moment—the door opened again. I expected Marian Foy to trudge out. But no, it was the PA again. "Thank you all for coming, but we have filled the role."

Some of the women groaned. One of them flung the script into the trash bin, where it landed with a papery thud.

I should have stomped out of there like I was wearing combat boots, but no, that role was filled. So I merely tried to walk in a ladylike fashion to my car. Ladylike to me meant with small, crisp yet unhurried steps, my eyes on the horizon, hoping like hell the fake smile on my face didn't look ridiculous.

Never let them see you cry. Dad never said who "them" was, but I took it to mean everyone.

CHAPTER ONE

REAL LIFE

GWEN

By the time I arrived at the Forum, the concert had already started. Thank goodness Ricki had gotten us VIP parking permits and backstage passes. The VIP lot was next to where the band's tour bus was parked—a massive thing with THE ROUGH logo painted on the side—and I could see a security guard standing outside a side door into the arena.

I clutched my purse to my shoulder as I approached him. He was wearing black and the band's crew jacket, a lanyard hanging from his neck with a cluster of laminated passes at the bottom of it. "Hi, yeah, is this the right door? I have a backstage pass waiting for me," I told him.

He looked me up and down. "Oh, really," he said, as if he didn't believe a word of it and was merely humoring me. "And who exactly would be responsible for putting you on the list?"

"My sister. Or her boyfriend. Axel Hawke? Perhaps you've heard of him?"

He laughed. "Try pulling the other one."

"Okay, seriously, I'm Gwen Hamilton." His attitude was really starting to piss me off.

Amusement twisted his mouth. "You know, honey, if what you really want is a good banging, plenty of guys in your hometown would oblige."

"Excuse me?"

"Okay, okay, I get it. You came all the way here to get some genuine, grade-A rock star dick. Which one do you want? I'll tell you if you're his type. The only one who's off-limits is Axel. He's monotonous and his girlfriend's here to boot."

"You mean monogamous and that's what I told you—his girlfriend is my sister!"

"He's into some kinky shit but I don't think incest is—"

The door opened and a guy stuck his head out. He was long and lean with a partially shaved head. "Gilbert, you got a problem here?"

"Excuse me," I said. "Have you got the guest list? Because I am on it and this dimwit thinks it's funny to sexually harass me."

The guy came all the way out with a clipboard in hand. "Name?"

"Gwen Hamilton."

"You got ID?"

"Yes." I dug my driver's license out of my bag and showed it to him.

"All right, come with me." He punched Gilbert on the arm. "Be nice."

Gilbert rubbed his arm and held the door open. "Come on, Nick, how was I supposed to know she was on the list? She looks like every other groupie."

"By checking the list," Nick said, waving the clipboard. "She's probably some fan club contest winner or something. Be nice or you'll go viral on YouTube." As the door shut behind us, he said,

"My apologies, miss. Here." In the hallway stood a podium on wheels. From behind it he pulled out a lanyard with a laminated pass on it, and he signed his name on the bottom with a Sharpie.

I slung it over my neck.

"When the band comes offstage, they'll go through there to the green room." He pointed down a hallway to the left. "Main party'll be over there"—then he pointed to the right—"and if you want to watch the rest of the show, straight ahead."

I thanked him and went straight ahead, the music getting louder as I went. There was a handwritten sign taped to the cinder block at a stairwell leading up that said STAGE OVERLOOK. Up I went.

As I was climbing the stairs, I was still fuming a little about what an asshole the security guard had been, but then it struck me: He had treated me like a groupie trying to sneak into a concert because that's *exactly what I looked like*. He'd bought it. Even when I'd told him who I was, he'd either not believed it or didn't know my name. That was possible; I was far from a household name. But a thrill ran through me as I realized how convinced he'd been.

I came out on an upper platform where a couple other people with passes around their necks were watching the show. Several of them looked like groupies and I wondered if the guard had been partly serious when he'd said some of the guys were "available."

But I didn't spend long looking at the other people there once I started watching the band. Axel, the lead singer, was at center stage, but on the side of the stage closest to me was the guitar player, Mal. We'd met once or twice in passing at industry functions. My impression of him from those occasions was that he never smiled and rarely spoke, looming in the background like a judgmental gargoyle.

On stage, however, he was animated, explosive, leaping into

the air with his guitar and then landing, flinging his long dark hair forward and then flipping it back with a head toss. He still didn't smile, but he matched Axel's energy with a feral grimace as he sang, and then he sauntered out onto the long runway into the audience, playing a solo and practically humping the guitar as he went.

Pure sex. One hundred percent pure sex that walked on two legs and played the guitar. When that song was over, he tore his shirt off and flung it into the audience. His arms and chest looked like something from a fitness-craze infomercial: *You, too, can have these abs! These biceps!* I certainly wouldn't mind if he let me touch them for a while.

I was so caught up in the performance that I didn't notice the others had left the viewing area until the band was taking their bows. One of the women I'd seen before came back up the stairs just as I was trying to figure out what to do with myself. "Come on," she said. "If you want to get picked, right after the encore is the time."

Get picked? I wasn't sure what she meant, but I had some ideas. I followed her downstairs and toward the green room. We passed several doors with paper signs taped to them: VOCAL WARMUP ROOM, WARDROBE, BAND ONLY. She led me into a room that was unmarked.

About a dozen women were there, some drinking bottled water from a tray on a table, some applying new lipstick, some gossiping. A few sat on folding chairs, but most of them were standing. I took my own lipstick out of my bag to give myself some time to figure everything out.

"I've been with Samson before," a woman with thick black cat-eye liner similar to mine was saying to another. "But he tweeted this morning that he's got a cold, so I don't know if he's partying tonight."

"Last night of the tour? You better believe they're *all* partying tonight," the woman who'd come back to get me said. She had red hair and a thick studded belt wrapped twice around her hips. "I don't care if he does have a cold. I wouldn't mind being the bread on a Samson meat sandwich." She gave the other woman a high five.

Okay, so it seemed as if "getting picked" did in fact mean what I'd guessed—that is, being chosen for sex.

"What's your e-mail again?" Cat-Eye asked. "I want some of those photos you were taking tonight."

"Oh, sure. I'll be posting them on my website, too." The redhead dug in her purse and pulled out a stack of business cards with a photo of the band on one side and her contact info on the other. "Here." She handed them around. I took one so I wouldn't be the only one refusing.

I should go to the party, I told myself. I didn't really belong here. But I was curious how long I could keep it up. When would someone notice I didn't belong?

A third woman joined us, downing a bottle of water. She looked like she had been dancing, her thin T-shirt sticking to her skin in places. "Is it true Mal is really rough?"

"Never been with Mal," Cat-Eye said with a shrug. "You figure with all the bondage and stuff in their videos that at least one of them is mondo kinky. Mal seems the type."

The woman who had brought me downstairs shrugged. "I saw them in Indianapolis with a friend. She said he's huge."

"Pictures or it didn't happen," I put in, and several of the women burst out laughing.

"Yeah, no pictures but she did have trouble walking the next day," she said, which caused even more laughter.

The roadie who'd helped me earlier came in then and everyone quieted down instantly. He had a flashlight in one hand. "Okay, pussycats," he said. "Mal's ready."

No one moved.

"Are you seriously telling me none of you is into the kinky shit?"

"I am," I said, starting to raise my hand like I was in grammar school; then thinking a wild child wouldn't do that, I ended it with a snap of my fingers.

"Great. Come with me."

I followed him out into the hall and was surprised when we stopped only a few feet from the door and he turned to me. "Just gotta check—you *are* into the kinky shit, right? Mal is not your typical lay."

"Neither am I," I said in the sassiest voice I could muster.

"If it's too much for you, just leave, all right?"

Which was exactly what I planned to do before things went too far, but I certainly couldn't let on that was my plan. If anything, this little chitchat made me all the more intrigued about what "kinky shit" Mal was into. Floggers? Canes? Bondage? None of that would faze me. I was getting a bit turned on just thinking about it—and the gorgeous abs and chest he'd displayed on stage. "All right."

"Good enough. Come on." He led me farther down the hall, past several more doorways, until we came to one that had a paper sign taped to it that read KENNEALLY, GUITAR. The roadie took a Sharpie from his pocket, added the words *DO NOT DISTURB* to the bottom, and then said, "Okay, honey, go on in. And be careful."

I wasn't sure exactly what he meant by that but I opened the door, slipped through, and closed it behind me, with no idea what I was going to see on the other side.

What I saw in the dim light of electric candles flickering was Mal Kenneally, leaning back on a couch that had been covered with a batik-print cloth. The whole room had been hung with patterned fabrics so that it looked like laundry day at a pasha's harem, and lush, exotic-sounding music was playing from somewhere. A woman was raking her long nails through his hair, spreading it out behind him like the glossy black wings of some legendary raven. He was wearing leather pants and nothing else. Well. He opened his eyes when he realized I had come into the room and murmured something to the woman, who patted him on the shoulder and then quickly left. In the low light I could barely make out her face and I doubted she could see me all that well either.

And so what if she could? I wasn't here to play demure, good-girl Gwen. I marched up to the coffee table, put my hands on my hips, and announced, "They told me you like to play with fire." I tossed my flame-red hair for emphasis.

He let his eyes travel up and down me slowly, as if he were drinking in every detail from my black lambskin boots up the fishnet stockings to my denim cutoff shorts, tank top, and fake tattoos. (Well, I had one real tattoo, but he couldn't see that one.)

His voice was low. "The question, my dear, is whether *you* like to play with fire."

"I'm game," I said, thrusting my chin into the air.

His smile warmed slowly. "Are you? Everyday sex bores me."

"I'm not an everyday groupie," I answered. Well, that was certainly the truth—maybe too close to the truth? My heart rate sped up as I worried he might see through my ruse. That would be humiliating.

Just how far are you going to let this go? a little voice in the back of my head asked. *You can chicken out anytime,* I answered. I decided I'd leave as soon as he got too rough. If he grabbed me or manhandled me, I'd tell him it wasn't my thing and walk out. That wasn't my kink and that was the truth. Otherwise, I figured I'd play along and see what happened. *Wild child,* I thought to myself. *Wild child.*

"Lose the shorts," he said.

I swallowed, my cheeks reddening as I realized he was about

to see my underwear. My silly, peach-colored cotton underwear, not the slightest bit sexy, but I hadn't exactly planned to show them to anyone when I'd left for the audition that day. *Maybe I should just run away now...*

But I wasn't ready to yet. I didn't want to. I put on a bit of a sneer, unbuttoned my cutoffs, and let them drop. I stepped gingerly out of them.

His gaze lingered over my underwear but seemed neither surprised nor judgmental about them. "Come closer."

I moved to the other side of the coffee table, then even closer as he somehow communicated to me with his eyes that I hadn't come far enough. I stopped when I was near enough for him to reach out and touch me.

But he didn't. He still hadn't even sat up. "Your middle finger," he said. "Put it in my mouth."

Part of me was startled, but the part of me that was playing the role showed him my middle finger in a rude gesture first, before gently placing the pad of my finger against his tongue.

He held my gaze while his tongue rolled back and forth against my finger. He drew it in deeper with sensual suction and it felt like waves of velvet were lapping against my skin. If that felt anything like what a blow job feels like to a guy, no wonder they're so fixated on them. How can I explain it? His mouth was gentle and firm at the same time, his tongue both soft and muscular, and the longer it went on, the deeper his eyes seemed to bore into me. It was only my finger but somehow it felt as if his oral skills were being plied on other sensitive parts of my body.

When he opened his mouth to let me go, his lips glistened and the tip of my finger was slick with his saliva.

"Now use that finger on your clit." His voice was never raised louder than a suggestion, yet it felt like a command.

I lifted the waistband of both the panties and the fishnets and did as he asked, sucking in a breath as my wet finger slid easily over my swollen clit. Far more swollen than I would have guessed it would be from merely what had gone on.

"Naughty girl," he breathed. "Nasty girl. Touching yourself like that."

"Yessss," I said through clenched teeth. That was exactly it. I was the wild child who touched herself instead of doing her homework or practicing her violin.

"Let me see it," he said next.

"See what?"

"Your slick, swollen clit." His tongue darted out to touch his lips. "Unless you're faking it?"

My heart hammered as again I wondered if he'd figured out I was only playacting—why else would he say that? But my arousal was real. I suppose he said it as a kind of dare. I put one boot onto the armrest of the couch and yanked my panties aside. One strand of the wide fishnets dragged across my clit and I hissed, but there was plenty of space between strands for him to see my aroused flesh.

His tongue came forth again, this time making a slow, sinuous pass across his lower lip. He beckoned with one finger, crooking it back in a "come closer" motion.

I pulled the panties a little harder to make sure my clit was completely uncovered, and I bent my knee as I leaned toward him.

He lifted his head from the couch at last to meet my throbbing pussy with his mouth, to put that tongue exactly where I had imagined it earlier. God, he was good. Every touch felt good, every slide of the velvety body, every tweak of the wicked tip. After a few minutes it was becoming difficult to stay upright and he reached a hand under my rump to support me. Between saliva and my own juices, wetness was soon running down his wrist.

My arousal went up and up and I forgot where I was, forgot

who I was supposed to be; the only thing in my universe that mattered was how close I was to orgasm. Very close but not quite there. Damn it. I needed something to get me over the hump. That was true even when I used my vibrator at home. It often took a pinch or something to send me over the edge. I had thought maybe that was because the vibrator desensitized me and it took something painful to get through to the nerves, but this? This was every nerve ending on fire, electric, fully charged.

I wanted him to bite my clit, to trap it between his teeth while torturing me mercilessly with his tongue tip, or to jam all his fingers inside, but he didn't do either of those things, just kept on pleasuring me, which was a different kind of torture.

My voice came out a whine. "Put your fingers in me. Please, God, I need something."

"If you want something in you, I'll give you two choices," he said, licking my juices from his face while he talked. "Neck of an ice-cold beer bottle or my cock."

"Oh, fuck!"

"Does that mean cock? You're not being clear."

Oh fuck, indeed. I wasn't ready to go there, mentally I mean; I wasn't ready to go all the way with this rock star sex god. And the thought of cold glass on my superheated flesh sounded ridiculously good. Does anyone really think rationally that close to orgasm? I definitely wasn't at that point. I grunted and threw my head back. "Where's that beer bottle? That sounded like a dare."

His laugh had an edge of delight in it. "Daring, indeed." He set me on my feet and got up, retrieving a bottle from a cooler and popping the top off. He took a swig of the beer and then set it on the coffee table.

"You might want to take your bottoms off," he suggested. "Much as I hate to see your fishnets go."

I toed off the lambskin boots and stripped the fishnets and

panties off my legs. Then I put the boots back on, not to be sexy but because I thought I might need the traction.

He thought it was sexy, though. I looked up to find him lying back on the couch again—he'd stripped off his own pants while I'd been wrestling with mine and was running one finger up and down his rigid, gorgeous erection. Entirely naked, he somehow looked less ridiculous than some men. His legs were well muscled, his chest lean, his neck strong and graceful, and his cock even more so. I began to rethink my choice of the beer bottle.

But a dare's a dare. I turned around so I was facing away from him and put one foot on either side of the coffee table.

I held the bottle in one hand and gradually lowered myself until I could feel the glass rim touching me. The glass was cold and dewy with condensation.

I lowered myself still more, the slick hardness sliding into me easily. I made a sound of surprise. It felt good. I rose up and pushed myself down again. Very good.

"Naughty girl," he rasped, voice rough with lust. "Nasty girl."

"Very," I whispered. "Oh fuck, it feels good."

"Go farther, all the way down, fuck yourself."

There was no thought in my mind but to do as he directed, the bottle widening me and sending waves of pleasure through my core.

"Now, lift," he said, "all the way off, all the way up."

I whimpered at how empty I felt and looked over my shoulder at him.

He took the beer bottle, licked the glass rim, and then drank deeply from it as he lay back on the couch. "There, now it's cold again."

This time he held the bottle on his stomach, mere inches from his cock, daring me again.

I climbed onto the bottle, facing him this time, bracing myself with my hands on either side of his head. The bottle was unforgiving and I had to move myself up and down slowly. He positioned his thumb so that as I raised and lowered myself I was brushing my clit against his finger, too. That tempted me to go faster but I just couldn't—anytime I went too quickly the hard glass reminded me to keep it slow. I whimpered and moaned. I don't think I'd ever wanted to come more than I did at that moment.

"May I . . . ," I heard myself panting. "May I have that choice again?"

"Do nasty girls get a second chance?"

My brain was in overdrive. We'd reached a point where it was no longer even a question whether I could go all the way with him. It had become a moral imperative. "They do if . . . their masters are pleased with them."

"Oh, I see. Well, this master is very pleased with his girl's performance so far. What would his girl like as a reward?"

"His cock? May this girl have it? Please? Oh fuck, please . . ."

"If she puts a condom on it, perhaps. They're in the case behind my head. Up."

I scrambled off him to open the black case, a combination toolbox, first aid kit, and sewing supplies. Half a dozen foil condom packages sat between the Band-Aids and the Phillips-head screwdrivers. I pulled one free and tore open the package.

He sat up. "Put it on with your mouth."

I gave him a saucy look. Little did he know Madison had taught me this trick just the other day. We'd practiced on bananas.

This was no banana in front of me, though. Whatever word you used for it—cock, prick, dick, pecker, penis—it was a beautifully engorged staff of manliness. The condom was unlubricated. Like Maddie had taught me, I got the convex side good and spitty before sucking the tip into my mouth and then positioning it over the head.

I used the force of my lips to unroll it over the spongy bulge and he groaned low in his chest. I worked my way down another inch or two before I had to give up and take a breath. He was longer than the banana I'd practiced on, too, and deep throating wasn't in my skill set. I nibbled my way down the side of the shaft then and used my lips and jaw to unroll it a little farther.

He took over then, using his fingers to make sure he was sheathed all the way to the base. "Come and get it, girl."

I straddled his legs and rubbed my wet pussy back and forth on his shaft, getting the condom completely slick.

"Sit up. Let me see it," he said. "Let me see."

I thrust my hips forward, giving him a good look at my glistening opening. He ran his thumbs along the edges of my labia, admiring.

Then he saw my real tattoos: black letters where my thigh met my labia. On one side the letters spelled out the words *LOVE PAIN*, on the other *EXCRUCIA*—the name of the heroine of a fantasy book series I loved, *Pain of the Sword*, about a concubine who rose to be empress. I wondered if he could see them well enough to read them. He let his thumb drift across my clit almost casually, his voice carefully neutral. "That was the name of my first band." Apparently he *could* read them.

Oh no, he thinks I'm a stalker. "It's from a book," I blurted defensively.

"I know. About a painslut." He drove a finger into me, and I gasped as he wiggled it. "A woman who craved it."

"A woman who thrived on challenges," I said. I'd never heard the word *painslut* before, but hearing him say it made things inside me clench with need.

"Mmm-hmm. Challenge yourself to make me come with that hungry cockhole of yours," he murmured.

The dirtier he talked, the hornier I felt. "Challenge accepted." I straightened my legs to lift me higher, and then I took him inside me, lowering myself a few inches and then letting him admire the sight. He felt incredible, far better than the beer bottle.

He jiggled his thumb against my clit, making my legs give way, and I sank down farther with a groan.

"Holy fuck, you're tight," he said, his hands gripping my hips as he pushed upward into me. He held me still while he ground his hips in a circle.

He was coring me from the inside with a pleasure so intense it bordered on pain. I wasn't about to explain that the dildo that was my usual "inside" toy was smaller than him. Instead I simply said, "Oh fuck," in agreement.

He let me move at my own pace, sliding his hands under my shirt to my breasts. I barely noticed when he pulled the shirt over my head while his thumbs and fingers played with my nipples.

He hummed appreciatively when he discovered that pinching my nipples produced a ripple of tightened muscles in my pussy. "That's my girl," he said. "Milk my cock with your body. You're going to suck the come right out of me."

Speaking of coming, I wanted to. I really *really* wanted to. But I'd reached a high plateau where everything felt fantastic but nothing moved me any closer to the release that was just out of reach. My movements became more frantic and so did the little cries in my throat. He pushed one of my hands between my legs, encouraging me to get myself off, but even that wasn't enough. Sweat was streaming down my skin. I was taking so long, too long; I was never going to get there...

"What do you need, sweet girl?" came his voice, low and insistent. "Tell me."

"Bite me," I said, and for one horrified second I thought he might take it the wrong way, but no, he knew what I was asking for. He didn't stop pumping his cock inside me, moving me up and down with his hands, and I didn't stop fingering myself desperately. With one hand behind my back and one clamped onto my ass, he latched his mouth on to one of my nipples and bit.

I screamed. I screamed and came with a spasm of shudders so intense my teeth chattered.

He flipped me onto my back on the couch, driving two fingers into me while his tongue attacked my clit again with its sensuous onslaught. Another orgasm followed quickly on the heels of the first, or maybe it never even quite ended, rolling right into an even bigger one like a peal of thunder.

And then I was blinking up at the ceiling, breathing hard, shivering with aftershocks but very definitely on the downward side of the peak. Wow.

I looked up. He had rocked back onto his knees. His hair was a sweaty mess plastered to his forehead and shoulders. He rested his hands on his thighs and caught his breath. His cock was still half hard, the now-full condom still clinging to it. Apparently he had come sometime during all that. I felt slightly guilty for having been so overwhelmed by my own release I'd somehow missed his.

He caught my eye. "A good girl would help her master with this."

I bared my teeth. "I'm not a good girl, but I'll be good for you." I sat up and cupped his balls gently in one hand while I palmed the condom. He groaned and shuddered, pumping one more gout of seed into my hand as I pulled the rubber free.

He nodded toward a doorway. "That's the bathroom."

I went and disposed of the condom, used the toilet, and gave myself a bit of a wash. Wow. My tender bits felt extra tender. Then I washed my hands, folded up some paper towels, and wetted them with warm water.

I came out and wiped him down, all around his balls and pubic hair, and then lovingly washed his now-shriveled cock. He lay still, watching me, saying nothing.

Clearly we were done and he was the very definition of "spent." I pulled my shorts back on, leaving the fishnets as a lost cause. I found my shirt behind the first aid kit. I pulled on my jacket.

"What did you say your name was?" he asked as I picked up my purse.

"I didn't," I said, blowing him a kiss and then quickly going out the door.

* * *

MAL

"Good party, huh?" Axel said as he bounded past me in the hall toward the catering area, not waiting for a reply. Axel is a whirling dervish, an Energizer Bunny of charisma and charm. Some performers get tired of being "on." Axel, on the other hand, has no off switch.

He doubled back before he got far. "Good show tonight, too," he added. "Great way to end the tour, don't you think?"

I stretched, every part of me feeling whole for the first time in weeks. Truly excellent sex always had a good effect on me, but this was beyond even that. "Yes. Definitely."

He looked me up and down. Axel is my oldest and best friend and he knew me well. "You got laid already, didn't you?"

I merely nodded. I'd had a shower and pulled my hair back into a long wet tail, and when I'd been unable to find a clean shirt, I'd opted to shrug my leather jacket on anyway. "You can tell?"

"You look more relaxed than I've seen you in months," he said. "Good. Maybe you won't bite anyone's head off at this party." It being the last night of the tour, our record company was treating us to an epic after-party.

"I shall try to be on my best behavior," I assured him. I am not a fan of small talk, especially with small people, but I realize it comes with the job. No doubt Marcus, our record company rep, was here, as were various other staffers from Basic Records on whom I should be endeavoring to make a good impression. Some of them no doubt thought of me as difficult, especially after what happened during the last recording sessions.

Perhaps they considered anyone who put artistic concerns in front of monetary ones "difficult." If so, please, label me difficult. I wondered if Larkin Johns, the producer I'd thrown out of the recording studio, would dare show his face backstage tonight.

I was following Axel toward the noise of the party when my phone vibrated inside my jacket pocket. I let him get ahead of me as I paused to check it. A text had come through.

Mal, this is Layla, long time no see! I'm so sorry to bother you but I need your help.

I stared at the words. That was all she had written. No doubt expecting me to reply. *I'm so sorry to bother you.* I let out a bitter laugh. *So sorry to have had to ferret out your private mobile number in order to send this passive-aggressive message,* she meant. I had not seen her for years and she had been told not to contact me. Did she think anything had changed? I wondered how she had gotten my number and whether I was going to have to change it again.

Layla had once been a fan, a groupie, and then I had made the mistake of trying to make her into something more. The breakup had been ugly and damaging for both of us, but that was years ago. For a moment I considered replying to her for old time's sake. But no, what had she gone through to get this number? I added her number to my contacts list so if she called

I would see her name and know not to answer. That was all I could do at that moment.

I caught our head of security in the hallway, heading toward the designated catering area. "What's up?" he asked the moment he saw me make eye contact.

"Nick. I just received a message from Layla. She shouldn't have this number."

He dragged his hand through his shorn black hair. "You worried it could turn into a stalker situation again?"

"Hopefully not. I didn't reply. I don't even know where she is these days, but I thought I should inform you."

"She was the blonde, right?" Nick had been working for us for a couple of years and had a very good memory.

"Yes."

"I'll keep an eye out. Lotta people here tonight." He glanced toward the catering area. "Bunch of fan club people, the folks from Basic, VIPs, everyone and their brother seems like. Speaking of fans, hope everything went all right?"

Nick was the man we'd put in charge of vetting groupies who wanted to have a much more up close and personal experience than a mere selfie and autograph. "Perfectly," I said. So perfectly that I considered asking him to let me know if he saw that woman again. But no. It was better not to confuse the issue, and if anything I should have taken the text from Layla as a sign not to get involved. "Thank you."

"Anytime," he said with a little salute, and moved off to his next errand.

I continued on to the catering area that had been set up in one of the large sports team locker rooms. I waded through the mingling crowd and shook hands with a few people. Thanked the members of Breakwater for doing a good job as the opening band. Posed for a selfie or two with some of our superfans. Allowed one of the promoter's staff to prattle on at me for a while about something—I'm not sure what since I tuned out what he was saying. I let my eyes roam the room, desperate to find someone decent to talk to. After six weeks on the road, I had nothing left to say to anyone in the band or crew. Axel was with his girlfriend, the heiress Ricki Hamilton. They were more or less glued together, side by side, having not seen each other since we left. Ford, our bass player, was introducing his father to Killian, the lead singer of Breakwater. I wouldn't have minded talking to Mr. Cutler about his guitar collection, but I wasn't about to elbow my way across the room and interrupt them.

Sometimes in the middle of a crowd is when I feel the loneliest.

Christina, our manager and a whirling dervish of energy herself, cornered me when she saw I was at loose ends. "Mal, I have something serious to talk to you about."

I braced myself for a talking-to about my insistence on a new producer when we next went into the studio. No one, including me, wanted a repeat of last time. "Of course you do."

She surprised me, though. The next album wasn't the foremost thing on her mind: "With the tour over, we need to strategize some ways to keep the band high profile in the media."

"I thought Capitol/Basic was going to release another single from the album and wanted us to make a video for it?"

"I mean besides that. You're going to be staying in LA for a while, right?"

"Yes, Christina." In fact, I was looking forward to some downtime at my condo in Santa Monica.

"Good. I need you to seriously think about arm candy."

"Excuse me?" Christina grew up in the Philippines, I grew up in England, and though we both spoke English, I was sometimes entirely unsure I'd heard her correctly. "Did you say 'arm candy'? Oh." I figured out the expression then.

"Yes. Seriously. We need a woman for you to be photographed with at events. Look at this."

By all the saints and sinners, the woman had spreadsheets on her phone identifying the frequency with which certain types of photos appeared in certain types of magazines and media. *Spreadsheets.* She had it broken down into an analysis of whether the musician in question had hit the Top 40, what genre of music he played, and the hair color of the woman he was photographed with. I kid you not.

"For maximum publicity effect, we should find you a blonde."

"Christina," I said firmly, "data is all well and good, but you know I do not date, and I especially do not date blondes."

"I know, I know. You're allergic to relationships. That's why this plan is perfect."

"Wait, what?"

"It's not a real relationship. It's just for show."

"That's not an improvement." I pressed the heel of my hand to my forehead, as if that could forestall the headache. "I have standards. I have rules."

Axel snuck up behind me. "Of course you do, Mal. What is it this time?"

"Explain to Christina why this plan of fixing me up with blond arm candy is not going to work."

Axel shrugged. "I told you he wasn't going to like it. If only because of his blond exes."

"Mal?" Our manager gave me her best questioning look.

I tried to keep it simple: "When I was growing up, my parents were forever attempting to match me with the so-called right sort of girls from the right sort of families." In other words, girls who were filthy rich like we were and so very often blond, as my father tried to "erase" my mother's half-Spanish blood, hoping for grandchildren without the jet-black hair and tawny skin I'd inherited.

Apparently I could escape England and my father's archaic attitudes, but not the pervasive need to keep up appearances.

Christina kept on. "Don't get too stuck on the blond thing, okay? But you know this isn't a real *date*-date, right? We're not saying have a real relationship. This is purely for image."

Before I could interject that doing it "purely for image" was in fact the basis of my original objection, more so than the "blond thing," Axel piped up in a knowing voice. "I know who would be perfect."

I growled disapprovingly. "Quit tag teaming me."

Axel ignored my comment. "You know who would be perfect? Gwen Hamilton. We could double-date."

"Your girlfriend's sister? Wouldn't that be a bit incestuous?" I asked.

He punched me in the arm. "I love you like a brother, Mal, but not like that."

I rolled my eyes. The truth was that I liked Gwen Hamilton well enough, but she set off every one of my alarm bells. She was Hollywood royalty and happened to be blond, and how awkward would it be if I did get involved with her and then Axel and Ricki were to break up? I never wanted to have to choose sides between a lover and Axel or the band. That was a recipe for disaster. Besides, Gwen Hamilton was undoubtedly far too nice a girl to satisfy my darker urges.

I tried to put all these thoughts into a glare.

"He's not buying it," Axel said to Christina.

"No, he's not," Christina agreed. "Won't you at least think about it, Mal?"

"Think about what, conducting a charade of fake romantic hypersexuality in public for the sake of increased album sales?"

"Mal, don't be like that," Axel wheedled. "It'll be *fun*. We're going to have to go to movie premieres and awards shows and who knows what else. It'll look weird if I have a date and you don't."

"It doesn't have to be Gwen," Christina said. "We could just hire a model. Would that be simpler? Just pay someone. That wouldn't be as good as someone with name recognition, but—"

"I'll think about it," I said, cutting her off and trying to close this tiresome subject as quickly as I could. "All right, Christina? I'll think about it."

"Excellent! Gwen is supposed to be here tonight, isn't she, Axel?"

"I didn't mean—"

"Ricki said she would be. I haven't seen her yet, though..."

I closed my eyes and pressed my hand against my sinuses, thinking, *Angels and devils, just get me through this night without having to fend off the fawning of some simpering innocent paragon of feminine virtue.*

When I escaped being reintroduced to Gwen Hamilton for the rest of the night, I considered it a victory. Perhaps Christina and Axel would change their minds. I could only hope.

CHAPTER TWO

SILVER SCREEN

GWEN

The next morning I felt wonderful and terrible at the same time. On the one hand, I'd slept amazingly well, all the tension from my back and neck had disappeared, and deep in my bones it felt like an itch was gone. On the other hand, I had teeth marks on one boob, a couple of bruises, and I felt like I'd had sex with a fire hydrant, not a...

Oh. I'd really done that. I would never be able to look at a bottle of beer without blushing again.

And of course today would be the day Ricki and I were supposed to discuss the upcoming dungeon party. After lunch, I gathered up my catalogs and information and we got together in the kitchen where I could spread them out on the table.

Ricki looked perkier than I'd seen her in weeks. She'd been working super hard on launching a new media start-up company, but I had a feeling the glimmer in her eye today had mostly to do with seeing Axel last night for the first time in almost two months.

"What do you think of this?" she asked, glancing at some of the tastefully photographed sex toys in the glossy catalogs. "What if we had a theme?"

"What kind of theme?" I was surprised. When we'd first learned that to keep our inheritance we needed to keep throwing play parties in the secret dungeon in the family mansion's basement, Ricki had been less than thrilled. Then she met Axel, who had apparently introduced her to the pleasures of kink, and her attitude had changed considerably. He was a dom; she was his sub. Anyone who attended our parties knew that now. I was, frankly, a bit envious that she'd found a dom so quickly—and she hadn't even been looking for one. I'd wanted to find someone like that for a long time, so it seemed a tad unfair she got there first.

I let out a breath slowly as a memory of Mal commanding me to serve him echoed in my ears.

Ricki's voice was drawing me back to the present, though. "I was thinking we could make a couple parties a year themed. You know, like do Mardi Gras in February."

I tried to focus but I wasn't really able to keep my attention on the details, as Ricki hashed out some ideas for party themes and how to spread the word among our super-secret membership without leaving a trail of incriminating e-mails. Telling people at the August party was really the only way. "We've got . . . four new members now?"

"Yeah. Sakura, Diff, Dara, and Paul." She chuckled to herself about the assistant she'd inherited from our grandfather. "I can't believe Grandpa Cy didn't let Paul come to the parties."

"Maybe he was maintaining boundaries for his employees?"

"Oh, I'm sure he was, but still, poor Paul! To be the one person who knew all about these parties going on but not be allowed to attend?" She shook her head. "I mean, it would be one thing if he wasn't interested, but you should have seen him light up when I broached the subject. He's been pretending to be vanilla all along."

"Paul's a sweetie pie." He really was. I never would have guessed he was into kink if Ricki hadn't told me. Then again, most people wouldn't have guessed about me either. We spent the next half hour or so planning out what to buy and how to decorate. I enjoyed running the club, honestly. Sex should be good clean fun and not something people had to hide, but I understood why we had to hide it.

Oh God. Good clean fun. *Is that what you call what you did last night?*

I tried to put last night out of my mind. *That wasn't me,* I thought to myself. That was all an extreme experiment in Method acting. And it had worked. No regrets. Time to move on.

Right?

Ricki was saying something about the film premiere she was going to tonight. "Gwen, are you even listening to me?"

"Yep. Yep. Right here." I felt bad for spacing out on her so tried to be enthusiastic and interested to make up for it. "What film?"

"I don't even know. Some pseudo-indie thing that Brad Pitt executive produced. The party needs another girl to round it out. Want to go? I'd love it if you would."

I love my big sister and I like making her happy. Now wasn't the moment to repeat why I wanted to stay out of the spotlight until it was shining on me because of my acting talent and not the family name. "Will it be fancy-fancy?"

"Not like Oscar night but party-fancy, sure. Oooh, hey, you could wear that sunset-red dress that was the wrong color for me. I've still got it."

See, I told myself, *not Oscar night, just an indie film, so every media outlet in the world won't be there.* "The Vera Wang? Let me try it on. And I better make sure all the temporary red is washed out of my hair or it could clash."

"I'll get the dress and meet you at your room."

It's handy to have a sister who is almost the exact same size as you, even if she is two years older. As I gathered up the catalogs, I heard her make a phone call, telling someone I was coming along tonight.

In short order she was laying the dress across the chaise longue in my "dressing room," the room with the floor-to-ceiling mirror and my light-up makeup table. "I'm glad you're coming out with us tonight," she said, "since I didn't get to see you last night. Was the audition that bad?"

Acting, acting, acting, I thought as I tried to act casual. "Oh, it was such a pain," I said as I held the dress up to my chest, then began working it off the hanger. "They kept us there forever and then in the end announced they'd filled the role without even looking at most of us. I never even got to read."

"Seriously, Gwen, cattle calls aren't the way to do it. Maybe at this thing tonight you'll meet someone—"

Here we go again. "No, Ricki, don't. I don't want some director casting me because we met at a cocktail party or because he thinks he'll get the family money backing his project. I want to prove I'm a good actor." I slipped out of my clothes while facing away from her so she wouldn't see the teeth marks on my breast and stepped carefully into the dress, which left my shoulders bare but covered the marks handily. Phew. "Otherwise, what's the point?"

"There are tons of great actors who don't get parts." Ricki helped to zip the dress up. "You have to have connections, too."

"I suppose. Am I wrong to want to make it on my own?"

"No, of course not, but... This'll be good for you. Go out, be seen, get some fresh Google hits on your name." She flattened the zipper against my spine. "You know, WOMedia's launching that app in a couple of weeks and we want to shoot a promo video for it. You could totally do the part of the woman using the app for the first time."

"I suppose..."

She stepped back to look at me. "I didn't even get to see you with the red coloring in your hair. I can't tell it was there at all. Jamison said he didn't even recognize you yesterday."

"I know. He almost called security when he saw me walking through the house." I looked in the mirror now, though, and saw perky, friendly Gwen Hamilton all dressed up. The knee-length dress was just on the orange side of red—blood orange, maybe—and the hint of yellow in the undertone had made Ricki's complexion look sallow. On me, though, my skin glowed healthy and golden. "How long will the promo video be?"

"Probably two minutes? I don't know if there'll be any speaking in it, mostly just footage of a happy woman or women gazing lovingly at their phones. You'd be perfect. And it'd be a line on your résumé." She watched as I turned to check the back of the dress in the mirror. "It would also help me out because then I won't have to do a talent search."

"Oh, all right. If you really need my help, Ricki, all you have to do is ask."

"You'll be perfect." She smiled.

I pulled at the limp strands of my hair. "Do you have a stylist coming? Or are you going to do your own hair and makeup tonight?"

"I was planning to do my own."

"Let's do each other's," I said with a grin. "Like we used to when we were teenagers."

"But no braids, beads, or French twists."

"Deal."

* * *

MAL

I'd had about enough of Axel and Christina chirping at me by the time Tashonda was finished with my hair. She was just giving it one last spritz of something before pushing me out of the chair when I said, "Enough! Let me get one thing clear. I am attending this function tonight because you insist that being seen with Gwen Hamilton on my arm is a good career move. It's work. Fine. I'll work. But don't expect me to *enjoy* it."

Christina was satisfied with that and left me alone. But Axel wouldn't give up entirely.

"You have the weirdest hang-ups, Mal." Axel knew me better than anyone else on Earth. Axel had been there the night I lost my virginity, the weekend we'd snuck away from my parents and took the train to London...

I didn't know *that* girl's name any more than I knew the name of the mystery woman with the labia tattoos. I wrote a lot of songs with women's names for their titles. Was that why?

That one at the Forum. She had to be from Los Angeles, hadn't she? Was there a chance I might run into her again?

I wanted to, rules or no.

I wanted to because even though she'd left me sexually sated, a gnawing feeling inside me flared up whenever I thought of her. I called this feeling *the Need*, a term I'd borrowed from the fantasy novels of Ariadne Wood. I wanted to do depraved things to this woman. To her and with her. My "rule" was that I never did a groupie twice because I didn't want them getting attached or obsessed the way Layla had, but honestly most of them didn't come back for more.

But it's not your run-of-the-mill sex kitten who has the words *Love Pain* tattooed on her inner thigh where only a very intimate partner would ever see it. I still wanted to ask her about that. When a woman doesn't tell you her name, should one take it as a sign she isn't interested in another go or merely that she has secrets of her own?

"Mal, you're not even listening to me."

"Sorry, what?"

"Never mind. Here, put your jacket on." Axel handed me a black jacket that I shrugged on easily. It was cut like a dinner jacket but with leather lapels embossed with a dragon design. I had a black dress shirt partly unbuttoned, black pants, and black leather boots. I was never seen wearing another color in public except as an accent to the black, fully conscious of its weight as the color of both mourning and villains.

Axel, on the other hand, had pumped up his blond highlights so much one could be forgiven for forgetting that his natural hair was actually light brown, and he had opted for a jacket that appeared to be light blue with green imitation snakeskin. At least I'm fairly sure it was imitation.

"Come on, Mal," he said, poking the corners of my mouth as if trying to get me to smile. "Bask in the attention a little, will you?"

Basking in the attention is your job, I wanted to say to him. *That's why you are the lead singer and I am not.* But I didn't have the energy to argue. "I'll try," I said, without specifying what I was trying. "Now, let's go."

* * *

GWEN

One of the things about my sister is that she's sneaky in an understated way. She simply doesn't tell you things that she thinks might change your mind. But I should have known. When she said they needed "a girl to round out the party," I should have known what she meant was "a double date with my boyfriend, Axel, and his best friend, Mal."

Why wasn't that obvious to me? Maybe because I thought Ricki would have come out and *said* that. But no. Why make it obvious that she was trying to fix me up with her boyfriend's friend? She was obviously hoping something might work out and didn't want to jinx it, I guess.

She also had no way of knowing I was kind of hoping something might work out myself, although I was worried he'd flip if he realized I was the same girl. I had to remind myself that Ricki didn't know about last night. No one did.

No one, not even Mal. As he took a seat next to me in the limo, there wasn't any recognition in his eyes beyond the slight flicker that we had met in passing before. He did bow his head in a gentlemanly way and kiss my hand as we were reintroduced, and he was quite a gentleman in other ways, too. I certainly hadn't expected that after yesterday's raunch-fest, but there he was, doing things like offering me a handkerchief after I sneezed. I suppose the years of finishing school came out in situations like this. It certainly did for me, as I pretended that kiss on my hand didn't start a chain reaction of sense-memories of his lips touching me all over. His hair was tamed back and his suit was impeccable, but the scent of his skin seemed to tempt me like the warm familiarity of a favorite candle.

When we reached the theater, the limo came to a stop and he exited first, then offered his hand to help me step out of the car. My hand in his reminded me of how he'd held it to steady me as I'd stepped over the coffee table—and what I'd stepped over the coffee table for.

A flurry of flashes and shutter clicks showered us and he extended his elbow so I could take his arm. He placed his hand atop mine, almost protectively I thought—or maybe wished—as we made our way along a barrier crowded with people. He had to let go of me to sign a few autographs and I felt the absence of his touch keenly.

A large blond girl with blue streaks in her hair was waving a photo frantically as he drew closer. "Mal, Mal! This is the photo we took last night! I got it printed!"

He smiled graciously and looked at the glossy picture. "Our selfie. Well, now we have to take a selfie while holding it up, don't we?"

"Here, I'll take it," I said, and she handed me her phone. The two of them squished close together and held the photo under their chins. Mal had the same smoldering, serious look in both photos, the girl the same elated grin. An innocent grin, I thought.

And he was a gentleman to her, too. I was still trying to reconcile the sexual animal who had dared me to use a beer bottle as a sex toy with this polished public persona. "Remind me how to spell your name?" he said to her as he picked up the pen to autograph it.

"Aurora," the girl said. "Like the Disney princess."

"I didn't grow up on Disney, I'm sorry," Mal said.

"You know. Like the city in Colorado," she tried instead.

"I don't think I've been to that part of Colorado." Mal held up the pen. "Does it start with *O*? *A*?"

She finally spelled it and he handed the photo to her. "Now, where's my copy of it?" he joked. Or, no, he was serious.

"Really? You want a copy?"

"Yes. Would you e-mail it to my manager? Here, take down this e-mail address."

While he was reciting the address to her, another photographer elbowed his way in with a big flash protruding from his camera and nearly blinded me with it. Mal glared at him and got a flash to the face, too. At that point, Mal hurried us away from the barrier, his arm across my shoulders in an unmistakably protective gesture. He was tall, six feet easily, and no one else tried to stop us.

"My apologies," he said with a small bow once we were inside the theater. "I should know better than to let a feeding frenzy start."

"Oh. Um. I'm fine. It's all right, really."

"You haven't done many of these events before, have you?"

"Not really. Just starting to." I hadn't been in the public eye much. Yet.

"Let me get you something to drink." There was a reception set up in the lobby. We had lost Ricki and Axel completely in the delay. Mal steered me to one side and up onto a raised part of the floor, slightly out of the way, and then waded into the fray.

I stood there lost for a few moments, trying to compose myself. Be sweet, be nice: that was a role that came naturally to me. For a moment, though, I wondered if he had abandoned me now that we had passed the main gauntlet of photographers. No sooner did I start to wonder than he returned with two bottles of cold water.

I couldn't help grinning as he handed one to me. He couldn't have brought me a more perfect choice and the choice surprised me.

"Something wrong?" he asked.

"No, no. I just somehow thought you were going to come back with champagne. Or Jack Daniel's or something." *Mal Kenneally,* I thought. *What's going on under the image you project?* I started to wonder if maybe the suave gentleman was any closer to the "real" Mal than the backstage bad boy was, or if they were both hiding the truth.

He raised an eyebrow. "Would you rather—"

"No! Water is awesome, actually. That's why I'm smiling."

He removed the cap from his bottle and said, "Cheers." We tapped our plastic bottles together and I caught him smiling a little before he smoothed the expression away as he caught the eye of someone in the mingling crowd. "Is that Roderick Grisham?"

I looked and saw an older gentleman with a distinguished streak of gray in his hair and deep laugh lines around his eyes stopping to greet another man. "Yes, that's definitely him." He was British and had played some of my favorite film villains—well, everyone's favorite film villains, actually. If there were an Oscar for best villain, he would win it every year. In typical Hollywood fashion, that meant that in person he was known for being one of the most gracious, generous people in the business, tirelessly supporting charities and mentoring young actors, that sort of thing. "Do you know him?"

"We met very briefly once at a party in London. Barely exchanged two words," Mal said, but even he sounded a bit awed.

The man was headed toward us again, and as he approached he held out his hand to shake Mal's. "Ah, Kenneally, wasn't it?"

Mal stood up very straight. "Yes, sir. I'm honored you remembered. May I present Ms. Gwen Hamilton."

Roderick Grisham took my hand, kissed it with a bow, and made it all seem perfectly smooth and natural. "Charmed, Ms. Hamilton. Truthfully, Kenneally, the reason your name stuck with me is I thought, well, that's an odd name for a man I'm quite certain is English, not Irish."

"It's a stage name, sir. Chosen to irritate my father."

I tried not to stare in amazement that Mal was calling him "sir" like it was second nature to him.

"Ah, so you know the history of the name?" Grisham asked.

"An English bastard who was awarded the Victoria Cross after he joined the Irish Guard, yes. As the story goes, Kenneally's valor caused Winston Churchill to express love for the Irish, somewhat ironically."

"Just so," Grisham said with a laugh. "The troublemakers are the most interesting people in history. And which irritates your father more, your stage name or what you do upon that stage?"

Mal chuckled. "It is all of a piece to him. I am the black sheep of the family."

"Black sheep make the best art," Grisham said, and then turned his charming smile to me. "And you, Ms. Hamilton. Are you a budding impresario like your elder sister?"

"Oh, not really," I said, feeling every bit charmed by his attention. "I'm trying to break into acting, actually. Any . . . any advice?"

"Let's see. The best advice I can give in a short amount of time is this." He paused for dramatic effect and we both leaned toward him in anticipation. *"Always get it in writing."*

All three of us laughed and then he was nabbed by a member of the press with a microphone. Mal and I edged to the side to let them pass.

"I am not normally one to be starstruck," he said as he watched Grisham recede across the crowded lobby. "But something about that man is quite striking."

"I agree," I said. "And I grew up with Harrison Ford and Denzel Washington hanging around my backyard pool."

Mal's glare returned suddenly as he caught sight of something.

The annoying photographer from outside was making a beeline for us. Because of the crowd and the ridiculous amount of equipment the guy had hanging off his shoulders and neck—three different cameras and a bag—he had to weave and pause, trying to get to us. The man himself was not small, either.

"Let's go in," Mal suggested. He shepherded me up the stairs and I felt the warmth of his hand at the small of my back through my dress. I wanted to lean toward that touch like a flower toward the sun, but I kept myself poised and proper while we were in full view.

"Do you know that guy?" I asked as ushers opened a set of velvet ropes for us.

"Not him in particular, but I know his type. Like a bulldog. It's best not to engage." We made our way down the aisle. In the theater, it was relatively hushed compared to the high-energy schmoozefest going on in the lobby. "He'll move on to easier targets."

"Okay, but isn't the whole point to get lots of photos taken?" I asked as we took seats in the second row.

Mal looked at me with an even more serious glare than his usual look. "Have you been talking to Christina?"

"No, I haven't even seen her yet tonight," I said, confused.

"Hmm." He took my hand and placed it on top of his forearm on the armrest, then put his other hand on top of mine. I felt a little thrill run through me. He certainly didn't seem to mind touching me. "If she asks, tell her they took *thousands* of photos of us. Which they did. I just don't like to reward assholes for assholish behavior."

"I can certainly agree with that." I was starting to like this righteous gentleman. So different from the raunchy sex god of last night, and yet so controlled. So firm. I wanted to hear those gentle yet unyielding commands again. Knowing it was the same man only made the thought even more appealing.

I reminded myself he had no idea it was me. And this was not the place to be bringing up such subjects anyway. "There are too many boors and trolls out there."

"Manners have their place," he said.

"They certainly do." I found myself blushing, though, as a little voice asked me, *Where were your manners when you practically tore your stockings to show him your "cockhole" last night?* "Speaking of which, here come Ricki and Axel."

Mal stood, and they took the seats directly in front of ours.

"So what is this film about?" Ricki asked. "From the posters it's hard to tell."

"It's a modern fantasy, I think?" Axel said. "The film is titled *Midnight*, but the actual book was called something else."

"I've read it," Mal said. "*On a Midnight Far*, by Ariadne Wood."

I felt my blush deepen as surprise hit. Ariadne Wood was the author of *Pain of the Sword.* I managed to sound pretty cool about it, I thought: "I read a lot of her books as a teenager but I don't remember that one. Is it new?"

"It's one of her vampire books," Mal said, looking up at the frescoed ceiling of the restored theater. "The other one was *The Need.*"

"Aren't vampires kind of done now?" Ricki asked.

"I believe you Americans have been saying that vampires are 'done' since before we were born," Mal said. "Which is why *On a Midnight Far* was never published in the States. Ariadne Wood was my favorite author when I was growing up."

"Well, I bet they published a movie tie-in edition of the book now," Ricki said. "Don't tell me about it. I want to watch the movie without spoilers."

"She wrote all kinds of fantasy." Mal stopped looking at the ceiling and examined his hands instead. "Some medieval orientalist mélange, some Arthurian, some modern."

"One of our early bands was named for a character of hers," Axel said. "When we were, what, eleven, twelve years old?"

"Indeed. Starting a long series of failed band names." Mal did not smile, but something about the way he looked at Axel made me think he was amused.

"Really? Like what?" I asked more to keep myself in the conversation than because I wanted to know.

Mal began to name them. "Jackhammer, Twister, Cuffboys..."

"That one only lasted about a week," Axel said.

"...Florentine, The Highwaymen, Flashbang, Trembler..."

"Some of which were already used by other bands," Axel added.

"I can't even remember all the ones we tried and abandoned." Mal shrugged. "Trying to capture the right spirit in a name was difficult."

"You're the one who insisted it have a sexual innuendo in it," Axel said.

"All the best band names do," Mal said sagely.

"You mean like the Sex Pistols?" Ricki asked.

Mal made a dismissive noise. "Far too obvious. I'm referring to bands such as Cream or Pearl Jam."

"Oh my God, I never realized those were references to—" I put my hand over my mouth as I laughed.

Axel grinned. "There are even more that are, er, anatomical. Nine Inch Nails, anyone? Tool? Whitesnake? Third Eye Blind?"

"Third Eye Blind is about the...?" Ricki stage-whispered and looked around at the seats filling up all around us. No one seemed to be eavesdropping, thankfully. "I never would have thought of that."

"Ideally it shouldn't be too obvious. Something like Steely Dan," Mal said. "It's a literary reference. To a William S. Burroughs book."

"Who was Steely Dan?" I asked. Burroughs had not been in my reading curriculum.

"Not who, what. It's the name of a dildo in the book *Naked Lunch*."

Now I was blushing so hard I wanted to fan my face. The last thing I needed to be thinking about—while sitting next to the man who had given me a knee-trembling orgasm last night with a beer bottle—was a steel dildo. But I could imagine what Mal would do with one so vividly, right down to the wicked glint in his eye.

He sounded thoughtful, satisfied. "I'm glad we settled on 'The Rough.'"

"Yes," Ricki said, "I like The Rough."

Axel put an arm around her. "I know you like it rough, darling."

"You are terrible," Ricki said with a mock slap on his hand.

"He corrupted me," Axel said, pointing at Mal.

"You're each a bad influence on the other," Ricki concluded. "Now *shhh,* they're about to introduce the film."

The lights went down and I settled into my seat, trying to tamp down the feelings raging through me. There was a tall, dark, and handsome gentleman sitting beside me, the same man who had seen my hidden tattoo. The same man I had begged to hurt me.

It suddenly occurred to me that almost no one saw both sides of Mal.

Except me. My stomach dropped like I was on a roller coaster as the realization took hold in my mind. We were alike in that way. Except Mal had separated his "bad boy" side from his gentleman side and somehow still managed them both. I'd been fighting that battle for a long time, good girl versus bad, and good girl had pretty much been in charge ever since the disaster of secretly dating a much older tattoo artist when I'd turned eighteen.

His name had been Chuck; he had been pushing thirty at the time, and thinking back on him now I knew he was nothing more than a sleaze. But at the time I had been giddy with having moved to the East Coast, with the freedom of college life, with the temptation to explore who I could be where no one knew me.

The night we'd met, I had gone to a club. One of the guys in my dorm had a band and they were playing at a bar downtown and I'd promised him I'd go to see him play. They were great, and he was cute, but after their set, I didn't find him.

What I did find was Chuck, sitting on a motorcycle outside. He had a tattoo of a bullwhip on one arm; I had a lifetime of fantasies built on pirate movies and Westerns and books like Ariadne Wood's, full of dragons and heroines who sacrifice themselves to save the day. Somehow those two things added together to him taking me back to his place and spanking me until I came.

Three weeks later, I had the "Excrucia" tattoo and was convinced I had found the perfect man for me, the only guy who had ever successfully made me come.

Three weeks after that, on the day I'd gone to his house to confront him about the STD I'd come down with, I found him in bed with two girls I didn't even recognize. The bubble burst that fast. Bad girl went back into the fantasy closet and good girl took over with a big, fat "I told you so."

I retreated into college life, studying, joining a sorority, a theater improv troupe, a campus pro-environmental group. I'd tried to put my fantasies aside and figured if I was going to get into kink, it would have to wait until later. I dated a bit within my social circle but that's all it was, really, "social" dating, not good sex and certainly not love.

And here was Mal Kenneally, a perfect "society" date in public and a perfectly wicked match for every "bad girl" fantasy I'd ever had in private. I'd convinced myself that I would never meet someone right for me.

But here I'd already met him. And I already *wanted* him. The man who had seen my tattoo. Who had left bruises on my skin. Who knew I needed him to hurt me. Except he didn't know it was *me*.

I pressed my knees together as the memory of yesterday swept through my body again. I wanted him and I wanted him to do it again. How was I supposed to play nice society date when my panties were getting damp just from sitting next to him?

The lights went down and the film did not help distract me. All of Ariadne Wood's books have a sexual undercurrent, even the ones supposedly written for teenagers. *Midnight* was about a girl who dreamed about an angel coming to rescue her from her cruel existence at a remote boarding school for girls—and those dreams were intensely erotic, at least as depicted in the film. But when she is convinced to open her window in the middle of the night looking for her angel, it is of course a vampire who has been sending her the dreams, a monster who then ravages her.

Or perhaps ravishes her. With gorgeous cinematography, of course, filmed in loving detail. I know it wasn't intended to be interpreted as an actual sex scene—right?—but I couldn't help but see it that way. The slow-motion close-up of his teeth against her skin in the moment before the bite gave me flashbacks to Mal's mouth on my breast and the hungry way he had wrung every ounce of pleasure from me.

I squirmed, wanting to escape to the ladies' room but unwilling to make a scene. So I sat there in the dark, awash in desire, intensely aware of the scent of leather from the man beside me and wishing I could climb into his lap.

CHAPTER THREE

INSIDE

MAL

I have never seen a pornographic film while in formal wear in a crowded theater, but the experience of watching *Midnight* was very nearly that for myriad reasons. I wondered if the director was a closet kinkster or if it was merely my reaction to the scenes, perhaps to my adolescent memories of reading the book and masturbating furiously.

At first I chided my imagination for tricking me into thinking Gwen Hamilton was also finding the film arousing. Her bosom heaved enticingly, the hint of cleavage that showed beyond the edge of her dress far more erotic to me than the projections on the screen. I warned myself that reading too much into a woman's signals had gotten me into trouble before. But then she gripped my arm during the ravishment scene, her nails digging into me. Was it my imagination after all? Even if it was, the scene was so rapturous that the sensation of her nails against my skin transformed from pain to pleasure.

By the time the credits rolled, I was painfully hard. As such, I was not going to be very polite company. The moment the final applause died down, I stood.

"Coming to the after-party?" Axel asked.

"I think not. I've...had enough glitz and glamor for one evening."

To my surprise, Gwen said quickly, "Me too. Ricki, you and Axel go on to the party. I'll have Riggs drop Mal off and then take me home."

"If you're sure?" Ricki asked, glancing around at the three of us. Everyone seemed to be on the same page. "All right. See you at home."

Hence, far sooner than I had thought possible, we were ensconced in the spacious, quiet back of the car, out of the public eye. That in itself was a relief. Gwen's driver had engaged the privacy screen. Now I only had to keep up my manners for one.

"Ms. Hamilton, thank you for the gracious offer of a ride home. I truly appreciate it."

"Don't mention it. I'd had about enough of the spotlight for one night. Whew." She crossed her legs, her thighs looking creamy white in contrast to her fiery red dress. I curled my fingers against my own thigh, trying to curtail the desire to reach out for that flesh, to pull her toward me and ravish her like something from my fantasies. Or like something from last night, for that matter. I scolded myself. *Down. Just because this woman is beside you doesn't mean you can put your cock in her.*

That girl from last night, though, I found myself wishing she were sitting beside me. A woman I could command to straddle me, to use her body to satisfy my needs and who would do it without hesitation. Or perhaps only enough hesitation to heighten my anticipation. She had been glorious. Perfect.

Against my better judgment, I had made up my mind to search for her. A plan was forming in my mind—the fan network? Aurora?—and I found myself unable to resist it. The warning bells were ringing in my head—but then again, I liked my music loud and chaotic.

It was making it hard to concentrate on being polite to Gwen Hamilton, however. I tried to steer the conversation to a safe topic. "You said Ariadne Wood was your favorite author when you were growing up?"

"Oh, yes. I bought every book of hers I could get." She pressed her finely shaped hand to her cheek and I had a moment of déjà vu about last night. I was so obsessed with that Excrucia girl that the littlest things were reminding me of her.

Don't be ridiculous. Focus. Wait until you get home and get off and then your brain will work again, you dolt. "Same here. And as I got older, I... discovered more and more of her hidden themes."

With a sly smile, Gwen gave me a sideways look. "Sex, you mean."

So much for finding a safe topic. "Well, yes. What else would a book that hinges on a werewolf finding his fated mate be about?"

"Oh, God, I loved that one," she said, all slyness gone. "*Nightfang.* I think I read it so many times the pages fell out."

So had I. What a curious thing to find in common with her. "Indeed. Somehow she managed a plot in which the hero must have sex with all his prospective mates without ever triggering the censors." The indirect language and tasteful fades to black hadn't stopped me from vividly imagining what had happened between the pages, though. In that book and in many of her others.

"I was fascinated by this film adaptation. So sensual! Was it very different from the book?" The graceful expanse of Gwen's neck seemed to stretch out before me as she tilted her head, almost as if she were beckoning me to bite her.

She couldn't possibly know the effect she was having on me, sending my fantasies into overdrive. I wanted to pull her head back by her hair and dapple her neck with the marks of my teeth. I wanted to bury my face between her legs and feast upon forbidden fruit.

But those things were for the groupies, the wild women, the fly-by-nights. The ones who could take it, who wouldn't cry foul in the morning, who would worship my cock as a source of pleasure or pain, not of baby-making sperm. The women who knew what they wanted from me, a sexual conquest, an erotic adventure—not a boyfriend or a husband or social status. This is why I lived by the rules I did.

I was not going to terrorize this nice society girl with my depraved desires. I was not. I was *not.* I cleared my throat, trying to keep the conversation on a clean and polite path. "Hard to say." I failed. My mouth gave me away: "Perhaps the images themselves reflect a sensuality inherent in the book, or perhaps it's that the memories they invoked of my reading experience, but I found it highly . . . stimulating."

Her cheeks were nearly as aglow as her dress, but I felt her hand on my arm. "I found it stimulating as well."

Did she? Her hand felt as if it were burning my skin right through the sleeve of my jacket.

"Ah." I gave her a nod of acknowledgment, at a loss for what else to say or do, other than apologize for crossing the line.

Before I could do so, however, Gwen Hamilton crossed the line herself. "I want you to know, I don't have a chance to meet a lot of guys like you."

"Oh? Like me in what way?"

"Um, in th-the way that I am attracted to you," she said, stumbling over her words slightly. "I mean, I know this was just a publicity date, but I'm actually very, very attracted to you, Mal."

She didn't know what she was saying. Of course she didn't,

because she didn't know the real me. She had met only the polite version of me, the public veneer that I was, even now, struggling to keep from peeling away.

I took her hand to try to reduce some of the sting, because I knew my next words were going to come across very cold. "I'm sorry to be such a disappointment, then. You are lovely, Gwen, an ideal and charming companion for an event like this, and I thank you for that. But I cannot have sex with you."

"No?" She looked truly puzzled. "Why not?"

"For one thing, my tastes may shock you. For another, I do not invite romantic entanglements."

Her eyes flashed in challenge. "Who said I wanted romance?"

That startled a laugh out of me. Was she for real? Or was she playing? "Oh ho, are you saying you're only interested in a bit of casual sex? I find that hard to believe."

"It's rude to judge a person by appearance." She thrust her sharp chin at me. "Why is it so hard to believe I might be as turned on as you are?"

I let go of her hand. "I am not turned on."

"You're so hard I can practically see the tip of your dick sticking out of your pants."

I glanced down to see if that were true—not *quite.*

"Seriously, Mal Kenneally, you're a consenting adult. I'm a consenting adult. If we're both horny, I don't see why we can't do something about it." She gave a shrug like she was being wholly reasonable.

And I admit, it did sound wholly reasonable. But like the monster in *Midnight*, once the Need took hold of my brain, my ability to judge logic was severely curtailed. The beast inside me smelled prey. She was *offering* herself. How dare I say no . . . ?

But, no. *No.* "You don't know what you're asking."

"Sex? I know what sex is, Mal." Her eyes had an enticing

depth, a playfulness and a sensuality that I wanted to plumb. "I've even had it before, if you're under the misguided notion I'm some kind of virgin."

Well, thank goodness for that...? I'd taken my cousin Camilla's virginity a few months after I'd lost my own. At the time the forbidden fruit had been irresistible, but we'd both come to regret it and I'd avoided virgins ever since. But Gwen still truly did not know what she was asking. "I mean, you don't know what sex with me entails. You don't know the slightest thing about me."

"So tell me. Enlighten me." She bit her lip and my mouth nearly watered at the sight. "I would love to know more about you."

I focused my mind on a bracing dose of the truth, to splash some cold reality on both of our superheated libidos. "I have boundaries. Strict rules."

"Boundaries are good," she agreed.

"For example, one of my rules is that I don't do... repeat engagements."

"Repeat engagements?"

Perhaps vulgarity was necessary for the shocking effect I hoped for. "I don't fuck a woman twice."

Wrong. "Who said I wanted you twice?"

"Ha. Another is that I don't fuck bossy women." The Need surged and I fought to keep my voice calm and dispassionate. "I fuck obedient, pliant, submissive women who have to work very hard to earn my cock."

If I thought that little speech was going to scare her away, I was quite wrong, again. Her tongue darted against her lower lip and every instinct in me screamed that I should grab her and devour her mouth rather than allow her to speak. But I did not. "What... what would I have to do to earn it?"

"Could you be taught to obey?"

"By you, I could," she said.

Gods and monsters. This could not be happening. "May I remind you"—and myself!—"this is not a negotiation, Ms. Hamilton. This is... me telling you the reasons why we cannot have a sexual relationship."

"I haven't heard anything to convince me of that yet," she said. "I thought it was you telling me about yourself so I could make an informed decision about whether to pursue a sexual relationship with you."

"You still haven't heard it all!" I snapped. My emotions were definitely getting the better of me.

A reflection of my anger flared in her eyes before it settled to a simmer of concern. "I'm sorry. Go on, Mal."

"One of my biggest rules," I growled, trying to tamp down the turmoil roiling inside me, "is that I do not date."

"Yet... here we are on a date?" she probed cautiously.

"I mean, I do not date women like you."

"Like me?"

Rich, heiress, cultured, blond... I couldn't explain any of those things without it seeming insulting. Maybe there was no way around it, though, other than to plow ahead with the truth. "Before I cut off contact with my family, they were constantly arranging dates with women like you. By which I mean moneyed heiresses and, yes, nearly always blond."

Her voice was slinky with skepticism, her intelligence sharp even if her manner was gentle. "And you can't date me because your family might approve of me?"

"No. That would be juvenile. It's that my repeated negative experiences with those women taught me my needs lie elsewhere. And regardless of my reasons for erecting my boundaries, I still expect them to be respected."

"Ah, true." She settled back against the plush seat of the car with a sigh and I felt another surge of desire despite everything

I had just said. After all, those boundaries were all to protect my heart. My cock could not care less what my heart felt or my brain thought about the situation.

And it wasn't just my cock that wanted to plunge into her. My fingers ached to grip her flesh, to sink into her hair, to pull her nipples until she cried out. My mouth wanted to taste every inch of her pliant skin, discovering what was hidden by the fabric of her dress, leaving it marked by my teeth, my nails, by whatever implement I wished...

I needed to find the girl from last night. That was the only solution. I needed someone as an outlet for my most twisted desires. What could be more perfect than a woman with the word *Excrucia* tattooed alongside her most intimate place? *Love Pain.* Did that mean she loved pain or that love was pain?

Both, perhaps.

Gwen was talking, though. "I swore off prep school boys and fraternity brothers for much the same reasons, I guess." She looked at me with one eyebrow raised. "Now you're going to try to convince me you're the ultimate prep school boy, but you're going to fail, Mal. I know you're not like that."

"Do you?"

"I don't know too many of them who are rock stars, for one thing," she pointed out. "It's all right, Mal. If you don't... want me, I can take it like an adult. You don't have to invent a bunch of excuses."

"They're not excuses," I heard myself say earnestly. Somehow she kept wrong-footing me with her own mix of sincerity and honesty. I wasn't used to anyone—much less heiresses—being so open or aware. Axel had warned me the Hamiltons were different. I tamped down the temptation to find out how different. "It's nothing personal. I've... found you to be a charming companion for an evening such as this, Gwen."

She relented with another sigh. "Well, for what it's worth, I liked going out with you, too. I predict my sister and Axel are going to try to get us together again."

"Seems certain."

"Are you okay with that? Because I suppose if I have to go out and be seen, I'd rather it was with you than, well, some actual grabby, selfish prep school product who thinks boobs are like the dials on his daddy's yacht."

She made me laugh in spite of myself and the burning need below my belly. "Likewise. It is far more pleasant to talk to you than to some model they would hire for me out of a catalog or something."

"Good," she said, and folded her hands above her knee, looking through the dark-tinted window away from me.

I could make out that we were on Santa Monica Boulevard and we would be at my condo soon. We lapsed into silence. Did she feel how fragile the balance was between us? Did she understand how tenuous my position could be? The need for a public image that hid the truth of my desires yet projected a dangerous sensuality to my fans was a tricky strait to navigate. As Christina would say, my image was an asset to be maintained. My publicity value was an asset to be guarded. I reminded myself being seen in public with Gwen was a tactic for doing so, and I found myself grateful that she seemed to understand this.

And gratitude was a feeling I should express when felt, or so I had learned. "Thank you," I said quietly.

"You're welcome, Mal," she replied, just as quietly.

She was an intriguing woman, wasn't she? Try as I might to encase her in my mind as nothing more than a stratagem, my curiosity was piqued.

Curiosity could be even more dangerous than flat-out lust, though. I forced myself to think about Excrucia instead. In her, had I found a woman whose interest in pain complemented my own?

I'd dabbled in the organized bondage and fetish communities

in both the UK and the States, but as fame had grown, I'd pulled back from anything that could be scandalous—much as I would have relished my family's horror had I landed in the tabloids for it. The classes and seminars on safety and technique made sense to me but also left me feeling cold and unmoved inside. No one seemed to value pain for what it was: actual pain.

I'd discovered pain as a secret friend at a childhood Christmas party, candles everywhere, tapers and tea lights. I've always liked candles, the flickering light making everything seem like a dream. At the dinner table I started playing with the flame of a tea light with the tip of my finger, flicking it back and forth. Did you know you can feel a flame without getting burned? It feels like air pressure, like gossamer, like the touch of a ghost.

I began to test myself. How long could I keep my finger in the flame without it hurting? And then the test became how long could I keep my finger in the flame *despite* it hurting?

That was when I started to feel alive.

I didn't discover that inflicting pain on others was just as good—better, even—until I was a teenager. I was sent to a boarding school with many longstanding traditions, most of them unacknowledged by the faculty and administration. I don't know about the girls at the school down the road, but among the boys, hazing rituals and tests of endurance—especially those involving nudity and jeopardy to one's genitalia—were commonplace. Points of honor were won through such activities.

Bullying was never my style. I was not interested in picking on the weak. Sadism without honor is madness. What intrigued me was the submission of willing victims. Everyone who wants pain has their reasons. Some feel pain as pleasure. Some experience emotional catharsis through it. Some test themselves and their mettle.

Some simply feel alive.

My imagination flooded with erotic images. If the redhead

from last night were sitting beside me, what would I do? My fantasy reeled off as easily as a porn film. I would say to her, *"If you are truly giving yourself to me, you'll climb onto my cock right now."*

"Right now?" she would ask.

"Yes, this second. Or I'll have the chauffeur take you to your destination and never see you again."

Her lip would tremble slightly and then she would ask, *"And if I do it? If I pass your test?"*

"Then we will proceed directly to my home, where you will spend the next two weeks as my fucktoy, naked and prepared for me to take you anytime the mood strikes me."

I would unzip my trousers and my erection would strain upward and I would command her to engulf me. The test: *"You have ten seconds to get me all the way inside you."*

In her haste she would climb astride me and simply yank her panties aside, struggling to get the head of me positioned between her lips. Yes, the struggle would be the sweetest part of all, as she would fight to accommodate my size without any preparation. Once inside, I would find her snug and slick with desire but the initial penetration would make her bite her lip and me gasp . . .

I nearly gasped aloud there in the limousine as I realized I had imagined Gwen and not Excrucia at all. Thank goodness we were pulling up to the privacy hedge that surrounded my condo. I opened the door, desperate to escape the allure of this woman. From the curb I turned to close it and saw she had crawled to my side of the seat and was looking up at me with huge, lust-filled eyes.

That's your imagination, I told myself. You're confusing her with every other woman who has sucked you into a vortex. "Ms. Hamilton," I forced myself to say in the most polite tone I could muster. "Thank you for a lovely evening."

She held out her hand and I took it gingerly, my fingers disconcertingly damp, and kissed the back of her hand. Her skin was smooth, perfect, and I knew all I had to do was tighten my grip, pull her out of the car, and tell her to come with me and I could have her.

And I could ruin her. And that would not be good. I let go reluctantly.

"Until next time. Good night, Mal," she said, before reaching out and closing the door herself.

I didn't even wait until I reached my bedroom. The moment I was on the other side of my front door, I tore open my trousers and relieved the pressure that had been building there as if I were a hormonal teen again, on my hands and knees like an animal, painting a series of grayish stripes on the foyer tile, my control utterly gone.

* * *

GWEN

As we drove away, I clung to the sense-memory of Mal's lips against the back of my hand. I don't think it was my imagination that his lips lingered a little too long. Mal Kenneally was obviously interested in me. For a guy who supposedly hid all his emotions, Mal was as readable as a billboard on the 101. I was sure I hadn't heard the whole story behind his sex and dating rules, though. Maybe it was as simple as him justifying his fear of commitment? Why else make a rule that he could only have sex with a given woman once?

I mean, I get the whole rock star thing. He had a steady stream of women throwing themselves at him. He didn't have to make a commitment to have plenty of sex, so why should he?

I, on the other hand, wasn't so lucky, and pretty much all I could think about while he'd been sitting there in the car with me was how his cock had felt inside me yesterday.

You're deluded, I tried to tell myself. *If he wanted you, he would have invited you in. He wouldn't have said no.*

Besides, you're making him seem more interesting than he probably is. Yes, the sex was hot, but come on, he's obviously got issues. He's clearly a big old cup of avoid-for-your-own-good, right? Buy a bigger dildo instead.

But while my insides clenched with need every time I thought about him, I knew it wasn't his cock I really craved. It was something else. His attitude. His . . . mastery?

This wasn't how it was supposed to go. If I was going to get into dom/sub role-playing, I was supposed to find a guy and exchange checklists and negotiate and talk about limits and aftercare before we even set foot into a dungeon. I was not supposed to hop onto a beer bottle on command.

But just thinking about it was making my insides melt all over again. Maybe with time I might have forgotten about Mal or reduced the memory to the status of a favorite fantasy, but now having spent the evening next to him—touching him and getting to know him—I was more attracted to him than ever. It was like getting hooked on a drug where a big second dose ensured the need took hold.

To think tonight we hadn't even had sex. Maybe we didn't have to. The film had stimulated all the right parts of my fantasies, even the deep hidden and forbidden parts. And Mal had as much as admitted that it had done the same for him, too.

I slipped back into thinking about that room backstage, draped with cloths and tapestries like a vestige of an ancient seraglio. He'd ordered me to put the condom on him and I'd done it, and obeying him was the best aphrodisiac ever. No, the second best. Him reducing me to a fuckable hole was the best.

What the fuck was that about, anyway? I lowered the window

to let the wind into the limo, to feel the air moving on my face. I'd always been interested in various kinks. Growing up, I'd known they existed. Bondage had looked like fun, spanking had sounded great, but I'd never fantasized about being a human sex toy. Had I?

Was that why Mal only did a groupie once? Because what got him off was treating her like a disposable fuckdoll?

Worry about Mal later, I thought. *Why did* you *get off on being treated like that?*

Was it a leftover vestige from Chuck? My first real lover, my first time doing kink, and Chuck had degraded me and ordered me around and spanked me and I had loved it at the time... until I'd realized he was actually a really degrading person. But I'd imprinted on that style of dominance, I guess. How else could I explain why I found bossy male entitlement hot?

But you don't find it hot in spoiled brat dudebros, I thought. They had entitlement up the wazoo, too.

But they were boring. They didn't even care enough to boss me around or *make* it hot. They'd just expected me to lie there and think of New England.

And they weren't Mal.

I tripped and fell right into a fantasy about Mal, like something out of a historical romance only much dirtier, Mal as viscount or duke ordering me to get on his cock... to milk him dry so that when the upper-crust seductress intent on tricking him arrived at his English country estate he wouldn't be able to impregnate her. He'd keep me hidden, naked and chained by my collar under his palatial four-poster bed, and after a lavish dinner in the formal dining room, he'd take the woman to bed. The bed would creak and groan while he tried to satisfy her. Maybe he'd even fuck her—yes, Mal would get it up, of course he would—and she'd be none the wiser that he had barely a dribble of seed to plant between her legs. Then when she was gone, he'd pull me out from under the bed and put me into the covers and snuggle with me all night long...

Oh, self. That was not a good fantasy. That was a degrading and useless and *fucking hot* fantasy.

Maybe I should talk to Ricki. I wasn't sure I really wanted to get into the intimate details of my fantasies with her, though. We were close, but still, we had boundaries, too. I wondered if Granddad thought about that when he left the running of the Governor's Club to us. Did he think about how two sisters like us would manage to run a secret sex dungeon for Hollywood's elite without it getting too incestuous?

For the most part, we just stayed out of each other's way. If one of us was playing in a scene room, the other one was "on duty" as hostess, so we never actually saw each other play. When Axel put Ricki in bondage, he never did it in the main central room. I got spanked by everyone in the club for my birthday, but that wasn't like a scene-scene; I didn't even take off my clothes. Come to think of it, Madison was probably a much better choice of someone to talk to. We'd really hit it off, and she had tons more experience with kink than I did. I knew she wouldn't judge. She was also great as a dungeon hostess.

Running the dungeon was fun. I really liked being part of people having good sex and having a safe place to get kinky. But I really needed to figure out what was going on in my own head.

And buy a bigger dildo. I took out my phone to mail-order one before I even got home.

CHAPTER FOUR

ALL WORK AND NO PLAY

GWEN

My sister and I have this in common: We're very systematic about things. We make lists. She loves spreadsheets. I like flow charts.

And I liked sex with Mal. No, *liked* was not the right word. Craved, needed, "would die without"—those were more accurate. By morning I had decided to set aside all my doubts about my underlying motivations and focus on concrete goals. I had tasted the forbidden fruit and all I could think about was how to have more of it.

I sat down with my tablet in my room and drew a circle on one end and wrote *GWEN* in it. On the other end I drew a triangle with *MAL* in it. Okay. Now to visualize the paths from one to the other.

One potential path was going to be through the publicity dates, so I wrote the word *DATES* in the middle. The obstacle there was Mal's rules. He would have to get over the whole rule thing—let's face it, he'd have to get over himself, too, and what were the chances of that? I suspected if he really grew to like me that he'd start to bend the rules or decide that they no longer applied, but he had also demonstrated a fairly iron will, so it wasn't going to be easy. I made a dashed line through the word *DATES* to indicate the shaky nature of that plan.

Of course another potential path was through the Governor's Club. C-L-U-B. Axel was already a member. Just a few weeks ago Ricki and I had floated the idea about whether the rest of the band, being so intimately linked to Axel, should be invited, too. It was obvious to me now that Mal was a kinkster at heart. Would he be able to resist me if the right situation in the dungeon came up? Maybe he'd consider anything that happened in the dungeon to be under a different set of rules from either groupies or dating. Certainly worth finding out. I drew another dashed line, this one through the word *CLUB*. There was still the question of whether he would accept an invitation, and even if he did, whether I could get through his resolve.

Then there was a third way. I wrote *SUPERFANS* on the tablet and swooped my finger through a thick black line. Obviously given what I had seen, Mal would have rock star sex regularly with girls he didn't know. I still had the contact information of the superfans I'd met at the show. I'd have to cook up a convincing disguise, but hey, if it worked once, it could work again.

I liked the third way best because it was another test of my acting skills and it was the plan that relied the most on me and the least on anyone else. Mal could just be Mal; he wouldn't have to change anything, and we'd both be happy.

Time to set up a fake e-mail address.

I had just finished setting up an alias and mail-ordering a black wig when a text came from Ricki:

Next week, Bob Monteleone fund-raising bash, you, me, Axel, Mal?

I pulled up my to-do list and drew a circle around the word

DATES. If it was going to work, I just had to be ready when he changed his mind. I called her instead of texting back. "Fund-raiser, you say?"

"Yes, a banquet. CTC has a whole table."

"Well, if he'll put up with it, I wouldn't mind having Mal Keneally as my date."

"Was he that bad? I thought you were getting along great at the premiere."

"Oh, he's a sweetheart, but I think he'd rather be sitting in his crypt pulling the wings off bats than talking to me."

Ricki laughed and then tried to stifle it. "Oh, Gwen. That doesn't sound like a ringing endorsement."

"Don't take it the wrong way! He's interesting to talk to and I could listen to his accent all day. But I'm not the one you might need to convince. Mal told me it was his manager's idea that we should be seen together for publicity purposes. I think I might be more willing than he is."

She clucked her tongue. "Does this mean you're getting used to the idea that raising your public profile could be good for your career?"

I held in a sigh. I still didn't really like that idea, but now that I had ulterior motives for being with Mal, I rationalized it. "Maybe I'm finally figuring out that being seen is part of the job description."

Besides, I was already planning the ultimate test of my acting skills.

* * *

MAL

Why do rock stars wear sunglasses so much?

Perhaps some enjoy the mystique. I have also been told that

those avoiding the paparazzi prefer them because photos that do not show your face are less desirable to photographers.

In my case the dark glasses were purely practical. Los Angeles is very nearly a desert and the sun shines as wretchedly bright as in the Sahara. Especially when one has spent most of the previous night on a glorious, whiskey-fueled songwriting binge. The five of us had played until nearly four a.m. before grabbing a few hours of sleep before a morning photo shoot. I didn't regret the night's activities one bit, but I did ever so slightly regret how bloodshot my eyes were.

I, at least, didn't scream like a schoolgirl when the stylist put the drops in my eyes, unlike Axel. Chino, not to be outdone, put on a full horror-movie act, complete with dropping to his knees and clawing at his face in agony. I held in a smile as the poor assistant stylist, who couldn't have been more than eighteen, stood beside him with her hands fluttering, a look of pure terror on her face.

Chino laughed, hopped up, and took a bow, the rest of us applauding and the stylist breathing a sigh of relief. I think he'd convinced her she'd accidentally put acid in his eyes. Which was what it felt like, but no.

Photo shoots are a test of both physical and mental endurance. The band would rather play a three-hour show in West Texas with no air-conditioning than do a photo shoot.

But they are a necessary brick in the path of success.

This one thankfully did not take all day. The photographer had just two hours with us before she had to move on to her next gig, which suited us fine. We changed clothes only once and needed hair touched up once. Doable. At least this shoot took place inside a studio and not somewhere ridiculous like the "LA River" (the giant concrete drainage ditch you always see in movies). Our previous one had taken place there, the Santa Ana winds had been blowing, and we ended up blanketed with wildfire smoke and ash.

A much more pleasurable task was that afterward we signed autographs for a few fans who had found out where we'd be—and there were nearly always a few, no matter where we went. A group of about a half dozen were patiently clustered on the sidewalk outside the building and we spent several minutes autographing things and taking selfies with them.

One of the women there was the zaftig blonde, Aurora, whose day I made by asking, "Aurora, have you e-mailed that photo yet?"

"I did! I did!" Her eyes, her face, her entire body lit up with euphoria. "Did you not get it?"

"Just checking. I had you send it to our management office but I haven't checked with them yet. I will inquire."

"Let me know if you need me to send it again! In fact, here, just to be sure, I'll e-mail it again now." She bent her head to her phone and I took the moment to study the faces of the other girls, looking for the mystery girl, "Excrucia." None of them were redheads and my memory of her face was as dim as the light in the room had been. In fact, my brain seemed to be conflating her and Gwen Hamilton, since the face I now pictured was Gwen with heavy black eyeliner.

We arrived at the rehearsal studio by midafternoon. Basic Records was pushing us to deliver the next album, but I was insisting we not go into the recording studio with a producer again until we had a better handle on the material to choose from. They had wanted to put an album into the pipeline before we went on the road, but given how disastrously the recording sessions had gone, we'd only managed to fully finish two songs. Now that the tour was over, we needed to buckle down and get back to work.

Between what we had in inventory and what I'd written while we were on the road, I think we had close to forty potential songs to work with, which sounds like a surplus but trust me, once a producer like Max Martin or Larkin Johns starts ripping your music to shreds, sometimes you have very little left by the end. Well, we hadn't worked with Max Martin, but our experience with Johns had left me with a very bad taste in my mouth—so bad that I was wary of producers as a whole now.

I sat down with my electric tuner and my current favorite guitar, a Paul Reed Smith with a dragon inlaid in pearl. Yes, a dragon. It was an indulgence in image and an insanely expensive guitar, but also an insanely good one, imminently playable with incredible tone. Not to mention beautiful to look at. But if it had merely been beautiful to the eye and not also to the ear, I wouldn't have bought it.

The rest of the band went through their own preparations. Ford tuned his bass across the room from me, doing the bottom string with a tuner and then using his ears for the other three, his eyes unfocusing as he listened, his dirty-blond hair hanging in front of them. Axel had gone into the bathroom to warm up his voice; everyone sounds better in the shower because of the echoes off the tile, and professional singers are no exception. Chino tightened his cymbals on their stands.

"Where's Samson?" I asked Ford.

He shrugged. "I'm not his keeper. Why are you asking me?"

Hmm. The reason I was asking him was because the two of them so frequently traveled together, but his defensive answer made me think perhaps now was not the time to point that out. "Just thought you might have heard him say something."

I heard the outer door open, though, and in came Samson. He had his hair up in a topknot and was carrying a stack of pizza boxes. "*Ta-da.* Aren't you guys hungry?"

Ford's eyes were shadowed and he said what I was thinking: "We should really get to work."

"Hey, we've got to eat sometime." Samson set the boxes down on the table against the wall. "Look, I even got it from the place you like."

Americans are strangely sectarian about certain things and pizza is one of them. Honestly I could not see why if one wanted melted cheese and tomato on flat bread it mattered so much whether the crust was thick or thin, crunchy or chewy, or a thousand other variations, but the others assured me it did. And we often let Ford pick what we ate because, we jokingly said, he was the runt of the litter and needed to fatten up. Ford wasn't actually significantly shorter than anyone else in the band but me. In fact, he and Chino were the same height, though Chino outweighed him by about forty pounds of muscle—but facts have never stopped a good round of ball-busting, and never underestimate the amount of ball-busting necessary to keep any band sane.

Ford set his bass into the stand and went to inspect what I strongly suspected was a peace offering from Samson. In a band, there are always undercurrents of who is getting along with whom at any given time.

Ford took a slice and tore into it with gusto, apparently approving of this pizza. I resigned myself to a lunch break and set down my instrument as well.

Axel joined us with a chuckle but did not comment beyond that.

"What do you think, Mal?" Samson said as we began demolishing the second pizza. "Can we work on that song from last night some more?"

"We could," I allowed, catching Ford's eye before he looked away. It was a song the two of them had written together. Axel and I wrote most of the band's songs but we were open to some compositions by the others if they were good. It was going to be up to the record company to choose what went on the album ultimately, no matter how much I liked it. I tried to be sure they knew I approved of it so if it got cut later they wouldn't think it was because of me. "I like that riff."

They shared fleeting smiles with each other and it appeared whatever rift had been brewing between them was healed.

When we were done working on that song, though, I wanted to work on one about sex. I'm sure that comes as a complete surprise.

* * *

We worked for several hours, running through our inventory of half-finished songs and favorite riffs, and Axel listed them on the whiteboard propped against the wall. Those without titles were represented by descriptive phrases that would hopefully spur us to remember which we meant: "So Many Drums" and "Chugga Chugga Wah" and others like that.

We took a break after sunset and I stepped out to see if some fresh air could be had—the term *fresh air* being relative to the smog level in LA. I drove to the nearest convenience store as much for the break as to actually look for some decent beverages.

Our rehearsal space was in a small strip mall, in what had once been a semi-private fitness training gym. As I pulled back into the parking lot, I was displeased to see a couple of women standing in front of the shuttered tanning salon next door. They approached the car as I got out.

"Hi, Mal," the blond one in the front said.

Aurora again. This time I didn't use her name. "You can't be here."

"Um, we were just wondering if—"

"No. We're working. All of you. How did you find out where we were?"

"Well, Krista thought she saw your car the other day at the Circle K down the street and—"

I shook my head. I knew getting the cherry-red 4C had been a mistake; the Alfa Romeo was too easy to spot. They'd probably seen us drive away from the site of the photo shoot today and knew the makes of our cars and our license plates. "This is utterly inappropriate and you should all be ashamed of yourselves," I said. "Do you not see enough of us at public events? Is it necessary to invade our privacy and interrupt our work? *Go.*" I pointed to the road. "And do not come back or we will close this location and go elsewhere."

"Okay, okay! We're going. I'm sorry, please don't ban us—"

"Go!"

They fled. They ran to a gray hatchback and drove away.

Chino was digging through the now-cold pizza as I came in the door. "What, did they not have the bottled tea you like, or did something else ruin your ever-sunny disposition?"

"Fans," I barked, and set the assortment of drinks I'd bought onto the table next to the stack of pizza boxes.

"What, out here?" We were in a nowhere part of town, not a place we'd expected to be found. Chino looked toward the front windows but they were completely tinted in and had blinds to boot. Back when this had been a small gym, the people working out hadn't wanted to be ogled by those driving by.

"Yes." I took a cold piece of pizza for myself and tore into it with abandon. Apparently running the fans off had worked up my appetite. "I told them don't come back or there'd be hell to pay."

The others gave me shrugs of agreement. Even if my stalkery ex wasn't out there, none of us wanted to deal with a horde of girls at the door every day. Most of our fans were wonderful people, and we quite enjoyed them, but some bad apples could do annoying things like steal pieces of our cars (not kidding), and even the presence of our best fans could be a kind of a pressure on the mind. The last thing I needed while working on new material was an audience standing right outside. Plus, if we let them gather, it would only be a matter of time before someone made bootleg recordings from a mic on the window. And the equipment—some boyfriend or desperate family member could decide our instruments and gear comprised a pot of gold waiting to be swiped. The alarm system on the building was a joke.

But then I mentally began kicking myself. If I wanted to find Excrucia again, I needed to be friendlier to those girls. They were probably my best chance of finding her again.

You're cracking up, Mal, I thought. *Pressures of fame are getting to you. This is a warning that you should forget her and stick to your rules.*

I've always been good at playing devil's advocate, though. *Just once. I'll see her just once more.* I rationalized that if we'd had more time, I would've gone farther with her, done more, that one time. *So if I see her again, that's all it'll be. It won't go any farther than that.* I wondered if perhaps she might show up at the Basic Records Beach Bash and—

No, don't be stupid. Put her—and Gwen Hamilton while you're at it—right out of your mind before someone gets hurt. Find some new biddable young body to torture.

I channeled that hidden inner angst into my songwriting. It had to be good for something.

* * *

GWEN

We arrived a little early to the Monteleone fund-raiser without our dates because Ricki wanted me to meet another guest: a talent agent named Simon Gabriel, who was there shepherding one of his clients, Jolene Hingham. I had met Jolene before, at the post-Grammy party at our house, but hadn't met her agent.

I got the message. I needed an agent and the way to interest a good one wasn't e-mailing my résumé cold. It also wasn't good form to just plow right into pitching myself as the next big thing, so I refrained from talking business, sticking to safe topics like recent film releases and the Dodgers.

Then Mal and Axel arrived and we had official photos taken at the backdrop in the lobby. Mal had his hair back in a long braid threaded with silver, highlighting the silver ring through his ear and emerald held captive on it. His shirt and tie were dark satin-silver and his tux jacket and pants were matte black.

I was never going to look that suave or sophisticated. I felt lucky I didn't fall off my Jimmy Choo heels. Although maybe that would have been nice as we posed together, if I fell against him...? Lucky for me the photographer was the one who suggested I put my hand on Mal's chest and that he put an arm around my back. Even with the heels, I was shorter than he was, and his pecs felt comfortingly solid. His hand found the crook of my waist and the sunny smile I put on for the photo was entirely genuine. His hand on me felt *right.*

I reminded myself not to overdo it, though. Slow and steady was going to be better than antagonizing him and losing the chance to see him again.

Once we were seated, I met the last two people at our table for eight, a CTC shareholder named Dr. Lionel Torres and his wife, Tyra. Mal was seated at my left, Dr. Torres at my right. He was brazenly gray haired and handsome, and his wife had a gracious smile.

"A doctor?" I asked as I shook his hand. "I didn't know we had many doctors as majority stockholders."

"I'm sure you don't," he said with a smile. "Except maybe the big money plastic surgeons."

I took that to mean he wasn't in plastic surgery. "So what type of doctor are you?"

"Originally I was an endocrinologist, which led me into fertility for quite a while, and I ended up in the business of what is politely known as 'men's lifestyle' medicine."

"You're a *dick doctor*?" Axel said from Ricki's other side, causing laughter around the table.

Dr. Torres grinned. "No, that's a urologist, but I do specialize in fixing erectile dysfunction. In fact, I was doing it before it was cool," he said, polishing his nails on his lapel.

"You mean before Viagra?"

"Yes, and let me tell you, the existence of the little blue pill hasn't put me out of business yet."

"That's fascinating." I ended up asking him a ton of questions about what he did and whether he could write prescriptions for porn and a bunch of stuff like that. ("One needs a subscription for porn, not a prescription, dear.")

We were done with salad and they were serving the main course when I realized suddenly that I had been completely ignoring Mal. The waiter put a plate down in front of each of us and I turned to him guiltily. "Um, hi."

I didn't know him well enough yet to be sure if the tightness across his mouth was him being disapprovingly unhappy or him hiding a smile of amusement. "Nice to make your acquaintance," he said dryly, and I still couldn't tell if that was a rebuke or a joke. He picked up his steak knife. "Hmm. What are the chances this is edible?"

I looked down at my plate. They had given us prime rib. Mine was swimming in blood and looked like it might have been still mooing when it was sliced. His was the opposite, with a rich, dark crust on the outside and gorgeously marbled with fat. "Do you by any chance happen to prefer it rare?"

"As a matter of fact, I do," he said, brightening right up.

"Because I like mine more done." I gave him a hopeful smile. "Want to swap?"

"You are a goddess among women and feel free to remind me I said that," he said as he deftly switched our plates.

"I'll get it tattooed on," I joked as I picked up my own knife. I could see Axel was smirking, too. I guess it wasn't the first time Mal had wanted the rare stuff. I was about to ask if there was a story there, but Ricki struck up a conversation with Tyra then and I concentrated on eating my meal as neatly as possible.

I was wearing red again, a different dress with a mini, high-cut jacket. I'd wanted to wear black, because I'd known Mal would like that, but I had also already planned what I was going to wear to the Beach Bash and it was black. It'd be a much better disguise if he didn't associate that color with me.

When Mal finished eating, his hand landed casually on the back of my chair. He appeared to be paying attention to the emcee, who was introducing the banquet speaker, but my heart leaped into my throat. Did he even notice he was doing it? I wanted to lean closer to him, maybe tuck my shoulder under his, but I didn't dare unless he was intending it to be flirtatious. Or at least look flirtatious...?

Oh, Gwen, you have it bad. I stayed still, enjoying the fantasy that any moment now that hand would move from my chair to my shoulder, and then he would lean down to whisper something lovely and intimate in my ear. I didn't care what. Something.

There wasn't much of a chance to talk once the speaker got going. When he was done, the auction started, and while that was droning on and on, dessert and coffee were served. Axel and Ricki kept themselves amused by feeding each other spoonfuls of chocolate mousse.

I glanced at Mal more wistfully than I intended, then looked away quickly, but he had noticed. He misinterpreted what I was longing for, though, and pushed his entire cup of mousse in my direction. "We're even," he murmured in my ear.

"Thanks." I dared to peck him on the cheek before he could withdraw. Something flashed through his eyes when I did and it didn't look like anger. I scooped the mousse cup into my hand and picked up my spoon, pretending to ignore him now.

All eyes were on the podium—except maybe Mal's—and I took the opportunity to test his resolve, carefully licking every trace of chocolate from the spoon before dipping it for more, and then doing it all again. I sucked the whole spoon into my mouth and hollowed my cheeks. I didn't dare check whether he was actually watching me but I sensed him shift in his seat. Impatient? Or were those tuxedo pants getting a might tight? I could hope.

His napkin landed on the table and he barked, "If you'll excuse me," before he hurriedly stood. As he stormed away, a waiter shied back out of his path and I wondered if perhaps I had overdone it.

* * *

MAL

I took far too long to return to the banquet hall from the men's room, but what else could I do? The Need had to be quelled. In boarding school I had perfected the art of wanking silently in the restroom, but it took time.

Gwen Hamilton had to know what effect her tongue-and-spoon games had on me, didn't she? Maybe she thought my gift of the mousse had been intended to provoke such a display from her? I'd merely meant to be kind.

The fantasies her mouth inspired! Sweet angels. I imagined her under the table, hidden from the glitterati and moneyed folk around us, alleviating my boredom with a talented oral exploration of my equipment.

In my fantasy world she was chained there, her hands behind her back, her mouth available for my use. When I would grow impatient with her teasing ministrations, I would grasp her by the hair and fuck her mouth, bringing myself to the edge before letting go, allowing her to continue her slow, sensuous stimulation of my cock.

To reward her for her excellence, I would stimulate her in return, pressing a polished shoe between her legs, giving her something to rub herself against, the poor neglected slave girl. I would challenge myself not to come until after she did, but when she did, when she would choke down on a cry of release, then and only then would I paint her lips and cheeks with my seed...

I came with a series of harsh breaths, into the toilet, my hand shaking as I wrung the come from my cock. *Mal Kenneally,* I thought, *you are not a man—you are a savage beast.*

This was a terrible sign for my self-control, the Need gripping me like that. I thought I had left fantasizing so vividly about sex—or about women in general—behind with other teenage behaviors. And yet here I'd lost myself in a full-blown adolescent porn fantasy. About my best friend's girlfriend's sister. This was not what I considered wise.

Was I encouraging her without realizing it? Before she had picked up that cup of mousse, I had been holding my fantasies in check by sheer force of will. During the photographing, it was all I could do to control myself. She had a gentle but intoxicating scent and each time she was near, I found myself wanting to pull her even closer, to bury my nose in her hair or seek out her pulse points with my tongue.

I'd tried to tell myself my lust was misplaced. The only reason Gwen was attracted to me was because of that blasted film we'd seen together, and surely she had recovered her senses by now. It was only me who hadn't.

But when she had made love to a cup of mousse with her mouth, I had fled before I did something inadvisable like . . . take that delicate hand of hers and slip it into my trousers under the table. My thoughts were at least less lust-clouded now, but I felt ill equipped to discuss this with her.

I could hear applause from the ballroom. At the very least to save face, I had best bid her a chaste good night. I hurriedly cleaned up, washed my hands, and made sure I was presentable again before I exited the washroom.

The crowd was already streaming through the lobby, apparently as eager to escape as I had been, though undoubtedly for a different reason. I ducked into the banquet hall but I could see the table was empty.

I caught sight of Axel, though, with Ricki on his arm, Gwen and the others behind them. I made my way through the crowd toward them, hoping to at least salvage a polite good-bye and to try to prove to Gwen I had been unaffected by her toying with me.

I had almost reached them when Gwen's heel caught on the carpet and she nearly fell, except that Dr. Torres caught her by the arm.

I felt the oddest thing—a surge of heat. Anger? Jealousy? Possessiveness? All of the above: a strange rage that I had not been the one whose arm was around her.

A photographer stepped in front of the group, impeding their way to the exit. He picked the wrong moment to do so. I strode forward with my teeth murderously gritted and he fell back hurriedly, the leech.

Outside the venue, I helped Gwen into the back of her limousine, Axel doing the same to her sister on the other side of the car. "Thank you for a lovely evening," I said, unable to come up with anything original to say that wouldn't betray far too much of what was churning inside me.

"Likewise," she said, patting my hand before letting go.

I would like to think that I played it cool, but unfortunately I suspect that she knew exactly what she had put me through.

CHAPTER FIVE

ROCK HARD

GWEN

I knocked on the door frame of the entrance to Ricki's office. The room had been our grandfather's office before he died but she'd brightened it up a lot. The bay window overlooking the grounds was now full of potted plants and the walls were a tasteful pale yellow. "Got a minute?"

She looked up from her computer screen. "Sure, what's up?"

"I just figured I'd pop down here to talk to you instead of e-mailing you from across the house," I said, plopping myself into one of the armchairs facing her desk. "I can't do the video filming this Saturday, but how about Monday?"

"Oh, I'm sure that's fine, too. Let me message them." She tapped on her keyboard quickly and then looked up at me again. Her phone rang seconds later and she put it onto speakerphone. "Hi, Mandy, what's up?"

"Nothing much, I just figured I would call instead of sending ten more e-mails back and forth. Is Gwen there, too?"

"Yep, right here," I said.

"Great. Let's see." Her voice was tinny through the phone speaker. "Monday, Monday . . . three p.m. All right? I expect it'll take about two hours to get the footage I want."

"That works for me."

"Perfect. Oh, Gwen, while I have you on the phone, I went looking for photos of you online to grab to make the storyboard with. Did you set up a Facebook fan page?"

"No, I haven't. Should I?"

"I thought you hadn't, but I came across one. Well, I guess that means you have a fan out there."

"Huh. What's on it?"

"Nothing much, just a couple of photos."

Ricki grinned. "See? Things are already starting to take off."

"Ha. I don't think one Facebook page is exactly the world beating a path to my door, but whatever." I got up. She hadn't even asked me what I was doing Saturday, which was good because that meant I didn't have to hide the fact that I was going backstage with a couple more superfans of The Rough.

I'd made this plan before the Monteleone fund-raising dinner, and now I was glad that I had. I was pretty sure I'd gone too far there and I was kicking myself a little about that. When Mal had stormed away from the table in a huff I had just about died. I didn't want him angry at me. I'd figured the worst that could happen was he'd ignore my flirting and teasing or tell me to stop. Apparently it didn't take much to drive him away. Overall, I considered the publicity dating plan to have taken two steps backward. Meanwhile, the next dungeon party wasn't for a couple of weeks. That left going backstage as my best current option, and still my favorite.

I had decided on a Gothic Lolita look this time. You wouldn't believe some of the amazingly great costume and tutorial videos there are out there. I found out about wig clips and sewed them into the wig: one video swore if I used them he'd be able to tug on my fake black hair during sex and it wouldn't come off. Black lipstick, double-layer fishnets, a skater skirt with satin waist-corset to make my hips look big and my boobs busty—neither of which they were—and I was all set.

Either it was going to work or it wasn't.

* * *

I met up with some of the other girls I had e-mailed with at a Target and we carpooled from there to the Beach Bash. One of them said she was definitely on the guest list, one of them claimed she knew Nick—the band's head of security—really well, and the third one had a friend who had supposedly been "picked" for sex once before. I didn't tell them I had been, too.

You might think that groupies would be competitive with each other, tearing each other down and hissing with jealousy. But it was not like that at all. A lot of these fans knew each other and they seemed to have a really supportive community, as if when one girl "won" and got to meet the band, they all won somehow. I was a little surprised to learn the ultimate goal for each of them wasn't necessarily to sleep with a rock star, even though they talked about sex openly. Some just wanted to meet the guys, be near them. Some had already met the band multiple times. Having grown up inside the world of celebrity instead of outside it, I was amazed and fascinated by the whole thing.

It turned out that in this group, each one of us had a different favorite. "Okay, but seriously," said April, the one who was driving, "what's this I hear about Axel being off the market these days?"

"I'm telling you," said Monica, the one who knew the head of security, as she applied fresh lipstick in the passenger seat. "He did not sleep with anyone this whole tour."

"That's unnatural," April said, shaking her head. "How does a man deprive himself like that? Especially a guy like him."

I put on my best funny-girl voice. "You know? There's this thing I heard about called masturbation?"

That made them all laugh. I hoped it was true, too, that Axel had been staying true to Ricki. It was certainly good to hear.

April didn't seem at all disappointed by the news. "That's actually really sweet. Only makes me want to meet him even more."

"The rest still party hearty, though?" asked Della, who was in the backseat with me. She had blond ringlets and her makeup made her eyes look huge. "Right? Chino didn't pair up with somebody and I missed it?"

"Nope, honey, he's still quite the party boy from what I hear," Monica assured her. "Speaking of party boys. Vera," she said to me, using the name I had picked off a designer label, "we knew you were a Mal girl the second we saw you."

That boosted my confidence. "He likes the vampire type?"

April snickered. "He *is* the vampire type."

I played dumb. "Oh, really? What have you heard?"

"Girrrl, I hear he is a cruel bastard. Kinky as fuck. A real hurts-so-good type. Which is totally okay if you're into that, you know?"

I looked at my fake black-tipped nails and said coolly, "I think I can handle him."

They all laughed. Then April said to Monica, "Are you still really into Ford? Even after all the rumors that went around?"

"Rumors shmumors," Monica said. "Just because nobody on the fan sites or bulletin boards has sucked his dick doesn't mean anything. Maybe he's just more discreet. He's obviously the sweetest of the bunch. Boy next door. Maybe he likes a quieter sort of girl."

"Or boy," Della stage-whispered, making us laugh again.

"You really think so?" Monica said. "I mean, I know he and

Samson do some crazy stuff onstage, but I didn't think it was *real.*"

"Do you think they do that stuff to start rumors about themselves?" Della said, her eyes wide and intense as she leaned forward. "Or do you think the rumors are true and they do that stuff to make it seem like that's the source?"

Monica waved her hand. "Psssh. No need for a conspiracy theory. I just hope he remembers me from Phoenix."

At the show things went smoothly: April was on the guest list and a quick discussion between Monica and the roadie I remembered from the Forum resulted in all four of us being given passes to a VIP area. Yes! Nick didn't apparently recognize me, which was a good sign.

The Basic Records Beach Bash was a big promo concert where each act was only playing thirty to forty-five minutes, and in the parking lot beyond the stage I could see dozens of trailers had been set up. Our VIP area was very close to the stage, but to the side and slightly behind it.

"Aurora!" Monica and April recognized a friend among the cluster of folks standing around and they introduced me as Vera. I remembered her from the premiere; in my head she had become the Disney Princess from Colorado.

"You guys, you guys, you're not going to believe it. I actually got an e-mail from Mal," Aurora said excitedly.

"Really? That's awesome! I thought he was really aloof online," Monica said.

"He is, but here's the thing. He's trying to contact a fan who was at the Forum show. And I have no idea who he's talking about."

Monica rolled her eyes. "That party was huge. There were probably fifty people from the fan club VIPs alone. Usually I know everyone, but not that night. What did she look like?"

"His description was, get this, red hair and fishnets."

April snorted. "That narrows it down to like... a quarter of the people there."

My heart leaped into my throat. Mal was looking for me. I mean, he didn't know it was *me* me. But still. I kept quiet, afraid if I jumped into the conversation my voice would be shaky. Why would Mal be looking for me if he supposedly never did the same groupie twice? I had a crazy thought: What if he knew it was me? But that made no sense. Then again, my mind had been turned into a complete jumble at the news.

Monica gave a shrug. "Sorry, can't help you."

"Well, whatever, I told him I'd ask around," Aurora said with a sigh. "I tried. Vera, your corset is so cool! I love it!"

I tried to pull myself back to the moment, but it was difficult when Mal was a hundred percent of my thoughts. All I could do was cling to the possibility that this meant his rules were bendable after all and carry on. "Oh, thank you!" I said automatically, then looked down to check what I was wearing. I chuckled. "This thing looks like a knee brace on me. I really don't have the figure for corsets. You do, though."

Aurora put her hands on her hips. "You think so? I've always wanted one."

"Oh, definitely. The more you have, the more there is to shape. I have these fantastic catalogs at home."

Monica chimed in. "You could get an electric blue one to match the streaks in your hair. You'd look amazing."

"Corsets are great for your back, too," April added. "And they're so much easier to find now than they used to be. I used to have to go to the renaissance faire to get one."

The chatter about how fetishy fashions were mainstreaming carried on without me for a while as my thoughts returned to Mal. Would he like the corset on me? Would he like the "Vera" look? I felt certain he would. Even my lipstick was black. I'd warned the staff this time that I was dressing up and, even with the warning, our head of security Reeve had reacted when he first saw me like he was seeing a burglar. It wasn't until he recognized my voice that he'd stood down.

When a band I didn't know began to perform and it got too loud for conversation, I went to check out the beverage situation and found there were a couple of large drums full of ice and cans of energy drinks for us. I dug down and found some bottled water in there, too, thank goodness. I was nervous enough without getting pumped up on Red Bull.

I saw Monica talking to Nick and gesturing in my direction.

After the next act had performed and I was starting to get restless, Nick approached me and asked me to come with him.

I followed him around the tent of port-o-johns to the other side where we had a tiny bit of privacy. "Look, your friend said you're interested in Mal. I'll be honest, I am Mal's scout."

I nodded, hoping this meant he was about to lead me to Mal.

"I don't know what you've heard, but I have to check. Are you sure you're okay with him being kind of rough? I don't know how to put this exactly, but . . . listen. I've known him for years, and he's a very good guy. But I want to avoid a situation where you get in over your head."

"I've heard about Mal," I said. "I'm okay with it."

He still looked unconvinced.

"I've got a dungeon in my basement," I added.

"Okay. You looked like the type who could handle it, but I just had to be sure. Lately he's been—" He broke off with a shake of his head. "Okay. Here's the deal. The last song they'll play is 'Kidnap My Heart.' When they're about halfway through the song, I'll take you to his trailer. I'll warn you. He's in a mood, really loaded for bear today."

"Oh?"

"Yes. You sure you don't want to back out?"

"Sounds like a man who needs to blow off some steam." I raised an eyebrow. "That only makes me more interested."

He nodded. "Just remember, if it does get to be too much? He's not a jerk. Just say stop and he will. You know that, right?"

"Safe words, blah blah blah, you mean?"

Nick breathed a sigh of relief. "See, I knew you would know how to handle yourself."

Uh-huh, that's why you took me aside to give me this little pep talk, I thought. But I smiled and said, "Thank you for checking, though. It can't be an easy job . . ."

He shrugged. "It's part of the job. Mal's tricky. If I bring him somebody too timid, neither of them has any fun."

"Timid doesn't really describe any of the women here," I pointed out.

"You're right. *Timid* isn't the right word. Well, anyway, you're perfect." He checked his watch. "They go on in ten, and like I said, last song, we go straight to his trailer. If you can, be as close to the edge of the corral as you can, at the rear."

"Will do."

He ran off to his next task and I wandered back to the gals, giving April a smile and a thumbs-up when she gave me an inquisitive look. She hurried over. "You lucky duck! If Nick gave you 'the talk,' then you're definitely in."

I nodded. "My heart is beating a mile a minute!"

"It should be!" She hugged me. "Good luck! You want us to wait for you?"

"Oh gosh, I guess so?" I hadn't thought that far ahead. "You don't have to, though. I can get an Uber back to my car."

"I've heard sometimes he can be really wham-bam-thank-you-ma'am. If you're quick, we'll wait. If you're taking too long, though, we may split. I think Della and Monica are somewhere right now trying to write Chino's name across Della's cleavage in lipstick. Nick told us we'll probably get a five- or ten-minute meet and mingle after they come offstage." She bounced a little as she said it. "God, I'm excited and all I'm going to do is take selfies and get autographs!"

"That's awesome," I said, not sure what else to say.

"I mean, I know, wow, there are millions of fans who will never even get this close to them. I'm . . . really lucky." She sighed.

"You're okay with that?" I asked, curious about how happy she seemed. "You're not really trying for . . . more?"

"Hey. Before this I was a megafan of Adam Lambert. And *none* of us have a chance with him, you know."

I shared a laugh with her. Adam Lambert was the most out and proud gay man in the history of pop music, but that didn't stop millions of women the world over from swooning over him.

"Oh, hey, here comes their set," April said, and we hurried to the edge of the VIP area.

Although we were very close to the stage, it was difficult to see from there. My view of Mal was partly blocked by light stanchions and some sound equipment. But I could barely pay attention to what was happening on the stage when my mind was spinning and spinning on what was about to happen.

When the familiar riff of "Kidnap My Heart" kicked in, my heart went into overdrive, and the next thing I knew, Nick was grabbing me by the hand and pulling me along a maze of barricades, behind some trailers, and then up the stairs into one.

He shut the door behind me and I looked quickly around. The trailer was divided into two halves with the door in the middle. One side was kind of like a living room with two small couches and a countertop. On the countertop was a makeup mirror and a couple of bags. The other half of the trailer had a bed folded into the wall to get it out of the way, a card table, and another makeup mirror.

I sat on the couch, then stood up again, trying to think of what I should say when Mal walked in, what I should do.

Stay focused on your objective, I told myself, thinking of it as an acting exercise. In any improv acting exercise, each character had a simple objective that the other characters did not know, a motivating factor that would drive the scene forward. *My goal is to... get laid.*

I looked quickly at the makeup kit partly strewn on the countertop. There was a penknife sitting there. I picked it up to look at it more closely. The pretty little knife had a couple of dark streaks on the blade; someone had been using it to sharpen eyeliner pencils.

I stretched my legs a little and then bent over the couch so my ass faced the door, and placed the open knife on my back, atop the corset's strings.

Not a moment too soon. The door banged open and in came Mal. I heard him slam the door behind him and then after a stretch where I could hear him breathing hard, another sound. Was that him shoving a chair against the door?

I guess he wanted to be absolutely sure we wouldn't be disturbed.

* * *

MAL

Did they think I wouldn't notice Larkin Johns hanging around the catering tent with Marcus and chatting up Axel? His gray ponytail, combed back from his receding hairline, was conspicuous as he schmoozed. Did they seriously think I was suddenly going to change my mind about his suitability to work with us or that he could turn the band against me? I'd thrown him out of the studio once; I'd do it again.

These were the thoughts churning through my mind during the Beach Bash show and were still smoldering hotly as I hurried back to the trailer where Nick had sent the woman he'd chosen for me. *Find me one who can really take what I dish out,* I'd told him. I threw open the door, not knowing what to expect, but my mood changed the instant I saw her.

Oh sweet universe, thank you for whatever I did to deserve such blessings as this. She was bent over, head down, hands on the back of the couch, in a fuck-me position. She was still wearing all her clothes but she had a knife on her back, balanced on the laces of her corset. A gift is made more special by being wrapped—and then unwrapped—is it not?

And I needed this gift. I needed this woman, this involving little puzzle, to make me forget my growing frustrations with our record execs and to supplant my growing obsessions with Gwen and Excrucia. This one looked ripe to satisfy the Need.

I took the knife and wiped it against my jeans, then flipped her loose black skirt over her back. Nice ass, what I could see of it through the fishnets. She wore no panties and a beautiful damp spot clung to the stockings like dew in a spiderweb.

I may have a tiny bit of a fetish for fishnets—specifically for fucking through a hole in them. Some things you imprint on early in life.

She still hadn't said a word. I ran a hand down her thigh and she trembled, but not in a bad way.

I started cutting the corset off her, revealing the strapless tank top she wore underneath it. The tank top I shoved upward until her tits hung free. Standing behind her so my legs touched hers, I reached around to fondle them until her nipples were so hard and tight they felt like buttons.

And then I ran the knife down her back and she shivered and let out a moan. Knife play is one of my favorite things. People who haven't tried it simply don't realize how sensual the tip of a knife feels when it isn't cutting you, when it's merely leaving a suggestive trail against your skin. It's like a fingernail only ten times more arousing.

Yes, I've been on the receiving end of the knife, too. That's how I learned.

I traced imaginary whorls of smoke across her pale white back, then yanked her skirt down. Now I let the point snag her fishnets a bit as I traced up and down her thighs until I was ready to cut a hole big enough for my dick.

"Step out of the skirt," I commanded, "and spread your legs as wide as you can go."

She did. *Yes, thank you, divine fate, for delivering this biddable gift into my life.*

I slid the knife carefully through the fishnets at the wettest place and then tore them with a backward slash of the blade, leaving her gasping...

...and me amazed. Her tattoos suddenly visible to me now: *Love. Pain. Excrucia.*

Fate, now you are just fucking with me. Thrill at having the very woman I was obsessed with delivered into my hands warred with the thought that she must have tricked her way in here. Or had she? Had Aurora found her? Did she know I was looking for her?

I shoved a finger into her and she groaned eagerly, so wet and slippery and ready for me that it had none of the punishing effect I was hoping for.

"Either you're a massive coincidence, or you're the woman I fucked at the Forum," I said.

She nodded but stayed silent, an intriguingly submissive choice.

"Did you hear I was looking for you?"

A more vigorous nod this time. Sweet angels. My cock strained against my fly as if it wanted to teleport into her. She came back.

She came back for more.

I decided to string her along a bit. "Do you know my rule?"

She shook her head vigorously no. I finger-fucked her hard a few times.

"I find that hard to believe and your disguise makes me think you know quite well. It's common knowledge I don't do repeat engagements." I jiggled my finger inside her and provoked a gasp. Knowing that she had returned to me even after the previous taste of my depravity emboldened me to push her further. "But as you must have guessed, I was searching for you for a reason. And it wasn't so I could return your panties."

She pushed back against my finger now, showing how eager she was to be fucked. I added a second and she moaned.

All this chatter wasn't merely building anticipation in her. It was stoking the Need in myself to furnace pitch. "It takes a very special woman to take what I dish out. Something about you made me think I could push you further, though. So I thought perhaps I could satisfy the rule another way. After all, I haven't fucked your other hole yet."

It was patently obvious I was playing fast and loose with the rule, but within the lust-logic of the Need it sent a surge of hunger through me—through both of us. She clenched around my fingers when I said that. I took the opportunity to jam them in deeper and pull out a good load of her lubrication, which I then spread up and down her asshole. I pushed one finger in and nearly swore.

"The truth, pet. Have you ever had anal sex?"

She shook her head.

By all ye gods and monsters. A virgin. This knowledge only sharpened my appetite for ravishing her, the beast in me roaring with approval. "Don't move."

I looked for my road bag and found it under the table. I carried it back to her, then paused to strip off every stitch of my show clothes. She was trying to catch a look at me through the long strands of her black wig hanging down. I wondered if her real hair was red. At the time I'd thought it was a dye job but maybe it had been a wig and I hadn't noticed.

I dug out the small bottle of lube, a strip of condoms, and the leather belt I'd taken off to do the show. If you don't take your belt off, or at least turn it to the side, the buckle scratches the back of the guitar.

"You test me, Excrucia," I said. "You test me, so I'm going to test you." I trailed the doubled belt over her ass and she stiffened. "Keep those legs spread wide. I'm going to whip you with this belt. I'm going to whip you until every inch of flesh exposed is red. In fact..." I tore away more of her stockings, exposing the full globes of her butt cheeks. "Your ass, your thighs, your cunt."

She nodded in agreement.

I did as I promised, flailing her with the leather until my arm was tired and her entire genital region was inflamed. Some women can't withstand pain directly to the cunny. But she never buckled, never begged me to stop, never crumpled or curled into a ball.

Which only made my desire to have her burn even hotter. What a prize. What an incredible prize. I'd known there was something about her that intrigued me, but I hadn't expected this...perfection. I brushed my fingers over her swollen clit and she shuddered. LOVE PAIN her tattoo read. I believed it now.

I found myself contemplating whether next time I could make her come with the belt and nearly came myself from the mere thought. And then the thought: *Next time? You've already decided there'll be a next time?*

Think about that later. Right now, think about where you want to put that cock of yours and what it'll take to get it in there.

So many possibilities. Use the belt to secure her hands behind her back and have her service me with her mouth for a while? No. I had no patience for that right now and I needed no assistance at all in the rigidity department.

Lube, fingers, preparing her, stretching her. That was next.

She stifled a soft cry, plaintive and hungry, when I drilled her ass with one well-lubed finger. This was going to take some time, but it was one of those tasks in which thoroughness would be rewarded and haste would mean ruin.

I was good at being thorough because I was good at denying myself temporarily. It took long enough to work in a second finger that I began to wonder if her arms were growing tired of her position, then decided to let that be another test.

Perhaps there was not as much weight on her arms as I thought. She began pushing back against me as I filled and stretched her. Very encouraging.

A third finger was difficult but inevitable with patience. My hands are large. But so is my cock.

"Time to take me, darling," I said when the amount of lube in the bottle was beginning to dwindle and my hand was moving easily at last. "You remember how big I am?"

She nodded. This silence thing was interesting. I would have to ask her about it... assuming she didn't run off this time.

I took my time tearing open the condom package and rolling it on. Her legs trembled with anticipation.

I drizzled lube up and down my length and then rubbed the head against her now supple and sloppy hole. I still had to push to get it in but *sweet angels and demons* it was worth the effort. Two inches of me were buried in her and it felt like my entire body was throbbing with pleasure.

I pushed another two inches in with a snap of my hips and she flung a hand back, trying to slow me. I allowed her that, taking the rest gradually—never letting up my weight but slowing the penetration, filling her bit by bit until there was no more to give.

"You have me," I whispered, and she shook. What beauty, what beauty in her obedience, her submission. It spurred such strange and sudden feelings in me, an urge to reward her, to glut her with pleasure, as well as to guard her jealously against those who would misuse or exploit that biddable nature of hers.

These were unhealthy thoughts for me to be having about a strange girl I knew nothing about, a mystery woman who could be anyone, have any motive. But I could not stop having them with my cock buried as it was.

Enjoy the moment, isn't that what they say? I seized her by the hips then and force-fucked her hard five or six times, making her use her voice at last. She cried out wordlessly and I froze with the echo of her cry in my ears.

I had just played a show and my hearing might have been off. But I knew Gwen's voice when I heard it.

Gwen.

I had to be hallucinating. I had been obsessed with Gwen and with Excrucia and my lust-addled mind had decided they were the same person. Right?

I fucked her hard, trying to clear my head, but the cries only sounded more and more like Gwen.

Enough. "You sound like you're not being satisfied," I taunted. "Shall I put another beer bottle in your cunny?"

Angels and devils, she nodded. Fine. I pulled out abruptly, went to the tiny fridge on the wall, pulled out a beer, and popped the top off. I drank a deep draught and poured the rest down the sink, then barked at her. "Turn over. On your back." *Now,* I thought, *I'll see it's not Gwen.*

It was Gwen. Heavily made up with black lips and false eyelashes and a black wig but *it was Gwen.* I could see why Nick had been fooled, but knowing her as I did now, there was no mistaking her. I pushed her knees up to her chest, stuffed my cock into her ass again, and teased at her slit with the beer bottle. She shuddered and wriggled until I realized she was trying to get her clit against the glass. This exquisite creature, for whom pain was pleasure, was the same woman who had sat prim and proper beside me at that banquet and had tittered amusedly in the theater at the sexual innuendos in band names? But she was also the one who had admitted that the works of Ariadne Wood turned her on, who had brazenly propositioned me in the limo, and who had tormented me with her tongue, a spoon, and chocolate.

She had been wanting this all along.

"You wanton thing." I rubbed the lip of the bottle up and down against her clit and was rewarded with a wail from deep inside her as she came, the throbbing around my cock almost intense enough to make me come, too. I pushed the bottle aside and went after her clit with my thumb, wanting another orgasm from her almost as much as I wanted my own, pursuing it relentlessly.

She screamed again, and then I thrust my thumb into her, fucking her in both holes at once, and any plans I may have been making to delay my own gratification further were shredded by an orgasm so intense I lost my vision, my breath, and probably my mind.

* * *

GWEN

People throw around the phrase *best sex of my life* a lot when what I think they mean is "most recent sex in my life." Like "best pizza I ever ate." It wasn't the best; it was just the most recent.

Well, this was the best sex of my life up to that point. I'd never come so hard or that many times in quick succession. Because it was anal? Or because it was Mal? More likely Mal—his style, his technique, the way he made me feel—it all added up.

When we were done, he moved to the small sink to clean up a little and I saw the tattoo on his back for the first time. Had I really not seen Mal shirtless from behind before? Perhaps I'd had a quick glance that time at the Forum, but his hair was so long it could hide the sinuous blackwork dragon that coiled up his spine and spread its wings across his shoulders. Right now his hair was in front, though, giving me a full view of the tattoo.

He returned and lay down with me side by side on the narrow couch, slipping one hand between my legs immediately. That made me feel really weird—warm and wanted and possessed. I was used to withdrawing into my own body after sex and it was like Mal was holding the door open.

I liked that feeling.

"That was great," I said, because someone ought to fill the silence.

He grunted in agreement. "I must reluctantly concur."

"Reluctantly?"

"Only in that you have forced me to reevaluate my rule."

How did he have the ability to speak like an English professor right after knee-buckling sex? I tried to engage my brain. "Did that rule exist because the second time is never as good?"

His chuckle was low, dry. "You could say that." He reached up to stroke my wig affectionately.

What was he being so cagey about? That wasn't a yes or no. I tried asking another way. "Is the problem that you get bored?" When he didn't answer right away, I figured I had hit a nerve. "Because you'll never get bored of me. I can be a different woman every time."

"Can you?"

"Sure." If I was looking for a test of my acting abilities, this would certainly be one. "You tell me what you want, or let me surprise you."

He slipped a finger inside me and I clung to his shoulders with my hands. He murmured into my ear. "You'll find that I'm very difficult to satisfy."

I couldn't answer for a few seconds, as his finger triggered waves of aftershocks through my body. Which gave me my answer. "So am I."

"And the reason I don't do repeats is I become increasingly difficult to satisfy." He chuckled again and I felt certain this was just more dirty talk, not the real reason for Mal's rule. That was probably still fear of intimacy after all—which was why my proposal that I could be a different woman for him every time was perfect. The thrill of victory surged through me as he said, "If we're going to do this, you need to understand I'm going to push you hard."

All I heard was *we're going to do this.* Yes! "What do you mean by that?"

He jammed a second finger in alongside the first. "I am first and foremost a sadist. I like pain. I like suffering—*your* suffering especially. Sexual suffering *most* especially. To me the purpose of bondage isn't to look pretty or to tweak your leather fetish. It's to make sure you can't escape while I'm torturing you."

My throat tightened at the same time as I squeezed his fingers inside me. The words he was saying had stoked the fire between my legs to raging, even as my brain was thinking: *Is he just playing around, or does he mean it?*

I really hoped he wasn't just playing around.

I tried to get back into character. "I don't have a tattoo that says *Love Pain* by accident," I snarled.

With the hand that wasn't deep in my snatch, he yanked my hair (thank you, wig clips!) and forced me to look into his eyes. "Why are you here?"

"For the sex," I said quickly.

"Why me?"

"Because your reputation says you're the roughest of The Rough."

He searched my eyes. "A beautiful woman like you could surely have her pick of bedmates."

I nodded as best I could with his grip at the back of my neck. "And I pick you." I tried to sound just as confident when I confessed the thing I hadn't been able to say aloud, even while Chuck had been tattooing me: "Because it's not just sex I need. I need pain, too."

"Perhaps this arrangement can be mutually satisfying, then," he said, sliding his fingers in and out of me. "I promise no permanent damage, no scars. Beyond that, my dear, here is my pledge. Accept any pain I dish out, any command I give, and you will never take your leave of me unsatisfied. But refuse me and I will send you away unfulfilled."

"That seems fair," I said, my hips starting to move in time with his thrusts.

"I cannot promise that our trysts will be frequent," he added. "Though I confess I would dearly like to see you next week."

Maybe it was just his accent but phrases like *dearly like to see you* sent my heart racing. "N-next week would be fine."

"I'll secure a hotel suite. How will I contact you?"

"I'll give you my e-mail address."

"Excellent. Then I will send you not only the location but also instructions on who to be."

"How much time will you give me to prepare? If I need a costume or—"

"Two days, at least. Now tell me honestly, Excrucia, do you want to come again?"

I tried to close my legs around his hand but he blocked me with his elbow, his thumb working up and down my clit. "You've been fingering me. Of course I—"

"A simple yes or no would suffice."

"Yes."

"The coin is pain, the return is pleasure," he said. "Tell me what pain you'll give me in exchange for this pleasure."

My heart beat in double time while I racked my brain. What pain? Did he mean what part of me I wanted him to hurt, or what way I wanted to be hurt? I was paralyzed by the possibilities.

But I suddenly realized what the only right answer was. "I'll give you whatever pain you want to inflict."

His grin was feral. "That's right. You will." With that, he bit down on one of my nipples and did not let up until I was screaming—from orgasm.

* * *

MAL

Sweet mother of angels, what was I getting myself into? I left her in the trailer, well fucked and sated, while I fled to the refuge of my car in the outer parking lot. I managed to escape without running into anyone else from the band, which was fortunate because the thing I needed most at that moment was to be alone to think.

It was already madness to have decided to go down this road with a groupie, but *Gwen*! I was full-on certifiably insane. I was putting myself on a collision course with everything I knew I should avoid. How long would it be before she came to realize that what I did to her was leaving unseen scars? How long before she renounced me and reviled me? How long before her self-esteem crumbled under the weight of submission? Risa had led me on for months before biting the hand that fed her. Risa, the woman I would have married despite my father's approval, despite the issues, despite everything, had she not broken every promise and recanted every moment she had spent as my supposed slave.

But Gwen is not Risa, I told myself.

No, in fact, Gwen is not even *Gwen*, technically, having come to me twice now under a disguise. Did she know that I knew? She was certainly playing it cool if she did.

I pulled onto the highway, letting my brain drive on autopilot while I thought. Either she had no idea that I recognized her or she was such a good actress that she didn't let on the slightest bit. Both were possible, I decided. Maybe what she wanted most was to get away from her prim and proper heiress life and this charade allowed her to? I could certainly sympathize with that.

If that was her strategy, it made a certain amount of sense. That way we could still be seen in public for PR purposes. She could pretend all we had was an arranged thing and so could I. We could keep all the rest locked away in our trysts.

There was a kind of safety in pretending. I wondered if it allowed her more resilience, feeling that a scene was happening to a character instead of to her true self. Role-play seemed to ramp up the intensity while simultaneously allowing a kind of emotional buffer.

I still had no doubt that after a few such experiences at my hand she would decide she'd had enough and pull away from me. She was too strong and smart a woman to let me have my way for very long. A time would come when I'd fail to rein in the Need, when I'd push too far. Then it would be time to separate...but perhaps not quite yet. My fantasies were straining for release as I dreamed of the possibilities we might explore together. I'd told her I would dictate where to appear and who to be when she did. If I was already her fantasy, what fantasy of mine could she fulfill?

The possibilities were so enticing to dream on I drove right past my exit.

CHAPTER SIX

SMACK YOUR LIPS

MAL

We took two days off after the Beach Bash and then we went back to rehearsing. I wrote some fragmentary songs while home alone, but I reserved judgment on whether they were excellent or pure dreck. When I am at my most heated emotionally, it is likely to be one or the other, but my ability to judge which was absent entirely.

Meanwhile, I finally confronted Christina and Marcus via phone while driving to our rehearsal space late that morning. "I've been waiting to hear what producer we'll be working with in the next session, you know," I told them.

"Well, given our timeline, we're a little constrained by who's available. Christina nixed the idea of Max Martin because you'd have to move to Europe for a month or two to work with him," Marcus said.

I grunted in agreement.

"I do wish you'd consider giving Larkin Johns another chance."

I pulled over rather than risk an accident while arguing, because I could barely see from rage. "You have got to be kidding me." My knuckles whitened as I stress-gripped the steering wheel.

"Hear me out, would you? I know you didn't see eye to eye—"

"I threw him out of the studio and locked the door behind him," I reminded him.

"I know, and I want you to know he doesn't hold that against you. Mal, he understands how passionately you want the final product to be good. I really believe you two have more in common than you think."

I couldn't very well say that the reason I disliked Johns was his tendency to side with the record execs rather than the artists. "I'm not some pop princess who will do as she's told," I said instead.

"No one expects you to be. May I point out that the two songs he produced on your last album are the two that have hit the Top Forty? 'Kidnap My Heart' wouldn't have done half as well without his sound. I truly believe that."

"I believe you have a self-fulfilling prophecy. The two songs you gave him to rework are the two you enthusiastically pushed as singles."

"I should also point out that right now in the UK, four of the top five singles in airplay were all his. He's got a really good grasp on the sound that will cross over to European markets. Not that we at Basic actually get anything from your UK deal . . . " He trailed off and I wondered if he was trying to hide some bitterness about that, especially since he then entreated Christina to change my mind. "Christina, what do you think?"

"Mal," she said, "I will fight for whatever you want. But I don't want to cut off the band's best chance for big sales over a personality conflict."

I was silent.

Marcus spoke. "You and Larkin are both professionals. I know you could work together if you stay focused on the common goal of a kick-ass album."

"The difficulty lies in our divergent priorities," I said, trying to be polite about it.

"Well, I'd like to sit down with you and him, and the rest of the band if you want, and discuss those priorities. Unless there's some other producer you'd like us to try to get?"

"You know I'd prefer Bart Cubbins," I said. Other than the tracks Johns had reworked, the rest of the album had been basically mixed by me, Samson, and Cubbins in a collaborative effort.

"He's not available," Marcus said quickly. "I know, I did check. Even though I didn't like that choice, I did check. If there were an easy alternative, I'd have suggested it, Mal."

"Fine. Set up a meeting in a few days."

"Great. Will do."

"See?" Christina said to Marcus. "I told you he could be reason—"

I hung up as I sped back into traffic. Maybe the meeting would make it obvious to Marcus how badly we got along.

Overall, rehearsal went well that day, and we were blissfully undisturbed for two whole days in a row. Almost. Late on the second day, Axel picked up his phone and said, "Now I know why bands go to the south of France or tropical islands to work on stuff." He stared at his phone, shaking his head.

I set my guitar down and signaled the others to take a break as well. "What is it this time?"

"Christina got us on the guest list for Jolene Hingham's birthday party." He cracked his neck and sighed. "Biggest see-and-be-seen event this season, she says."

"Two questions," I said. "One, when? Two, who is Jolene Hingham?"

"Three," Chino piped up. "All of us or just you two?"

"All of us," Axel said, "tonight, and she won best supporting actress last year for playing the schizophrenic best friend in *West Texas*."

"Ah. So not the one with the lips puffed to match her tits," I said. "The redhead."

"Yes, although I don't think she's normally a redhead," Axel said. "So don't go making a fool of yourself at the party saying happy birthday to the wrong woman."

"Will we even have a chance to greet this woman? How big is this party?" I asked, looking over Axel's shoulder to see if Christina had sent any further information.

Up popped the official invitation and I heard a few other phones chime in the room: Christina had forwarded it to all of us. The bright yellow graphic was a rose—the yellow rose of Texas?—and the font was some kind of coiled rope design. Not the sexy kind of rope, the fake cowboy font kind. "Please tell me there isn't a rodeo theme."

Axel looked back at me in sympathy. "I would, but I'd be lying. Hoedown all the way, it looks like."

I held in a groan.

"Aw, c'mon, Mal," Chino said, bumping me with his shoulder. "At least we get a break from tuxedoes."

"You can still wear black," Axel pointed out. "Put on that concha belt you got in New Mexico and all the rest of the silver and turquoise stuff."

"I suppose." It was just as well that we were being yanked out of rehearsal, I thought, given how it was going. I wasn't pleased with how the band was sounding and my own playing irked me. I picked up my phone to check the details of the location and saw I had a text.

From Gwen. How fortuitous?

I was going to stay home and watch Netflix tonight but did you see they got rid of all the BBC shows?

Just kidding. Tonight's the birthday party for one of Simon Gabriel's clients, Jolene Hingham, and I've been encouraged to make an appearance. Make it with me?

I strongly suspected that the female grapevine had carried the suggestion from ear to ear rather than it being a complete coincidence, but I supposed it didn't matter. I texted her back:

Apparently I've also been invited to the party. I would hate to disappoint Ms. Hingham and I would hate even more to disappoint you. I shall pick you up at 7pm.

P.S. The BBC is overrated.

* * *

GWEN

"What's so funny?" Ricki asked, because I was staring at my phone, grinning like a fool.

He said yes. He actually said yes!

"Mal agreed to be my date tonight," I said, setting the phone down on the kitchen counter and trying to act cool about it. "So I guess I'm going to this party."

"Well, I know I am." Ricki bent over to put the milk back into the fridge and then put a hand on her back as she straightened up. "Argh. What's the point of being the CEO who wears yoga pants if I never get to do any actual yoga?"

"The problem with working at home is you never go to the gym," I said, resisting the urge to do a little twirl while still looking at Mal's message. Why was I so elated? It's not like we were actually dating, right? But any chance to be near him thrilled me down to my toes. I wondered what he was going to wear. For that matter, what was I going to wear?

"You know," Ricki said, distracting me from wardrobe

thoughts, "we still haven't formally invited the rest of The Rough to join the Governor's Club."

"Have you talked to Axel about it yet?"

"Yes. He's fine with it. He let it slip to Mal already, of course. Those two keep no secrets from each other."

"Oh, really," I said neutrally, thinking it didn't seem likely Mal actually told Axel as much as the other way around. Axel was a much more open person. "Well, you're in charge of invites."

"All right. But I won't do it tonight. It's too public. There won't be a chance." She downed the small glass of milk she'd poured for herself. "What are you going to wear?"

"No idea. It's supposed to be Western style? I have some nice cowboy boots somewhere. I'll have to look."

"Likewise. You want to go in the limo together?"

I shook my head. "Mal says he'll pick me up."

She laughed softly. "Like a real date."

"Tsk. It's that we know what kind of shenanigans you and Ax get up to in limousines. Wouldn't want to ruin your fun."

She blushed but didn't argue. Ha.

* * *

Mal was right on time, pulling up in a sleek red sports car. As Jamison opened the passenger door for me, I was pleased to see I'd matched his color scheme—or lack of one, since every stitch of clothing Mal was wearing was black. So was mine. I'd found a black suede skirt in my closet with a vest to match. Over a white blouse and with super-dark cowboy boots it was suggestive of Western without being costumeish.

He had his hair loose, his shirt unbuttoned all the way down, his chest covered with multiple necklaces and adornments, giving him *almost* a Native American aesthetic but mostly just pure "rock star." I slid into the passenger seat and before he could say anything, I leaned over and gave him a peck on the cheek. The scent of his skin was familiar and made my insides purr.

He glared at me a little but didn't say anything, merely put the car into gear. The moment Jamison closed my door, he pulled away from the house.

"You look quite nice," he said, but it was a generic compliment.

"Did they teach you to say that sort of thing on society dates?" I asked.

A short bark of laughter escaped him. "Yes. Was it that obvious?"

"It's okay, Mal," I said for my own benefit as much as his. "We both know this is all for show." I reminded myself to keep my cool and that he didn't know I was the painslut who had agreed to let him do whatever wicked thing he wanted to me. A sudden wave of heat passed through me, though, as I wondered, *What if I told him?* I suddenly didn't know which idea was more dangerous and thrilling, keeping the secret or shocking him by revealing myself. I took a breath; I'd have to think about it later. On our way to a public gathering wasn't the time to shake things up. "You don't have to try to pretend on my behalf."

That provoked a softer laugh from him. "You're much more of a . . . realist than I expected."

"I grew up in show biz," I said. "You've got to learn where to draw the line between fantasy and reality or you'll go crazy." Come to think of it, maybe that was one of Dad's biggest problems. To this day, he still has trouble distinguishing image from substance. I was suddenly glad he was in St. Maarten for a couple of months. I didn't want Mal to meet him and get a bad impression of my family.

Okay, now who's pretending? I thought. Mal wasn't a suitor for my hand. We were publicity dating, that was all. Even if I did tell him that arm-candy Gwen Hamilton and his exotic fucktoy were one and the same, wouldn't that make it even less likely this could turn into a "bring him home to Dad" sort of relationship? I suddenly found my head spinning, like I couldn't get my bearings on my feelings. It seemed very warm in the car, like I was getting drunk purely from breathing his pheromones. I wanted to touch his forearm as he rested his palm on the gearshift.

"Oh, oh wait!" I said suddenly as I realized he'd taken the wrong fork through the estate. The main gatehouse was to the east and he'd taken the west loop.

"Did I go the wrong way?"

"You did, but it's okay." Maybe I wasn't the only one disoriented. "This'll come back around. We're not late or anything, are we?"

"We will be fashionably timed," he said with a nod.

"Well, welcome to an impromptu tour of the Hamilton estate," I said, waving my hand. "Here is a hill. Over there, another hill."

He cracked a grin; then as we came around a bend and a building came into view, he asked, "Is that a stable?"

"Yeah. From the brief time when we had a couple of horses. But no one in the family was equestrian enough to keep it up, so it's been empty since about the time I went off to college."

"A shame, but understandable. Horses require a lot of attention and upkeep. They're not like a car you can simply leave in the garage until you want to go somewhere." He craned his neck to look at the barn a bit better as we cruised past. "I had an equestrian phase as well. It stopped when they wanted me to go fox hunting."

"You mean with a live fox?"

"Yes. My father called it a noble tradition. I called it savage. He threatened to take my horse away if I wouldn't bow to his wishes."

His voice was flat and matter-of-fact, but I saw his hands tighten on the steering wheel. "Did he?" I asked softly.

"He did. Sold my horse." His eyes were on the road but I had a feeling he was seeing something in his past. His chin tilted up and I saw him swallow.

"How old were you?"

"Eleven? Twelve?" His voice turned bitter and I couldn't blame him. "Old enough to know it was only a matter of time before I was going to leave that wretched family behind."

And young enough to have your heart broken by losing your horse, I thought. How cruel. "How old were you when you knew you wanted to start a band?"

"Oh, I was already dreaming of that by then," he said. "The ultimate thing my parents would disapprove of. I'm quite chuffed to have succeeded at it."

"Chuffed? That means happy, right?"

He chuckled. "Yes, sorry. I try to speak American but sometimes I fail."

That made me laugh. "You never sound American to me."

"Oh, but I've learned to say things like 'in *the* hospital' and not to say words like motorway or"—he searched for a word—"telephone."

"Telephone? That's perfectly American."

He glanced at me. "I've never heard an American say *telephone*. You just say *phone*."

"Oh, hmm. That might be true." I pointed to the fork ahead. "Try the left one this time."

"Assuredly," he said, and I laughed at how British that sounded.

"I get the feeling your parents were kind of controlling."

That startled a laugh out of him. "You could say that. My father demanded strict obedience of everyone around him, staff, wife, and family alike. I can't say I took well to it. Being forced to go fox hunting was mild compared to his efforts to get me to date the girls he chose for me."

"Chose for you?"

"Yes. If I thought he was inhumane to the poor fox, you should have seen his attitude toward the young women he hoped to use as bargaining chips with their fathers."

"Oh my goodness, you mean like arranged marriage?"

"I mean exactly that, except perhaps for the ones he wanted me to woo until he secured whatever he needed from their families and then he wanted me to break off the relationship in order to get some other man like him to dangle his daughter in front of me. Sordid. The entire idea is sordid."

Hmm. Perhaps I understood a little better where his aversion to dating heiresses came from, even if it really didn't apply in my case. Maybe I should hint to him just how different things were in my own family. "I'm at the opposite extreme. My father's barely taken any interest in my relationships." I wondered if I should tell him about the dungeon in the basement, too. Now wasn't the time for that, though. We had a formal process about inviting and initiating people into the secret that was the Governor's Club. We were on the highway toward the city by then, and I decided maybe we should switch to some safer subjects. "So how is the album recording going?" I asked. "That's what you guys are up to, right?"

He shook his head. His hair was loose and I wondered if he'd object to me running my fingers through it—later, when he wasn't driving. "We haven't begun recording yet. We're still rehearsing and writing material. I don't want to enter the studio with a producer until I'm happy with what we've got to show him."

"Ah. So you're something of a perfectionist?"

"No," he said, but I had a feeling it was an obligatory denial. "I know when we sit down with the producer, their urge is always to make a lot of changes. My hope is if the songs sound truly outstanding, they'll leave them alone."

"But isn't the producer kind of like the director on a film? He—or she—isn't the writer or actors but oversees how the whole thing comes out?"

Mal shuddered. "Unfortunately, yes. While I appreciate a professional whose job it is to ensure we sound our best, I'm also aware that their priorities and ours may clash."

I realized if I kept asking him questions, he'd keep talking and that would give me an excuse to keep looking at him. He had a sharp chin and cheekbones but a sensuous mouth and gorgeous eyes. "How can your priorities clash?"

"Ours is to express ourselves through music. Theirs is to make the corporate overlords happy. When these two things can be accomplished by the same action, it's a harmonious relationship. When they cannot, it's a living hell."

"Was the last album harmonious?"

"After we fired one producer and got another one." Mal gritted his teeth. "My doing, mostly. It's usually me who argues with them the most."

"I never would have guessed," I said, teasing him gently. I was pleased to see he gave a self-deprecating smile, his long, glossy hair sliding over his shoulder as he dipped his head. "It's excellent you care so passionately about the music."

"Maybe it's the one blessing from growing up in a well-heeled family," he said. "I can make my decisions based on the purity of the music and not on money. I mean, of course I want the band to succeed, but we have to succeed artistically for me to be happy."

"That makes perfect sense." We lapsed into silence while I thought about what that must be like, pouring so much of yourself into a project and not knowing if it was going to succeed or fail. Maybe if I got some decent roles in films I'd find out.

"And how have you been, since our last date?" he asked. It had the ring of another of those etiquette school questions. I supposed he'd been taught to draw a conversation partner out by inviting her to talk about herself if she fell silent.

"Pretty good," I said. "I've been doing some soul-searching about my career, and I'm still figuring out what I want."

"Oh?" He glanced at me. When I didn't answer right away, he prompted, "Soul-searching?"

"Yes, about my as-yet-nonexistent career in acting," I said with a sigh.

"Ah. I would think you are ideally suited to succeed in that endeavor," he said.

"I know. Blond, skinny, and well connected." I held in the urge to shrug. "I had a wonderful time doing theater at school and summer stock plays, that kind of thing. I really enjoy acting. But I feel like using my family name to get roles is . . . cheating."

"Ah," he said with an understanding nod. "Because then you'll never know if they believe in your artistic merits."

"Exactly! Oh my gosh, exactly." Why couldn't Ricki understand that? I was so relieved that someone did. "So far no one has really believed in my merits anyway, since I still haven't gotten a part."

He cleared his throat somewhat uncomfortably. "You do realize if we keep doing this, keeping your identity a secret will be impossible."

Adrenaline surged through me as I thought for a second he was referring to "Excrucia"—had he figured it out? But when I didn't answer immediately, he went on and made it clear that wasn't what he meant.

"If we continue to be seen and photographed together, your face will become well known. Even if you audition under an assumed name, they'll know who you are."

"I know, I know." I settled myself back in the bucket seat, trying to restore calm. "I think I've resigned myself to giving up."

"Being an actress?" He sounded alarmed.

"No, no, I mean giving up trying to keep it a secret. After all, if I got a big role, that would let the cat out of the bag anyway, right? I'll still use a stage name, but I guess I better start working my family connections. I just filmed a promo video for my sister's media development company, so that's going to put my face out there, too."

"Any director would be a fool not to hire you," Mal said with an edge of protective vehemence in his voice I didn't expect.

"Oh, you know, half the time they think they know who they want for a role anyway, and no matter how good you are if you don't match what they have in mind, you've got no chance."

He wasn't dissuaded. "They simply don't know talent or beauty when they see it."

I found myself blushing and looking out the window. Mal had just called me beautiful and talented. I was starting to think he really liked me.

My heart was aflutter. But did he know the real me? He did but he didn't. I was suddenly afraid that telling him I was Excrucia was going to derail what felt like . . . something. Something I dearly wanted but didn't dare hope for.

* * *

MAL

The Hingham party would have been a difficult chore without Gwen by my side. Instead the evening was an unexpected pleasure. Gwen was charming and funny and even when she tried to put on a suave, sophisticated air, somehow her nerdy bluntness was never entirely suppressed, making her a delight—and a different kind of torment. I found myself making excuses to touch her, to shepherd her away from photographers with an arm around her shoulders, to help her down to the dance floor with a hand in hers.

I was not a fan of the music they were playing, but I was a fan of dancing with Gwen. I ignored the exhortations of the DJ to do whatever dance moves were being dictated, and pulled her waist against mine and twirled her as I liked. Seeing her smile with delight, knowing that my touch brought her a moment of euphoria: These are the bright moments of life, the moments worth living for.

They were a torment for me nonetheless, knowing that tonight I would go unfulfilled, having explicitly told her that our relationship could not be sexual. She had accepted the terms. If I were to make a move on her now, I'd be violating her expectations. No doubt the reason she was being so flirtatious tonight was that she felt safe in inflaming me, knowing that I would keep myself in check.

The time to let the Need rage would be at our next tryst. If she knew that I knew her identity, then that was where she would expect this raging ball of lust growing in my center to be directed. And if she didn't know? Well, that was where it should be directed in any case. That and into some very aggressive songs.

As I drove her home, I found myself seething with lust and burning with a dark rage that I fought to keep buried deep. This was the very rage that I needed most to protect her from, the destructive urge that always rose eventually if lust burned long enough or hot enough. I toyed with the idea of unmasking her, bringing it all into the open, and then burying myself in her as the only way to quench that flame. She would submit to my demands, I was sure. But no. That was exactly how I had pushed too far, too fast in the past. No one should merely be a repository for a lover's poisonous emotions—no one you truly care about, anyway.

I pulled up to the mansion feeling badly that I'd turned so

stiff and cold to her on the drive home, that my good-bye was so awkwardly delivered. She patted me on the arm as if to say it was all right and then exited the car.

I rolled down my window. “Gwen.”

She came around to my side of the car. “Yes, Mal?”

I lost my mind. I grabbed her by her suede vest and jerked her mouth to mine, half biting her lips in a kiss so rough it provoked a whimper from her.

By all gods and monsters, had I gone insane? I pushed her back from the car and sped away in a squeal of tires and smoke.

CHAPTER SEVEN

YOU ARE WHO YOU'RE NOT

GWEN

I stumbled into the house, giddy from the kiss and wondering just what was going on inside the dark and twisted mind of Mal Kenneally. *It's so obvious he wants me. Me, right? Not just some groupie?*

After the giddiness wore off, however, I started to have my doubts. Maybe he was just impulsive with all women. Maybe he couldn't help himself. Maybe it had nothing to do with me and Mal was simply a lustful cockmonster.

If so, he was the lustful cockmonster I couldn't wait to hear from. At the Beach Bash he'd said "next week," so I knew he'd be contacting me soon, and a few days later Excrucia got an e-mail from him.

The message came on Wednesday afternoon. I'd been sitting in the gazebo, looking through audition listings online on my tablet when I saw the alert pop-up indicating that Excrucia had mail.

I forced myself to go into the house, put my glass in the sink, and then walk slowly to my wing of the mansion. I wanted to run and slam the door and dive into bed to read it, but I didn't want anyone to think something was up. A couple of servants were around, as was Ricki. So I tried to act normal until I got on my side of the door.

Then I dove into bed and logged into the Excrucia e-mail account.

Excrucia,

I assume because of your tattoo that the books by Ariadne Wood were as formative to you as they were to me. Hence, your role:

Excrucia herself, dressed to meet the Linder Mage.

You will have access to the room between the hours of 8 pm and midnight this Saturday night to prepare yourself. The key will be available at the front desk under the name of Wood. At the stroke of midnight, I will enter and we will begin. If this is acceptable to you, reply with the word "yes."

Mal

Attached was a map to a hotel in Los Angeles and a room number. I sent back a "yes" immediately and then realized I had better check my calendar. It was clear, thankfully.

I hurried to the bookshelf in my bedroom to look for the book where Excrucia battles the Linder Mage. It had been years since I'd read them and some of the books were missing. I bought the whole set in ebook format.

The scene I was looking for was in book three. Excrucia at

that point has been studying magic, but because of her past as a concubine, she's treated poorly by the other women studying with her. When they are attacked by the mages of a more powerful school, she is chosen to be a sacrifice, sent to the Linder Mage as a tribute.

I had to search for the actual description of what the women wore and when I found it, I had to read it twice. Was this really what I read as a kid? "From a chain around her waist hung a cunning contraption of silverine, allowing for the passage of necessary wastes but preventing the entry of any intrusion into her sacred space other than the contraption itself. A wrap of the finest silk encircled her hips and loins and another her chest and shoulders, with a short cloak covering it all, exposing only her bare knees down to her feet." As a child, I'd read "her sacred space" as merely the area between her legs but reading it now I realized a chastity device had been inserted into her.

And what was *silverine*? In the books it was a metal forged with magic. I Googled chastity devices and decided chrome or stainless steel would have to do. I would need a fire-engine-red wig, too, and some colored contact lenses. Time for some shopping, quick.

* * *

The hotel was upscale but out of the way and very private. I pulled into an underground garage and took the elevator up to the front desk where they had an envelope waiting for me. I felt a little like a hooker taking the envelope, which clearly held a hotel key, while carrying my bag of clothes for sex. Well, Excrucia had been a concubine, right?

Upstairs was a bland but large hotel suite. One wall was glass overlooking the valley and the curtains were all the way open. I closed them in case someone, anyone, could see in and looked around a bit more. I recognized the leather bag on the couch as Mal's, but I didn't dare touch it. There were no obvious ropes or bondage cuffs attached to the bed or anything like that.

It wasn't quite ten. I got out the pieces of my costume and spread them out on the bed, but I wasn't ready to put it on yet. Everything I had read about the chastity device said it *should* be comfortable to wear for long periods of time, but I still wanted to wait to put it in. The insertion piece was a chrome ball on the end of a short stalk that jutted up from a metal piece that ran between my legs. The ends had loops for a leather harness to go through, but I'd improvised with some chains and clips (thank you, pet store) that fit over my hips. The whole effect when I was wearing it was that I had on a stainless steel thong.

I got out of my clothes and paced up and down nervously. What was he going to make me do? Was he going to be cruel like the villainous Linder Mage? The sex all took place offscreen in that book, but it was strongly implied.

I reminded myself of our deal. I'd get all the sex I wanted if I agreed to his price of pain.

Nnnnnf. Just thinking about it was making me wet. Maybe it was time to put the chastity device in after all.

I went to the bathroom to put it on and didn't even need the bottle of lube I had brought. All I needed was to think about Mal being cruel to me and my insides were gushing. *I know this fixation on pain probably isn't healthy,* I thought, *but damn it feels good.*

And the chrome ball felt very good going into place.

I wrapped the long scarves of silk I'd bought around me, one like a sarong and one around my breasts a couple of times and then tucked in. Nothing too fancy. And then I put on the cape. That had been the hardest part to find, but I'd ended up with what had once been part of a nurse uniform.

Then I paced around again. He hadn't said where I should be in the room. Should I be standing, sitting, or kneeling? I checked the book again.

Excrucia had been sent to the tower to await him. As she sank to her knees, a great calm descended as she surrendered herself to her fate.

Kneeling, then. I knelt on the rug near the couch, facing the door, but a great calm did not descend over me. This position pushed the chrome ball farther up inside me and if I rocked my hips slowly, I could give myself a deep, sensual stimulation.

So much for "chastity."

I fell into a slow rhythm of it, hypnotizing myself with it, until I was shocked to hear the click and hum of the door lock engaging. I glanced at the clock.

Midnight. He was right on time.

I forgot I had intended to bow my head as he entered. Mal stormed into the room, a vision of fury, head to toe in leather, a shiny medieval-looking dagger in his hand. Had I not been so aroused, he would have looked terrifying. Instead, he looked gorgeous and my mouth hung open in awe.

"Witch," he spat, and hauled me onto the bed by the collar of the cape. The button broke as he threw me down and he tossed the cape away, leaving me covered only by thin silk. Though he never broke character, I could see the way his eyes swept up and down my skin and that he liked what he saw. "Temptress. Spy. You think I'll succumb to your charms?"

My mind raced. This wasn't in the book. This was what went on behind closed doors. I wondered how many times Mal had fantasized about this and whether I could live up to that fantasy. I raised my chin. "I am yours to do with as you will."

"We'll see about that." He tore the silk off me with his hands and then held the point of the dagger to my throat while he pretended to examine my skin. "You have no mark of evil on you."

No, I had goose bumps from the air on my bare flesh and the way his tongue darted out to touch his lips as he looked at me hungrily. "The magic we practice is not evil. It's the same as yours, only we're women," I improvised.

"If that's so, then why are you caged thus?" He tapped the dagger against the metal of the chastity belt.

"That is to keep any interloper from entering where he is not invited."

He tugged on the chain, making the metal of the device rub against my clit. "Then tell me, Witch, am I invited?"

"I told you. I have been given to you. The device is yours to remove or to leave as you wish."

He sneered. "Perhaps I shall leave it in place until I am convinced you harbor no demons under your skin. Lie flat. Arms out. Legs wide. Make any move to cover yourself or close your legs and I will throw you from the tower."

Oh yes. His commands affected me as strongly, maybe even stronger, as they had the last two times, sending waves of desire deep into my center. God, I wanted him. I spread myself in answer, wondering if I was about to feel his belt again or what. But he unzipped the leather duffel bag and drew out a suede flogger. I felt almost relieved seeing such a familiar sight. We had lots of them in the dungeon, and Madison had tested a few of them out on me for fun. Suede wasn't particularly challenging—in fact, it could be quite soothing.

He swung the tails in an even rhythm, covering my breasts, my belly, and my thighs with blows—*thwap, thwap, thwap*—a pleasurable sensation overall, waking up my skin and senses. I sank into the rhythm, letting the blows rain down on me without resisting.

When he stopped, it felt like all my skin was throbbing. I arched upward with a gasp as he ran his fingernails down my breastbone and stomach—they were sharp! When I looked in surprise, he twirled his fingers before my eyes—each was tipped with a shiny metal claw.

He then dragged the claws all over my sensitized skin, down the insides of my thighs and around my swollen breasts, pausing to pinch teasingly with the needle-sharp tip against each nipple. It was like knife play, only more sensual, and I felt myself sinking deeper and deeper into a lust-addled haze.

Suddenly another flogger sound drew my attention half a moment before the tails—these of hardened leather—bit into my inner thigh. I screamed. Each of these was as painful as the end of his belt had been last week, but they hit all at once.

But I remembered his command not to cover myself or protect myself. The flogger bit again, this time closer to my snatch. And closer and closer. I knew what was coming. He was going to whip me right on my swollen clit and pussy, like he had with his belt, only this time I was even more exposed.

In fact, he didn't feel I was exposed enough. "Bend your knees and put the bottoms of your feet together."

Now I was wide open. Except for the chastity device. I was almost thankful for the metal that shielded my clit and inner labia from the worst stings. It was probably the only reason I was able to stand it.

When Mal said pain, he meant pain. The thought was surprisingly freeing. He wasn't expecting me to beg for it, nor for mercy. He was expecting me to take it because that was our agreement. I loved it, loved how the burn of each stroke seemed to leave my whole heart and soul on fire, yearning for him.

"No sign of demons yet," he said with a growl as he tossed the flogger aside. I felt the sharp tip of one steel claw tapping against the chastity device. "Remove this."

I unclipped the chains and slid the metal free of my body. He took it from me and laid it aside. When he returned, he gestured for me to spread my knees again.

And began flicking a sharp claw up and down on my clit. I sucked in a breath, caught between how much it hurt and how aroused it was making me. I was surging up my arousal scale to a whole new measure, it felt like.

"Are you going to come?" he asked, his voice hard and almost scientific.

"Y-yes! I think so—" I had barely finished saying that when my words turned to a long wail of release. I rode his hand as he ground his knuckles against me, letting me eke out every last shudder of pleasure.

When I opened my eyes, he was staring down at me as if entranced.

"It would appear you have driven a demon from me, my lord," I said.

He blinked, remembering the scenario. "Indeed. But I remain concerned that one still lurks deep within you. Spread your legs again. I must examine you."

I lay back again and opened my knees. This time he attached four clips to my labia and stretched them open by clipping the other end of each chain to one of my nipples or my inner thigh. The clips bit into my skin at first with a pinching sensation but the feeling soon turned to a deep ache.

He fingered me first, then held up the dagger in front of me. I swallowed and he gave a small nod, as if reminding me he'd promised no permanent damage. He ran a finger along the edge of the dagger, showing me that despite how wicked it looked, it was blunt.

He slid it into me, his gaze boring into mine as he pushed it inch by inch into me, and then with his fist around the blade, he fucked me with it. It was one of the hottest things I had ever done in my life and I think if he'd been touching my clit I would have come again right then.

Then he pulled the blade free and licked my juices from it.

Hotttt. I desperately wanted to slip my hand between my legs and rub my clit.

He unbuckled the leather vest armor he was wearing and shrugged it off, baring his chest, and then unzipped his leather pants but didn't take them off. "Only one way to really get deep inside you," he said, sounding somewhat breathless, more like Mal and less like a character.

I nodded in reply, praying that he would take the clips off before fucking me.

I almost got my wish. He rolled on a condom and penetrated me with the head of his cock first. And then he tore away the clips, which hurt like a motherfucker. But the moment he tore them away, he drove all the way into me and began banging me hard and deep. Is it any wonder that pain and pleasure were all mixed together in my mind?

Everywhere the clips had been touching me was pure agony, while his cock driving into me was pure pleasure, and my overworked nerves counted it all as one.

* * *

MAL

I could not have dreamed of a better scene. Did she know how enticing she was, costumed cunningly and playing her role so earnestly? I was entranced by the image burning in my head of the witch-woman willingly submitting herself to whatever violation the villain might choose, overlaid with the undeniable reality that here was *Gwen* submitting herself to *me*. If I thought she would shrink away from the knife—dulled for safety—I was wrong. She accepted it the way she accepted all of my attentions: with zeal.

Was it the condom that thrust me out of scene or was it Gwen herself? The moment I pushed into her, the last scraps of the Linder Mage fantasy were torn away and I was nothing but myself, a man burning with need for her, with the need to claim her as my own. I discarded the clamps, unable to tolerate anything that might get between me and her, my blood surging with the need to make us one.

What strange creatures we are. Humans are mammals, warm-blooded animals who reproduce through the oddest activity, requiring the male to insert a piece of himself inside the female's body.

We could dress it up with costumes or contraptions, but with Gwen ultimately I was reduced to this primal drive to put my cock inside her. This wasn't sadism or dominance or mastery; it was raw hunger.

Fast, slow, deep, shallow, from the side, from the rear—I didn't care. All I cared about was pushing inside and the only reason I pulled out was so I could push in again.

This is the animal that Gwen reduced me to, a fucking machine, unable to do anything but pound my flesh into hers like my life depended on it. No woman had ever stripped away every pretense of mine like this before. She screamed, she cried, she wailed, she moaned—every reaction made me want to do it again, do it more. It wasn't even that I was hunting down my orgasm; I was in such an animalistic state I couldn't even think that far ahead. There was only this, this moment played again and again, of penetration, of *needing* to penetrate.

I don't know how long I fucked her that way. Several positions, several changes of rhythm... half an hour, perhaps? An hour? Long enough that I was giving myself friction burns, where my knees rubbed against the insides of my leather trousers. Yes, my need to put my cock into her had been so great I hadn't even bothered to remove them. Time to regain control. I pulled free now and shucked the trousers, my erection bobbing angrily.

I stripped off the condom, which had gotten somewhat bunched and wrinkled, and put on a fresh one, aware of her watching my every move.

"On your front. Cunt in the air. Open it for me," I snapped. My heart rate doubled and my lust spiked as I watched her do it with alacrity. Her over-the-top poppy-red wig was bright against the white hotel duvet and her cleft was invitingly pink between her white thighs.

I pushed into her again and she pushed back, ensuring I sank to the hilt. I held her there, my hands on her hips. "Squeeze me."

She made a little sound of dismay, but she obeyed as I felt the velvet grip on my cock tighten and loosen as if she were pumping it with her fist.

I pulled out suddenly, my arms shaking, on the brink of coming but consumed with the need to prove to myself that I was the master of my orgasm, that it was not the master of me.

I shoved two fingers into her and she groaned and pushed back against them, squeezing. This pussy of hers—I was rapidly becoming obsessed with it. With possessing it. With possessing her. "Tell me how many men you've fucked."

She looked back at me, her hands slipping from holding her wide, questions in her eyes.

"In real life. Not the book," I clarified. The wall between fantasy and reality had crumbled once again. That seemed to happen often when I was around Gwen. "Tell me."

"Three," she said.

For a moment I felt a thrill that made no sense, as if I had somehow conquered these three anonymous men. Then I remembered she was supposed to be playing the part of a groupie and I wasn't supposed to know she was Gwen Hamilton. I twisted the fingers inside her as I asked gruffly, "Three? Is that all? You present yourself as more experienced than that."

She grunted and fucked herself on my fingers as she answered. "I've been holding out for the one I really wanted."

I jammed my fingers into her brutally, as if I could punish her for lying, but instead she simply soaked up the rough treatment, her wetness nearly gushing. Did that mean she'd spoken the truth? Logic did not work when most of the blood in my body was in my prick instead of my brain and the Need was surging.

I clearly wasn't thinking straight. "Do you want my cock?" I asked.

"Yes, yes, please!"

"Do you want it again in the future?"

"Yes, of course!"

I pulled my fingers free and teased her with the head of my cock, rubbing it up and down her pussy lips but not putting it in, no matter how she squirmed. Madness. What I spoke next was pure madness but it was everything I felt and I could not hold back. "Then I want to be the only cock you'll take."

She froze for a moment and I knew she was considering what I said seriously. "I... I would *love* for yours to be the only cock I'll take."

The surge of victory thrill coursed through me again. Mine! She was mine. "I want you to be as hungry for me as I am for you," I said, putting it in an inch and then pulling it away. "So no dildos either."

"Yes, Mal." She sounded breathless, elated.

"No fingers. Even your fingers would be cheating."

She gave a little sound almost like a sob. "But... but am I allowed to come? Without you?"

"Only if you are thinking of me." Sweet mother of angels, I had truly gone insane. I was guaranteeing that her obsession with me was only going to grow.

It was only fair, though, given how huge my obsession with her was becoming.

"I'm going away for three weeks starting tomorrow," I said, putting my cock into her again and then pulling out. "Can you stand three weeks with nothing inside you?"

"Not even the chastity device?" she asked plaintively.

"No. Cunning though it is, it goes inside you and that makes me jealous." I pushed into her again, freeing my hands to grab the stainless steel toy and examine it. Fascinating. The insertion ball was detachable.

I detached it. "There. Now not only may you wear this, but also you're going to. For three weeks. Remove it only to bathe or if you need to eliminate."

"Really?" she asked excitedly, then more seriously, "I mean, yes, Mal!"

I had no idea if what I was asking her to do was reasonable or not. I was beyond reason at that point. I did know they made these things for long wear. How she would hide it from the people in her life was not my problem. How much it tortured her with constant arousal was not my problem.

Three weeks without her was my problem.

"I'm going to fuck you now and spank you until I'm satisfied while you reach between your legs and make yourself come."

"How many times?"

"Until I say you can stop."

Oh, how she squeezed me internally when I said that. This woman loved being tormented with pleasure as well as pain. I laid a heavy hand onto her buttock as I drove into her and quickly fell into a rhythm, alternating hands right and left.

By the time she came her sixth time and I came my first, her cries of ecstasy had turned to whimpers of pain. I emptied my bollocks with a great bellow and then pulled out all too soon. Even utter perfection must come to an end, unfortunately. I discarded the condom in the bathroom and then returned to the bed to find she had barely moved.

Seeing her lying like that—spent, exhausted, aching from the things I had inflicted on her—made my chest tighten and my eyes grow soft with a sudden protective urge. *You're insane,* I told myself. *You're the one who hurt her and now you want to be the one to kiss and make it better? Madness.*

But a madness I indulged. Now I wanted nothing more than to coddle her, to care for her. "Excrucia, dearest," I heard myself say as I encouraged her to roll onto her side. She groaned a little but did as I asked. I pulled back the covers and coaxed her under them, sliding in with her and cradling her with one arm. Her warm skin against my own was a luxurious pleasure unto itself.

"That was unbelievably amazing," she said. "Thank you."

"I did promise to satisfy you, did I not?"

"You did. And you definitely kept that promise."

"For your part, you did quite well, too," I said. The memory of entering the room and seeing her for the first time in full costume, kneeling at the ready, was burned into my brain. A more gorgeous sight I could not imagine. "I was unsure if you'd go so far as to obtain a chastity belt. I am pleased that you did."

She wriggled happily against me and it was as if that happiness soaked right through her skin into mine. I even smiled. "I'm glad you like it. Re-reading that part of the book, do you think Ariadne Wood knew when she wrote it that things like that existed?"

"I have no doubt of it. Chastity devices are not a new invention, you know." I petted her hair, luxuriating in the bliss we had both strived so hard to earn. Such a rare feeling. My mind was rarely so quiet. I had to wonder if part of me didn't crave that even more strongly than the primal rutting. "I do have to wonder what the author intended for us to imagine in the scene in the tower."

"Maybe that's the beauty of it," she said. "People could imagine whatever they wanted. Whatever they needed."

"Hmmm." I rolled her onto her back and toyed with the bright red strands of her wig. "The power of imagination serves up whatever we need most—is that the idea?"

She nodded.

"Three weeks," I said. The band had agreed to go into the studio with Larkin Johns for another try. I needed to keep myself free of distractions, but I had a strong feeling when we emerged from recording I was going to be burning with the need to see her again. "I'll message you with who to be when we reunite."

CHAPTER EIGHT

HEAT

GWEN

Of course the day I was supposed to meet Mal again would turn out to be the day of Ricki's app launch. Originally they called the app Stargazer, but it turned out there was an astronomy app called that already, so they renamed it the much more on-point Man Candy. The app showed you photos of hot guys—models, actors, pop stars, and so on—and let you rate them by hotness. The app would not only serve up new photos of guys from all the syndicated newsfeeds like Getty and AP, but it would also learn what type of look you liked and show you new hot guys you didn't already know about. The app was intended to be a sideline for her media company WOMedia that would simultaneously let them do market research into what women liked while giving them a direct marketing tool right on women's mobile phones.

Genius. That's my sister.

Not that I was a slouch in the intelligence department myself, of course. My challenge was to figure out what to wear to a press event that would hide the chastity device I was wearing, and how to meet Mal in secret without Ricki getting suspicious.

"Your calendar's clear, right?" she had asked.

Right, because I didn't put my secret trysts with Mal on the calendar that she could see.

Thankfully Ricki didn't ask for any more details when I said the afternoon was free but I would be out that evening. I knew it would sound weird if I was too vague if she asked later, though. I settled on telling her a college friend was in town and wanted to reconnect.

Mal's instructions included the address of a different hotel from the previous one, as well as a scene from an Ariadne Wood book I hadn't read but that featured a virgin sacrifice to a dragon.

Black wig acceptable, he wrote, *but put it up, atop your head or in a bun.*

To match the character in the book, who was described as wearing ritual garments made of spider silk, I packed a see-through lingerie gown. I had my full makeup kit, so I could do the heavy eyeliner and facial contouring that I figured had to be the only reason Mal hadn't recognized me yet. My face is actually pretty generic when I'm not made up.

There were moments during the last scene when I'd felt like he was going to say something, especially after I'd dropped character completely. I was sure he'd figured it out. But then he didn't say anything.

Maybe he knows but wants to keep up the fantasy that it isn't me? It seemed plausible given that I wanted to keep the fantasy up for as long as possible myself. It was working so well. I felt freer somehow, less judged, less self-conscious when I was pretending to be someone else.

Maybe in order to keep it up, he really did need to pretend I was a groupie and not the kind of girl his father would have fixed him up with. I had to hope that by the time he either figured it out or dropped the charade he had decided I was worth bending another one of his rules for.

First I had to get through the press conference. I was distracted, trying to imagine what Mal was going to do to me tonight. The chastity device was very odd: I'd gotten so used to it I'd forget it was there, until I thought about Mal and suddenly I couldn't ignore it. I know, scientifically, it was probably that thinking about him aroused me and made my clit swell, but it felt a lot like magic. As if thinking about him invoked him, as if that were his hand tugging at the chain, tightening the device.

The scene he had sent described the priests binding the sacrifice to the altar with "inescapable" bonds and then leaving her there alone. The dragon had then entered the stone grotto and, tongue flicking like a snake's, had tasted the sacrifice's skin to determine whether she would be accepted or rejected. If rejected, she would be burnt to a crisp.

In the original scene, the dragon becomes enraged by the spider silks and tears them away with his claws. "And then the dragon's tongue performed a most thorough and complete exploration of her skin, leaving not an inch untouched by that muscular appendage. Yes, it would seem the dragon deemed her an acceptable sacrifice."

There the chapter ended. I had bought and devoured the ebook to find out more, but the next scene began with a priest coming to collect her charred bones and finding her surprisingly alive and whole. Perhaps Mal was going to dress as the priest?

Ricki nudged me from behind and I smiled, suddenly realizing I'd been fantasizing and hoping my face hadn't been showing my feelings. Then again, for what the app was supposed to do, maybe some drooling was appropriate.

She was right; literally all I was required to do at the event was nod and smile. There were tons of cameras and lots of photos were taken. They showed the promo video as part of the presentation. The rest of it was blather about their business plan; I thought about Mal instead of listening.

And then, at last, it was over. I went to say good-bye to Ricki before hitting the road. She was talking with their publicity manager, Thalia Rashan, a tall woman with her hair in an upswept knot at the back of her head. I took mental notes, wondering if I could put the wig up that way.

"Oh, Gwen," Thalia said when she saw me. "Thank you so much for doing that video. You were perfect."

I wasn't sure what to say to such a compliment; I hadn't done much but goof around on my phone making faces while they filmed it. "Um, you're welcome? It was fun."

"We might do a follow-up video at some point. It's great having you in the family so we'll always know where to reach you," she said with a smile. "Oh, one more thing." She reached into her blazer pocket for a business card. "This photographer wanted you to contact him. Says he has some great portfolio shots and his work's often in *EW*."

I looked at the card but didn't recognize the name: Beau Lavern. His phone number and e-mail were printed next to a generic logo of a camera. I tucked the card into my purse. "Is he here?"

"He said he couldn't stay." Thalia shrugged.

"Well, speaking of not being able to stay, I've got to go off to my next stop. Don't wait up for me, Ricki."

She chuckled. "Do I ever?" She suddenly looked at me. "Who are you meeting again?"

Thank goodness I had cooked up what to tell her in advance so it came out smooth. "Oh, a college friend who's in town!" I embellished it a little. "Recently broke up. I don't know if we're going out partying or if she's looking for a shoulder to cry on."

"Well, have fun either way, I guess."

* * *

The new hotel had private villas with high-walled patios, each with an outdoor Jacuzzi tub. A note from Mal on the bed told me to remove the chastity device, "prepare myself," and await him on the "altar." I searched the suite for what he might mean by that and didn't find anything... until I went out onto the patio. Beside a hot tub large enough for eight was something altar-like draped in dark cloth. Under the cloth I discovered a massage table. The cloth had an odd feel to it, like it had been waterproofed.

I also found there were Velcro straps attached to the legs of the table and a blindfold with an elastic strap sitting on top. I unhooked the chastity belt and set it on the edge of the hot tub and then climbed onto the table. Did he expect me to put the bonds on myself? It felt like he had left me a puzzle to solve. What did I think would please him most? And should I be faceup or down? I went back inside and reread both his instructions and the scene on my phone. Faceup, I decided, although the text was a little ambiguous. Then I stowed my phone and all my clothes in a drawer and put the see-through lingerie on.

After I finished applying my makeup, I set about pinning the wig up on top of my head as he'd specified. Imitating Thalia's hairdo turned out to be the right thing, twisting the dark locks into a single curl and pinning it at the crown of my head.

Now to solve the self-bondage puzzle. On the "altar" it was easy enough to strap my ankles down and my left hand, but how should I do my right hand? If I looped it around my wrist loosely, I found I could "tighten" it by wrapping it around my arm a few times. I took one last look at the scant pinpricks of stars in the dark sky before I slipped the blindfold over my eyes, lifting the elastic strap easily over my pinned wig. Then I lay back on the table, put my hand back through the last of the Velcro loops, and made the necessary twists of my wrist.

Bound. Ready. Trying to be calm but heart racing and clit throbbing.

I had been lying there on the table for only a few minutes when I heard the glass door from the suite slide open.

I heard the creak of leather as he walked across the stone patio.

And then I felt the brush of a finger along my lower lip. I tipped my chin upward reflexively and felt the sharp metal of the claw-tips he wore.

"Sacrifice," he whispered, and I found myself nodding, as if that were a question to be answered.

And then: "Mine," and I nodded again as he began to tear open the lingerie. He was not gentle, rending and ripping, occasionally catching my skin with his claws until I was laid bare to the sky and to his gaze, his touch.

His hot mouth upon my nipple. Yes! I could feel the points of his claws as he gripped my rib cage, holding me still so his tongue could rasp across one nipple and then the other, and his mouth could wander up and down my breasts, suckling and biting while I fought to keep myself silent. He hadn't said I should be quiet, but what if there were other guests on the patio next door?

He dragged his claws down to my hips as his mouth traveled down my stomach. And then his tongue was teasing my clit out from between the inner lips where it usually hid, until he could suck it between his teeth and grip it, trapping it for his tongue tip to torture.

The sweetest torture ever. So much for staying silent. After a few minutes of that I couldn't keep my voice quiet and whimpers began to escape me, then moans, and as I drew close to the peak of orgasm, outright cries.

But he pulled back before I could climax. I heard a scissors snip and felt the last shreds of the lingerie being tugged away. Then his hands—without the claws this time—running up and down my torso, caressing me all over while my legs shook with the need to close, to clamp down on my clit. I was that close to coming.

"I'm going to set you on fire now," he said.

I was startled into saying, "Really?"

He chuckled and kissed me on the pubic mound. "Yes, really. I am a dragon, after all."

I felt him moving around beside me, preparing for whatever he was going to do.

"It's very important that you don't make any sudden moves," he said.

I decided this might be a good time to bring up this fact: "Um, my right hand is bound kind of loosely."

He made a grunt of acknowledgment and untangled my arm, reattaching it with the Velcro snug around my wrist.

The next thing I heard was the unmistakable sound of a lighter—*chttt, chttt, chttt*—and then I felt something warm near my face.

"Open your eyes," he ordered softly as he lifted a corner of the blindfold.

I looked up into a blazing orange flame on what looked to my lust-addled brain like a marshmallow on a stick in a campfire. I sucked in a breath, more excited than truly afraid—if I feared anything, it was the fear of the unknown. What was that going to feel like? He'd promised no permanent damage, so that thought hadn't even entered my mind. The only thing in my mind was whether I would be able to stand the pain or not.

The first place he touched me was on my stomach and all I felt was a moment of coolness, then warmth, then the caress of his palm. I sighed as he petted me.

Several more touches like that followed and I realized he was swiping me with the flame, leaving a dab of lit fuel behind and then extinguishing it with his hand before the heat could build up in intensity. I groaned with pleasure. He worked his way down my stomach onto my thighs and then up to the swells of my breasts, letting the fire burn longer and longer, until I began to let out little gasps of pain. And yet it still didn't really reach the point of actually hurting.

When he yanked the blindfold off, it got caught partly in the wig but then came free, and I found myself looking up at him. He tapped the flame with his fingers and then tapped his tongue, the flame burning momentarily there before he closed his mouth. I stared in amazement.

Dragon. Like the tattoo on his back. He had stripped out of his clothes and I drank in the sight of his bare skin, muscular chest, his hair up in a topknot.

He did the flame trick again, transferring it to his tongue with his fingers, this time closing his mouth around my nipple, just a moment of heat and then wet. I groaned again.

The place I was wettest though, by far, was between my legs. He slid his fingers into me and then pulled them out, sucking them clean and then transferring the flame to his tongue again before snapping his jaw shut.

When he positioned himself between my legs, I wondered if I knew what was coming.

Yes, I did. He spread my labia with one hand, tapped my clit with the fire wand, and doused the flame with his mouth against my flesh. He did it again, letting it burn a moment longer and then soothing the pain with his incredible tongue. He brought me close to orgasm again, then returned to teasing me with the flame, sometimes setting me on fire, sometimes his tongue, but always dousing it with his tongue against my clit.

My cries were loud echoing off the stone.

But again he didn't let me climax. Next, he knelt down out of my sight and rummaged in a bag—I sensed he'd put the flame out even though I couldn't see him do it. I missed its cheery thrill, but not for long: When he stood, he was holding a wicked-looking black and green dildo, carved with ridges like a dinosaur's tail.

He let my legs free and lengthened the bonds that held my arms. "Bend your knees."

I did, trembling with anticipation. "I . . . I . . . "

Mal slipped a finger into me and wiggled it. "Speak. Does something concern you?"

"Just, you remember I've had nothing inside me for weeks, right?"

"I know," he said with a serious nod. He held up the dildo and examined it. "Do you think it's going to be hard to take this?"

"I do."

He looked me in the eye. "Good."

When he said that, my entire insides gushed with need. It was like my pussy said to my brain, *Screw you, we need that thing more than we've ever needed anything before.*

Without breaking eye contact, he began wetting the thing by rubbing it between my lower lips. Before I knew it, he was pressing the angular, ridged head against my opening.

The tip went in easily, of course, but the thing felt like a ziggurat, widening quickly from the top. It went in until it stuck, not from lack of slickness but from the odd shape and size.

"Take it," he murmured, and pushed harder.

It went in another inch, another ridge, and then I tightened around it reflexively, panting.

"I know you can do it," he encouraged, brushing my clit with his thumb, which made me tighten even more but only for a second. When that wave of arousal let go, he pushed in even more.

"Oh God."

"And heavenly angels," he said, as if answering me. "Almost there. It's almost in."

It felt huge and strange and that only increased my craving for it. I wriggled my hips, trying to will myself to open up.

"Knees up," he said as he pushed them toward my shoulders.

I sucked in a breath as that tightened everything between my legs and made the thing sticking out of me sharply visible to me. "Oh God," I said again.

And then a new wave of longing swept through me as I held my legs where he had put them while he rolled a condom onto his cock. He slipped a lubricated finger into my ass and I groaned, wanting something more.

He teased me mercilessly, slipping fingers in and out of me for several minutes. Oh, I knew he was making certain my ass was stretched enough to take his cock, but it still felt like merciless teasing.

Mal climbed onto the massage table and then crooked my legs over his bent knees, one hand on his cock, steadying it for entry, the other on the dragon dildo, keeping it in place.

"Oh, fuck," I said as he thrust, thrusting both his cock and the dildo into me. He gave me a moment to adjust, to savor the wave of pleasure that poured through me on that penetration. "Oh, fuuuuck."

When he drew back, it was slow, tantalizing, and then he thrust again, and I wrapped my legs around his back out of reflex. It felt amazing but overwhelming at the same time.

"Down," he commanded. "Lie still. Let me fuck."

Three simple words that thrust into me as hard as any penetration: *let me fuck.* I relaxed my legs and closed my eyes, taking a deep breath. When I let it out, I whispered, "Sacrifice."

"Yesss," he said, and rewarded me with a kiss on the heart.

Thus began the hardest fucking of my life.

I loved it.

* * *

MAL

The look on her face was incredible as I plowed into her and matched the explosion of euphoria I was experiencing. She looked like she was seeing God and I don't mean that in some self-inflated dom sense; I mean it in the sense of the revelation of miracles. Perhaps we have the keys to heaven, to divinity, locked deep inside us, and it takes going deep to reach them. I'd made an altar, after all, and here we were atop it, worshipping together under the open sky.

Her cries of ecstasy only egged me on to take her harder, faster, driving relentlessly toward my release. Everything that had pent up in the weeks apart, everything I had been holding back tonight as I'd played with her and teased her, I let loose. I roared when I came, and it echoed from the stone, sounding as loud as any dragon I could imagine.

When my hips ceased moving, I opened my eyes. My hair had come loose from the topknot and hung in sweaty strings over my eyes. One of my hands was clamped so hard around her upper arm I had left bruises.

I eased out of her but held the dildo in place. I could manage only short, brutish words. "Did you come?"

She shook her head.

I twisted it back and forth. "I did promise to always leave you satisfied if you would submit to whatever I inflicted," I said.

A final round of licking her and fire play would do for a finale. I eased the dragon dildo out of her and set it aside, massaging her pussy with my fingers until she purred. Then I uncapped the fuel and soaked and lit the baton again.

She was beautiful, sweat-soaked, radiant, clearly pushed to her limits but still eager to comply with any command of mine. Who could resist that? It was beyond human endurance to expect not to be moved by such a sight. That baffling protective urge welled up again; it felt as if the more severe the pain she suffered, the stronger that urge became. My beautiful treasure. Surely there could not be another woman like Gwen in the world.

I swiped the flame across her belly, putting it out with my palm. Sweet tender lover, her skin, her life, in my hands. I held the flame off to one side while I licked her, thrusting two fingers into her with my free hand.

She built to a crescendo quickly and in mere moments she was coming, much more quickly than I expected.

Accidents don't happen because a single thing goes wrong. Not when you're careful. No, when you're careful, a whole host of things has to go wrong, and when they do, people get hurt.

I had forgotten her legs were no longer tied down. One knee jerked up as she spasmed in her climax, bumping the arm that held the fire baton. That in itself wouldn't have been harmful except having been so recently loaded with fuel, the baton jerking forward threw a gout of burning flame onto the fireproof cloth. Which wouldn't have been dangerous if that had been all. But when I'd removed her blindfold, I accidentally unwound a lock of her wig.

Her flammable wig. I felt a twist of dread lance through me as I saw what was happening in that split second. The stray lock caught fire and even as I hurriedly flung the baton into the hot tub and reached to smother the flame with my hand, she screamed and jerked her head in fear. My dread exploded into horror as her motion jerked the flaming lock onto her own face and set the rest of the wig on fire as well.

I grabbed the lock, pulled it away from her skin, the melting strands of wig burning my palm, but I could not have cared less about that. With the other hand I tugged the wig from her head—the damnable thing was pinned on!—and then tossed the entire partially melted mess into the hot tub as well, leaving a searing pain in my palm and a very blond Gwen under me.

I patted out the last bit of fire guttering against the flameproof cloth with my other hand and then ripped open the Velcro holding one of her wrists.

Her hand flew to her face and then we held still, both panting, me looming over her, the pain in my palm starting to register dimly in my brain.

"Are you all right?" I heard myself ask.

"Yeah. Think so. That was . . . that was close. I think."

Oh, Gwen, dear nerdy innocent Gwen, are you sure? I climbed carefully off her and discovered my hand would not open on command. It wanted to stay clenched tight.

I released her other wrist and she sat up immediately. "Are you all right?" She was reaching for my hand.

I pulled away. "I'm fine. I'm much more concerned about you."

"I'm fine, I told you. Let me see that."

"No." I cradled my hand to my chest and realized how petulant that sounded. "That is . . . let's get inside and assess in better lit surroundings."

Inside the suite, we decamped to the bedroom and then into the attached bathroom where the light was best. She examined my still-closed fist. "I'm going to get some ice," she declared.

She pulled on the T-shirt I had shed on my way through the suite earlier and my long leather duster and out she went.

When she returned, she had a bucket of ice. She added some water to it and then set it on the bathroom counter. I dunked my hand into it without any urging and held it there until the ache of the cold was stronger than the pain. Then I gradually unclenched my fist.

That was a mistake. I nearly screamed and I think came close to cracking a tooth. I closed my fist again.

She looked rather worried. With my good arm, I pulled her

close to me, still addled by the scent of sex coming off her skin mixing with the savory essence of the leather she was wearing. "I'm afraid your wig is ruined." The burn mark on her cheek sent my blood roiling, as if I could rush out to seek revenge on the scoundrel who'd harmed her, and met the heavy stone of dread in my stomach that was the knowledge *I* was that scoundrel. I swallowed hard, trying to think of what to say, trying to keep my anger at myself well in check. "And you should get some burn cream onto that."

"Onto what?"

I reached up and ran my thumb close to her cheek, but not actually touching the dark red mark, a crescent shape like a downward frown that might have been starting to blister. *Sweet angels, let it not leave a scar.* I felt bile rising at the thought I had broken my promise never to damage her.

She looked in the mirror. "Oh. Oh my."

I handed her an ice cube and she pressed it to her face as she sank down onto the side of the bathtub.

"Gwen," I said, and she looked up sharply, her eyes wide, her other hand flying to her hair.

"Did you... How long have you known?" she demanded. Then before I could answer, "Please tell me you only just figured it out?"

I cupped her unblemished cheek. Dear, precious beauty. "You know I won't lie to you. I figured it out in the trailer after the beach party."

Tears welled in her eyes. "Oh." She blinked them away. "Oh."

Oh indeed. I wasn't even sure where to start untangling this mess. Maybe it was for the best that the truth came out now, before anything truly disastrous happened to body, mind, heart, or soul. "You've been deceiving me. Lying to me."

"I know." She shrank down. "I... I know. I'm sorry."

I should have asked her why, but all I could feel was sorrow and loss. I hated what I had to do next. But the euphoria of the scene faded and was replaced with the dread knowledge of how close to major disaster we had come, how close I'd come to ruining the most beautiful woman I'd ever met. And for what? To bring an adolescent sex fantasy to life? Only one course of action made sense.

"We can't do this again," I said, shaking my head.

"I'm fine," she insisted.

"For how much longer? No, Gwen, this whole thing is clearly dangerous beyond all reason." I realized suddenly that her deception was the lever I could use to pry us apart. "And I don't just mean physically. You've been *lying* to me."

"And you've been *letting* me!"

"Which only proves how fucked up we are!" I forced myself to look at my palm, regretting it immediately as blood was beginning to well out of the horror-movie wound. I showed it to her for a split second before I clenched it again. "That could have been your face, your head. Your career—"

"Career isn't everything!" she cried, hopping to her feet and grabbing another chunk of ice out of the bucket.

"—your life," I finished. I took one more breath, putting a heavy lock on my emotions and clicking into post-emergency response mode. I looked around. I needed to take myself to the hospital but first I felt it prudent to remove any trace of what had happened. In the bedroom I dug a pair of track pants out of my bag and stubbornly pulled them on one-handed.

Fishing the burned wig out of the hot tub wasn't difficult, but there was no sign of the swab baton I'd used. It must have been sucked into the filter. Fine. Your average person certainly wouldn't suspect it was a sex toy.

I carried the dildo and the chastity device into the bathroom. Gwen had moved to sitting on the lid of the toilet, looking shell-shocked.

In fact, she was probably in shock, and I meant that in the medical sense. Especially when I went to wash the dildo and realized I was washing off blood. So much for keeping my emotions in check. "Gwen!" I barked in alarm.

"What?"

"Are you sure you're all right?" I slammed the dildo down onto the counter, my own hands shaking.

"Why?"

"This . . . this . . ." I gestured at the thing. What was I thinking, using it like I did? Why did they even manufacture such monstrosities? "It's got your blood on it!"

She squinted at the green and black object and made an unimpressed face. "Oh, come on, Mal, don't tell me you're freaked out by a little blood. Women bleed, you know."

Why did the worst explanation—that I'd torn her somehow—seem more believable to me at that moment than the more likely one? I stared at her, trying to reassert my rational mind.

"Stop being such a freak case, okay?" she entreated. "I'm all right. I'm perfectly fine. You, though, you probably need to get your hand taken care of."

My rational mind. If I had been listening to it instead of the siren song of the Need all along, I never would have been meeting her in secret in the first place. I knew perfectly well pursuing my extreme sexual fantasies was a mistake.

Time to own that mistake.

She had taken the clips out of her hair and I allowed myself one last caress, brushing her bangs off her forehead. "I think you may be in shock," I said, trying to sound as calm and authoritative as possible. "At the very least, you're probably experiencing some intense after-scene effects. Drop in blood pressure, chill . . ."

Gwen rubbed the burn on her cheek with her fingers as if to prove it didn't hurt. "I'm going to be fine."

"Come get in bed," I said, trying not to sound gruff but failing. I drew back the covers for her.

"All right." She climbed into the bed but quickly realized I wasn't getting in with her. "Where are you going?"

"To the ER." I held up my fist.

"I'll come with you."

"No. Neither of us needs that kind of publicity."

That seemed to convince her, and she sank back into bed with a sigh. "Okay, but we need to talk."

I sat down on the edge of the bed and kissed her on the forehead. "You want to talk about how close to the edge of the precipice we can get? We shouldn't be on the cliff in the first place." Wasn't it obvious I couldn't be trusted? And if she trusted me anyway, it was just proof how fucked the whole idea was.

"Oh, Mal. I'm sorry."

"I'm sorry, too." I bent to kiss her one last time and she tipped her head so that I caught her mouth instead of her forehead, stealing one last kiss from me before I forced myself to leave.

CHAPTER NINE

GUNPOWDER PLOT

GWEN

I could not believe he left like that, but then again, it made some sense. His hand was badly injured and I was in no shape to go anywhere. Seriously. I was wobbly and weak in the aftermath of the scene. Just getting from the bathroom to the bed had been a dicey proposition. That didn't stop me from fantasizing about getting in my car and tailing him to the hospital. But I'd taken a first aid class in college and knew better than to try driving while in shock.

Not that he should have been driving himself, I thought, after I'd had a while to think about it. I should have insisted on an ambulance, or at least a taxi...?

I didn't even know which hospital he might have gone to.

He's probably fine, I thought to myself. He might get bloodstains on the inside of his car but that would be the worst of it.

And now that no active crisis was going on, I could barely

keep my eyes open. It felt like sleep was ambushing me despite my worries. I was that exhausted and drained by the scene and the aftermath.

I woke again in the wee hours of the morning and he wasn't there. I searched around the main room of the suite to make sure he wasn't sleeping on the couch or out by the pool, but he still wasn't back. I dragged myself to the bathroom and checked myself out more thoroughly than before. I was fine. I was going to be sore for a while, but it was the good kind of sore. The blood definitely wasn't from an injury and the burn on my face didn't seem that bad. It was red and visible and I wondered if the skin might blister, but it really wasn't worse than a bad sunburn. I'd burned my hand worse while making coffee.

He's completely overreacting, isn't he? He totally is. Surely once he had a calmer look at things it wouldn't seem that dire to him, either. *I'll tell him when he comes back.*

I went back to bed, but when I woke up in the morning, I discovered he'd managed to slip in, take his things, and leave again without waking me. The massage table, the dildo, even the chastity belt—which was mine!—everything was gone except for my own bag of clothes.

The only thing he left was a note.

Gwen,

I'm truly sorry but it's for the best. Your health is too precious to be risked gratifying my twisted fantasies. Your deception and my compliance with it is all the proof I need that we should have known better—that deep down we <u>*did*</u> *know better but we did it anyway. Every woman I've cared for, I've pushed too far. I care for you too much to break you. I have to stop before things get even worse.*

Please respect this boundary of mine and accept my good-bye with grace.

Mal

I read the letter over several times, trying to make it say something other than what it did.

But he wants me and I want him, I thought. Shouldn't there be a way to work it out when that's true? I was angry that he wanted me to "accept his good-bye with grace" but didn't have the balls to say it to my face, and I was sad that he felt his fantasies were somehow to blame. He was right about one thing, which was that I should have told him sooner who I was, but that made our lack of communication my fault, not his. Did that mean I deserved to lose him? I didn't think so.

I called Maddie on the drive home.

"Hey, Gwen, what's up? Planning for the party?"

Our regular dungeon party was in two weeks. "No, I'm calling about something else."

"You sound upset."

"I do?"

"Well, you don't sound like your usual perky self. Are you driving? Do you want to meet for coffee or something?"

"Um, I think I'd rather not be in public when I tell you what I've got to tell you."

Her voice was soothingly firm. "I've got coffee in my pantry, you know."

"Oh, I don't know, Maddie. I don't want to impose."

"Stop it. I'm texting you my address."

Forty-five minutes later, I was pulling up to a Spanish-style condo on a side street in West Hollywood. The front courtyard was surrounded by ten-foot-high walls and crowded with palms and banana trees. To the side of the main door was a stairwell up to the second-floor unit and at the top of the stairs Madison was waving. Her auburn hair was pulled back in a scrunchie and she was in sweats.

She ushered me into a high-ceilinged great room with a sectional sofa and glass-topped coffee table. One corner of the room had been made into a mini-office, with a desk, computer, and printer, while the back of the room was delimited by a kitchen island. A hallway to one side presumably led to the bedroom and bath.

"Nice place," I said as she urged me to sit and poured us both large mugs of coffee. I didn't argue as she added cream and sugar to mine.

"Yeah, I lucked out with it. My grandmother left me a pile of money just big enough to buy the place, and the way rents have gone, I cover the mortgage with what the downstairs tenants pay." She sat back against the couch, cradling her mug in her hands. "Should I ask what happened to your face?"

"Oh, God." I set my mug down and took a deep breath. "Does it look bad? I've been flipping back and forth between thinking it's the worst thing ever and that it's nothing. Well, okay, most of the time I've been telling myself it's nothing, but that's because Mal overreacted so much it's like I had to underreact to balance him out."

She took a sip. "I think you better start at the beginning."

"Okay. You know that rock star I've been publicity dating?"

"Yeaaah."

"It's more than publicity dating. A lot more. But it's complicated."

"Oh, honey, it always is. Go on."

So I told her. I told her about how I showed up backstage still dressed for a part and ended up having wild sex with him that first time. I told her about the beer bottle, *everything*. This was the main reason I went to Madison and not my sister or another friend. I'd never be able to tell them stuff like that, but I knew Madison wouldn't be fazed. Sure she was a gorgeous, voluptuous redhead, but I think the real reason my grandfather hired her to be a dungeon hostess was because she simply wasn't ever shocked or put off by anything sexually weird. She was sensible and levelheaded and didn't judge. And I needed that right now.

"So let me get this straight. He has, or had, a bunch of rules? Doesn't date rich girls, except that he did, and never does the same woman twice, except that he did?"

"Pretty much. The dating thing was just supposed to be for show, you know? But we went on a publicity date and saw this really sexy film and..." I stopped myself and started again. "I mean, when the film was over, I was like, oh, let my chauffeur give you a ride home because I basically just wanted to get him alone so I could ask him to have sex with me. Like, I would have done him right there in the limo if he'd wanted. God, when did I turn into such a pushy bitch?"

"Asking for sex doesn't make you pushy or a bitch," she pointed out. "And if he thinks you're either of those things, he's not worth talking about."

"No, no, no, you're right. He's not the one saying that. I am. Forget I said that. Except then I kind of tricked him into having sex with me anyway."

"Kind of?" She cocked her head, waiting for the explanation.

"So I had kept in touch with a couple of other fans, and I got dressed up in a different disguise and went backstage at another event and got chosen to be Mal's girl again."

"Aaah, so the roadie doing the screening didn't realize it was you or that he'd seen you before."

"Exactly. But—" I suddenly remembered what had happened, what the women were talking about. "But here's the thing. Talking with some of the other groupies, it turned out Mal was trying to find me. I mean, find the girl he'd had sex with at the Forum.

So I kind of wonder if he was getting ready to break his one-time-only rule anyway."

"Interesting. Go on."

So I told her about putting the knife on my back and about not saying anything so he wouldn't hear my voice until after he'd convinced himself I was someone else. "I hadn't realized keeping quiet was going to make the scene so hot! It was like, I don't know, we switched to communicating through touch, through our skin. What am I saying? It was my imagination; it doesn't matter."

"Whoa, whoa, whoa, when we're talking about a scene, your imagination certainly does matter," Maddie said.

"Especially given what happened later. But I'm getting ahead of myself a little. Well, later he told me this was the scene where he figured out it was me."

"Ah, I wondered."

"Yeah. But he kept up the act like he didn't, I guess because it was obvious I was pretending not to be myself? Then he agreed to meet me—I mean her—again for sex. For a role-playing scene."

"Interesting." Her eyes narrowed as she listened.

"Yeah. So much for the one-time rule, eh? He sent instructions on what to wear and stuff, based on a fantasy book we both read as teenagers. You know, one of those books where there's no sex but you know it must be going on between the chapters? We acted out a scene that could've happened."

"This is getting more interesting all the time." Maddie tapped her finger against her mug like she was trying to solve the puzzle of Mal, which I hoped she would. "What kind of a scene? You mean like a rape scene?"

"Not exactly. Our heroine is studying magic at an ancient castle where it's all women and they wear these chastity belts. She's given to an evil mage as a kind of tribute. I guess the sex is implied in the fact that she's not wearing the chastity belt anymore in the next scene? Anyway, I wore a chastity belt, we had an amazing scene, and then he told me to wear it for the next three weeks until our next meeting."

She nodded, impressed. "That's commitment."

"I thought so. So I wore it. I'm wearing it in the WOMedia video and I wore it to the press event yesterday." I sighed. "I'm not wearing it now because he took it when he snuck out this morning after we had a scene go wrong."

I described the scene in as much detail as I could recall, the Velcro straps on the massage table, the flaming "marshmallow" on a stick, the "dragon" dildo. I found it comforting that Madison had seen those before; they even sold them at the sex-toy store where she used to work. And of course I told her how it all went wrong.

"You know," Madison said when I was done, "not that I'm blaming you, of course, but if he'd told you it was going to be a fire play scene, you might have at least had a chance to check if your wig was flammable or not."

"I should have guessed, though! I knew it was going to be a dragon sacrifice scene."

"Nope nope nope, no blaming yourself for this one, Gwen. That falls squarely on him. Secret tryst or surprise scene or what, he could have still given you some warning. Besides, who would've thought he was going to play the dragon himself and not a temple guard or priest?"

"Maybe I really didn't know him well enough."

"Of course you didn't know him well enough! You were pretending to be someone else. He was letting you pretend to be someone else!"

Oh. That made sense, I supposed. "Well, anyway, now he's saying we can never see each other again. That it's for my own good and also his mental health and so please respect his boundaries. And that makes me feel like I really stalked him, you know? I was the one who snuck backstage in disguise, twice, to have sex with him, and I gave him a ride home so I could proposition him—"

"I dunno, Gwen." She set down her coffee mug, now empty, and rested her chin on her fist. "On the one hand, part of me says yeah, respecting limits and rules is sacrosanct, but on the other hand what the actual fuck. Especially if he knew it was you but played along anyway. Just goes to show it wasn't an actual hard limit for him."

"So do you agree he's overreacting?"

"Totally." She turned my chin with her thumb, examining the burn mark. "I don't think this is even going to blister. He thinks he's being responsible and doing the right thing by breaking it off with you? No, he's being chickenshit. The responsible thing is to accept that accidents can happen and that you deal with them responsibly when they do."

"Look at his note. Look at what he wrote. He says he always pushes things too far."

"What, can this guy not get off unless someone's on fire or there's live blood or something? I think he's being chickenshit again. Unless he's actually a psycho, which I don't think he is. This is just another form of the same old song: men afraid of feelings."

I pressed my hands together. "The thing is, I've always got that fear in the back of my mind, that things *will* go too far, because of how my mother died."

Madison scooted a little closer to me on the couch. The whole world knew my mother had died in an accident on a movie set. Some knew the accident involved ropes and rigging. Because of the tabloids, some "knew" that it might have been suicide. Only Madison and a few others in our family's inner circle knew the whole story of how much our mother enjoyed rope bondage and suspension and that she was likely playing with someone when the accident happened. "Oh, honey, I know," Madison said. "But so many things went wrong there."

"I know. I also know having a car accident is way more likely than having a bondage accident, and that doesn't stop me from getting in cars." I sighed again. "But it's always lurking in the back of my mind."

Maddie took my hands. "Listen. BDSM is a part of your sexuality. Part of who you are. Forget Mal for a second. Remember what you told me about that guy in Providence?"

"The dirtbag tattoo artist?"

"Yeah. He was a guy who fulfilled your fantasies when you were in the dungeon but was a totally reprehensible human being outside of it. You're on a search to find a guy who isn't a jerkwad and who can give you what you need sexually. It sounds to me like Mal really worked for you and you really worked for him. You're a heavy-duty masochist, Gwen."

"And Mal's a sadist."

"There's more to it than that," Maddie said. "All the stuff about fantasy and dragons and that stuff: that gave you both a context for the pain, which can feel a lot better than just a guy being like hey, I want to cut you, burn you, hurt you. His note makes it sound like he doesn't understand why his fantasies are important to you both."

I let go of her hands and pulled my knees up on the couch. "Why do I need pain? Why can't kink just be good, clean fun for me?"

"Maybe for some people it can be. Maybe some people only need a little slap and tickle and they don't go very deep psychologically. I don't know very many of them, Gwen. We like the dark stuff for a reason. It gets at what we really need, deep down, and it's why you don't connect to vanilla guys. You need someone who will connect with you on that deep core level, the level that wants pain, wants intensity, wants adrenaline and domination."

Just hearing her talk about it like that set off a yearning ache in my heart. "Mal's the closest thing to that I've found."

"You haven't exactly been looking," Maddie said. "Until Mal, I think you'd convinced yourself all you should have is a little slap and tickle from time to time."

"What makes you say that?"

"Oh, come on, Gwen. You could be inviting anyone you want to the dungeon in the mansion's basement, but I don't exactly see you out there recruiting."

"Well, it's complicated. I mean, first of all, how do I know if a guy I meet is kinky enough to rate an invitation? And second, I'm submissive. How do I go about approaching a dom without being too forward?"

"Can I remind you that submissive is something you are *in the dungeon*, not in real life? Any play partner who expects you to act like anything but an independent, confident adult woman when you're not in the dungeon isn't someone you want to play with anyway."

"True. That isn't Mal's problem, though."

"Seriously, Gwen. Your grandfather started the club as a way to find play partners for himself."

"I thought he started it as a refuge for all his kinky friends."

"That, too, but he definitely used it as a recruiting ground. You'd just be continuing that tradition."

"Ricki and I have been talking a lot about expanding membership. She thinks we should invite the rest of Axel's band to join."

Madison smiled slyly. "Aha. Are you thinking right now you don't want to invite him because he's a big jerk and you're done with him?"

"No!" My heart skipped a beat.

"That's what I thought." She gave me a sympathetic smile and then her look turned thoughtful. "So you still want to find a way to convince him not to break it off?"

"Yes."

"One question—if you invite him to the dungeon, are you prepared for him to potentially... play with someone else there?"

"Someone he'll play with once and then refuse to do again?" I pointed out.

"True. So here's a related question. How do you think he'd feel about watching you play with someone else?"

"Are you thinking this might be a chance to wear down his resistance?"

"That's exactly what I'm thinking."

That brought a smile to my face. "I love the way you think."

Madison was good at covering all the angles. "Assuming he doesn't refuse the invitation to join the Governor's Club in the first place, of course."

"You know what?" She had given me a huge boost of optimism. "Something tells me if he accepts the invitation, that's a huge indicator right there that he's not as ready to break things off with me as he appears."

She nodded. "Definitely. Let me know if he says yes, and then we can commence planning Operation Dragon Tamer."

* * *

So. Ricki invited The Rough to join our secret dungeon club. They said yes. I tried to act appropriately happy—as opposed to conspicuously super-stoked—when she told me later that week during dinner. "That's excellent," I said, keeping my voice neutral. "They all seem like very nice guys." *Nice, hah! Is that what you call men who like to play with actual fire?* I knew the scene had gone wrong, but if anything, now I found myself longing for the parts that had gone right and wishing fervently for a different ending. What if it had gone perfectly? Would Mal have told me he knew it was me all along? Would I have told him myself? Would we be planning a scene together for the dungeon party or would he be dropping me hints about his plans? Would he be sitting there at the table across from me right this second, amusing Ricki with his commentary about the entertainment industry or the wine? I could almost picture him there, or he and Axel together, the four of us enjoying a grand evening of cuisine and company...

"How's that orientation curriculum coming along, by the way?" Ricki asked.

I nearly breathed in a forkful of rice pilaf in surprise, too caught up in my daydreams. I coughed and set my fork down. "I made a checklist. Do you think we should put the guys through it?"

"Yes. With four of them joining at once, I want to make sure we don't leave anything out. What do you think about the two of us leading them through in the hour before the party starts? Or should we do it the day before?"

"You mean get them into the party next week?" We were eating in the small dining room, where we usually did when it was just the two of us. The table could easily seat six and I couldn't help imagining her and Axel sitting on one side, me and Mal on the other. Right at that moment I found myself wishing he would hold my hand under the table. Real kinky, I know. Why was I thinking about that when we were discussing the dungeon? "Aren't they kind of busy with their album stuff?"

"They're supposed to go to Montreal to record, but not for another two weeks. At least according to Axel," Ricki said. She sat back in her chair and picked up her wineglass.

Thank goodness I had the Ricki connection to find out that sort of thing since Mal himself had, of course, been silent since the "good-bye" note. "Montreal? Why there?"

"Axel didn't give me the details but I'm under the impression if they go somewhere they know hardly anyone they'll get more done."

"Makes sense." I decided to leave my wineglass right where it was. I was prone to klutz moments whenever I talked about Mal, and right now my hands were feeling especially shaky. Maybe because I was having flashbacks, not to the wig accident but to how his cheek felt against mine when he pulled me against him, to his hair in my mouth and the sound of his voice. Plain and simple: I was missing him. "You want to check with them on when they want to do the, um, orientation?"

"Sure."

"Should we do, like, two and two?" *Play it casual, Gwen. Casual.* I tried to put up the walls in my mind: *All those things happened to Excrucia, not to you. You're just sweet little good-girl Gwen.* "Like you do Mal and Chino and I'll do Samson and Ford?" I suggested.

Ricki chuckled softly and patted my hand. "You're so cute. I thought you would *want* to be the one who led Mal around down there."

Ricki doesn't know anything, I reminded myself. She thinks we've just been on three dates. "Whatever made you think that?"

"Oh, come on, Gwen. It's completely obvious you really like him."

"It is? Why is it obvious?"

"You're a terrible actress," she said, then put her glass down quickly. "Oh goodness! I didn't mean it that way. I meant, you know, you're bad at hiding your feelings. That wasn't an actual comment on your acting ability—you know it wasn't, Gwen."

I sat there stunned, though. My sister had just called me a terrible actress. "You really think that."

"No, *of course not*! It's just a phrase. Don't think that, Gwen."

"Okay, now who's being a terrible actress?" I crossed my arms.

My heart was beating a mile a minute. "Why didn't you tell me before?"

"Don't be ridiculous, Gwen. I'm no judge of acting talent. What would I tell you? I want to support you, not tear you down."

She was just digging the hole deeper. I thought about how easily Mal had recognized me. Maybe I really was terrible at acting. Maybe I was completely wasting my time.

Panic set in as the longing for Mal and the worry that I wouldn't be able to change his mind crystallized into spiky general anxiety.

My phone buzzed on the table, interrupting my thoughts, and I picked it up hurriedly. Normally I wouldn't answer during dinner unless it was someone important, but I needed something to distract me, to derail the rising anxiety. "Do you recognize this number?" I asked, showing the screen to Ricki.

"I think that's Simon Gabriel's number," she said.

The agent I liked. I stared at the phone, trying to take a deep breath. Ricki mistook it for career nerves. "How exciting! This could be your big break, Gwen. Deep breath! But you better answer it."

Right. Answer it. Think about something else. "Um, hello?"

"Gwen? This is Simon Gabriel." His voice sounded friendly. Approachable, even. "You may not remember me—"

"Oh, Mr. Gabriel!" His open manner helped me answer in kind and pretend I wasn't hanging on every word. "Yes, of course I remember you. From the banquet. And, um, Jolene's party."

He laughed warmly. "Yes. Look, I won't beat around the bush. I understand you're looking to get more serious about acting as a career pursuit. At least, I hope that's true. I took the liberty of Googling you and I have to say, I like what I see."

"Oh." There couldn't be very much out there, I thought. I

knew there were a few scenes from a university production on YouTube and the WOMedia promo probably came right up. That reminded me to look up the Facebook page someone had made for me. Last time I had Googled myself, most of what popped up were photos of me on Mal's arm at the *On a Midnight Far* premiere. I tried to push Mal out of my mind for a few moments and focus on the man on the phone. "Um, thank you, I guess?"

He laughed again. "You're smart, beautiful, and it never hurts that you know the business. So if you're open to the idea, I'd very much like to discuss the possibility of representing you."

I met Ricki's eye. She was smiling. I couldn't help smiling myself. "Great!" I tried to keep my business voice on, though. "I mean, of course we can discuss it." Roderick Grisham's advice came back to me. He'd said it as a joke but I realized he'd also meant it. "I've been, ah, advised to get everything in writing."

"Of course. I'll send over a client contract for you to examine."

"Thank you, Mr. Gabriel."

"Oh, please, Simon, call me Simon. Another question—how would you feel about doing music videos?"

A business question was even better than flattery for grounding me. "Is there something particular about videos?"

"Some consider them almost more like modeling gigs, since there's no dialogue, but some of them really require emotive facial abilities like yours, the complete opposite of modeling."

"I'd love to do some music videos if the chance comes up. The promo video I just did has no dialogue in it, just miming."

"Good. I'll be looking around for some opportunities for you. To that end, there's a music industry party I'd like you to attend, if you're free? I believe it's Tuesday. I'll have my assistant send you the information."

"That sounds good, Mr. Simon. My schedule's fairly open right now."

"Excellent. I'll look forward to seeing you then. Gotta run now. So glad to be working with you, Gwen. Bye now."

And, poof, Simon was gone. I set the phone down. "Did you hear that?"

"Sounds like you've got a talent agent," Ricki said.

"Yeah. Yeah, I guess so."

Ricki was smiling. "For a 'terrible' actress, your career seems to be starting to take off."

"Oh, stop. I'm sure even Meryl Streep had her moments of crushing self-doubt when she was my age." Yes, but did she crave the attention of a distant dom? My moment of angst had passed, and I told myself to focus on the party. Until Mal was in the same room as me, there was no use worrying myself to death over what might or might not happen.

"Dessert?" Ricki asked.

"No way. The camera adds ten pounds," I said as I pushed my chair back and picked up my phone.

"Gwen, you don't need to lose ten pounds."

"No, but I shouldn't put any extra ones on, either."

"It's pumpkin pie, though."

"Drat." I pulled my chair in again. "My weakness."

"I know." She smiled and dialed our chef Mina. "With fresh whipped cream?"

"Definitely."

"Pie with whipped cream for two, Mina. Thanks," she said into the phone.

"I'm not crazy about how they're trying to make everything taste like pumpkin pie, though," I said. "It starts happening earlier and earlier every year and the only thing that should really taste like pumpkin pie is, well, pumpkin pie."

"Almost makes me wish for cold weather. Almost."

For two California girls like us, the hardest part about going to college in the northeast had been getting used to the winters.

"Yeah, almost." I realized there were a few more things about new club members I had meant to ask before I'd been sucked into my little angst vortex. "Hey, so did you tell Schmitt about inviting the band to the club?"

"I did. He just grunted affirmatively, which is about all he does when I talk to him these days." Ricki seemed quite pleased about that. "He'll contact each of them to sign the confidentiality agreement."

"We ought to see about recruiting some more people, you know," I said. "Didn't you say Sakura had some more leads?"

"Yes, she recommended a couple more people, but we already got Difford and Dara through her. I worry about too many people who already know each other becoming a bit of a clique."

"Yeah, but it's not like we're going to invite total strangers, are we?" It was a puzzle. How did you find people in celebrity circles who were kinksters if everyone was in the closet and "word of mouth" about your secret club was forbidden? "Kinky people will meet other kinky people and it'll grow. Especially now that we're in charge and it's no longer just older couples."

Mina came in and set two plates of pie down, one in front of each of us, then added a dollop of freshly whipped cream right from the whisk out of a metal bowl.

When she was gone again, I was too focused on enjoying my pie to talk about the club any further, and my mind had circled back to Mal. He'd said yes to joining the club. I took it as a good sign that he wasn't avoiding me completely. I wondered if I should text him in advance, or if I should just play it cool?

My phone pinged, startling me, but it was just the details about the event Simon wanted me to attend. Turned out it was the record release party for a band called Breakwater. I'd heard the name but couldn't think of one of their songs.

I finished my pie and excused myself, staring at my phone as I went to leave the room.

I had just reached the door when Ricki called my name again. "Gwen."

"Yes?"

"You know I really would have told you if I thought you couldn't make it."

"I know." I smiled at her. The truth was I don't think she would have told me. I think she would have supported me no matter what I wanted to do, and that included saying what I wanted or needed to hear at any given time.

What I needed to hear right then was Mal's voice, telling me he was sorry and that everything would be all right. Right then that was my favorite fantasy.

CHAPTER TEN

GOOD COMPANY

MAL

Axel drove and I quietly seethed.

"Look on the bright side, Mal," he said as he stopped at a red light. "If you can't play guitar right now because of the burn, at least it came at a convenient time. Until we hear back from the Powers that Be about those tracks we did with Larkin, we shouldn't work on new stuff anyway."

We had managed to work with Larkin Johns briefly without incident, but that only made me more impatient to move forward and my injury made my mood black. "I would still rather be home licking my wounds."

"Ew. I don't think it'll heal faster if you do," he said.

I didn't mean it literally of course, but Axel was always happy to make a quip at my expense.

The bandage went around my whole palm and also immobilized my thumb. It was covered in black veterinary wrap, at least, so it looked almost like a postapocalyptic-punk accessory of some kind. If it had been bulkier or uglier, I would have refused to go out under the theory that it would make for bad press: speculations about the injury and unsightly photos.

As it was, I had lied to the band about how I'd done it. Burned myself while cooking, I'd said. Grabbed the handle of a hot cast-iron pan. It burned my pride more than anything to make myself sound incompetent in the kitchen. I'd worked hard to learn to cook after all those years of having every meal prepared for me. And it felt sickening to lie to my bandmates. But I could not even begin to explain the situation with Gwen. I could imagine Axel's reaction: *You've been fucking my girlfriend's sister in secret so you could do* what *to her? You kept it a secret because you* knew *you were going to go too far and then you* did*?* Never mind trying to explain the whole thing about how I didn't even know it was her at first...

Never mind about the entire affair. I should have known better, full stop.

I tried to keep the conversation to business because if I let myself think about Gwen, then I really was going to insist he turn around and leave me at home. "Will Marcus or any of our team be at this party tonight?"

"I expect so, since Breakwater is one of Marcus's bands," Axel said. "Are they playing at this or is tonight 'booze and schmooze' only?"

"I have no idea." Christina had given me no details beyond that we were expected to be there to add hype to the event. Grammy-winning, chart-topping blah blah blah. Breakwater had opened for us on the western leg of our U.S. tour and they were a good band who deserved success. I wanted to help them. I simply wished I didn't have to leave the house to do it.

"Help me look for the place," Axel said as we eased our way up Sunset Boulevard. "I think it's in the block coming up."

The nightclub was actually quite easy to find, a large stand-alone building with a billboard advertising its name. Not exactly a speakeasy. There was a line of people outside waiting to get in.

We parked the car and walked around to the door. There was a bottleneck of people on the guest list being approved to go in.

There were also some fans behind a set of sawhorses near the entrance, not trying to get in but merely there to see who they could see. At first I assumed they must be Breakwater fans, but then I recognized Aurora. I nudged Axel as we drew close. "My stalker is here," I said, only half joking.

We paused to take some pictures with them and sign autographs. Aurora was again over the moon that I spoke to her by name, perhaps taking it as a sign that I had forgiven her for showing up at our rehearsal space.

It's a strange thing to have so much power over another person's happiness. I took it as a good sign, though, that no other fans had appeared at our rehearsal space since then. It restored my trust in them somewhat.

"Sorry, I haven't been able to help you find that girl you've been looking for," she said just as we were about to rejoin the line.

I had forgotten I had enlisted her help in trying to track down the red-haired temptress from the LA Forum. "Ah. Thank you." Best to keep that Pandora's box of emotions firmly shut while in public. "I did eventually get her e-mail. Mission accomplished."

"Oh, good," she said with smile. If she had any curiosity about why I had wanted to find her or what had happened when I did, Aurora kept it to herself. Perhaps she sensed my reticence. "Well, have fun in there tonight."

"I'll try," I said with a not-entirely-fake scowl that made her giggle.

Once we were inside the venue, it became obvious there would be live music because a stage at one end of the dance floor was set with instruments. The place had a faux posh feel, with gold-colored banquettes and lit-from-beneath promotional vodka displays. Many people were already there, and a shaven-headed disk jockey in a prominent booth was spinning unobtrusive tunes; this crowd was there to schmooze, not dance. People were clustered near the bar, where they were pouring free vodka cocktails as part of the promotion while another small mob pressed around a catering table. I circulated until I was able to extend my congratulations to the members of Breakwater, the last being their singer, Killian. His hair was fire-engine red tonight. We gave each other one-armed backslaps.

"Oh, a photo, a photo please," said a photographer who was roaming the event. He was a large man with multiple cameras, and as someone bumped him from behind, he motioned for us to get closer together.

I put my arm around Kill and he gave a thumbs-up toward the camera. The flash went off multiple times.

"One more, one more," the photographer exhorted. He motioned to some people crowded right behind us to get out of the picture and then snapped a few more.

Killian was then pulled away by an assistant, presumably to get ready to perform, and the photographer mopped his bald spot with a handkerchief. I wondered why he carried so many cameras when surely these days they were all digital. With them hanging off him as they were, making movement difficult, I supposed there must be some professional reason.

Suddenly he was in my face again, one hand on my arm. "Oh, here, here," he urged. "The happy couple."

"What?"

With his other hand he had seized a slim blonde from within a knot of people and pulled her next to me.

Gwen.

She plastered her public smile on her face. "Mal."

I merely cleared my throat and turned toward the camera, trying not to scowl too hard. Wouldn't do for it to look like Gwen and I were fighting.

However, I couldn't help but look sideways at her, checking to see if the mark on her cheek had healed. Perhaps it had? I quashed that flare of optimism as quickly as I could. They could do wonders with makeup these days. Maybe I simply couldn't see how well hidden it was in the few moments of bright flash, especially since I was trying not to look like I was looking. She put a hand on my chest in a classic "couples photo" pose and I caught the gentle, enticing fragrance of her skin.

I needed to get away from her before we descended into rehashing our previous argument or I did some other rash thing. The guy took another dozen or so photos of us and then I tried to make my escape. "If you'll excuse me, I need to get a drink."

"Bring me one, too?" Gwen said.

The photographer was too close for comfort—close enough that if we bickered he would notice. "Of course," I said, falling back on etiquette. "What would you like?"

I was expecting to see a triumphant light in her eye but she was giving me an entreating sort of look. *No, Gwen, not here. We're not doing this,* I thought.

"A club soda with a twist of lime," she said.

"I'll be back as soon as I can," I said, and then pushed my way through the crowd.

* * *

GWEN

My heart sank as Mal disappeared into the thicket of people on the dance floor. Well, not disappeared completely since he was tall and I could still make out his head as he made a beeline for the bar. I was trying to keep my attention on him and not on the photographer, who was giving me a creepster vibe. Maybe it was how he'd just grabbed me by the arm but something about him made me feel like I didn't want to be stuck talking to him.

Maybe if I ignored him he'd move on to other people to photograph. But no, he was still standing there a few feet from me.

I should have told Mal I'd go with him, but he would probably think I was being clingy.

I hadn't even known he was going to be here tonight. I was only here because Simon had suggested I come.

The photographer finally stopped staring and came forward. "Er, Ms. Hamilton? Sorry to bother you," he said, edging close to me as the crowd around us pressed in, "but I've been trying to get in touch with you. Ms. Rashan said she'd give you a message from me?"

No wonder he'd looked unsure how to approach me. He must have thought I ignored him on purpose. "Oh my goodness, I'm sorry!" I said. "She did give me your card but I lost it before I could e-mail you." Which was true: I'd forgotten to e-mail him and now I had no idea where the card was. Maybe it was among the things Mal had "cleaned up" after our last scene. "You had some photos, you said?"

"Um, yes. I wanted to send them to you directly, you know. Not to a . . . a shared address." He seemed nervous all of a sudden and I started to wonder: Were they upskirt shots or something? I felt goose bumps go across my back as I thought about how the fire scene had been in the open air. But wait, this guy had been trying to get in touch with me *before* that. So it wasn't that. Maybe he was just socially awkward around women?

I really didn't want to give him my personal e-mail, but I also didn't want to piss off a member of the media unnecessarily. "I don't actually read my e-mail that often because my assistant does it for me," I lied, since I didn't have an assistant. I just wanted to get away from the guy. I had a sudden idea. "I do have a personal address I rarely use, though." An address I wasn't planning to use at all anymore. "Here, I'll write it for you."

It felt like an interminable wait while he dug a pen out of his pocket from under the straps of the cameras and a small notepad. I wrote out my "Excrucia" address and handed it back, thinking that would be the end of it and he would go away.

But he was still standing there, only looking at the floor instead of at me. "Ms. Hamilton, I want you to know, you're one of the most beautiful women I've ever seen."

"Why thank you, that's very nice of you to say!" I enthused, but I was thinking underneath it all, *Jeez this is getting more uncomfortable by the second.* Where was Mal?

Thankfully, Simon Gabriel came to my rescue. "Gwen, here you are. Come meet some of the other folks from the agency."

"Oh, of course!" I gave a little wave good-bye to the photographer. "Bye, um, Beau."

After we got a little ways away, I breathed a sigh of relief. I wondered if I should tell Simon thank you or that I was creeped out by the guy, but I didn't want to seem like a problem client so early in our working relationship. If I couldn't handle one socially awkward photographer, how would I handle a whole press conference? I decided to keep quiet.

I felt much less awkward a short while later when I was able to introduce Christina, manager of The Rough, to Simon, and they seemed to hit it off really well. See? I'm not completely dead weight at an entertainment industry function even if I'm not the power schmoozer that my sister is.

* * *

MAL

I accepted two plastic cups of soda water from the harried-looking bartender and retreated from the bar, feeling rather mortified that I did not have a few small bills to jam into his tip jar. I'd gotten used to using my credit card for everything lately, and the only cash I had was the well-folded "emergency" hundred-dollar bill in my wallet. It hadn't occurred to me I'd need cash at a function like this and I wasn't about to try to interrupt the poor fellow to break a hundred so I could give him back a buck or two when there was a crowd clamoring for attention. He hadn't even made eye contact as he'd plopped the cups down in front of me and moved on.

Now all I wanted to do was give Gwen her drink, find Axel, and leave. We'd done our penance at the temple of publicity. But before I could find either of them, a young woman I recognized as an employee of our record company found me. She had dark hair and glasses, with her hair in a bun, giving her a bit of a librarian look despite her sharp business clothes.

"Mal? I'm Penny, Marcus's assistant."

"Ah, Penny, right. I'd shake hands but they're full," I said.

She smiled, humoring me. "No worries. Kill wanted me to ask you to come backstage."

I gave a last glance around for Gwen, didn't see her, and said, "Lead the way."

Penny brought me to a VIP room in the back, where I wasn't surprised to find most of my bandmates hanging around with Breakwater. Killian accosted me the moment he saw me. "Hey! I have an idea I wanted to run by you."

Axel often looked at me with that same mixture of eagerness and mischief. Perhaps it's a lead singer trait. I responded with my usual skepticism. "Idea?"

"You guys get up and jam with us. Tonight."

"Ah." As lead-singer brainstorms go, that wasn't a bad one. Unfortunately, I had to decline. "The others are better candidates for that than me at the moment." I held up my bandaged hand.

"Whoa, I didn't even notice that before!"

"It's nothing major, but I can't play until it heals."

"Dude, that sucks." Kill pushed cherry-red hair out of his eyes and looked like he was about to ask me how I hurt myself when Axel jumped in.

"Did you know Ford plays the mandolin?" he asked me.

"I am under the impression Ford will play anything with strings," I said seriously. I had never seen him with a mandolin before, but I can't say I was surprised.

"He showed me a little while we were on tour," Killian said. "Perfect for the kind of rootsy vibe we're going for tonight."

So that is how it turned out that our quiet blond bass player was tabbed to get onstage with Breakwater to do a punk-folk acoustic rendition of one of their songs. Which meant we had to stay for the set. I suppose it would have been rude to leave before it regardless, but I especially did not want Ford to think I was being dismissive of his talent. I'd known him the shortest amount of time compared to the others in the band. We'd first gelled when Axel and I had met Chino, and the three of us had recorded a demo album where Axel and I had traded off dubbing in the bass and keyboard parts. Thank goodness most of those original tracks were binned. After Marcus signed us, he'd played matchmaker, hooking us up first with Samson, and after we'd auditioned a few bass players and hated them, Sam had suggested he knew a guy and, voilà, along came Ford.

Ford was the son of a well-known rock-blues musician and I was still unsure about his true ambitions. Or maybe it was Ford who was unsure. Like with that song he'd brought us a couple weeks back, sometimes he seemed hesitant about us actually playing what he wrote. Granted, the last thing we needed in the band was another strong ego vying for expression, but I sometimes wondered if he didn't yearn for a little more time in the spotlight. If so, it was good that tonight he would get some.

I made my way back into the main room to try once more to find Gwen and deliver her now-somewhat-lukewarm drink. Amazingly, I managed to find her near the poorly lit entrance to the restrooms. I caught sight of her blond head and made a beeline for her. The mere sight of her sent my emotions simmering.

She saw me coming and bit her lip for a moment before she composed her face into a neutral, friendly look. "Thank you," she said as she took the plastic cup from my hand, a small, bemused smile bending her lips.

"You're welcome." Now that I had found her and she seemed unhurt, unscarred, I gave vent to the annoyance that had been brewing in the back of my mind since I'd seen her the first time: "I don't appreciate being stalked."

The smile disappeared. "Stalked? Who's stalking you?"

"Y-you," I sputtered, trying to say more. "You're... you're... What are you doing here, anyway? I don't appreciate you using your sister's connections to create opportunities to run into me."

Her eyebrow was sharp as she frowned. "Mal. Hate to break it to you, but I'm not here to stalk you."

"What are you—"

"In fact, Ricki wasn't even invited so far as I know. My agent invited me. I didn't know *you* would be here. Why are you here, anyway?"

"I... because..." I forced myself to slow down or my explanation was going to come out defensive and angry. How had she put me on the defensive so quickly? "We're friends of Breakwater."

"Ah." She sipped her drink through the tiny red straw and continued to regard me critically. "Well. That was pretty low of you to sneak out the other night."

"It was pretty low of you to deceive me," I said, but I could feel myself losing ground. That cannon had already been emptied.

"We have a saying in America—*Two wrongs don't make a right.* Do you know it?" She looked... disappointed. "If you think you're doing the 'mature and responsible' thing by breaking things off, maybe you should think about that."

"So noted," I said, and looked around for an escape from the argument. "Perhaps that's merely another tally in the evidence against my suitability. Since I clearly am no judge of what counts as mature and responsible."

"So you should just stay home like a monk or something?"

"Just so. Now if you'll pardon me, this monk needs to answer the call of nature." I hurried past her into the men's room, my head a maelstrom of thoughts and feelings.

She's right, you're right, you're no judge of these things and that is exactly why you shouldn't even try. But you know you're going to... How long until you give in to the Need? How long until you go on another search for a woman who will let you have your way?

You are deeply, deeply, deeply fucked up, my friend, if you truly believe the only women you should be allowed to fuck are those you'll never have to look in the eye again.

"Hey, big guy," came a familiar voice behind me. "You okay?"

I realized I was leaning against the wall with my head on my arm above the hand dryers. I looked up at Chino, who was giving me a wry smile.

"I'm fine."

He shrugged and looked around the restroom. "Coulda fooled me."

All right, I conceded it looked bad to be hiding in the men's room. "Female trouble," I admitted, hoping that would put an end to it.

"Isn't it always?" he said with a shrug. "You want to talk about it?"

"No."

"I don't mean now. Let's grab a bite to eat later. Something other than this rabbit food. Just you and me." He gave a vague wave toward the door. "I get the feeling Axel's getting sucked into an after-party with the Breakwater guys and I'd rather eat than drink."

I considered this plan of action.

"Come on. I heard you complaining there's no good food in this town. You just don't know where to go."

Chino knew LA; there was no doubting that. "All right. After the set, we'll go."

He grinned and smacked me on the upper arm. "Now you're talking."

The set was mercifully brief, four songs, including Ford's mandolin jam, which brought the house down. I was glad about that. Gave me something to talk to Chino about besides myself.

"I sometimes wonder if being our bass player is going to be enough for him," I said as Chino pulled his SUV out of the parking lot. He had what I assumed was a rosary hanging from his rearview mirror but on closer inspection I realized it was a figurine of Elvis on Mardi Gras beads.

"I know what you mean. Ford's a cool caterpillar now, but one day he might butterfly on outta here." He turned on the car stereo and the orchestral sound of a movie soundtrack filled the car. "Ah, you young'uns."

I snorted. Chino was the eldest of the group by about five years, and he often lorded it over us as if he were a different generation just because he was closer to thirty than we were. "So, you promised me good food."

"What are you in the mood for? Seafood? Best tacos on the

West Coast? Thai food so spicy it'll leave a stump where your tongue was?"

"How does one judge the best tacos on the West Coast?"

"By how little English they have on their menu," he said seriously. "Really, though, there's a crab shack up the coast. They'll have fresh Dungeness—"

"No, no, you've intrigued and challenged me with this best tacos idea."

"All right, but you gotta promise me none of your gringo bullshit."

"Which would be what exactly?"

He laughed. "Just play it cool. If anyone gives you a dirty look or whatever, you know? It'll be okay. You're with me."

"You know I have Spanish ancestry, do you not?"

He laughed again. "Boyyy, that won't get you far in this crowd. Trust me. Let me do the talking. You know how no matter what kind of restaurant you go into around here, you'll find Mexican busboys and cooks? This is the place all of *them* go to eat."

The place was the very definition of a hole in the wall, a former Chinese restaurant in a strip mall in the middle of nowhere. They'd boarded over the old restaurant sign but left the neon dragon in the window.

The menu was written in magic marker on pieces of paper taped to the wall. I could read many of the words thanks to a few years spent trying to teach myself Spanish as a teenager, but that didn't mean I knew what they *meant*. "Old clothes?" I asked. "Is three Marias a religious reference I'm missing?"

Chino's startled look was deeply satisfying to me. "You can read it?"

"Only a little," I admitted. "And my pronunciation is atrocious."

"Well *ropa vieja* is called 'old clothes' because it's a stew with shredded beef in it, so it's like when your clothes shred in the laundry. No really!" He waved his hand emphatically. "I'm not making this shit up just to get back at you for the explanation of what 'spotted dick' is."

I held in a chuckle. On the tour one of the shows had been in Victoria, British Columbia—the one place on Earth I've been that tries to be more British than Great Britain—and while eating in the hotel pub I'd had to explain much of the menu. "Spotted dick is a pudding," I reiterated, as if he still doubted it. "You can Google it."

He shook his head. "I guarantee you Jell-O has no 'spotted dick' flavor pudding."

A waitress came over and had a rapid-fire conversation with Chino that I could not really follow except for the English words peppered throughout. I gathered he was ordering an assortment of food. And beer.

She brought us two glass bottles of beer and plastic cups. Chino merely wiped the mouth of the bottle with a paper napkin and drank directly from it. I did the same.

"Okay, so you said female trouble," Chino said, settling back in his chair with his beer in one hand. The general hubbub around us was in Spanish, and no one was listening to what we were saying. "I thought you had a foolproof system for avoiding exactly that?"

I leaned against the wall. "I did. And if I had stuck to it, I wouldn't be in the mess I'm in now."

"Uh-huh."

"You sound skeptical."

"Mal, I love you like a brother, but you know we all think your tactic of only ever fucking a woman once is whack."

I took a pull from my beer before mounting my defense. "The entire problem is with inappropriate emotional attachments. My tactic prevents that."

"You mean you do it so you don't get attached to them?"

"You have it backwards. It's that I don't want them getting attached to me."

"Hmm. I guess I can understand that with groupies, but with a woman like Gwen? This is Gwen we're talking about, right?"

There was little point in denying it. "Yes, Gwen, who I wasn't supposed to get involved with emotionally, you might recall. The rule isn't only for groupies." I tried to decide how much to tell him. Chino knew me fairly well, but only Axel really knew much of my past. "I've had a few serious attempts at relationships. All have been disastrous, more so for the women I was involved with than for me."

"Disastrous, how?" He had a concerned look on his face, so unlike his usual wry smirk.

Perhaps that's what convinced me to tell him. "I have this tendency to be attracted to submissive women," I began.

"That's not news," Chino said, "and you're hardly alone there."

"It's not just that. It's things like—" I broke off with a shake of my head. "It never works out well."

"It's okay, Mal. You can tell me whatever it is."

"Well, there were a few clingy ones to begin with when I first started exploring dominance and submission, and then I'd have to explain I wasn't recruiting a slave, I was just sowing my wild oats. I began to make that part of the negotiation up front—the no repeats thing—and that cut down the clinging on a lot. But then I—" The specter of my failure with Risa hovered in the back of my mind. So many things had gone wrong there. So many. But my worst mistake had been in thinking love justified all. "I met a woman—not through the scene. Someone my father arranged for me. I thought, well, I'll scare her off with my whips and chains."

"Let me guess," Chino said, his beer completely forgotten now. "She wasn't scared off."

"Indeed, she was quite excited and more than willing. In fact, she begged me for more and more extreme treatment as time went on. She was... the first submissive that I let love me."

Chino nodded as if he heard what I implied but couldn't bring myself to say aloud, that she was also the first one I'd loved, truly loved.

I tried to explain it as simply as I could. "She wanted to 'serve me,' to 'be mine,' so very much that any small fault I found with her crushed her self-esteem, and she would beg me to punish her to 'make it right.' No, that's not even the right way to put it. She wanted me to hurt her, to do terrible things to her, to damage her."

"Physically? Mentally?"

"Yes and yes, and emotionally." I couldn't even separate the tangle when it came to Risa. "This was the woman who very nearly talked me into branding her labia."

Chino's mouth hung slightly open. He tried to play devil's advocate. "Some people like the extremes."

"It wasn't a matter of 'like.' At first I thought she was a perfect match for my sadism, but I eventually came to see she was using me as an elaborate form of self-harm. I put my foot down about the branding." The burn on my palm seemed to throb in time with my heart as I remembered her fighting with me. "She accused me of not loving her enough to give her what she needed. When I wouldn't give in, she showed the scars to her father and told him I'd not only ruined her, but I'd also been torturing her."

"What! Did they go to the police?"

I made a dismissive noise. "Of course not. A man like that fears scandal more than he fears having his daughter violated. Her father and mine then agreed to keep us apart."

"Man. Real Romeo and Juliet stuff."

"Quite." I set my bottle on the table and rotated it slowly, seeking out the cool condensation with my fingertips. I had to tell him the final piece. The story wouldn't be complete without it: "She tried to kill herself shortly after."

"Mal, holy shit. Seriously?"

I nodded. After she was committed, I'd left for the United States and hadn't spoken to my own father since. Axel had been at university and I'd slept on his floor for a couple of weeks until I sorted a place to stay. "She used to drop hints to me all the time about breath play. I have to wonder if she had a death wish the entire time."

"That's just... not healthy."

"No," I agreed. I had been looking at the beer bottle but I forced myself to raise my eyes so he'd see how serious I was. "I avoid going that far or that deep again by avoiding repeat engagements. Or I had successfully avoided it until recently."

"You think Gwen Hamilton is like that other girl?"

"Yes." I felt a sudden urgency to be sure he knew I didn't wish to speak ill of Gwen, or even Risa. "Listen. It's not my way to air my private affairs, especially in sexual matters."

"I guess you didn't leave all your British traditions behind, then," he said with a raised eyebrow.

He was irritatingly correct, but I held fast.

"That's not what I'm trying to say, but yes, your silence would be appreciated. What I'm trying to say is just... what I've told you... I would normally never speak of."

"And it's important to you that I know that?"

"Yes." Hearing him put it that way did make it seem a bit silly that I felt he might judge my actions less harshly because I was a polite boy at heart. Stupid. "Anyway."

Of course our food arrived just then and we had to pause to devour a large platter of things whose names I didn't even ask about, although Chino did explain that *trés marias* referred to the three different sauces. While we ate, my mind turned the

Gwen question over and over: I had a gorgeous woman at my beck and call, and I knew exactly what I wanted to do with her. Lock her in a room and use her, toy with her, demand her obedience, and if she couldn't obey to compel compliance through force... except by all indications Gwen was completely willing to obey me. Was the problem that I wanted to see her both on my arm before the glitterati and over my knee? The problem was that love was no antidote for the damage that could result when her need for pain met my need to hurt—in fact, it was throwing more gasoline on the fire. By the end of the meal, I hadn't come to any new conclusions, but at least now my belly was full and that made me somewhat calmer than before.

"I told you there was good food to be had in this town," Chino said when we were staring at the empty remains of our plates. He then ordered a second beer for me and a cup of coffee for himself.

"Thank you for that," I said, and saluted him with the beer in my unbandaged hand.

"Now, you were saying."

"Yes. I was saying." Food and drink had mellowed me, which made it marginally easier to say. "Gwen and I have been playing a dangerous sexual game, and I broke things off with her before it went too far, but she's none too happy about it."

"Well, Gwen seems more down to Earth than your Juliet, but you obviously know her better than I do. When you say dangerous, how dangerous?"

I was blunt. "I... set to fire her the other day."

He seemed unfazed. "You mean like we did in the video for 'Short Fuse'?"

"Yes and no. I used the same fire-play technique, but we also had a... mishap." I held up my bandaged hand. "And it was nearly much worse."

"I knew your story about burning yourself cooking didn't

sound right." Chino sipped his coffee, frowning slightly. "And you're worried it'll happen again, or worse?"

"Yes." I hunched over my beer, staring into the dark hole of the brown bottle. "That's why I've decided we shouldn't go any further, but she's resisting my decision."

"Whoa whoa whoa. You didn't think she'd have a problem with you unilaterally declaring that something you did together was over, without her input? Are you telling me you set it up so that you were the one 'in charge' *all the time*, not just in the dom/sub role-playing? You dictated everything in the relationship?"

"First of all, it wasn't a relationship—it was a sexual affair at best—and secondly, yes, because I'm the dom." I held up my hand before he could jump down my throat. "And, yes, I'm not a complete idiot, I realize now—saying it aloud to you—how patently ridiculous that sounds."

"Do you? I mean, help me out here, Mal. I'm not exactly a shining example of responsible commitment myself, so, you know, pot-kettle-black, but I really was under the impression that when people are into role-playing that there's a pretty firm delineation between when they're in a scene and when they're not. And when they're not, they're equals in the relationship. Right?"

"Right. But like I said, this wasn't a relationship." Even as I said the words, I felt the lacerations in my heart, the yearning for a love I didn't dare admit. Instead I spoke the harsh necessity: "It was nothing more than a game."

"And what is it now?"

"Over," I said, and stood abruptly. "Game over."

I tossed the hundred-dollar bill onto the table and stalked out.

Of course, a dramatic exit loses its impact somewhat when you have to wait for the other party to unlock the door of their SUV. Chino came out a few minutes later and we got in.

"So this might not be the right time to bring it up, but listen. If you're dead set on breaking it off with Gwen, I'm the last person who'll try to talk you out of it. But to get back to something we were talking about earlier, let me tell you, Mal, when you're in a mood, it's hard on all of us."

I buckled my seat belt.

"Plus," he went on, "how does this tie in with the fact that we're supposed to go to some kind of secret kinkster shindig at Ricki and Gwen's house?"

When the invitation to the orientation for the Governor's Club party had come, I'd accepted because at the time I had taken it to be an olive branch from Gwen, perhaps even an indication that she was moving on—that both of us should move on. A party would be the ideal situation for us both to find new play partners, would it not? But my optimism had been dimmed by her attempts to argue with me tonight. "I'll leave if Gwen can't control herself around me."

"Okay, fine," he said. "I'm basically saying, given what we've got on our plate right now with the album and laying down the new tracks, we need everybody working together. We can't all be tiptoeing around wondering when you're going to bite somebody's head off next."

"I—" I couldn't really defend myself from that accusation. "I'm very passionate about what we do."

"I know. We all know, which is why we stick with you. It's why we put up with your weird groupie shit, because when you're getting regular pussy, you're a hell of a lot easier to deal with."

"What. Are. You talking about?" I kept my eyes on the road ahead of us instead of looking at him.

"Come on, Mal, seriously? The entire band and crew have a vested interest in making sure you get your rocks off. Whether that's with Gwen or some other way, you clearly need to be getting your freak on somehow. Mal, your sex life is unfortunately *all* of our business."

It takes a lot to make me blush. But my cheeks felt hot and I wanted to crawl into a cave and hide. "Am I truly that difficult to get along with?"

He laughed. "Yes, Mal. You're the dragon we send the virgin sacrifices to so the rest of us don't get eaten."

CHAPTER ELEVEN

EVERYONE LOVES A PARTY

GWEN

I gave Ricki the orientation checklist when we had lunch the day of the party. We were sitting at the kitchen table where we could grab a quick bite without the help of any staff. On party days they were all sent home early except for Jamison, who manned the door, and our security staff.

I pointed to the section on the paper about rope suspension. "I wasn't exactly sure what to put here."

Ricki took a pen out of the caddy on the table and wrote something.

"What are you putting down?"

"That no one should try to use the suspension rig in the Inquisition Room without first having a one-on-one training session with an approved senior member, and there must be one monitor on duty during any scene." She met my eyes over the top of the paper. "Though no one but me and Axel have dared to use it so far."

"Well, this group is mostly older. You have to be kind of in good shape for rope suspension," I said, knowing that probably wasn't the reason they avoided rope.

Ricki wrinkled her nose but didn't argue. We'd always known our mother had died in some kind of accident, but we hadn't learned that it was a bondage accident until several months ago. Ricki had been really shaken by it. I had a feeling a lot of the reason she and Axel had gotten into rope was that it was helping her work out her issues about it.

I hadn't felt the impact as hard because I didn't have any memories of our mother at all, really. When we'd found out, I'd already long since explored my kinky side. If anything, finding out my mother had been into bondage had given me something to feel kinship with her about, and it had validated my feelings a lot. You know, the acorn doesn't fall far from the oak.

But rope suspension wasn't particularly an interest of mine. Obviously there were safety concerns, too—not because rope suspension was so much more dangerous than other things, but because it would have seemed extra tragic if an accident were to occur, given the family history. I didn't like tempting fate.

Speaking of which: "So, we didn't have any rule at all concerning fire play, but I thought we should put one in prohibiting it."

"Oh, has someone asked about doing it?"

"Um, no," I lied. "I just saw a how-to on YouTube, and it seems to be getting popular." Well, it wasn't a total lie: I actually had watched a YouTube video to find out more about it and concluded that generally speaking, Mal had done almost everything right. The way I remembered the accident, I'd kicked my leg and jostled his arm holding the flame and that's what had set my wig on fire. If we were ever going to do something like that again, I'd know not to wear a flammable wig and to keep still if I wasn't tied down.

But what were the chances I was going to convince Mal to get over himself enough to try it again? Slim, perhaps. He'd texted a terse message to me after the Breakwater party: This event at your home: shall we be civil to one another?

I'd replied: I plan to be the perfect hostess.

Two oddly sincere-seeming words had come back: Thank you.

I took his request to mean I shouldn't harangue him about "us" the way I had at Breakwater's thing. Well, I had no intention of doing so. In fact, I'd resolved not to talk to him at all unless he talked to me first. Madison had agreed: playing hard to get was the oldest play in the playbook, but it was there for a reason.

"Make two copies of this, I guess, one for each of us?" Ricki suggested. "Then we'll, what, shred them after the orientation is done? Wouldn't want to have incriminating evidence lying around. Let's have Madison and Bradley go around with us, too, because they might think of things we forgot."

"Sounds good. I'll update the file on my encrypted hard drive." I took her notated version and went to make changes to it.

I called Madison while I was typing in the additions. Time to work on what we had in store for Mal, and it definitely did not involve speaking to him, though I sincerely hoped it sent a message.

"Did you read the book?" I asked her when she picked up the line.

Her voice was gleeful. "Oh my goodness, that was a book for kids?"

"Well, twenty years ago, I guess. What did you think?"

She laughed. "That was definitely the kinkiest thing I ever read outside of a porno shop. I mean, you had to read between the lines but there's so much implied."

"I know. So what do you think? Can we do a scene with Excrucia and the Headmistress?"

"Oh, totally. There's the whole description of how the Headmistress has the two punishment floggers hanging over the doorway to the correction room. I have two floggers, a matched set, that'll work for that."

"Awesome." I sent my document to the printer. "You're sure you're okay with being a little more intense than we usually are? I mean, people are used to you and me playing, but, well, *playing*. As in playfully."

"Gwen, no one in this crowd is going to be fazed by actual play-*acting*, least of all me. I mostly want to make sure it's okay with *you*."

"I'm thinking of it like an audition scene, you know, to see if I can," I told her. "I know I'm in good hands with you."

Her laugh was warm and genuine. "I do love giving the husbands of the older couples something to break the ice and get them going. Their wives always thank me when we do, you know?"

"I know! This is going to be fun." Good, clean fun. Maybe I'd find out that role-playing with other people was just as much fun as it was with Mal. Maybe the game of Let's Pretend was what really made things so intense, and I'd find that there was a way other than Mal to fill the aching gap in my chest.

Truthfully, that ache had only gotten worse since the last time we'd seen each other. You'd think seeing me healthy and unscarred would've calmed him down, but his text had made me think he was as defensive as ever. *At least he's coming to the party,* I thought. To me that meant there was hope.

* * *

MAL

Chino and I took separate cars to the Hamilton mansion but we arrived at the same time. While the butler drove Chino's vehicle down the drive to a parking area out of view from the front door, Ricki Hamilton showed us inside. She was in a blazer and pencil skirt looking almost like a stewardess from a vintage poster.

"I know you guys have been here before, but of course today Madison and I are going to show you a part of the mansion you haven't seen," she said as she led us through the main foyer. "Mal, I know Axel's told you some but I'm going to pretend you know nothing, just to make sure I tell you everything I should."

"That sounds like a solid plan." I followed her to a door with a numeric keypad, Chino coming up just behind.

She punched a four-digit code too quickly for us to see and then opened the door to a stairwell downward. "This door is always locked from upstairs but unlocked from downstairs, so you can always exit if you need to, but if you need reentry, you'll need to page us to come let you back in. All guests are expected to arrive between eight and nine p.m. and the staff is here to provide continuous access during that hour."

We followed her down the stairs to another doorway where she introduced us to two dark-suited members of her security staff who would be on duty that night. I had the feeling they were memorizing our faces. Just beyond them we met our other "tour guide," Madison, an auburn-haired woman with the legs and posture of a Rockette dancer. Chino said something to her, but I didn't register what, too distracted by the sound of voices coming from down the hall, my ears listening instinctively for Gwen.

Madison opened the door into a bathroom. "This one has a shower stall big enough for three, but it's intended for cleanup purposes only." She flicked on the light, revealing a tastefully tiled room. "The next one down is for actual bath or shower scenes."

"I'm easily confused," Chino joked. "What happens if I do a scene in the wrong one?"

Madison gave him a sharp look. "Then you might get spanked."

"But what if I *want* to get spanked?" His smile was cheeky.

She didn't look amused. "Are you a bottom?"

"I am if it means a pretty girl like you looking at my ass," he said, adjusting his jeans.

"Chino," I said in my have-some-respect voice.

Ricki, at least, seemed to appreciate my effort. "There'll be plenty of time to flirt later, guys."

"I'm not flirting," Madison said at the same moment Chino said, "Who's flirting?" so that the word *flirting* matched up. Then they both bafflingly said, "Coke!" at the same time and then burst out laughing.

"Is this some American courtship ritual I'm unaware of?" I asked Ricki.

She was smiling and shaking her head. "You could say that. Come on, let's continue and they can catch up." She turned on the light in a changing room that had wood-paneled lockers and electronic code locks. A matching leather corset and thigh-high boots, richly dyed a reddish cinnamon brown, were sitting on the polished wood bench. "We of course prefer if people arrive wearing their discreet, usual clothes and wait until they're out of the public eye before they slip into something less comfortable."

Was the outfit Gwen's? I couldn't help but picture her, the way her golden skin would look against the brown leather, remembering how her back had looked while laced into the corset she'd worn to the Beach Bash, the knife balanced on her back as she'd awaited me in the trailer like a gift...

Waiting to be torn open, I reminded myself. *No. We're not going down that road again.*

Now I was certain I could hear her voice, and a part of me was aware we were drawing nearer to her.

As we entered the main room, I saw her, leading Samson and Ford on a similar orientation tour with another man I did not recognize. I immediately wanted to know who he was. Gwen merely waved to us as she led them out the other side of the room, leaving us in a wide open socializing area that reminded me of a gentlemen's billiards room or library, except there was no billiards table and only a few small bookshelves set into the walls. Everything was dark-paneled wood and leather, with a bar that seated four, several low leather couches, and a Catherine wheel against one wall.

"Who was that with Gwen?" I asked Ricki, trying to sound casually curious instead of agitated.

"That's Bradley, one of our other hosts. You can bring any problem or question to any one of the hosts, or to me or Gwen of course."

Oh. An employee. How sensible. "How did you hire them? I can't imagine the job listing."

Ricki smiled. "My grandfather hired them. I'm not sure how he found them, but they're great. Now, play is allowed in this room, but we generally keep it to the equipment, not the seating area. Let me show you the Catherine wheel, which can be locked so it can be used like a Saint Andrew's cross."

I watched, trying to act as if I were paying rapt attention, but my mind was wandering the back hallways, wondering what Gwen was telling my bandmates.

She was probably telling them exactly what Ricki was telling me. Most of the rules seemed to be common sense, but the Hamiltons made no assumptions that their guests knew everything (or anything) about safe sex. Chino and Madison caught up and Ricki walked us through the kit in each room, which included not only condoms but also dental dams, gloves, and disinfection supplies, and also drilled us on several other rules, including no fire play, never leave a person alone in any kind of bondage even for a minute, and a full rundown on earthquake preparedness.

I still hadn't gotten accustomed to living in a place where the Earth might suddenly decide to heave. But like so many thoughts, it was necessary to shove it to the back of my mind in order to carry on with day-to-day life.

Like the thoughts about what I wanted to do to Gwen Hamilton. Tonight would be the ultimate test of whether I could keep a lid on that Pandora's box, wouldn't it? *This is good for Gwen,* I told myself. *This is a safe environment where she can't get herself into too much trouble. That Bradley person is a trained professional. Surely that is all she needs...*

I discovered I was clenching my fist, which was still sore from the burn, though I only needed a simple Band-Aid now. I forced my hand to relax, forcing myself to pay attention to Ricki's words as she brought us to another doorway.

"This is a new room we just opened up that had been storage. We thought it would be fun to have a medical play room that really looked like a doctor's exam room." She stepped into a small room that was an impeccable re-creation, right down to the drawer of sterilized and packaged instruments. Medical play was not my cup of tea—too precise and fussy and anti-erotic for my style—but I appreciated the attention to detail.

Then there was the large room that was made up like a, well, *dungeon,* complete with faux flame sconces and iron manacles set in the stone walls. That was more to my taste. "We call this the Inquisition Room," Ricki said.

"No one expects the Spanish Inquisition," Chino said with a sage nod.

We returned to the main room after that, prompting Chino to ask an actually intelligent question. "Do you serve alcohol at this bar?"

"We do," Ricki said, "though we don't allow anyone who's

drunk to play, and no drugs. This crowd gets high on the endorphin rush and tends not to drink much in the way of alcohol to begin with. Any other questions?"

Yes, I thought to myself. *Isn't it a bit... odd?... to run a secret bondage establishment with your own sister?* Instead I said, "It all seems very well organized."

She smiled. "We try. The club got sort of dropped in our laps after our grandfather passed and it turns out there's still a need for it. I mean, yes, BDSM is less stigmatized than it used to be, but there's also more intense interest in our private sex lives than ever."

"Very, very true." At that moment Gwen and her group returned with a short, plump woman in tow, solving the mystery of whose boots and corset we had seen earlier. Her skin was almost as dark as the leather and her smile was brilliant.

"Hey, everyone, if you haven't met her yet, this is Chita," Gwen said. "We have a staff of three hosts—Chita, Madison, and Bradley. They're fully trained with all the equipment and are available to be invited to play, but let me emphasize the word *invited* because they are never required to do anything they don't want to do."

I feigned interest in meeting the hosts, enough to seem believably polite, whilst armoring myself to ignore Gwen further.

That plan worked for a few short hours. The guests began arriving after our orientation ended, and it was pleasant enough to socialize with a few people I'd met before like the model/performer known as Sakura and the people who were new to me like Madison, who seemed to always be there with a ready conversation whenever my attention lagged.

Perhaps inevitably I ended up in a conversation beside the bar that included Gwen, and when the other two moved off to play together, I was unable to simply walk away from her. That would be rude.

For her part, she was fulfilling the role of perfect hostess, as promised. "Can I pour you a drink, Mal? Some soda water? I'm going to have some."

"Um, yes, that would be very thoughtful." I made small talk to fill the silence while she went around to the other side of the bar and got out glasses. "So. Your new agent. You like him? Or her?"

"You met him at that banquet," she said as she scooped the ice. "Simon Gabriel. Did he make a good impression on you?"

"Good enough, anyway." My eyes followed her as she put the ice into the glasses. Her hands were entrancing me. "Seemed a reasonable fellow."

"He says he's going to try to get me some gigs in music videos." She shrugged.

"This idea doesn't thrill you I take it?"

She poured from a bottle into each glass and then set one in front of me. "Oh, it's not that it isn't a good opportunity, but it's the whole thing of being a pretty face but not getting a speaking part."

"Aaah, I see." I wasn't particularly fond of the mimicry and vamping that filming a video often required of the band, either. I picked up the glass and raised it to her in thanks. "What is it that drew you to acting?"

"I resisted it at first, actually." She took a sip and looked off into the distance instead of at me. "But I fell in love with that feeling of inhabiting a character, of becoming another person. Talking like them, thinking like them, it's like a whole new internal logic springs up in my mind."

I murmured in agreement, barely aware that we'd slipped into an easy intimacy: me asking, her answering from her heart.

"It can be really… intense sometimes. Like I've changed how I thought or felt about things personally as a result. Like the first time I did a death scene. It wasn't even for a show; it was just an acting class. But it was like . . . I died and woke up a new person."

The ghost of Risa in the back of my mind would not let that go unremarked. "New how?"

"Less afraid. More willing to embrace the mysteries in life. It sounds weird, I know, but it was almost like a . . . religious epiphany. One of my theater professors warned us about it. Even though you're 'just acting,' real emotional change can happen." She paused for a second before going on. "You know, now that I think about it, that must be true for role-playing in a BDSM scene, too."

"You think?" I tried to keep my voice neutral, knowing I wanted to avoid anything that smacked of "relationship talk" and yet part of me craved hearing what she was saying. Perhaps I was unable to stop picking at a wound as I asked, "Did you have any epiphanies when we played?"

Gwen met my eyes. "I don't know about epiphanies exactly, but I do feel like, even when you told me who to be, the character I became, the person I inhabited, was actually the best possible version of myself."

Sweet Gwen. I was speechless. How could I explain to her that once I gave in to my cravings I felt I became the worst version of myself? I was unable to muster even a polite automatic response.

She glanced at the clock and took a hurried last sip from her glass. "Ooh. Gotta run! I've got to go get ready for a scene Madison and I are going to do. Talk to you later, Mal."

And away she went. Gwen and Madison? I was still trying to absorb what she had said about becoming her best self while in scene. If that was so, then what was she trying to prove by doing a scene with Madison? I wondered if I could go through watching it. Perhaps I should leave.

I knew I wouldn't, though. I was as drawn to Gwen Hamilton as the proverbial moth to the flame.

* * *

GWEN

Oh, man. Here I'd promised myself I'd keep my distance and I'd gone right for the jugular instead. Why did I tell him that? If Mal needed a reason to think I was turning into an obsessed stalker, telling him I found BDSM a potentially life-changing experience probably just handed him one. He'd stared at me like I'd told him I liked to kick puppies. Maybe I was overreacting. Maybe he was just so moved by my confession that he was speechless.

Yeah, right. I tried to put it out of my mind while Madison showed me what she'd brought, laying them across the bench in the changing room.

"Oh, Maddie, these are absolutely beautiful." I ran my fingers through the tails of the matching pair of floggers. The leather was dark blue and managed to be both thick and soft at the same time. The handles were braided with dark blue and silver strands. "Where did you get them?"

"A woman in Virginia makes them, I think. Maybe it's Maryland. I loved the color but I had to get both because they only came as a matched set. They're moose hide." She stepped back and swung them, though there wasn't quite enough space in the changing room to really flail them around. "They're a little on the heavy side, but if you like more thud than sting, they're exactly what you want."

I felt myself blush a little at the thought that flashed through my mind: If it had been Mal, I would have wanted it to sting like crazy. But to play with Madison, thud was probably better. She wasn't really a sadist. We were just having fun.

Well, having fun *and* provoking Mal.

"That's all you're going to wear?" she asked.

"I couldn't come up with anything better given the description in the book," I said, looking down at my feet. I was wearing thin, strappy flat gold sandals, a plain black knee-length skirt that was slit all the way up the sides, and a gold string bikini top.

"I better double-knot the bikini in the back if you don't want the flogger to untie it," she said.

"Sure." I held my hair up so she could double-knot the string behind my neck, too, even though that one wasn't going to be directly struck with the floggers.

"To save time, I brought the wrist and ankle cuffs in here." She dug them out of a tote bag on the bench.

"Great idea." I held out my wrists and she buckled the soft leather and sheepskin around each one. The chrome quick-release snaps dangled. If there was an earthquake or anything like that I'd be able to free myself easily, but not accidentally if I wanted to thrash around and pretend to struggle. I bent over to do one ankle while she did the other one. "Okay, ready?"

"I think so." She grinned at me. Her red hair was in a bun and she wore a short black cape over her sleeveless mock turtleneck, the closest we could get to her looking sort of like a nun without an actual nun outfit. "Okay. Walk in front of me, head down, wrists crossed."

I stepped out of the changing room into the hall and we made our way into the main room. With each step, my heart rate seemed to speed up and I felt my palms grow damp. About a dozen people were socializing and they quieted down as soon as we stepped in. Mal was still by the bar, but I didn't dare look at him. Club regulars were used to me and Maddie doing an "ice-breaker" scene, and I could feel their anticipation sharpen as Maddie cleared her throat.

"Kneel," she said, and I did, in the space between the last two couches and the wheel. "Excrucia, you have been found guilty of wanton conduct. However, the tribunal has determined your behavior is most likely caused by demons. Rather than banishment, we offer you the choice to have the demons beaten out of you. Do you accept this sentence?"

"I do," I said, my breathing getting shallow and quick, the way it always did in a scene—any scene where I was acting, not just a BDSM one.

"Then place yourself on the punishment wheel." She tested that it was locked in place and then I stepped up. Maddie quickly clipped the cuffs to the attachment points so that my face was to the wheel and my back was to the room.

That was it, all the setup required, and then she began to swing the floggers and hit me, slowly and softly at first, then gradually increasing the pace and force.

Those heavy moose hide floggers felt wonderful. Didn't hurt at all. The closest thing I could compare it to was one of those massages where they thump on you until everything relaxes. I moaned into it.

"That's it," Madison ad-libbed. "Let those wanton demons escape."

Yes, of course, the logic of the scene suddenly clicked. I moaned louder as she hit me harder, thinking, *Ariadne Wood must have been a kinkster.*

But the scene quickly plateaued; her hitting me only went so far. I ground my mound against the leather padded surface of the wheel but there was no way I could come from that. Where was this scene going? Or were we just going to play it like the demons were eventually banished? That could work. Maybe if I screamed a bit louder she would decide at some point I'd had enough?

There was a pause in the blows and I wondered if Madison was taking a short break. I dared to peek behind me.

Mal had stepped up beside her. His hair had been pulled back into a ponytail and he'd stripped down to a tank top and jeans.

As he spoke, I swore I felt the vibrations of his voice. "There's a way to use the two floggers in tandem."

Adrenaline coursed through me and I tried to send a telepathic message to Maddie: *Let him! Let him!*

No message was necessary. "Here, why don't you show me?" she asked as she handed him the floggers and then shot me a wink.

Mal took one flogger in each hand and, without looking at me, twirled them in the air as if testing their weight. First one, then the other, then he twirled them together like something out of a kung fu film. My jaw fell open. That looked amazing, and so did the muscles in his bare arms as he swung the floggers through intricate variations.

My neck was getting stiff from craning to watch. He stopped then and came up to me, and I quickly straightened, pretending I hadn't been watching.

Mal lifted the back panel of the skirt, folded it, and tucked it into the waistband so that my butt and thighs were exposed.

He said one word before he stepped back, with a bit of a low chuckle. "Demons?"

* * *

MAL

I could not stand by and watch Madison struggling with two floggers that were too heavy for her upper body strength and that she didn't know how to use to full effect. She had stepped back and was testing whether she could swing them both together with both hands like a baseball bat when I asked to cut in.

Though this was no ballroom dance, she bowed out and let me take over. Gorgeous instruments, these floggers, though they paled in comparison to the beauty pinned to the wall in front of me, a beauty so clearly pining for release that it felt like a moral imperative to step in and relieve her need.

And my own. A bound, half-naked, needy Gwen was too much to resist. I was utterly seduced, as ensorcelled as any character in an Ariadne Wood book. I took the floggers in my hands as if I were sleepwalking, almost like I was someone else. I had to hope that clarity would return in the aftermath of the scene, as it usually did once the air was cleared and the Need ebbed away.

I began to strike her with one flogger with a simple side stroke and the tenor of her cries immediately sharpened. Yes, I could hit harder than Madison and direct the blow at the surface of her skin with the tips, and I could also feel how much Gwen needed it, as if the craving were visible on her skin. *Ah, sweet pain, old friend, I welcome you into my bed once again.* I watched as Gwen rose on her tiptoes, tension building in her as the sensation intensified. I covered her from thighs to shoulders with wicked blows, reddening her skin, laying my claim to her inch by inch.

I backed off the sharpness of the strikes, changing to more of a swiping blow, one that would send the impact deep and resonate throughout her body. *Yes.* Her cries changed to low groans with shuddering breaths between them. She was losing the sense of herself, losing her self-consciousness and moving into a state almost akin to meditation, and I was taking her there.

The release from a beating like this is not, strictly speaking, sexual for most bottoms but is more of an emotional one, a kind of catharsis that some truly need and crave and something that cannot be achieved solo. I didn't know if Gwen had ever experienced that before but now would be the perfect time for it. It was time she let go of whatever petty emotions she was clinging to that made her think it could work between us. Clean out the cobwebs and surely she would see how wide the gulf was between what she actually needed and me.

Yes, there was the note my ears were straining to hear, the first hint of the tightening of her chest that would lead to tears. I needed her tears as much as she did. I changed to swinging the floggers in tandem, "Florentine" style, doubling the rate of the blows and pushing her rapidly toward complete emotional breakdown. *I am a destroyer, Gwen. Now you'll see.*

* * *

GWEN

I'd seen a number of couples who would spank or flog until the bottom burst into tears, or even past that point, and they always seemed blissfully, euphorically happy afterward. Chita had told me it was like having a really good cry at a romantic or sad movie but that she could only get there with a partner she really trusted emotionally.

I wasn't sure if it was Mal's intent to make me cry, but by the time I started feeling the urge to, with tears pricking the corners of my eyes, I knew if I didn't, I was going to feel unfulfilled.

But Mal was always so good at fulfilling me, wasn't he? Just when I feared he was going to stop, the blows came raining down so quickly I could barely catch my breath. He must have been twirling the floggers the way I had seen, but now I couldn't look; I could only stand there and feel every nerve in my body going into overdrive.

Each swipe of the flogger seemed to wear away a little more of my natural resistance to crying, to letting it all out, to letting go. And when the last bit of reserve was washed away under the lashing torrent of leather, I cried as loud and as hard as I could ever remember. As hard as I'd ever cried for my mother or when my father had disappointed me or when I'd fallen on the playground and no one had come rushing to pick me up.

Everything comes pouring out at a moment like that, everything, and any emotions you haven't been facing are suddenly staring you in the face, raw and undeniable. *Mal!* I was crying too hard to actually say his name but my heart was saying it. I wanted him, I needed him, and I was terrified of losing him. Terror. Terrified that I'd already lost him. That it was too late, too late . . .

And then strong hands were holding me up while my wrists came loose, and I felt him pick me up and carry me. I clung to his neck, my eyes closed as the feeling of being carried gave me a moment of vertigo, or maybe that was the intoxication of breathing in his scent. He was real and he was here and I pressed my wet eyes against his chest as relief swept through me. I gulped as if I could breathe Mal like air, soaking him in, and every breath now seemed to stoke the flames all along my skin and deep in my center. I'd never felt such a heady mix of arousal and emotions before and him carrying me only made the feeling that I was floating all the more intense.

He'd worked up a glorious sweat while beating me and I licked his chest.

He growled and threw me down onto a bed, or tried to. I held on to his tank top and pulled him with me and a moment later his mouth was at my neck, licking and suckling while his body covered mine. I wrapped my legs around his hips then and wished there were a magic spell that could make our clothes disappear.

"You," he said, when he had to pause to breathe. The word came out harsh, like an accusation.

I didn't care. Guilty as charged. I pushed at his jeans, trying to get them off, open, anything.

He shoved them down until his cock was free and then quite suddenly the bulk of his erection was crushing my clit as he sank his teeth into the join of my neck and shoulder again.

"Oh please, oh please," I urged him, writhing to try to get the right position.

The thick head of him suddenly caught the proper angle to penetrate, and penetrate he did, all the way in, prompting a scream of ecstasy to tear free of me. Yes, yes, yes! That primal need to be completed, to be filled, roared. Did he feel it, too?

"So much for a beating exorcising your wantonness," he hissed in my ear as his hips shimmied.

"Not when it's you doing the beating," I answered.

"You're wetter than I've ever felt you." His hand worked alongside his cock and a thumb brushed my swollen, slippery clit. I realized that his hip shimmying had been him pushing his jeans farther down his legs without disengaging from me.

"It's because of how much I need you," I said, gripping a fistful of his tank top. How could I explain it?

"Need. Greed," he said, and began to fuck me hard, mercilessly, exactly the way I liked it.

Needed it. Needed it so much he made me come twice without even having to work that hard. Needed it so much it wasn't until after he came with an anguished cry that I even gave a thought about safe sex.

He pulled out hurriedly and looked at me with a look of pure panic and self-loathing in his eyes.

"It's okay—" I started to say.

But he backed completely off the bed, hands shaking, unaware of his own hair in his mouth, eyes wild.

"Mal, it's okay," I said, sitting up slowly. I saw we were in one of the small playrooms. "I'm on birth control." When that didn't seem to sink in, I tried, "Mal? It's *Gwen*."

He drew a rough breath and blinked, seeming to come back

to himself a little, pulling his underwear and jeans up. He smoothed his sweaty hair back from his face. "That was..."

"Wonderful."

"Completely... inappropriate. Out of control."

"I think it fell well within our negotiated limits, actually," I said, crossing my legs. "Though we should've had the condom discussion first, I think we could both work on talking about our limits in the future."

"Future?" he spat, zipping up his fly and clearly getting ready to run off. "Gwen, this is exactly why I said we couldn't do this anymore."

CHAPTER TWELVE

UNDER THE MOON

MAL

"Mal, for Pete's sake, why are you so freaked out? I'm not hurt, am I?" She made a show of checking that she wasn't bleeding anywhere. "The only thing that'll hurt me is if you walk out that door without a proper explanation."

The minx somehow knew exactly what to say to take the wind from my sails. Nothing ruins a dramatic exit like someone telling you they're expecting it. I looked around the room where a few hours before her sister had lectured us primly on safety and rules.

What a sham. No matter how many precautions we could take, there was nothing that could keep me from being consumed by the Need. I didn't belong in this neatly ordered world of checklists and negotiations. I was a wolf among the sheep.

Well, but she expected me to play along with the sham, to keep up appearances. Disappointment burned bitter in the back of my throat. Appearances. I'd had about all I could stand of keeping up appearances, but I supposed I could pretend for a short while longer, at least until I could make a more graceful exit.

"Fine. If you would like the explanation to be 'proper,' then let us wash and make ourselves presentable again." I let her precede me to the bathroom with the shower stall large enough for four to use at once.

She seemed to respect my silence as we went through the motions of showering. She soaped my back and I hers, and my heart ached to see the graceful curve of her neck as she tipped her head back into the spray. I had left marks where they could be seen. How was an actress going to explain those bruises to a casting director, to the makeup artist who would have to try to hide them before sending her onto the red carpet for a thousand photographs?

I wanted to claim every inch of the lithe beauty before me for my own. But I knew perfectly well that could never be more than a fantasy for so many reasons. The Need does not recognize petty human concerns like career or emotional safety. There was only one way to keep her safe and that was for me to absent myself from her life.

Her affection, in the face of our inevitable separation, was painful. She toweled my skin dry with sweet care and allowed me to do the same to her, pressing a wistful kiss to the back of her shoulder, her neck, so near to where my teeth marks doomed me.

"I'm sorry," I whispered, wanting to apologize for the marks but only those two words made it past my lips.

"Mal, hush," she said, and handed me a plush bathrobe to put on. "Let's go for a walk and we can talk when we're away from the hubbub."

The sounds of spanking, laughing, orgasmic cries, and other play-party sounds echoed down the hallway. "All right."

She belted herself into a robe as well and took me by the

hand, leading me upstairs, down a hall, and through a large parlor to the patio.

The swimming pool lights glowed softly through the placid water. The air was crisp but not cold, and some kind of frog or insect called from the trees in the shadows beyond the patio's edge. We walked together by silent agreement along the edge of the pool.

We made our way into a back garden, but the path was poorly lit and she turned us back toward the pool. "So where'd you learn to use twin floggers like that?"

"Took a class," I said. "A few years ago." Before the smug complacency of the kink scene had begun to grate on me and before it had been a liability to fame.

"I've kind of wanted to check out some of the classes I see offered on the Internet," she said, "but I worry about keeping everything a secret."

"You think it's easier for other people?" I mused. "The stakes are perhaps different but no less high. Any teacher or doctor could find their job in jeopardy if they're associated with kink. Or any job if one's boss is a prude, for that matter. Divorced parents have to worry that if their ex finds out they went to a kinky party or a BDSM class that they could lose visitation rights to their own children."

She shook her head. "That's so wrong."

What's truly wrong is that they're right when it comes to me, I thought. Most kinky folk were harmless. Gwen and her sister and their safe little secret dungeon were proof of that.

Gwen pulled me down to sit next to her on the diving board. "Mal. Talk to me."

I forced myself to look at her face. "I don't have anything new to say, Gwen. We shouldn't continue. I shouldn't come to these parties. I shouldn't be tempted to hurt you. Because I will. I don't know what's worse, that you don't realize how seriously out of control I was tonight or that you do realize and you want me anyway."

She tried to take my hand but I pulled it away. I ended up jamming it into my robe pocket and she burrowed her hand in beside it.

Her fingers felt chilly. I sighed and put my arm around her, pulling her close, keeping her warm. It seemed the polite thing to do given that the only reason we were in exile from the festivities was because of me.

"Mal," she said. "You make it out like you're some kind of monster."

"Yes."

"No. You know who the real monsters are? The users, the abusers, the jerks who would never even consider whether they're a problem or not. That's obviously not you."

I said nothing.

After a while she went on. "My first lover, the first guy I met when I was out of the house and on my own, was a sleazebag. I didn't know that at first. All I knew was I had met a kinky guy who made me feel like no one else had. Who didn't think my fantasies were unhealthy or sick, who, if I told him I had a fantasy about being locked in a cage naked for the weekend, instead of laughing and telling me I was a weirdo, would look up the price of dog crates on the Internet."

I nodded to keep her talking.

"And he talked the talk: consent, boundaries, negotiation. It was all so thrilling and new to me that I didn't realize he was actually terrible at those things—the mere idea of bringing them up was enough to convince me to trust him." She nestled closer to me and I breathed in the scent of her damp hair, mixing with the hint of creosote from the breeze coming down the hills and the chlorine tang of the pool water. "What I didn't know was that he took me being submissive as equivalent to me being a doormat.

He gave me an STD, and when I went to confront him about it, I found him in the middle of a threesome with two women I didn't even know. And when I tried to confront him about *that*, he tried to order me to get in bed and lick pussy until I 'learned my place.'"

I tightened my arm around her, disgusted by this man and wishing I could time travel back to kick down his door. "I take it you refused his order."

"Damn right I did. I learned right then and there that he was the worst kind of fuckhead, and it was super obvious he was preying on my fantasies, on my willingness. I was just a piece of tail he used. And it took me a while to untangle that from the fact that I *liked* the feeling of being used sexually. But that's the key, right? I did figure out there was a difference between actually being used, or abused, and creating a consensual situation where that feeling could be experienced without it being the actual thing. Just like people who like to role-play and scream *no no no!* don't actually want to get raped by a stranger in a dark alley."

I kissed her hair. "An important distinction, if you don't actually wish to be hurt."

"Plus you promised not to injure me."

"And I broke that promise."

"It was an accident."

"Not tonight it wasn't!" I held her at arm's length. "Did you see the marks I left on your neck?" The ones I wanted to leave so much that I had done so against all rational judgment.

"Mal—"

"Hear me out, Gwen. You think you can tell the difference between good and evil, that your sleazebag first lover was evil and that I am somehow good? You're wrong. You say you become the best version of yourself when you are in scene? I don't. The absolute worst in me comes out and I can't stop it."

She was shocked into silence. "Right now you can convince yourself that you don't mind the bruises; you can forgive the careless accident. But when the infatuation starts to fade, you'll realize I'm right. At some point I won't be able to stop myself from going over the line, and then you won't have forgiveness for me anymore. It'll be the same as it was with your first lover. You'll be left with nothing but contempt, self-loathing, and perhaps a permanently damaged capacity for love."

Her eyes glistened with tears, but her voice was clear. "Speaking of self-loathing... Mal, why are you so convinced you're going to go over the line? *What line?*"

"Try to look at this from your sister's point of view. Do you think she'd approve of the many lines we've transgressed? The unprotected intercourse? The fire accident? Pretending not to know each other? The fact that you won't be able to show your neck in public for a week, maybe two?"

She withered a little under this line of inquiry. "Ricki doesn't need to know everything."

"You've kept secrets from her because you know perfectly well, deep down, that you were foolish and that what we did was *wrong*." I stood. "You said it: two wrongs don't make a right. It's only a matter of time before I wrong you even more severely than I have."

She hugged herself and I felt ill for hurting her emotionally, but better a small hurt now than utter devastation later. "Mal, it doesn't have to be that way."

"I like you, Gwen. You're intelligent, clever, funny, insightful, kind, and good-hearted. You're so beautiful that sometimes it's painful to look at you. But my desire for you rages like a fire that can't be contained. I..." I reached down and took her hand. "I love you too much to destroy you. I'm not as noble as you make me out to be."

"Do you hear yourself?" she said.

I pulled my hand free. "You like when I play the part of the villain for you: the Linder Mage, the Dragon, the Beast. There's a reason these characters always die in the end, Gwen. Because they're the villains. Don't you see it? The reason I identify with them all? I'm a villain, too. Maybe for a while it would work out, but ultimately there will come a day when it'll be too much for you. When I'll demand too much, go too far." Now I was repeating myself and it was time to stop. "I should go."

Gwen stood up, too. "Tell me about who hurt you," she said softly, reaching for my face. "Or who you hurt."

I shied back. She had struck far too close to the truth. Having so recently admitted it to Chino, I might have found it easier to talk about Risa, but no, it was as raw and sore a subject as ever. "No."

"Is talking about your past a hard limit?"

"Don't joke about that."

"It's not a joke."

"Then, yes. It is." I knew I was being unfair, but monsters do not have to be fair. And it worked. She let me go that time and did not follow when I went back into the house. I found the butler, who retrieved my car and who was too impeccably trained to say anything about the fact that I drove away barefoot in a bathrobe.

* * *

GWEN

Well, that didn't go as planned, I thought as I watched him storm away. And when Mal stormed, it was like a dark cloud with lightning bolts shooting out of it followed him.

The thing that struck me most about what he had said was the bit about how keeping things secret from Ricki proved it was wrong. The moment he said it, I had bought into it, like, *Oh shit, he's right*, but after the party, when I was in the kitchen trying to figure out if we had almond milk, things didn't seem anywhere near as dramatic.

That was the thing, I guess. When Mal was around, everything seemed super dramatic. Passionate. Intense. But that meant nothing really made logical sense either. It was like seeing a really good movie and then on the drive home realizing there was a hole in the plot or a gap in the continuity.

Why *was* I hiding everything from Ricki, anyway? I'd told Madison the whole story, after all, and she was just a close friend. But I knew Maddie wouldn't judge. I didn't want anyone to judge me, to criticize my choices or my mistakes, especially not my sister.

Was I ashamed to have done some down-and-dirty things?

I know I was supposed to be. I had even embarrassed myself a few times thinking about that beer bottle, but the feeling had faded. I didn't really feel any shame about it anymore.

And shame didn't mean something was wrong or evil. How could Mal make that mistake? Obviously. Churches, politicians, homophobes, and so many others were always trying to make us feel ashamed of any sex, of any pleasure, and *that* was clearly not valid.

I was too tired to make hot chocolate and just put a mug of vanilla almond milk into the microwave. While it went around and around, I thought it through. People needed sex, love, and pleasure. Some of us got that pleasure through means that seemed unusual to others, but we couldn't let their judgment control us. That was pretty obvious.

So how did Mal end up thinking if a person was afraid of being judged that meant they were doing wrong? I *felt* that fear, that under it all we were sick or twisted, broken inside. There were books and movies that made it seem that way, like people only needed kink if they were unhappy.

But Mal is *unhappy.* I carried my hot mug to the kitchen table. Mal was unhappy because he was making himself unhappy. *Does Mal really believe that under it all he's, like, a serial killer or something?*

How could he not see that in the same breath he was claiming he wasn't as noble as I thought he was, that he was leaving for *my own good*? Does it get more noble-hearted and self-sacrificing than that?

I scalded my tongue a little on the almond milk and then sat there sucking air through the O of my lips to cool it. That was when I knew what my next step had to be.

If I wasn't ashamed to tell Ricki everything, it was time to bring in some help. No one knew Mal better than Axel, and maybe the two of them could help me untangle the puzzle.

I turned on my phone to add "Enlist Ricki/Axel in Project Mal" to my to-do list and then checked my e-mail while waiting for my milk to cool enough to drink.

There was a message to my regular e-mail account from an address I didn't recognize, GHlover16@hotmail.com. *Who uses Hotmail still?* The subject line was "Gwen, please accept this sincere career advice." If not for my name, I might have deleted it as spam.

It wasn't spam, but it was very weird. The attachments were all photos of me. One with Mal at the *Midnight* premiere. One with Dr. Torres at the Monteleone fund-raiser. One with Simon Gabriel. One kind of blurry and dim, of me talking to some random guy I didn't even know or remember, one who must have been at the record company party.

The e-mail read:

Dear Gwen:

I want you to know that you are the sweetest, loveliest person ever to come out of Hollywood and you are the best role model for our young people because of your purity and angelic nature.

But I wanted to bring to your attention that in the public eye it looks like you are turning into some kind of slut. This is very bad not only for your career but also for the youth of America being seen with so many different men. Please think of the children.

An Admirer

My *purity and angelic nature*? I could feel the whip marks on my back burning. Well, I had just had the demons beaten out of me, hadn't I? I had to laugh. People had the weirdest ideas.

I forwarded the e-mail to Reeve with the subject line: "Should I be worried about this?"

The last thing I needed was some weirdo on the Internet latching on to me. Well, that was why we hired security. *See, Mal,* I thought, *I can take care of myself. I'm doing the responsible thing.*

Thinking about him now, though, in the calm and quiet, I felt tired and vulnerable. The fear that he would successfully abandon me surged up again and I clamped down on the lump in my throat. I'd never felt like this about anyone before, not Chuck, not even my high school crushes in the worst of my teen angst. Yeah, being rejected hurt, but this wasn't that. This was like when Mal left, a piece of my soul went with him.

Tomorrow I'd talk to Ricki and Axel and ask for help. I'd tried every way I could think of to get through to Mal, and he had shut me out again every time. Even while he was saying he loved me he was slamming the doors of his heart. *I love you too much to destroy you.* His words echoed in my head. I tried to only hear the first few words and I whispered them to myself: *I love you too...*

CHAPTER THIRTEEN

BACKS AGAINST THE WALL

MAL

I wasn't in my best emotional state when we flew to Montreal for the next recording sessions, but I'd at least assumed that throwing myself into working on the album would be my best bet to get my mind off Gwen. I suppose in some ways that was true, because there was enough drama and strife during the sessions to occupy any man's full attention.

Working with Larkin Johns lasted until our fifth day in Montreal, which was the day he finally turned the band against me, whereupon I bit his balding head off and threatened to mail it to Los Angeles in an international mail sack. He stormed out rather than prolong the confrontation, and confirming my worst fears, Axel and Chino immediately went after him, no doubt to placate the idiot.

"What say we take ten, everybody?" suggested the Quebecois engineer whose name I hadn't learned, and then he, Ford, and

Samson made themselves scarce, perhaps to the cafe across the street where a gaggle of our fans had taken to gathering each day. I did not care. I went to the fire escape to cool down in the first hint of chill autumn air and look down over the shadow-filled alley between us and the next building.

I gripped the steel railing hard enough to make my palm hurt. The injury had mostly healed but underneath some tender spots lingered.

Things were not going well.

Our previous studio stint, the three-week "trial run" with Johns, had been productive to a point—we'd narrowed down the prospective song list somewhat and had fully finished the recording for two more songs, bringing the total to four. It had made me optimistic that continuing with Johns was a viable option. But since we had been in Montreal, he had systematically undermined me, drawing the members of the band to his side until I stood alone in the face of withering idiocy.

I supposed I had best call Christina, who hadn't come to Montreal with us. Johns was probably on the phone to Marcus right now. We had the studio booked for another two weeks here. What I wanted to do most at that moment, though, was heave large objects from the fire escape. Perhaps I was still not calm enough to speak to anyone.

I heard the sound of knuckles rapping against the metal door frame behind me and expected to see Axel standing there to confront me when I turned.

Much to my surprise, the blond head that greeted me with a tentative smile belonged to none other than my superfan Aurora. Her blond hair was loose and her top was dangerously low cut for such chilly weather.

"Hey," she said.

"How did you get in here?"

"Axel sent me up here to talk you off the ledge."

"I am not on a ledge!"

"Uh-huh," she said with a knowing look. "What say we go back to the hotel since you're not getting much done out on that fire escape?"

I remembered what Chino had said, that my sex life was the whole band's business because I was so difficult to deal with if I didn't get off regularly. Had they really approached this woman to throw herself at me? Apparently they had.

The moment we were alone in my hotel room, I turned and pinned her with a mere look. She had her back to the door. I hadn't let her get more than a step or two into the room. Now was the moment when I should command her to pull that top down and expose her breasts for my admiration. Or perhaps strip down entirely before she should be allowed into my domain, my small kingdom where no woman could enter unless naked and on her knees...

The fantasy image in my mind raged out of control. Not Aurora crawling naked into the room, but Gwen. I could see it, hear her voice, imagine the look in her eye. I banged my fist against the wall and Aurora squeaked.

Poor scared soul. She didn't dare move.

I ground my erection against the corner of the wall where the bathroom jutted out. Mother of angels and devils, I was trapped in a torment from which there was no sane escape.

"Axel put you up to this?" I heard myself ask.

"Y-yes," she said. "Well, he approached the group of us and asked for a volunteer. And I volunteered."

"Did he... did he..." I couldn't bring myself to ask if he'd screened her the way Nick always did. I knew perfectly well he hadn't.

"I... I know your reputation," she said, her voice halting. "I'm not a kid. I'll... I'll try anything once."

I want to fuck you until you bleed. I want to leave bruises like flower petals all around your nipples from my bites. I want you to scream for me to stop as much as you scream for me to take you . . .

But not you.

"No," I whispered, my hands against the wall. "No, angel, you're not . . . what I need." Not who I need.

I ducked into the bathroom and locked the door behind me, tore open my jeans and smacked my erection with my hand against the marble sink top. Even if I didn't have serious doubts about Aurora's actual willingness to have sex with me, she wasn't the one I wanted. Even the most brazen partner wouldn't have been able to supplant the burning image in my mind of Gwen.

Gwen on the porch of my condo, stripping off her clothes and setting them on fire before I would allow her through the door . . . I let the fantasy play behind my eyelids while my fist pumped mercilessly on my dick. Naked, defenseless, crawling into my presence, ripe for debauchery.

Iron. I would have iron manacles made for her, brutal things that would weigh on her skin, and new chastity devices, all of which she would wear for me, bear for me, to prove her worth to me. And then, one by one, she would earn their removal by pleasing me, by pleasuring me and submitting to whatever tortures I might devise . . .

I came suddenly, my heart racing and a bellow escaping my lungs as I pumped line after line of glistening seed into the bowl of the sink.

It took some time for my breathing to slow to normal and for the flush to recede from my face. Once it had, I washed up, tucked myself away, washed my hands, and then listened at the door. Had Aurora left?

No. She was sitting by the window with the teapot and two cups, reading a book like a civilized woman.

"You made tea," I said, as if stating the obvious would help it to make sense to my brain.

"I thought it might help you calm down." She put down her book and poured both cups. I picked mine up while she added milk and sugar to her own.

"You look confused," she said after taking a sip.

"I confess that I am. I didn't expect you to stay."

"Mal," she said. "Maybe this will come as a shock to you, but some fans aren't after sex."

"What do you want, then?"

"Just to help, honey. Just to help."

I leaned back in the chair, exhausted. "I... appreciate that. Thank you. I apologize if I was uncouth."

"You've been through a lot. Is there anything I can do?"

It was soothing to hear a kind voice. "Yes. Please take a message back to Axel that..." That I need to be alone to cool down and get my head together. That's what I should have said, but what came out was: "They can expect me back in the studio after the four of them come to their senses and stop listening to the poisonous drivel that Johns has been feeding them. Can you do that?"

"I can do that." She patted me on the hand, more motherly than romantic. "Don't do anything rash, okay?"

I had to laugh at that. Was this all a karmic payback for being too rash with Gwen? Or was it merely that I was so distracted and out of my head about her that I was unable to communicate with the people around me?

I did the only sensible thing I could think of. I called room service and asked for a bottle of whiskey. The helpful Canadian staff was happy to oblige.

* * *

GWEN

The bellman opened the cab door and greeted me in French and then English. I thanked him and let him pull my tiny rolling suitcase into the lobby for me. I handed him a U.S. dollar as a tip without thinking, only realizing as he walked away that I should have changed some money at the airport.

Axel swept up to me. "Gwen! Thank you so much for coming on such short notice. We've got a room for you upstairs." He held up the card key to a hotel room.

"No need to thank me," I said as I followed him to the elevator bank. "You know I've been trying to find the thing that will let me break through to him. Maybe this will be it."

"We can hope. As I said on the phone, we're kind of desperate ourselves." We got into the elevator and he slid the key into the slot there, activating access to the executive level floor. "Do you want to freshen up after the trip?"

"I could wash my face."

"Sounds good. I'm really hoping you're the solution, Gwen. When you and I talked after the party, I thought, aha, that explains why he was so mellow in our last recording session. He'd just been with you."

"What's he like now?"

"Oh, you know. Angry, irritable, quick to offense, believes everything's a conspiracy to ruin what's good about our music. He's refusing to come back to the studio until the rest of us, I don't know, tar and feather our producer and run him out of town on a rail or something." The doors opened onto a quiet, thick-carpeted hallway and Axel led me to a small but richly appointed suite.

I shed my coat and washed my face while he waited nervously.

"He's my best friend," Axel blurted when I came out of the

bathroom. He looked worried, like he hadn't slept, not at all like the happy-go-lucky guy I was used to. If Axel was like that, I could only imagine what a ray of sunshine Mal himself must be right now. "I don't mean to speak ill of him, but understand... he's not shallow."

"If you're afraid I'm going to think it's silly that an orgasm"—or giving a spanking—"could change his mind, I assure you I'm not," I said.

"I've seen it happen," Axel said, as if I were doubting it, which I most certainly wasn't. "I know he's carrying a lot of baggage, but somehow it still works."

"Should I know about the baggage?" I wasn't sure knowing more about Mal's past would change my actions any, but it couldn't hurt.

Axel shrugged. "Here's the thing. I know his reputation is that he's a total Lothario, tons of women, all that. But there have only been three really serious ones. All three left him kinda fucked up."

Hmm. "Were all three submissive?"

"Well, the first one was a slightly older cousin of his who spent the summer with his family the same time I was there. We got up to all kinds of trouble. She got it into her head that she wanted to lose her virginity before she went to college but she didn't want me; she wanted Mal. He eventually gave in to the temptation and then when her family disowned her, he blamed himself for it."

That sounded like the Mal I knew, that noble streak hiding a guilty conscience. "Sounds to me like he blames himself for something that was her idea."

"Yeah, well, then there was Risa, the one he actually fell head over heels for. He used to call me long distance from England to talk to me about her all the time. She was a serious masochist, so I thought they were perfect for each other. In reality, she was begging him to do even more extreme things and when he refused, she told her family he'd been raping and torturing her and showed them the scars."

My mouth hung open. Was that why he was so paranoid about leaving marks? "He blames himself for that?"

"Well, then she tried to kill herself. He fled the country and hasn't spoken to his own family since."

"Oh my God."

"I know. The last really serious one was a fan he got involved with. Layla. Pretty nice girl—we all liked her—but you know how when one partner pulls away the other clings on tighter?"

"I can't imagine Mal reacts well to clinging," I said.

"Yeah. When it went south, she just wouldn't let go. He cut her off entirely and she went full-on stalker for a while."

"That's where his one-and-done thing comes from?"

"Yeah. And it's worked for a good while now, for Mal to have 'maintenance sex,' enough to relieve the pressure and then get back to work. But he rejected a fan we know he was friendly with and that's when we called you." I'd never seen Axel so serious. "I'm pretty sure it's because you're the only one he wants right now, even if he won't admit it to us. Or himself, maybe."

He'd rejected a fan's advances? My heart gave a flip in my chest, hoping it was true that deep down it was because he wanted me and me alone. "I'll give it a shot. Seriously, Axel, I welcome the chance."

"Okay. Would now be all right?"

"Waiting won't help anybody," I said. The truth was I was as impatient to see Mal as Axel was to have me do it. Sitting around was only going to make me anxious. Amazingly, at the moment I didn't feel anxious. I felt ready.

"I'll call him right now." He picked up the phone from the night table by the bed and dialed a number.

I heard Mal's sharp anger right through the tiny syllable that leaked from the earpiece pressed to Axel's head.

"Mal, it's Axel. Listen. I'm, ah, sorry about Aurora. I thought you liked her. I've been talking with the guys, though, and I think I have a much better alternative here now."

Mal let loose a long-winded argument of some kind.

"No, no, no, but really, Mal," Axel said when he could get a word in edgewise. "We're going to pay through the nose for the wasted studio time; you know that. We've still got nothing to show Marcus. If we miss the delivery deadline, they'll have to push off release of the next album for six more months. Who knows what it fucks up with the UK. I'm serious. Very, very serious."

There was silence at the other end.

"So for the sake of the band and our friendship, will you please just try? I'm sending you a girl I *know* you'll like."

My pulse went into overdrive when Mal's two-syllable answer was clearly audible: *okay.* The curtain was about to go up.

Axel rubbed it in: "*Promise me* you'll fuck the living daylights out of her when she gets to your room."

The response was louder, more exasperated: *Okay!*

"Great. She'll knock." Axel hung up and breathed a sigh of relief. "Room 1243," he said to me. "Good luck."

Showtime. I slipped my panties off from under my skirt and left them on the floor as I marched out the door.

* * *

MAL

When the knock came, I was barefoot and in sweatpants and hadn't left the room since sending Aurora away the day before. I could tell from Axel's voice on the phone that something was up. Was I going to open the door and find Christina there, ready to read me the riot act about how I was endangering all their careers? Or Chino in a wig to break the tension?

The last person I expected to see when I opened the door was Gwen Hamilton.

Gwen. I think I kept the surprise off my face with a scowl. I had one second where I could have engaged my mouth to argue, to be rational, to tell her to go away.

I gave in to the Need instead. I grabbed her by the wrist and yanked her into the room, slammed the door behind her, and pressed her back against it. Chino had said it: They sent the sacrifices to the dragon so they wouldn't get eaten instead.

This time they'd sent me the woman I wanted most but knew I shouldn't have. I ground my teeth. "I promised I'd fuck the living daylights out of you."

"I know, I heard," she answered, voice breathless.

My Gwen. I kissed her hard enough to bruise her lips and she kissed back harder. That only inflamed me more, and I had long ago lost sight of where anger ended and passion began.

She hitched one leg over my hip and I cupped her calf with one hand. She was wearing knee-high brown boots, a wool skirt, and a downy-soft cashmere pullover sweater. I slid my hand up her thigh as my tongue explored the reaches of her mouth, and she moaned against my lips as I discovered she wasn't wearing anything under the skirt.

I worked a finger between her pussy lips and to reassert my claim I forced it inside her, the way suddenly eased by a generous flow of her natural lubrication.

"You were made to be fucked," I heard myself saying. "This hole was made to be fucked."

"Yes, Mal, by you," she said.

Sweet mother of angels, I could not get my cock into her fast enough. I stepped out of the sweatpants and lifted her against the wall, pushing myself into her. Her cry of pain was loud in my ear as she clung to me.

"Does it hurt?" I pressed.

"The best pain in the world," she whispered, panting. "*Best.*"

"Squeeze me now." I wrapped my hands around her buttocks and rolled my hips. She contracted her muscles around me and I heard myself groan.

I carried her to the bed, fucked her hard until I was winded, and then pulled out abruptly. I stood, my cock dripping with her juices. "Strip."

She wasn't even wearing a bra. She tossed the sweater and skirt aside and then all she was dressed in was her skin, sweat, and desire. She lay back unbidden and spread her labia with her fingers, beckoning me.

No flogger, no fire, no knives, or claws—all I had were my hands, teeth, and cock. Plenty to make her suffer. I ran my hand loosely up and down my length. "Spank your clit. Do it."

She swallowed and gave herself an experimental pat, jerking in surprise at the sensation even though she'd barely put any force behind it.

"Harder."

She gritted her teeth and smacked herself audibly. "How many times?"

"Until I tell you to stop," I said, pulling her toward me by one leg until her buttocks were at the edge of the bed. I cradled her leg against my chest and pushed my cock into her while she continued to hit herself. She caught me with her swats a bit but I didn't care. Pain and I are old friends.

I pulled free. "Stop. Hands behind your head." I lay down beside her on my back and bent my knees. "Keep your hands there, and get on my cock."

She got to her feet and then straddled me, and I enjoyed the sensation as she struggled with nothing but motions of her hips attempting to get my cock inside her. Stiff and heavy with blood, it lay along my abdomen, curving slightly toward my stomach. This was a trick, of course. I didn't think there was any way she could succeed at my order, but while she tried oh how sensual it was, her clit and her lubrication dragging up and down my length. I tightened my abs a few times, making my cock lift slightly, making it seem as if she might have a chance, but no.

Her frustration and my glee grew in tandem, the noises from her throat increasingly pleading in tone.

"You want it."

She nodded.

"Would you like help?"

"Yes, please...?" She sat up straight, her arms trembling with fatigue.

"You know how our trade works."

"Pain for pleasure, I remember."

"Exactly. Keep your hands where they are." I reached down and took hold of my cock. She lifted herself and I held myself steady, pointing directly up, until she had engulfed me and lowered herself with a deep groan.

I smacked her on one breast and she rocked back against my bent legs.

"Uh-uh," I scolded. "No escaping the pain."

"Right. Sorry." She thrust her nipples at me. I grabbed them with my fingers and pinched mercilessly. She screamed and the way her interior muscles squeezed me I wondered if she came.

I demanded to know. "Did you just come?"

"No, Mal."

"I would love to train you to come from pain itself," I heard myself say.

She made a happy, needy noise in response.

"Make yourself come. I'll stop torturing you when you do."

I went back to smacking her directly on the nipple and then pinching, which didn't go on anywhere near as long as it might have because it took her only a minute or two to bring herself off. She was always beautiful but never more radiant and alive than in that moment, screaming from release while she rode me.

I pulled her down against me, driving my cock into her and letting my heavy hand fall onto her bare bottom at the same time. No warm-up swats. I went directly to my heaviest blows with my open palm. Her cries were only quieted by her need to inhale a fresh breath.

After many deep strikes, I switched to the other hand, the other buttock, and spanked her until it was as scalding hot as the first. Then I dug my fingernails into her sore flesh and dragged her up and down on my cock until she began to come again.

"How many times do you think you can come before I do?" I asked her.

"I don't know," she confessed easily. "I might be getting overstimulated."

"Excellent," I breathed into her ear. "I shall enjoy forcing you to come until either you are begging me to stop or I can't stand it any further and empty myself into you."

I felt her insides squeeze me.

"Hmm, yes, that will help move both possible outcomes along," I said, spanking her for another ten or twenty blows before I returned to dragging her up and down, knowing her clit would be rubbing against the roughness of my pubes.

She came again, gratifyingly soon, her body going limp and allowing me to drive into her even deeper. I kept that up for another two or three orgasms, spanking, spanking, grinding, until she didn't cry out any longer but merely trembled all over with a paroxysm.

I pulled free and rolled her onto her front, entered her again, and then slid a hand under her until her clit was trapped between two of my fingers. A pinch produced a squeak from her but no resistance, and I set to sawing against her clit with a finger while fucking her again.

I was going to lose this challenge in that I was going to come before she begged me to stop, but of course this was a game that had no loser.

"I want you to come one more time," I said as I drove into her slowly, teasing myself, rolling my hips in a circle. "I will not be denied."

"No," she said, then realized it might sound like she was protesting, and added, "No, of course you won't, Mal."

The heat of the moment had taken me utterly. I was not myself. And yet I was. "I fantasize about you, Gwen. About keeping you like a pet, a slave, a captive whom I can do this to anytime I desire." I suckled her neck, deliberately bringing up a dark purple hickey and making her moan. "I imagine you naked in my house, no clothes at all, not a stitch, perhaps chained, perhaps restrained, depending on the day."

"Mal," she said with a gasp as my fingers sought out her clit again. "Oh, yes, Mal."

"When I come in the door, you'd present your cunny to me for immediate filling."

"Yes, I would."

"Would you be wet and ready for me, my slave, my toy?"

"Yes!" She tightened as her arousal heightened again. Her eyes were closed as if she were picturing what I described. "And . . . and even if I wasn't . . ."

"That's right. This cock would be yours to take. As many times a day as I wished."

"Yes, oh yes, Mal . . ."

"Would you do it? Would you let me chain you to the bed with your legs open and fuck you four times a day? You might not even come."

"Only if you wished it, Mal."

"Or I might make you come. Like now. Come, Gwen. Come!"

By all ye gods and monsters, she came on my command.

* * *

GWEN

Mal must've come when I did. I was so overwhelmed by my own orgasm and the fantasies he was describing to me that I didn't even realize it at the time. As my own climax ebbed away, though, and I gradually floated back to Earth, I realized he was doing the same, breath slowing, muscles relaxing, mind returning.

He shifted and cradled me against him, pulling one edge of the duvet over us so we wouldn't get chilled as we cooled down from the white-hot intensity of the sex we'd just had.

I shifted myself onto my side and he moved with me, tucking my cheek against his chest. I lay my hand on his breastbone thinking, *Is this the first time we cuddled together like this?* We were both too spent to move much, and for once no one was about to run away or storm off.

And he wasn't. I could sense it, feel his inertia, as if he were a great weight come to rest at last.

"What am I going to do, Gwen?" he asked, his voice humming against my ear.

I ran one palm soothingly over his skin. "Axel said your head would clear after sex."

His arm around me tightened. "It was not mere sex that has improved my mood."

I took that as a compliment and smiled to myself. "Does that mean you're ready to talk about the band and Larkin Johns?"

"Yes, I suppose it does."

I lifted my head a little so I could see his face. He looked thoughtful and somber. No, not somber. Sad. I had never seen Mal sad before. "Why don't you tell me what's been going on? Maybe I can help you sort it out."

He sat up enough to pile up the pillows behind us and then lay back again, welcoming me into the crook of his arm. What can I say? I felt such a rush of happiness as I settled against him. I felt like I belonged there. At least for the moment he seemed to have given up trying to convince me he was bad for me.

"They say I'm too passionate," he began.

That sounded a little like his I-love-you-too-much thing. "They say, or you say?"

"They say I care too deeply about the music. That I'm fighting tooth and nail to defend it from the forces I feel will destroy it…but that I'm fighting the wrong people, for the wrong reasons." His fingers found the stray strands of my hair and smoothed them into place as he spoke. "I feel the producer's been gradually seducing the other members of the band, convincing them of his ideas, until I am the lone voice clinging to the integrity of our music, our songs."

I frowned. "Mal, the guys care about you. I know they do. I know they care about the band, not just…whether the band has hits or makes money."

"That's the thing, I suppose. The record company and Johns, they only care about whether we make money."

"You think Larkin Johns has convinced the guys to care more about money?"

He let out a long sigh. "No. If it were that obvious, they would resist. But he has his ideas about what will 'make hits.'"

"Like what?"

"Like…*horns*." He said the word like it was disgusting, which I suppose to him it was.

"You mean saxophones, trumpets, that sort of thing?"

"Exactly." He shook his head. "Horns are all well and good if you're Lord Lightning doing a massive show production or some pop band doing a little turn through soul or R&B. But that is not The Rough."

Something clicked for me in that moment. Mal seemed very clear about his vision for the band, but I wondered if he communicated with Larkin Johns as badly as he had with me about what he wanted. Like with me, had he assumed there was some reason why he couldn't have his way? "Did you tell Johns that horns were a hard limit?"

He twitched, then carefully said, "Don't joke about that."

Déjà vu. "I'm not joking. It sounds to me like you're positively offended by his suggestion of horns, but I have to wonder if he has any idea why you're so upset. It would be one thing if you had said 'no horns' and then he trampled your boundary and insisted, but it's something else if—"

"He should know perfectly well that horns are a terrible fit," Mal said, but he didn't sound sure.

"He doesn't know what the image is you have in your head of what the band is," I said. "It'd be great if he could just 'get' that from listening to the songs, but maybe he can't. Maybe he's hearing something else. Maybe you have to tell him flat out, no horns."

"Well, I did, eventually, but it isn't only the horns." As agitated as he was about Johns, his fingers continued to smooth my hair. Perhaps it was as soothing to him as it was to me. "I can't deny that he's produced many hits, but he can't leave anything alone. He's constantly wanting to change things that don't need changing. As if he doesn't truly understand what makes a song work."

"Or doesn't understand what's important to you about a song?"

"Hmm." He seemed to be ruminating on the possibility. "You may be onto something there."

"I hear you talking about specifics when maybe you should be talking in generalizations. I also hear you making generalizations and expecting Johns to figure out the specifics. Maybe you and he just don't draw the line in the same place. You need to negotiate the individual things and the bigger picture, too."

He let out a huff that might have been the start of a wry laugh. "You mean he's like a submissive who says yes to whips, paddles, and nipple clamps, but says no to pain?"

"Kind of? More like a submissive who might say yes to obedience but not assume that implied punishment?"

I could feel him nodding slowly. "You may have a point. The thing is, our goal isn't simply to make a song that people will *like*. It's to make a song that *we* like. Otherwise, what's the point? Why even write the music ourselves if they can manufacture something that will be universally accepted? I'm not interested in sounding like Justin Bieber, or Justin Timberlake, or Justin Moore for that matter. No matter how many records they sell."

"I'm betting that Johns has no idea you feel he's turning you into Justin Bieber."

Mal slid his fingers under my chin and tipped my face until we were looking into each other's eyes. "What makes you think that? Truthfully, Gwen."

"Mal, honestly, I don't think you realize that things you think are obvious or self-evident are only obvious *to you*. Everyone else needs to hear it out loud."

"At this point, I have made my feelings unambiguously clear, though. I've told him to go fuck his horns, his reggae backbeats, his—"

"No, I mean have you actually said, 'Hey, mister, I feel like you're trying to make the song sound like *yours* and it's more important to me that it sound like *ours* and that's non-negotiable'?"

Mal narrowed his eyes as he thought back. "Not in so many words, no."

"That would at least give you a basis for discussion, right? If he still doesn't get it, well, at least you set your boundaries, and if it comes to firing him you'll have a clear reason why. That's what will make him the bad guy, not you."

"And the rest of the band?"

"Mal, I think you're so used to playing devil's advocate that you've forgotten they really do agree with you. They all have a stake in the music." *And they love you,* I thought, but didn't say.

He sighed and kissed me on the forehead. "It all seems so clear when you boil it down like that."

"I have the benefit of an outsider's perspective," I told him. "I'm not weighed down by everything you have going on in your head. Plus"—I stretched up and kissed him on the forehead—"there's your whole postsex clarity thing."

He rolled me onto my back and pressed a trail of kisses down my face and neck, licking at the sore spot he had made. "You are the only person I am interested in having sex with, Gwen."

I wrapped my legs around him and looked up into his eyes. "Then let's do it. Your fantasy. Keep me here in the room, naked, ready for you to come and take anytime while you're working on the album. Anytime you need a break."

He leaned down to take one nipple into his mouth, suckling it gently until it hardened to a peak and then trapping it between his teeth. He bit down for an excruciating moment and then let go just as I gasped. His tongue soothed the hurt he'd made and then he raised his head again, his eyes darkened with lust. "Two weeks. We have two weeks left in the studio here."

A thrill ran all the way down to my toes. He was going to say yes, I could feel it. "My calendar is open."

"Your pussy is open," Mal said, rolling his hips. He wasn't hard again yet but I felt the tension in his muscles rising just as deliciously. "You'll really do this? No clothes at all. My captive. You might grow bored if I'm in the studio at all hours."

"And you might find yourself needing to vent some steam in

the middle of recording, too," I said. "I'll be at your mercy, Mal. Your fantasy and my fantasy are the same."

"Who will you be in this fantasy?" he asked.

"That's the best part." I licked my lips. "It's just you and me. No roles. Gwen and Mal."

"Gwen the obedient," he murmured as he nuzzled my skin. "Gwen the willing."

"Mal the cruel, Mal the demanding," I answered. "My keeper."

"Mine."

"Yours."

Perhaps the idea was simply that arousing or perhaps we had talked long enough that his refractory period had passed, but I felt him hardening between my legs, and a moment later he thrust into me, right where he belonged.

CHAPTER FOURTEEN

THE MUSE

GWEN

That first morning I woke up in Mal's arms, I felt such a thrill run through my whole body that I instantly grew damp between the legs. He was still deeply asleep, snuggled close, one of my hands cradled in his against his cheek.

Two weeks. He'd promised me two weeks of glorious imprisonment. At least, I hoped it would be glorious. All I knew was no clothes would be allowed, and I was to be ready and willing for sex whenever he demanded. No clothes undoubtedly meant no leaving the room. Other than that I couldn't really imagine what was going to happen, but at that moment reality felt very far away. Or rather the reality of being here, with him, blocked out all thought of anything else. He rolled onto his side then without waking, and I found myself gently tracing the wings of the dragon on his back. His skin was uneven under the black lines of the tattoo and I wondered why. Bad acne when he was a kid? That could leave scars.

The next time I woke, he was kissing the bruises on my neck. I stiffened for a moment, sensing how sore I was, but his lips were soft, and his teeth stayed behind them. I was laughably unsure how to react, half expecting a sudden bite at any moment yet melting under the pleasure of his touch.

He drew aside the covers and his hand sought between my legs, an appreciative hum escaping him as he discovered me already wet. He thrust a finger inside me and merely held it there, not stimulating me, not pushing in or out, just sitting there like it belonged where he'd put it.

Like I belonged to him. I felt a deep pulse of lust as that thought sank in.

He sat up without removing his finger. His hair fell in wild, dark strands across his face and over his shoulders.

"Good morning," he said, fingertips of his other hand brushing the inside of my thigh.

"Good morning." I smiled and stretched against my pillow, tightening my inner muscles around that digit inside me. "How are you?"

"Calmer than yesterday, certainly," he said. "We shall see when I arrive at the studio whether that equanimity is sustainable."

"I hope so. You can always come back and have another dose of Gwen's Common Sense if you need it."

His hand gripped my thigh warmly. "Or another dose of your delicious body." He shrugged his hair back over his shoulder. "Speaking of delicious. Order room service if you're hungry. Half the TV channels here are in French but you can rent movies if you like."

I felt excitement spread through me. This was going to be fun. "May I use my tablet? It's in the other room with my suitcase."

"I'll retrieve it and your toiletries, but I was quite serious about no clothes for you. If I find you wearing anything, or find out you did, I will throw what you were wearing out the window."

I grinned. "You won't find me wearing anything. I don't even think I'll be tempted to."

He returned my smile. When had I ever seen Mal smile like that? Maybe it was my imagination, but he seemed as happy as I was. "Did you ever read *The Story of O*?" he asked.

"A long time ago. I think I snuck it out of the library when I was a teenager."

"Hmm, likewise. It's funny. I remember only two things about the book. One was the fur-trimmed shoes she wears when they get to the Château. The other is a scene in which her lover casually penetrates her with his finger. I think she's naked on a table and he's socializing with other men, and he inserts his finger into her as casually as slipping his hand into the pocket of his waistcoat."

"I really can't remember any of that book, either," I said. "Although the finger thing does sound sort of familiar." I squeezed again. "I can see the appeal of that."

He gave a quiet laugh through his nose, shaking his head slightly. "Neither of us remembers one of the foundational works of BDSM literature, but we can practically recite *Nightfang* word for word."

"I know. For me the kinkiest books were always the ones where my imagination filled in the details." The two weeks ahead seemed a thrillingly blank canvas, awaiting whatever Mal and I might dream up. "I've been meaning to read all her UK-published books that we didn't get over here. Maybe that's what I'll do while you're out."

"An excellent idea. But if you're going to be lounging about reading stimulating literature, I had better put a prohibition on your orgasm. Save it for me."

Another spasm of lust ran through my body, primal and unexpected from the mere suggestion that my orgasm belonged to him. "Yes, Mal."

He eased his finger free of me and licked it as he stood and turned toward the bathroom. The dragon tattoo across his broad shoulders seemed to move its wings as he stretched. "Time for breakfast. Real breakfast, I mean. The room service menu is in the side drawer. Strong tea, two eggs, poached, with back bacon, and order yourself whatever you like. When you're done placing the order, come join me in the shower."

* * *

MAL

After a long discussion that resembled a marriage counseling session more than a business negotiation, Larkin Johns and I had established enough mutual ground to get back to work. Gwen had been right. When I told Johns I felt what he was doing was trying to make the songs *his* instead of *ours*, he was defensive at first, claiming that wasn't his intent.

Surprisingly it was Ford who spoke up as the voice of clarity, Ford who normally didn't speak unless asked. "Lark, listen. Your intent doesn't matter. What we're saying is that it *feels* like you're taking the music away from us. If it doesn't feel like ours, we may as well just do an album of cover songs. Do you see what I'm saying?"

Larkin pushed his overlong, prematurely graying hair out of his face as he leaned against his arm on the table. "I don't think you guys realize how distinctive you sound. It still sounds like The Rough to me even after the changes, and it'll still sound like The Rough even if we add backing vocals or a horn line. But I get what you're saying. Mal, I'm sorry—I didn't realize you actually felt insulted by my suggestions."

"Not insulted so much as offended," I said, my booted feet crossed on the table as I leaned back in my chair. "Though I realize the difference between the two is subtle. Apology accepted, regardless."

So we got to work. It wasn't a perfect session. Everyone was still a little sensitive about things. We stopped after getting basic tracks laid down for a song and strategized which songs would be our priority for the rest of the week. It was midafternoon when we took a break.

I took my break at the hotel and had Gwen for lunch. She was delighted I had returned so quickly and I delighted in emptying my balls into her with an urgent, unbroken rhythm. There would be plenty of time for imaginative cruelty and erotic games later.

We did another three hours in the studio and then called it a day. The rest of the guys went off to see a band play at a local club.

I went back to my room and had dinner delivered from room service. I sat Gwen across my lap and fed her gravy-dipped *frites* with my fingers while we talked.

"So I guess recording went okay today?" she asked.

"Yes. There's still tension, but we at least produced some music today that I'm happy with." I sipped some water, sucked an ice cube into my mouth, and then bent my head to suckle on her nipple until the ice had melted. "And you? Did you start your reading project?"

"I did! The entire Ariadne Wood library is available for download. I decided to read them chronologically so I started with *The Crow Prince*."

"I used to imagine myself as him," I told her. "My cousin played the part of Princess Sun. We were nine or ten, I think? She came to stay with us one summer. I don't think I've read the book since. I wonder what I would think of it now."

"You can read it when I'm done," she said, licking gravy off my fingers.

The tender touch of her tongue sparked my lust, and my hunger for her body overtook my hunger for food. I don't know which was more gratifying, the orgasm I experienced while buried in her or the knowledge that I needed only snap my fingers to have her.

We slept skin to skin that night, as if even while asleep I did not want to cease touching her.

* * *

GWEN

A few days rolled past, and although I expected to get restless or bored at some point, I hadn't yet. For one thing, it had become something of a game to hide from the hotel housekeepers that I had no clothes. One day I would pretend to be sleepy and tell them to come in and clean the bathroom anyway while I didn't get out of bed, and then I made the bed myself. The next day the sheets really needed to be changed so I had them come and do the rest of the room while I was in the shower. One day I wrapped my hair and body in towels and painted my toenails, sitting in the corner in the room's one armchair while the maid vacuumed around me. It was not always the same maid, so I figured it would be a few more days before they started to wonder.

The only "work" I had to do was answer a few e-mails here and there. I got one from Thalia telling me they wanted to film a follow-up promo spot for the next phase of the WOMedia app when I got back. She also said they had gotten a couple of weird messages from an anonymous e-mail address with nothing in them but photos of me. She wrote:

> Not sure but maybe they were trying to sell us promo photos of you? Probably pirated photos, though, given the sketchy nature

of the address. There's a ton of that going on in Eastern Europe right now. I'm ignoring them.

I ignored them, too. What a delight to lounge around reading to my heart's content! The only thing more pleasurable than devouring books was being devoured by Mal and then talking with Mal. Sometimes he came in seething with frustration about the recording sessions and used sex with me as an outlet. Other times he wanted my advice on picking through the minefield of personality conflicts and the dynamics of the band.

We talked. A lot. After all, even with all the sex and play, there were still generous hours to fill. And Mal had become generous with his words. I hadn't had conversations like that since my undergrad days, conversing late into the night about politics, history, art, people.

I was also delighted to find I could easily access some of the BBC shows I couldn't get legally in the United States. One evening Mal came in and discovered me watching one of them. He swept the tablet up and moved it from the bed to the table, letting the show continue to play while he pointed to the bed. I lay down immediately and then he crawled over me, greeting me with a kiss and the words, "I told you before, the BBC is overrated."

"It's research," I teased. "I'm, um, learning British accents."

He laughed at that and then bit me on the neck, letting up only when the imprint of his teeth was deep enough to last for a day or two. The sensation was intense and made me giddy with desire. "It might be a useful asset for you in acting if you could speak convincingly British English. Shall I teach you?"

"Are you serious?"

"Quite. I shall have to get a cane, though. Grammar lessons are not authentically British without punishment for errors." He nuzzled in my hair possessively.

"You're kidding, right? I mean, I know you're not kidding about getting a cane, but . . . " He had already bought a few toys from shops in the city. "They didn't really cane you in school, did they?"

He lifted his head. "I assure you sadistic schoolteachers are not what made me kinky. In the primary school I attended they used a shoe to administer the punishment, but corporal punishment in the elite boarding schools was outlawed when I was still a child." He tilted his head, giving me an odd look. "Did your father spank you when you were growing up?"

"No. Spanking was purely an adult recreation for him," I said seriously. "What about you?"

"My father's punishments were always centered on privilege or deprivation. Sent to bed without supper, for example. He was much more likely to torment me psychologically than physically."

"I would like to think if I ever had kids I wouldn't torment them at all," I said.

"Likewise," he answered, and then turned his attention to leaving a matching bite mark on the other side of my neck.

* * *

MAL

I was surprised to realize that knowing Gwen was waiting for me had a calming effect on my interactions with the band. It was not so much that I had "mellowed" as that I was less prone to extremes. It was as if she were emotional ballast, keeping my feelings from being rocked or tossed too violently by the weather.

That was not something I had experienced in any of my previous relationships. If anything, those experiences had the opposite effect, creating more potential for chaos and angst, even when they were going "well." But Gwen seated herself deep in my soul and centered me.

I tried to tell myself to be cautious, but her presence was a balm. I warned myself that Layla had seemed like the cure for Risa, and Risa had seemed like the cure for Camilla, and that my delusions had only gotten worse with each successive relationship. However, I was unable to hold back with Gwen. I could speak my mind and be myself in complete comfort with her.

She did not "tame" me, though. No, I was just as demanding as before, sometimes cruel, because that was what bonded us most tightly, like two wires twisted together. I was always sadistic. Well, almost always.

* * *

GWEN

One night late in that first week—I was losing track—he stripped down and beckoned me into bed, no restraints, no toys in evidence. By then of course it had become abundantly clear that Mal didn't need bondage to restrain me—one word or even a gesture was all it took to make me immobile—and he didn't need toys or implements to inflict intense pain.

He began by kissing me on the lips, something he usually did only after other activities, to soothe me after pain or to lay claim to my surrender. This time, though, it was a foray into tenderness, a gentle sweetness parting my lips and sharing my breath.

His mouth traveled down my neck, and he murmured, "The bruises are fading."

"Does that mean it's time to create new ones?" I asked.

He kissed along the top of my shoulder. "Perhaps. If I wish."

His hands massaged their way down my torso, firm and sensual, and before long he had encouraged me to lie back against the pillows while his tongue searched between my legs. Gentle swipes brought my clit out to play, and I thought for sure any moment he would clamp it between his teeth. But no, the only torment was in my own mind, wondering whether this tenderness was going to be enough for me. I almost never came from oral sex given by my old vanilla boyfriends. It had felt like nice foreplay but lacked the edge that I needed. Sometimes to come while they were doing it I had to pinch my own nipples and hope they didn't notice.

My breath hitched as I feared I might disappoint Mal if he wanted me to come.

He gently slid a finger inside me, slowly penetrating and pulling free repeatedly while his tongue languidly played at my clit. Some women couldn't come unless they were relaxed. I was the opposite. I needed to be wound up. I was like a match that needed a rough surface to spark against. This was...

Nice. I realized I didn't have to try to come. He hadn't said anything. All I was supposed to do was lie there and let him have his way. Besides, who said I was going to come, anyway? More than once he'd stimulated me to the edge of coming and then laughed and left for a recording session, leaving me absolutely itching with need until he returned. Maybe tonight would be like that.

I stopped worrying about how much time he was spending down there. He was in charge. If he wanted to stop, he would.

He didn't stop until my entire pussy was completely sopping, utterly swollen, and I was far more aroused than I thought I could get from such gentle sensation.

He kissed me again, hips settling between my legs, his spine undulating so slowly it could barely be called a thrust as his cock moved. He seemed in no hurry to penetrate me, our bodies moving against each other, his tongue seeking the erogenous hot spots on my neck.

When at last we connected, his cock pushing through my swollen folds, I let out a low groan. He did not hurry, keeping to the slow pace as he worked his way inside. I lost myself in the sensual haze created by Mal's rhythm, surrendering myself to his patient lust. The steady penetration was like a small boat rocking on waves, floating, riding the tide, drifting on pleasure.

My eyes flew open. Was it possible? "Mal?"

"Yes, lover," he answered without lifting his head, his lips brushing the tender skin behind my ear.

"I think I'm going to—I mean, may I come if I can?"

"Yes, you may," he said simply, and returned to his gentle fucking.

I hooked my feet behind his knees, tension in me rising, rising, rising, and then shuddered as the tension snapped and pleasure dappled all over my skin like a torrent of beads from a broken string.

He responded with an increased pace, the build of his own tension pulling me with him, and at last he began to exert some force in his penetration as he chased after his own release. I was coming again before I realized it, this time with a wordless moan of ecstasy that he answered with one of his own as he pumped hard, finishing and then milking the aftershocks until his cock went soft and slipped free.

I found myself clinging hard to him, the orgasm over, but my mind spinning, my heart pounding. What had just happened?

He kissed my cheek, my ear, my throat, then looked me in the eye. "Are you all right?"

I must have had a wild look in my eye. He brushed my bangs off my forehead and laid a tender kiss there. "Gwen?"

"I'm... I'm fine..." I blinked. Something had shifted. Something had changed.

Me, possibly.

We got cleaned up and then settled back in bed, as far from the wet spot as we could manage. Fortunately it was a large bed.

He massaged my hair as he cradled me close, but he didn't demand to know my thoughts. Perhaps he sensed I was still trying to figure them out myself.

How did that work? How did he make me come from gentleness alone? That wasn't how I was wired. That had never worked before.

Did that mean I didn't need kink after all? A flutter of panic went through me. After all the work I'd done to accept that I needed pain, that it was part of my sexuality and who I was, now I was finding out it wasn't true... My thoughts were in a spiral of turmoil. If I didn't need pain, did that mean I didn't need Mal? *No!*

Then the thought rose from the murk like a clear, bright star. No. The key wasn't the pain itself but the way the pain made me feel. Taken. Owned. His. That was the thing I needed, not a sensation but an emotion, not what happened to my skin but what was going on in my mind, my heart.

I burst into happy tears. That was the moment Mal began to worry. "Gwen? Oh, Gwen, what did I do?"

I hugged him around the neck. "It's just that I'm so in love with you! I'm so in love that it hurts. In a good way. Oh, God, it's like nothing else I've ever felt."

I felt that momentary stab of panic that he was going to be one of those losers who flips out over the L-word. But no. He smiled. He hugged back as hard as I hugged him and he murmured soothing words like "My beautiful Gwen" into my hair.

Before I could begin to worry that this was the start of a new vanilla lovemaking phase of our relationship, he added, "Tomorrow we start training you to come from pain itself."

A ghost orgasm rocketed through me at those words alone.

"Yes, Mal! Ooooh, yes." We had more than a week to go in Montreal and I wondered if we would succeed.

* * *

MAL

Of course the night that I wanted most to hurry back to Gwen would come on the recording day when we made the most breakthroughs. When everything is working musically, you feel like you can't get enough of playing a song, like you want to play it over and over because it gets better every time. I dubbed two guitar solos for a song we were calling "Fire" and they were both so good we couldn't decide between them. That was a good problem to have.

It was nearly two in the morning when I returned to the hotel, wondering if I would find Gwen asleep. I opened the door to see a gratifyingly arousing sight: She was asleep on a blanket curled on the floor near the door. She woke as I came into the room and rolled onto her back, pulling her knees apart with her hands.

"Don't move," I said, pulling my cock out and tugging it quickly to hardness. I dropped my trousers and knelt in front of her, spanking her pussy hard about a dozen times—that was all it took until I saw a trickle of her natural lubrication issue forth.

"That's all the foreplay you're getting," I whispered, climbing over her and positioning myself. "Hold on to me if you need to."

I thrust deep and she sucked a sharp breath through her teeth, no doubt trying to be polite to the other hotel guests by not screaming. She took my suggestion and clung to me, the cold still emanating from my leather overcoat, as I pulled almost all the way free and then thrust as brutally as I could again.

Through clenched teeth her words were still intelligible: "God, yes!"

"Does it hurt, my love?"

"You know it does." She panted and moved against me, though, impaling herself, taking me even deeper. "But it doesn't last."

"Nor should it," I said as I moved in time with her. "Your body craves me too much to resist for long. I could not resist taking you when I saw you awaiting me here."

I did not let up fucking her until I had come, taking my full due of my willing captive. When I pulled free, I sat back to watch my seed ooze from her, the sight satisfying to some primal part of me I could not rationalize.

"Did you come?"

"No, Mal."

"Good. Stand up." She still had my come dribbling down her legs. I retrieved a cloth from the bathroom and wiped her down roughly, then shrugged the duster from my shoulders and put it around her. "We're going out."

"Out?" She buttoned it closed but I could still see her bare neck and the marks that marked her as mine.

"Put on your boots." I don't think I would have dared this in an American city, but Montreal was French in its soul, and something struck me as so very French about taking a naked woman out for a stroll. I cleaned myself up a bit and then out we went.

The hotel lobby was deserted at that hour and so was the street outside. I held Gwen's hand as we walked toward some bars and restaurants, most of them closed but I knew a few were open until four a.m., some all night.

We settled at a place that served smoked meats, sandwiches, and other fare. The food was good but I was distracted by the constant looks from the waiters. It was patently obvious that Gwen had nothing on under the leather coat far too large for her, and the gazes were by turns intrigued, jealous, and lustful. I felt quite decadent, even as their attentions set me on edge.

"I was surfing the Internet today," Gwen said, drawing my attention back to her. "Do you remember the stable? It's currently unused."

I wasn't paying enough attention to her flirtatious tone, I suppose, because I said, "Are you thinking of getting a horse?"

She laughed. "I was thinking of *being* your horse," she said. "Er, pony, I guess is the term. Although you know, if you wanted to get an actual horse you could keep one in our stable."

I found myself caught off guard more by her than by her mention of pony play. Going out into the real world like this was more discomfiting than I expected, and the talk of her home only exacerbated it. "Thank you, but . . . " I tried to steer the topic to sex and play and avoid thinking about what awaited us in the future. "Pony play, you say?"

Gwen described some of the human pony tack she had seen online and I let her go on about it for a bit before I stopped her with a single finger to my lips.

"I think I prefer the real Gwen to pony Gwen right now," I said.

One of the waiters came and filled our water glasses, even though they did not really need refilling. I had a strong feeling he was trying to get a better look at Gwen, perhaps hoping she might flash a tit. I was certain if I took her into the men's room he'd fuck her without hesitation while I watched. My cock hardened in my jeans as the fantasy progressed to me tearing him limb from limb for daring to touch what was mine.

When the waiter was gone, disappointed, Gwen kissed my finger and said, "Real Gwen wants you to know that when we get back to Los Angeles she still wants to be your captive."

"Does she? Should I keep her in the stable?"

"You should keep her wherever you want." Her smile started

out innocent but somehow curled into wicked as she said, "I do still have that fantasy about being kept in a cage, you know."

"Didn't that cretin in Providence do that to you?"

"He never actually mail-ordered the cage, just showed me pictures of it on the Internet to get me hot." She raised an eyebrow in delicate challenge. "I mean, I know you'll be gone on tour again soon and all that, but when we're both in town, on weekends, maybe . . . ?"

Another waiter appeared to inquire if everything was all right. I might have answered with a glare and bared teeth. No, everything was not all right because the real world was intruding rudely on our delicate balance. I didn't mean the waiters, either. I meant the looming challenge of how to maintain this when we had to live normal lives. The artificiality of it was thrown into sharp focus when contrasted with the real world.

I was not ready to face that. Not with another week of studio time to go, and not with Gwen right there within my reach. I caught the eye of the first waiter, furtively watching us, and imagined locking Gwen into that cage . . .

"Penny for your thoughts?" Gwen asked.

I gave a harsh bark of laughter, then took a calming sip from my water glass. Maybe it had been a mistake to try to leave the room and the safe, small circle of our own little world. It was the first hint of a dark mood I'd had since her arrival. "Just wondering what kind of fantasies the waiters are having about us."

"There's always a lot going on in your head, isn't there."

I nodded. "Most of it not pretty." I reached for her, running my thumb, wet from the condensation on my glass, against her lower lip. "Only my fantasies of you are pretty. Would you do it if I told you to expose yourself to one of them?"

She swallowed, her eyes looking directly into mine. "If you told me to, I would." She licked her lower lip, her voice low but clear. "I'll suffer through anything you say, Mal."

"Exhibitionism would be suffering?"

"Tolerating a stranger's gaze? Only if it was what you wished."

I leaned across the table and kissed the sweet taste of her words right from her lips. I left cash on the table and we swept out of the eatery, curious gazes following us as we went.

Back in the room, I lifted my leather coat from her shoulders as if it were a priceless fur, but it was what I uncovered that was truly priceless. I hung the coat in the closet and then took one hand in mine, my other at her hip, turning her in a circle as if we were beginning a ballroom dance.

I pressed my mouth into her hair. "Tonight we begin training you to come from pain."

"Yes, Mal."

"As mine, you've experienced many kinds of pain. Paddle, flogger, cane, belt, my hand, my teeth on your skin, your nipples, your ass, your genitalia." I left out flames. I did not want to tempt myself, and this hotel room was not a suitable place for fire play. Too many sensors and alarms, too dangerous. "There are more to explore, of course, but of the ones you've felt so far, which would you say is your favorite?"

Her head rested on my shoulder and I rocked her gently to imagined music. "You know which pain is my favorite," she said.

"Do I? Oh, yes, sudden penetration." She had called it the *best pain ever* that day she'd arrived in Montreal. "Very well. And second favorite?"

She hesitated before saying, "Y-your belt."

I tipped her face upward to look at me. Her cheeks were scarlet. "This admission embarrasses you?"

She nodded.

"Why?"

"I don't know. It just feels . . . " She pressed herself against me as she bit her lip. "Raw. Dirty. Intense."

"More so than other things?"

"Yes. Because... it's not like a fancy flogger that was made to be a chic upscale marital aid. Not that those are bad, of course, but there's something real and edgy about you using your actual belt."

I don't know which aroused me more, the breathless intensity of her admission or the fact that I agreed with her. This wasn't a costume, wasn't a role out of a book, wasn't even some typical punishment fantasy. This was... real. "Take my belt off now and I'll give you ten strokes with it."

She dropped to her knees immediately and worked the buckle open, then slid the belt free of the loops, looking up at me. I stroked her hair.

"Make me hard while you're down there."

She freed my cock and mouthed it enthusiastically. I was already half hard just from our discussion, so no real effort was required on her part to bring me to full stiffness.

"I'm going to use your mouth often for the next several days," I said, "while we deprive your cunny of any interior stretching. So when I do take you, you'll be at your tightest."

She moaned in agreement around the flesh in her mouth. I pulled her off of me with a fist in her hair and took a kiss before pushing her toward the bed. "Bend over. Legs spread."

I delivered the first three blows of the doubled belt directly across her ass cheeks and then massaged her clit gently with two fingers.

"You find being beaten arousing even without me doing this, don't you?"

"Yes, very much," she said.

"I think you're the only lover I've had who would literally get wet from being struck." I slipped a finger into her. I could not resist. "It makes me want to fuck you all the time."

She laughed. "You already want to fuck me all the time."

I joined her laughter. "True. But even more. It's going to be a trial for me to resist while training you."

"There's always my ass, too," she pointed out.

"Also true. Yes, I predict your ass will be getting a regular workout as well." I pulled my finger free and teased at her pucker, then stepped back to deliver three more hard strikes with the belt.

Her quivering turned to quaking as I ran my bare hand over the welts. "The first time I beat you with my belt, I didn't know it was you until after I turned you over," I said. "But I had been thinking to myself, what a strange coincidence that there are two women, at the same time, both of whom I'm suddenly obsessed with seeing again. Normally I wouldn't even be interested in one, and now there are two? What a wild coincidence. But of course it wasn't a coincidence: you were actually the same person."

I struck her again and then ran my hand over the welt that came up. "I think deep down I knew it was you."

Her spine arched and she ground herself against my touch with a delighted noise.

I stepped back again. "Three more to go."

She nodded against the duvet.

I put the full force of my arm into these, no gentle or playful slaps now, fierce savagery in every motion. She bit the duvet, trying to keep from screaming but instead giving out only a high-pitched whine and then going limp after the final blow.

I pulled her upright against me, then pushed her against the wall. "Hold yourself up, ankles together, hands against the wall. That's it."

She was bent over partway now, and I spread my feet to lower my hips to hers, working my cock between her legs.

"That's it. Keep your thighs together tightly." I fucked the intercrural grip made by her thighs and cunny, gripping onto the sore, hot flesh of her ass. "This is how most of the so-called sex took place when I was in boarding school," I said.

"I thought you went to an all-boys school."

"There was an all-girls school down the road. Some of the girls claimed to come from this. Some liked it better from the front."

"Well, you do rub against... some very... ungh." She grunted as I thrust harder. "I never would have thought of doing this."

"I never thought I would do it again, but I confess your pose is fetching and the sensation is a satisfactory replacement for me—for tonight at least." I planted my hands on her ass cheeks and rocked her back and forth on my cock until I was close. "Now, on your knees, finish me with your mouth."

She chose a good time to swallow, as I'd already come earlier that night so the volume was not copious. She kept her eyes open, locked on mine, looking up as she swallowed everything I produced and then licked the head and shaft clean once the last dribbles had ceased. Any man who does not feel an intensity of emotions at such an upward gaze from the woman he owns has no heart at all. My Gwen.

One almost wonders if part of the allure of all the pain and brutality is how it heightened such moments of tenderness. I ran a finger gently over her cheek, over the spot where the burn mark had completely disappeared, and thanked my lucky stars once again.

After that we got ready for bed like any domestic couple might—brushing our teeth, et cetera—except for the fact she was completely naked. We got into bed together and I cuddled her close.

"You still haven't come," I remarked.

"No, I haven't."

"I'm going to wake you at some point during the night and let you come then," I told her. "But you have to sleep first."

"Why?"

"Because you're my plaything to do with as I wish."

"Oh right." She blushed deeply and snuggled close. "I'll try."

We both did fall asleep but after about two hours I woke again. She was deeply asleep, one of her nostrils whistling quietly. It was not difficult to very gradually, very slowly, work one finger of mine between her pussy lips and gently massage her clit until I felt her pulse begin to respond. She grew damp, then slippery wet as I carefully fingered her, her clit becoming more and more swollen with each passing minute.

I changed the motion of my finger to a quick flicking, spreading her with my other fingers and tweaking her clit with my index finger until the stimulation grew hard enough to wake her.

And wake she did, with a sudden gasp of "Mal!" and all her muscles freezing up as she reached the bare edge of her climax. Had I truly wished to make her suffer, I would have pulled back at that point, but my own body was suffused with sweet warmth as I kept up the motion, releasing her from the taut edge where she was held, pushing her right through a shuddering climax and denouement.

"Oh, Mal," she said as I tucked her against my body, and sleep reclaimed her.

No, I could not explain to myself why I did what I did, nor why I felt what I did for her. I knew it wouldn't last forever, that this magical equilibrium between us would fade once we had to rejoin the real world, once we had to face who we truly were.

But here, in this world of two that we created, the Need was sated.

CHAPTER FIFTEEN

CRACKS IN THE GLASS

GWEN

The next day I got an e-mail from Ricki saying there was a half page of photos of me in the latest *Entertainment Weekly* and wanting to know if I'd seen it, which made me laugh a little. I guess she hadn't taken it literally when I'd told her I was going to be Mal's sex slave for two weeks. I had been e-mailing her regularly while in Montreal to let her know everything was okay but I hadn't given her many details. I was sure she was hearing from Axel, too, but I wanted to reassure her somehow in case she was worried I was bored or tired of it or being coerced to going along with it for the sake of Mal's band. I was none of those things. On the contrary, I was indulged and stimulated and a little sad as the time went by that we were going to have to leave. I read the books of Ariadne Wood and watched BBC shows and did yoga in the room to keep myself limber.

And with Mal I needed to be limber. I don't think there was a single piece of furniture or surface we didn't have sex on or use as a prop for a scene. How strange that when he wasn't there I was absorbed in the fantasy worlds of books and shows but the moment he arrived we were Gwen and Mal, no role-playing, no contrived scenarios.

Which didn't mean we didn't have some intense scenes, of course. For one, a few times he quizzed me on my "BBC English" and caned me for each mistake, but that still felt like us being ourselves. It wasn't like playing the part of an Ariadne Wood character. The orgasms were plentiful for both of us—though once he began to train me to come from pain they never came without an equal dose of agony, and my poor vagina was restricted to penetration from one of his long fingers.

One night while we were lying in bed, ready to sleep but not quite sleeping yet, talking about art and life and all the things we usually did, he said, "Johns said something today about bands that fail, self-sabotaging because they have fear of success. I find myself coming back to that thought again and again because I don't understand it at all."

"Fear of success?"

"Yes. Who's afraid of success?"

I thought about it a moment. "I don't really get it either, but I know it's a thing. Maybe it's just part of fear of the unknown, fear of change. People get used to things being the way they are even if they don't like them. Maybe they subconsciously fight to keep them from changing even though they'd be happier if things changed?"

"Hmm. All the more reason to be aware of what one wants."

I snuggled close to him, basking in the scent of his skin. "I know what I want."

"Mmm, do you, now? Not sated yet, my pet?"

"Besides physically," I said, nudging him. "I want us to last. That's my dream."

"I thought your dream was to become a critically acclaimed actress."

"That's my other dream, silly," I said. I planted my hands and my chin on his chest so I could look directly into his face. "Tell me honestly, do you think I'm sabotaging myself from reaching that dream by being with you?"

He reached up to caress my hair. "No," he said, his eyes never leaving mine. "No, because I am not actually going to lock you in a cage twenty-four-seven."

"I don't have to be in a cage to know I belong to you."

His eyes softened for a moment and I wondered if he was going to kiss me. But then he went on. "You do belong to me, but think about the challenges it presents, Gwen. Going to auditions with visible marks, for example, or how speculation about the nature of our relationship might affect people's opinions of you."

I took it as a good sign that he replied so calmly, so rationally, and so positively. "The nature of our relationship," I heard myself say, as if tasting the words, trying on the way they sounded, felt. *Our relationship.* I couldn't help but smile. I felt warm all over.

Mal's thoughts had already leaped ahead, though. "There are those who would condemn the relationship for being consensually kinky and those who would wrongly assume it's abuse and condemn it for that."

"The only way to win the reputation game is not to play," I said. "I don't care."

"I do, though," he said seriously. "I care that your career could be much more negatively impacted than mine by the exposure of what we do." He sank his fingers into my hair. "Not that that keeps me from taking my due from you, so long as you're mine."

"I don't mind that the stakes are high." Relaxing into his grip instead of struggling had become a reflex over the past ten days. "It makes me appreciate being with you even more."

"This isn't a game," he said, pulling me onto my back by my hair and burying his mouth against my neck.

"I think if it was, I would've gotten tired of it by now," I said. "Instead, I still can't get enough of you, Mal." I gasped as he slid his hand between my legs as if to test what I said, two fingers working their way into me and finding me wet. It was the most penetration I'd had in days and I groaned with need.

"You're sure you're not tired of being treated like this?" he murmured against my skin, biting me for emphasis.

"I promise to tell you when I am." I spread my legs and angled my hips helplessly. "I need you, Mal."

"Because I have been depriving you," he said.

"No, that's not why," I said, then gasped as he moved his slick fingers into my ass, one at a time. I loosened quickly as he used my natural lube to prepare the way. "I've never felt so complete in my life."

He pushed himself atop me and his eyes looked like they were full of questions, his mouth moving as if trying to find the words. But then he mounted my rear hole, his cock filling me and filling the gulf between us, and in that moment all questions were silenced.

* * *

MAL

A glorious week passed, filled with sex and music and letting myself utterly drown in the world of Gwen. It was an indulgence I could not have imagined before. Knowing that Gwen was waiting for me put me on a completely separate mental plane from the rest of the band, but somehow that worked, that let me play and listen and flow through the sessions without constant strife.

Of course it helped that Larkin Johns had finally ceased making ridiculous suggestions. Or perhaps when we were playing so well together he no longer felt the need to constantly tinker or change. Chicken or egg, it mattered not to me, only that it was working.

And so was my regular torturing of Gwen. Favored though my belt was by us both, some variety was necessary. I had acquired an entirely new collection of toys and implements and plied her with them as each day we progressed toward the stated goal, the pinnacle of masochism, orgasm from pain itself. Concentrating on how well the recording work was going and on this delicious goal for Gwen's captivity allowed me to push aside all other questions. I thought not of the future but just of the days we had remaining.

The second to last day in the studio we'd pushed hard, working late, trying to nail down as much as we could while the mojo was flowing. But when midnight had come we declared a stop, leaving only a little for our final day, and I hurried back to the hotel with my other "project" burning in my mind. Gwen.

I stepped into the room and found her as I'd trained her to greet me, on the floor with her knees apart, her fingers splaying her pussy for my view. The pose was all the more fetching knowing that she had reached a stage of desperation over the previous week, deprived of vaginal penetration except for my fingers from time to time. She had tightened deliciously, her muscles contracted by repeated orgasms and relentless teasing, and each time I'd checked her with a finger I'd found her grip strengthened.

I stripped out of my clothes in front of her, leaving them in a pile at the door until I stood as naked as she, not a stitch on me. She watched, silent, her eyes as hungry as the rest of her, her breath betraying her anticipation and excitement.

My own hand hardened me, stroking myself until a glistening drop beaded at the tip. "Tomorrow is our last day in the studio,"

I said, trying to sound as casual as possible, as if need were not crackling between us like electromagnetism.

"I... Is it?" she said, as if she did not know.

"Yes. Which means tonight is your ultimate test. I'm going to hurt you tonight, Gwen."

"Yes, Mal."

"There will be no pleasure except what you derive from the pain itself," I said. "And perhaps this." I seized her, pulling her into a kiss, crushing her body against mine and ravishing her mouth before I pushed her onto the bed. "Facedown."

She flattened herself with her arms and legs spread, and I spanked her until my hand felt sore, knowing that every blow reverberating through her was as good as a caress along her clit. I left a series of bite marks across the tops of her shoulders and took another kiss, gauging her level of arousal by how supple her mouth was.

Then I brought the cane down on her buttocks, making her yelp. Unlike a formal punishment scene, where she'd be bent over and take the blows one at a time and ask for the next one between strokes, this time I laid the strokes on whenever I felt like it, playing her screams like an instrument and noting the way she ground her mound against the bed as I did it. What did I do to deserve such a gorgeous woman for my own? The vision of the red stripes appearing on her skin and the way she writhed against the duvet seared itself into my memory. "How do you feel?"

Her voice was light, giddy. "Like I love you."

That made me smile and rub my hand over the stripes. Sweet, wonderful woman.

"Now put your ass in the air," I commanded, knowing this would remove her ability to hump the bed. I had other plans for her stimulation. I forced her knees apart and splayed her feet, then began flogging her with the suede flogger first, then switching to a leather one, allowing the tails to not only strike her buttocks but also to liberally make contact with her labia and clit.

When I switched to the cruel rubber flogger, at first I worried that it would be too much for her. Her cries took on a note of distress, but I did not let up, and before long she had pushed through to the next level of arousal and endorphins.

Time for the finale. “Get me my belt.”

She crawled off the bed, not from submission but because her legs wouldn’t carry her, I think. She freed the belt from my trousers and then presented it to me on her knees, holding it up with both hands, her head bowed.

“Kiss it,” I said. “Show me you love it, make love to me through it.” My cock throbbed and leaked freely as I hungrily watched her press her trembling lips against the leather, doubling it over and rubbing her cheek against it before kissing along its length. Gorgeous creature, I could barely believe she was mine.

“Lie back. Run the edge along your clit,” I said.

She did as I bade her, hissing in pain as she sawed the hard edge of the leather against her most tender place. Her teeth were gritted but there was never a moment of hesitation to obey me.

At last I deemed she’d had enough. “Bend over the edge of the bed and spread your legs.”

I ran my hand over the tracks the cane had left and then began a new round of spanking, swatting her cunny as often as her thighs, pausing only to flick her clit hard with a fingernail, until I could hear she had reached a plateau of arousal, but remaining there was itself becoming a torture. I swiped a finger around her clit in a quick circle and was greeted with another needy wail. So close, so close, but she could not go over the edge without me giving her more.

I slicked myself with the ring of my fingers wet with her

juices and positioned myself behind her, one hand on each buttock. I scraped my fingernail across her welts again and then spanked her, once, twice, thrice. I insinuated the head of my cock between her cunny lips but held her still so she could not drive herself back onto me and then alternated striking her with one hand, then the other, driving the desperate note in her cries up the scale, up and up, until the moment was right.

And then I drove into her and loosed her cry of sweet release.

She came, screaming, clawing at the bed, fucking herself on my staff and crying out my name. Angels and devils, it was all I could do not to explode into orgasm myself at that moment, but I felt the promise between us—pleasure for pain, that I would never leave her unsatisfied—was sacred. I turned her over to face me and let her come twice more on my cock before I allowed my own release.

And then it was over. I covered her face with kisses and was rewarded with her triumphal laughter as she lay spent beneath me, unable to move a muscle after all she had been through.

My own feeling of triumph was short-lived, though. As my flesh softened and slipped from her, it was as if the walls I'd erected in my mind to keep me from thinking of anything outside this room, outside this city, also began to wither away. My goals had been reached, and everything I had been burying began to stir with unrest.

I tried to ignore it at first, cuddling with her, praising her, trying to enjoy the moment. She was so beautiful, so perfect, and had surpassed my every expectation. But my thoughts grew stormy. She had fulfilled every promise and yet a gnawing feeling ate at me from inside. A demon, maybe.

"I'm hungry," I declared. Would she drop her role now that she had reached that state of perfection? "Let's go out looking for something to eat."

"Should I wear your duster again?" she asked, looking somehow shy and sly at the same time. So much for the idea that she might be ready to leave her role on a high note.

I remembered the unease I'd felt on our last trip to the outside world. Had that been a reminder to me of all the issues I'd buried for the sake of these two weeks? "Yes, it's in the closet," I said. "Let's go back to the poutine and smoked meats place." Perhaps if I returned there I could meet my demons head-on.

* * *

GWEN

Walking through the chilly night air with only Mal's duster on was an experience. My boots stopped at my knee so goose bumps crawled up my thighs, and the coat's slick lining rubbed against my bare nipples. I felt flushed with success and the warmth of the man I loved beside me. Such a perfect match. Could I have even imagined it in my wildest fantasies? No, the real thing was so much better than role-playing.

With Mal I felt a kind of contentedness in my heart I'd never felt before. I'd read a lot of blogs and articles by submissives on the Internet recently, and I believed it wasn't simply love. It was a bond that could only exist between dom and sub, or master and slave, or owner and owned, no matter which words you used for it. Knowing that I was *his* I felt fully alive and fulfilled in a way that I hadn't before I'd come to Montreal.

At the deli meats place, the host indicated we could sit wherever we liked since it wasn't crowded; Mal chose a booth toward the back where it was warmest.

In contrast to my bursting with contentment, though, Mal appeared to be having troubling thoughts. He was always quiet, but he seemed quieter than usual, his brows drawn downward in a concerned expression. He was curt while ordering and neither of us said much until our food had come.

"Did the recording go all right?" I asked after we'd eaten a little and his mood still didn't lighten.

"Yes, yes, it's been fine." He gave me a half-smile but it didn't reach his eyes. He had eaten only part of his food and he pushed his plate away, uninterested in finishing it. "Apparently Axel and the boys were right: I needed my gonads wrung dry on a regular basis to keep me docile enough to work with."

Somehow I doubted that "docile" was a fitting description, but I didn't pry. "Last session is tomorrow, isn't it? Are you done with what you need to do?"

He drew a slow breath. "I believe we are close enough that if overdubs are necessary we can do those in Los Angeles." His eyes darted around. One waiter was wiping down tables nearby. The other was standing to one side, appearing to add up a check. There were only two other tables with customers at that point.

Is something wrong? I almost asked. But with Mal these past two weeks, being patient had usually brought me the answer to what I was wondering. Was he upset our two weeks were coming to an end? If so, couldn't we always plan to do it again? I made a gentle foray into the subject. "This trip has been blissful for me."

He nodded in agreement, his eyes wandering the edges of the coat lapels where my bare skin was exposed.

"They want me to film a new promo video for WOMedia when I get back to LA," I said with a sigh, and then joked gently, "I suppose they're going to want me to wear clothes for that."

His eyes were dark but his voice was calm. "I suppose many things will go back to the way they were."

"Oh?"

"You don't genuinely think we can keep up this charade of you being my captive?"

His words, though spoken calmly, tore through my heart. “Charade?”

“Come now, Gwen. This has been nothing more than a scene. A long one, a deeply involving one, but a scene nonetheless.”

Nothing more...? I had to swallow rising panic, trying to tell myself we were just talking past each other and if I stayed calm and talked this through, I'd find out we actually meant the same thing. “I... I thought what we had was... the real us.”

“Role-playing idealized versions of ourselves that would never exist in the real world is still role-playing,” he said.

“I...” My mind spun and I had to take a deep breath, trying to straighten out what I meant, what I felt. Was he trying to say he agreed with me, or not? Was it my imagination that we'd grown so close? “I haven't been playing, Mal.”

His face was closed, his eyes narrow. “You don't understand.”

“I understand that I want the real Mal. I want the Mal I've had for the past two weeks. That's the man I'd do anything for.”

“Anything?”

“Anything.”

He glanced behind him at the waiter and then focused on me again. “Flash your inner thigh at the waiter behind me.”

I swallowed. The last time we were here I'd told him I'd do anything he said, including that, even though I wouldn't like it. Did he mean for me to prove it? “You're sure?”

He gave a curt nod.

“Yes, Mal.” I licked my lips and extended my foot into the aisle, then my bare, bent knee, making eye contact with the waiter and then looking away with a blush as I pulled the coat aside for a few moments, then closed it again without checking to see if the guy reacted.

“He remembers you.”

“It would be hard to forget us,” I pointed out, trying to think of how this related to our argument. “How many naked sex slaves wrapped in nothing but a leather coat do you think they get in here?"

Mal huffed, a humorless laugh, then took a pile of Canadian money from his wallet and laid it on the table. The waiter hurried over with our tab. Mal beckoned for the fellow to lean down and said something softly into his ear. I think he said it in French.

The waiter answered in kind. *"Oui."* He then called out something to someone in the back. A third waiter came out from the kitchen and Mal gestured for me to get up to go.

But then he beckoned me toward the restrooms.

He steered me into the men's room. The two waiters who had recognized us were right behind him. One of them put the "closed for cleaning" sign out and then latched the door shut.

Mal's eyes were dark as thunderclouds. "Give me the coat," he snapped.

My fingers were shaking as I unbuttoned it. What was he going to have me do? These were total strangers. Had he set this up with these guys earlier in the week? Had he checked them out somehow?

I shrugged the coat free and one of the waiters swore. They were both dark-haired, one a little taller than the other, in identical white shirts and black pants.

"Show them your cunt," Mal said, putting the coat on himself and then rubbing his erection through his jeans.

I moved my hands to my thighs, then spread my legs a little, pulling my lips apart with my fingers. "Like that?"

"Put a foot up on the sink," he said. "Give them a better look."

I put one of my booted feet into the sink so it wouldn't slip against the wet ceramic, my thighs splayed and everything on display. Everything.

"I put those bruises on her tonight," Mal told the two men. "She likes it rough."

One of them made a comment in French to the other, who laughed.

"Pinch your nipples and then touch your clit," Mal ordered.

I did as he said, telling myself to trust him. He stepped close to me, saying something to the other men in French. He put a finger into me and continued talking to them as if he weren't paying attention to me.

It suddenly clicked: *The Story of O.* He'd talked about how the only scene he remembered was one where O's lover converses with other men while he has his finger almost casually inside her. They were even speaking French! It made sense now.

Mal sawed his finger in and out while talking. I don't even think he was aware he was doing it. I let myself sink into a pleasurable, submissive haze.

A touch I didn't recognize jerked me back to alertness. A hand on my breast. The other two had come close now, one fondling my breast while the other, behind me, ran a hand over my ass. I tried to meet Mal's eyes but he was resolutely staring at where his finger disappeared into my body.

Mal, is this really what you want? Do you really want to... share me with these men?

I yelped as the one behind me pinched my ass. The one in front pulled on my nipple. I put my hands on Mal's shoulders, the sudden sweat of fear breaking out all over my skin. How far was he going to let this go?

The one behind me kissed me on the back of the neck and I tried to pull away from him but that only pushed my upper body against Mal.

Then a finger was pushing at my ass. "Is that you?" I whispered, hoping.

"This is me," he said, and thrust his own finger harder.

"Oh," was all I could think of to say as the man in back kept touching me, trying to figure out how to get a finger into me.

When I'd said to Mal, right here in this restaurant, that I'd suffer anything he wanted me to, did that extend to this? When I flashed the guy earlier, was that my signal that I remembered I'd said that? But we never negotiated *this.*

The one in front at least had lost interest in trying to get at my breasts when they were pressed against Mal and had pulled his cock out of his pants and was masturbating instead. I heard the man behind me wetting his finger with his mouth.

"There are three of us," Mal said to me, "and you have three holes."

"No!" It came out before I could stop it. "No, Mal, this... I can't. *I can't.*"

"This is real, Gwen. You said you wanted it to be real. Feel how real." He put my hand onto his fly and I could feel how hard he was.

All four of us jumped then as someone banged on the door, and a male voice yelled in English, "Hurry up in there!"

The waiter with his cock out cursed and zipped up quickly and the one behind me stepped away. I practically had to tear the leather duster off of Mal and before I could put it on, he pulled me into one of the stalls and latched it shut. I could hear what sounded like the two waiters washing their hands—thank goodness. Mal sat down on the toilet and pulled me into his lap as the restroom door flew open.

Someone came in, presumably the impatient customer who had been banging on the door, pissed noisily into the urinal, belched, and then exited.

I put my feet down. My voice was shaky. "I want to go back to the hotel. I've had enough of this."

Mal stood and helped me to put the coat on properly but said nothing. He paused at the sink to wash his hands, and then we made our way quickly through the restaurant onto the street.

Mal stayed silent but kept his arm around me the whole way back to the hotel. I kept everything bottled up until we were in our own room.

Then I let it all out. "What the fuck was that about! Mal!"

"Merely trying to demonstrate to you the difference between reality and what you think you know about me." His voice was cold, with an edge of fury in it. "Apparently you desire a fantasy after all."

"I thought I belonged to you! I never thought you'd actually want to share me with anyone!" I burst into sudden tears.

"You certainly let it go quite far before you protested."

"I thought you were re-creating your *Story of O* fantasy! I was trying to do what you wanted because I trust you!"

"I've told you the real me isn't as noble as you think." He sat down heavily on the corner of the bed as if the strength to remain standing had suddenly left him. He was shaking his head and looking down.

I sank to the floor in front of him, the leather coat pooling around me, so I could be in his line of sight. "Mal—what is going on in your head? Can you clue me in at least a little?"

"Let me show you something." He stood and took off his belt, unzipped his pants, and bared his erection.

"I've seen that before, you know," I said, crossing my arms and not moving from my spot on the floor.

"This is everything that's wrong with me." He sat back down. "A good dom would never have allowed total strangers to have their way with his submissive. You're right. I hate the thought of another man touching you or even looking at you."

"Then why—"

"Yet, look at what my body did in response to it." He smacked his cock with his open palm. "This is the reality I live with every day."

"Mal, that's not *that* weird." I tried to give a sexologist-type answer. "States of arousal including anger, fear, revulsion, they can all be kind of wired close together, you know?"

He was shaking his head. "I am not a good dom. I'm afraid when you dig down below the veneer of consensuality, what you will find ultimately is . . . " He shrugged helplessly. "For lack of a better word, evil."

"Mal, you're not evil. What the hell gave you that idea?"

"Being sexually aroused by the wrong and perverse? As if being driven to expose the woman I love to danger isn't evidence enough?"

My mouth hung open, my next words unspoken, because I didn't want to erase the sound in my ears of him saying the words *the woman I love. Please don't just be saying that.*

He brushed my cheek with his fingers and then gently brought my chin up until my teeth touched. "I told you before that I loved you too much to expose you to the danger that is me. I'll hurt you."

I got to my feet and grabbed him by the shirt collar. "Guess what, Mal, that's the definition of love. The person you love, the person who loves you, that's who can break your heart."

"I told you I would."

"So you're saying, what, you have to leave me to prove yourself right?"

He pushed me away from him and got up off the bed.

"Think, Mal, think," I said, trying to keep myself calm, but it was difficult given what I'd just been through and the sudden rush of emotions that fighting with him brought out. "If we're together for any length of time, of course you're going to eventually push me beyond my limits."

He turned away from me toward the window, but I knew he was still listening.

"You say you're afraid to hurt me. But . . . but look at what happened tonight."

"I would have let those dirty ruffians traumatize you."

"No, you wouldn't, because I said no. The *fantasy* is that when I'm being your slave, responsibility for my well-being is one hundred percent on you, but the *reality* is I am still actually responsible for myself."

"If I hurt you because my lust drives me to cross your boundaries? I'll never forgive myself, Gwen."

"You're hurting me *now*," I said, my voice starting to shake again, tears blinding me. "With all this talk of throwing away everything, of throwing *me* away!"

He was there suddenly, his arms around me. "I don't want to do that. I don't."

"Then how do we get past this?" I sobbed, and pressed my face against his shirt. I really thought he'd changed his mind over the past two weeks, that I'd finally proved to him that it could work. But he was right back where he'd started, hating himself deep down for the very thing that I needed so very much from him.

"There's one way we could stay together," he said, his voice quavering with emotion. "Quit kink."

"What?" The words shocked me so much I literally pushed him away like he'd changed into a total stranger. I could also hardly breathe. "You can't... you can't..."

He tried to embrace me again and I found myself stepping back.

I saw the anger flare in his eyes, the disbelief that I'd defied him, then the defeat as he realized he could not order me to do anything and still "quit kink." He zipped his fly instead, settling himself uncomfortably in his too-tight jeans. "That right there, that I'd take a step toward forcing you, was the proof I should not be trusted as a dom."

"I think that was the proof that you know perfectly well the line between BDSM and being an abusive ass, and *you didn't cross it,*" I said, hugging myself. "If you ever did, you know what? We'd deal with it the same way we'd deal with any other mistakes or hurts in a relationship."

He shook his head but it was more of a violent shudder than a reply. His eyes were squeezed shut and his jaw clenched.

"Please, Mal," I said.

"Is that what it would come to? You begging me to hurt you? Tempting me constantly? Trying to entice me into hurting you?"

"You trained me to come from pain!" I cried.

"And it was a mistake!" he roared. "I never should have laid a hand on you. If you really love me, Gwen, then help me to stop."

I swallowed and my voice came out a rough whisper. "If you really love me, then treat me like I'm not just an addiction you need to kick."

He pressed his hand to his eyes and took a few deep breaths, then looked at me suddenly. "My coat." He held out his hand.

I shrugged off the duster and handed it to him.

"What if I told you to suck my cock right now," he demanded in a low voice as he put the coat on. "All I'd have to do is tell you I agree with you, you're mine, and a minute later I could choke you on this blasted erection."

"That's . . . that's probably true," I said, almost wishing he'd do it. Almost.

"That doesn't seem really fucked up and wrong to you, Gwen?" He adjusted his package like his balls were aching. "That I can snap my fingers and fill your throat with come just because I'm the dom?"

"There's a lot more to it than that, and you know it," I said, my own anger reddening my face. I put my hands on my bare hips.

"Psychobabble and window dressing," he said.

"You know what gives you clarity, Mal? Do you remember? Will you fuck me and then we can talk again?"

He shook his head. "Will you quit kink to stay with me, Gwen?"

"That's an impossible question."

"When a woman doesn't say enthusiastically yes, that means no," Mal said with a nod. He gave my naked body one last look and before I realized what he was doing, left.

Gone. Out the door. "Mal!"

I pulled the door open and looked into the hallway but he was already out of sight. By the elevator? He was counting on the fact that I wouldn't run after him while stark naked.

Unfortunately, he was right. I ducked back into the room. Where had he hidden my suitcase? In the closet. I dragged it out and hurriedly pulled on a pair of underwear and pants, a shirt, a sweater.

It felt so strange to be wearing clothes after two weeks naked. But even stranger to be wondering what the hell could be going through Mal's mind. A few hours ago I had been certain everything was solid, everything was perfect between us. And right now I didn't know what to think, what to feel. Give up kink? The thing that made us *us*?

I hurried out to the elevator: no sign of Mal. He wasn't in the lobby either. Should I go looking on the street? Had he gone back to that deli to confront those two waiters?

Running through the streets of Montreal at night was not probably the best strategy. I needed help. I went back upstairs and dialed Axel's room.

* * *

MAL

I walked. Stalked. Strode heedless through the empty streets, half hoping for trouble to present itself, as a violent confrontation would have been welcome just then.

But no attack came. The only trouble was brewing in my own head. How could she not see it? How could she let me do what she did? No: I could not rely on her to protect herself from me. To expect she would, merely placed the blame on her when it belonged squarely with me. The only solution was to stop altogether.

I was the one who could not leave well enough alone. I was the one who could not resist temptation.

Devil child. That was what my father had called me a very, very long time ago for defying him. Even at the time—eight or nine years old—my thought had been, *You don't know the half of it.*

Even Axel didn't know everything. In the years that we were apart, when he had gone back to the States and I was in boarding school? Those had been dark times.

Dark times. When I had hurt others as well as myself. The tattoo on my back largely obscured the scars I had inflicted on myself, in the days when I believed in penance, but they could still be felt.

I looked up and realized my feet had taken me all the way to the recording studio. It was located in an old industrial building that now had offices and art studios in it, and I could see the lights burning several floors up. Our studio's floor.

Curiosity, a desire to get out of the cold, inevitability, all pushed me to go upstairs. I punched the key code on the entry pad and rode the elevator up.

The music that met my ears when the doors opened was familiar, something Axel and I had listened to on repeat for days on end when we were teenagers. Nine Inch Nails.

I looked into the listening room to see who was there and was not wholly surprised to see Axel. The listening room was a conference room with surround-sound speakers, a boardroom table in the middle, and low black leather armchairs along two walls. Axel was at the head of the table, twirling a pen in his fingers. In front of him I recognized one of his old notebooks of lyrics and song ideas.

"Oh, hey, Mal," he said casually. "What are you doing up at this time of night?"

"I had a fight with Gwen," I said baldly, and threw myself tiredly into an armchair. "What are you doing here?"

He picked up the remote next to him and cut the music off. "Just trying to figure out if I can really live with some of these songs."

"What do you mean? I thought we settled on which songs we're using."

He ran his fingers through his hair, sighing. "I'm having serious second thoughts about whether I can really get up there in front of thousands of people and say some of the things that are in them."

That didn't strike me as much like Axel at all. "You're the one who has pushed the band's image the most in the kink and fetish direction. You can't be getting prudish all of a sudden."

He huffed, half laugh, half dismissal. "No, no, no. It's not the sex or kink that's a problem. It's all the... confessional self-loathing."

"Johns has no problem with the lyrical content," I pointed out, feeling my hackles starting to rise defensively. Most of the songs that we'd chosen, as it happened, were lyrically mine this time around.

Now Axel did laugh. "As you are fond of saying, Larkin Johns does not get the last word on what is or isn't a Rough song. I don't know, Mal. Maybe it'll be okay. I was just listening back to this old album trying to figure out where the line is. I mean, Trent Reznor really makes the dark self-loathing thing work, but... just... I don't know."

"Don't know what?" I moved to the table to look at what he had been writing but he closed the book.

"Never mind. I'll...come up with a way to make it work. I guess."

"Ax, you wouldn't be sitting in the studio at four in the morning if this was a small issue," I said.

"Well, all right, like this one, 'Inside.' It's kind of your version of 'Closer,' isn't it? In the second person, you can kind of read it as just an innuendo, but it doesn't have the uplift of 'Closer.' It reads as almost serial-killer level self-loathing."

I shifted uncomfortably in the chair. Axel was finally reading the song as I'd felt it was intended initially, but which I hadn't expected anyone to get. After all, songs like The Police's "Every Breath You Take," which was actually about a stalker, or R.E.M.'s "The One I Love," which is about an arsonist, were interpreted by most listeners as tender love ballads.

He leaned forward. "So... is this a bad time to ask about your fight with Gwen?"

I met his eyes. My oldest and best friend. "No. Now is the perfect time. I've decided I'm quitting kink."

Axel rubbed his eyes and looked at me. "You're what?"

"I asked Gwen to join me in quitting and she refused. I will not be adding her to the list of women I've ruined."

His jaw moved a couple of times before words finally came out: "*Ruined* is a pretty strong word, Mal."

"It's the word Camilla used for herself." I practically winced saying my cousin's name. I didn't even like hearing it out loud.

"You mean the cousin who pretty much cornered you and jumped onto your dick? Tell me again how you 'ruined' her? I was there, remember."

"I know. If you hadn't let slip that I wasn't a virgin anymore maybe she would have saved herself."

"For marriage, you mean?"

"Yes. I don't place any value on that rubbish but she—and her parents—certainly did."

"She's happily married and not even to some dickwad duke or something," Axel said with a shrug. "So maybe you did her a favor by 'ruining' her suitability to marry a prudish aristocrat."

"How do you know that?"

"Don't be thick, Mal. Social media. I checked her Facebook just the other day."

Axel was the type to friend everyone he ever met. "Just coincidentally?"

"Yes, it's a total coincidence I happened to look her up just when you need your head pried out of your ass. Listen. She's running a successful art gallery in London. Just finished photographing a whole series of nude self-portraits in famous British historical sites. Seriously, Mal. You might have been the spindle Cinderella pricked her finger on but it didn't put her to sleep. It woke her up. Camilla knew perfectly well what she was doing seducing you."

"Fine. Maybe things worked out for her. That doesn't mean I'm blameless. And there are others."

"I don't exactly see them lining up outside with torches and pitchforks."

"But you should."

Axel flipped to the back of his notebook where there was a pocket for loose sheets and pulled out several in my handwriting. Some of them were quite old. He flipped through them. "I don't know why I didn't see this theme before, but now it's really coming clear. You see yourself as a monster."

I stared at him. "You know I do."

He shook his head. "When I said Dracula was a phase you were going through, I was only kidding."

"It's not only Dracula, Ax. Think about it. The kinky one is always the villain. In every story."

He opened his mouth to argue, but I could see his eyes drifting as he tried to come up with counterexamples and could find none. From Catwoman to Baron Harkonnen to Zod. "Jeez. In the movies the kinky villain is always British, too. What is up with that?"

"Perhaps it reflects an inner truth," I said.

He laughed. "Or perhaps you've taken it entirely too much to heart. I mean, I know we all need role models, but Mal—"

I stood up, too discomfited by his flippant conclusions about my inner angst to subject myself to them any longer.

He stood, too, and caught me by the arm. "Listen. I know I don't sound serious, but I am. Just because the only representations of kink and desire you've ever seen are negative, are evil, doesn't make you evil. I *know* you."

"This isn't some facile air I fancy," I said, shrugging free.

"I know. Look, I remember us being ten years old and even then you were talking about the Need."

My blood ran cold. I didn't recall actually confessing that to him. "I told you about that?"

"You did. I let you hang me upside down from an apple tree and pelt me with apples until I begged you to stop."

I sat back down, my legs suddenly nerveless. "I don't even remember that."

"After you let me down, *you* were the one who cried, which made no sense to me at all. I wasn't actually hurt. I was quite proud of myself, actually." He made a fist like he was showing off his biceps. "But you told me you thought you were *possessed*, like in some book you'd read."

I had no memory of this. Had I meant what I said or had that been a story, too? "Did you read the book? Did I lend it to you?"

"You did, but I didn't really get into it the way you did. I'd forgotten all about it until we saw that film premiere." He sat down beside me again. "Listen, you think you want to quit kink? That's like gay people thinking they can be cured of homosexuality."

"This isn't the same."

"Pretty sure it is. I think the Need is just sadism, Mal. That's all. It's not good or evil; it just is. We've swallowed so many messages about sex itself being evil, desire being the devil, even before you get to talking about kink. You have to get past that, man."

"You've always had a more robust enjoyment of your sexuality than I have," I told him.

That made him cackle. "Robust enjoyment. I was a horny kid and I grew into a horny man, that's all. Jeez, there it is again, you know? Even the word *horny* is supposed to be the devil horns, right? How about *randy* instead. I was a randy kid and I'm randy now."

"But you don't get off on causing Ricki pain."

"Well, not exactly. I like to spank her and flog her and stuff, but it's all part of controlling her, of taking this incredibly powerful woman and knowing she bows to no one except me. It's why we're so into bondage and restraints, control and making her mine." He picked up the pen and twirled it again. "Sadism and masochism are just one small thread in what we do. For us, it's more about the total package of ultimate trust."

I looked at my hands. The fingertips of the left were dull from guitar calluses, the palm of my right seemed redder than the other, as if all the times I had reddened it while spanking Gwen had left it permanently ruddy. Perhaps it was my imagination. "For me, it starts and ends with pain. Pain is how I know I'm alive. But I learned long ago that it is even better to give than receive."

"So that's what you've been doing for two weeks in your hotel room? Smacking her around?"

"Yes," I said, for the sake of the argument, but I felt that burn in the pit of my stomach that I felt whenever I lied to someone close to me. "Well, no." My mind was full of the sensation of her sleeping in my arms, of the fierce protective urge that seized me whenever I pushed her physical limits. "A little of that, a lot of sex, and even more talk and sleep." I shook my head, as if it would make all the ideas circling in my head settle down. "I still fear that under it all, I'm merely a very well-behaved psychopath."

"What makes you say that?"

"How else do you explain these delusions that spring up? Like after I'm done hurting her, how I rush to patch her up and make sure she's all right. I gaslight her into thinking it wasn't that bad at all so that I can do it all again, so she'll keep letting me do it."

His face was skeptical. Incredulous. "You *really* think you convince her it wasn't so bad and that that's why she lets you do it again? Does she set limits and do you respect them? Do you negotiate?"

"Yes, but it's camouflage."

"I dunno, Mal, I think after two weeks if she didn't like it, she'd have said something. I really don't think she would have come to Montreal when *I asked* her to if it was because she was under some delusion you planted."

"She's never refused me."

"Never?"

Except tonight, I realized, when I'd tried to prove . . . what, exactly? "Once," I said. "Tonight."

"So she put her foot down to protect herself after all and you walked out in a huff?"

"No! Wait . . . " I felt like the cartoon character who gets tricked into arguing his opponent's point. Gwen *had* asserted herself. "I was . . . trying to make a point to her about fantasy and reality, that she needed to stop living in a fantasy world."

"And it sounds like she asserted reality pretty strongly, Mal."

He had a point, but so did I.

"I'm a terrible person for using her to further the band's ends."

Axel made a frustrated noise. "The only thing that will make

Gwen feel used is if you break it off with her now. Honestly, Mal, just because you want to run from your demons doesn't mean you have to run from *her.* You're afraid of hurting her? That's what you're doing by pushing her away. Trust me on this."

"I want to believe you," I said. "I want to believe that I actually love her and not that my twisted brain makes me act like I do so I can feed my sadism."

Axel reached over and squeezed my hand before letting it go. "Listen. We all love and accept you the way you are. But you bottle up a lot of rage, Mal. You know why I think you rush to patch her up?"

"Why?"

"Same reason you did it for me when we were kids."

"Because I was overcome with remorse for having hurt you?"

"No. I don't think that was it at all. I think it was that once you let the rage out, the positive emotions could finally come to the fore. I think that's your real 'Need.'"

"I think you have been watching too many pop psychology TV shows," I growled, and pushed back from the table. Was he right? I almost wanted to reach over and shake some sense into him, but maybe that only proved that he had hit close to home.

I walked back to the hotel with my thoughts as tumultuous as they had been on the previous walk.

What if you're wrong, Axel? Whenever one of these shooters is caught or killed, his friends and neighbors always say they never suspected he was violent.

Axel wouldn't say that about me. He knew I was a sadist. He knew me very well.

Maybe he also had to say whatever he could to keep everyone in the band on an even keel. Maybe he would say whatever he thought I needed to hear, whether it was true or not. Who was gaslighting now?

I sat for a while in the hotel lobby, but as morning neared I did not want to linger there. What was I going to say to Gwen when I got upstairs? I was fatigued and did not relish having the same fight all over again.

But when I reached the room I found her absent. A note that looked hastily written was on the bed. It read:

Mal,

I know who I am and kink isn't just a fun game or a compulsion—it's a part of me. I've never felt so rejected or invalidated as you made me feel tonight. Maybe someday you'll see that.

Gwen

CHAPTER SIXTEEN

FLY

GWEN

I was in the airport on the way home when I saw the e-mail from my agent about the video job. *I should have seen this coming,* I thought. Of *course* the music video Simon had been talking about was for The Rough. I'd even introduced him to Christina. In fact, reading his e-mail again, it made it sound like he thought I already knew it was going to be a Rough video.

Very rough. I wondered if Mal knew or if he would find out when he got back to town. Was he going to accuse me of stalking him for taking the job?

Should I even take the job?

As soon as Axel had called to let me know he'd seen Mal at the studio, that Mal was being as stubborn as ever and that he was on the way back to the hotel, I decided not to be there when he returned. There was no way I could listen to all that about quitting kink again. I caught a cab directly to the airport.

It had not been difficult to get a flight once the ticket agent realized I wasn't concerned with the price. I had just enough time to grab some coffee and breakfast before it was time to board.

The world felt strange around me—not just because it was Canada, where everything was almost the same but not quite—but because I hadn't been in the real world in two weeks. I fumbled taking my change from the cashier at the coffee stand while behind me a dozen people waited impatiently for me to get my act together. I juggled my open wallet, the coffee, and the croissant in a paper wrapper as I tried to get to a table before I dropped everything. Thank goodness a businesswoman got up and left the one near the counter. I made it there without spilling anything but then burned my tongue on my first sip.

I wondered if maybe there was something wrong with me, if maybe everything was somehow my fault.

I wanted to go back to being the best version of myself, not a klutzy, neurotic wreck. Was that what Mal had been trying to say, that the real me wasn't good enough? No, he'd never said that. If anything, all he'd said was that the real version *of himself* wasn't good enough, but maybe that was the message I was supposed to hear that he was too polite to say.

That was when I checked my e-mail and saw the one from Simon with the details. Where to be, what time. The concreteness of the news grounded me and immediately stopped my neurotic slide.

I was still contemplating whether I should back out, though, when I read a little farther into Simon's e-mail, which described the director's concept for the video and how it was like a mini-movie. They might even try to turn it into a short to enter into film festivals.

The director was Miles Redlace.

There was no way I was backing out of this job. I typed back an answer hoping I sounded enthusiastic, helpful, cheerful, and professional, or at least not like a sad weirdo who'd just been roundly rejected by the man she willingly served as a sex slave for two weeks.

I felt a flare of deep chagrin, my cheeks as hot as the coffee. I bit angrily into the croissant. Out here in the real world that was what it looked like, didn't it? I'd just let a man fuck me six ways from Sunday—*two* Sundays, in fact—and then he threw me away. All his talk about how he did it because he loved me seemed like just that, nothing but a story, a fairy tale.

God, I hate you, Mal Kenneally, I thought as tears prickled my eyes. Then I shook my head. What the hell kind of a thought was that? I looked down at the tiny hole in the lid of the coffee cup, at the wisp of steam coming out of it, trying to get a grip on reality. *This is the world,* I thought. *This is how the outside world would see us, if they knew.* The tabloid version of our story. But I also knew all too well that the tabloid version of reality wasn't reality at all.

It would be easy to fall into, though. A comforting, consensual delusion where nymphomaniac women are preyed upon by manslut rock stars. If I could believe in that reality I could hate Mal and move on.

The thought was almost tempting.

But my sister and Axel's relationship ran smack dab into that delusion. And so did the burning in my heart that had nothing to do with coffee, the solid fist grasping the core of the truth. I loved Mal, he loved me, and that love was built on *something* deep inside us that didn't fit the outside world's ideas. That *something* could only come out in music and acting and the reality we made for ourselves when we were together.

Maybe there was no way to prove it to him. Maybe Mal was actually incapable of seeing it. Maybe he truly didn't feel the bond between us, and it was my imagination after all. If so, maybe the relationship was doomed, and there was nothing to do but cry and try to move on...

No. Don't give up. You're not going to give up on your acting career or Mal's stubborn attitude. Hate the culture and the people who made him that way if you have to hate something. I cursed the family and the exes who must have taught Mal he didn't deserve love.

I looked up and realized I'd just heard "Los Angeles" coming from somewhere. A gate announcement? My coffee had gone cold, the croissant was still in my hand with a bite taken out of it, and they were calling my flight. I gulped down a few more swallows of the coffee, then threw it and the croissant into the trash and ran as fast as I could, panicking the entire way to the gate.

I made it onto the plane, and in first class they fed me, and then I actually slept almost the entire way to LAX. I decided to take it as a sign that things were going to start going right.

* * *

MAL

The phone rang. I picked it up, saying nothing.

Axel's voice: "Wake-up call."

"What makes you think I slept?"

"That bad, eh? Did you guys fight all night?"

"No. She's gone."

"Ah." He cleared his throat nervously. "Um, does that mean we should call off the studio session for today?"

"Of course not."

"Of course not?"

I was in no mood to explain. "See you there in an hour." I hung up the phone and then attempted to stand. I had been sitting at the side of the bed without moving for enough hours that my back and legs were stiff. Since coming in and discovering Gwen was gone—her toothbrush, her suitcase, completely gone—all I had done was sit there and think.

In fact, for a while I didn't even think. I merely sat there in shock. Her absence hit me hard, like a chunk of my head had been torn away.

You idiot, I thought. *You wanted her to leave.*

But it felt nothing like a victory to have her gone. Not that I had been expecting it to; I had been expecting it to hurt. When I told her I cared for her, loved her, it was true. That still wasn't enough to bridge the yawning chasm between what she needed and what the Need would let me be.

I stood in the shower for far too long, my mind caught in a loop, the water too hot but somehow I couldn't bring myself to lessen my suffering. Perhaps I was reminding myself I was alive.

The studio, the band, the album beckoned. How could things that were so important to me seem so insignificant all of a sudden? I felt as if I were deep down in a dark well, and everything in my life was contained within the bright circle that looked so small and distant above me it may as well not be real.

I forced myself to put on socks. To put on trousers. A band T-shirt would do. In the bathroom with the comb in my hand I discovered the folly of standing under the water for so long after such a wild and restless night: the bottom twelve inches or so of my hair were an impenetrable mass of tangles. I took the knife from the pile of sex toys that I had amassed in the past two weeks and sawed it off just below my shoulders.

Some fan would probably pay thousands for the mass of hair in my hand, I thought bitterly. I chucked it into the trash. So much for love.

I encountered Axel at the elevator. He looked openly shocked at my appearance. "She dumped you?" he asked, sounding confused.

I merely shook my head and said nothing.

"Look, we really don't have to go into the studio today—"

"If you are worried that the destruction of my relationship with Gwen will negatively impact my attitude with Larkin Johns, you are mistaken," I said evenly as we got into the elevator. "I promise you I shall be docile as a lamb."

"A lamb bit me at a petting zoo when I was five." Axel showed me one of his fingers. "You can still see the scar."

"You're not funny, Ax."

"You're not exactly a laugh riot yourself," he said. "Seriously, Mal, what happened?"

I shook my head. "She finally took all my exhortations to leave to heart, and she left. At least the record's mostly done."

"Small consolation," Axel said. "I feel like it's my fault. I mean, fuck, I—"

"It's not your fault." The elevator doors opened and I strode out into the lobby.

Axel caught up to me and we got in a cab together but he stayed silent this time, perhaps unable to come up with a suitable tactic to broach the subject again. Or perhaps, like me, he had decided to focus on the day's work instead. I expected a grueling day since much of what remained to be done was tedious redubbing work and filling in gaps.

Then again, perhaps that was a saving grace. Redubbing I could do with my brain and fingers on autopilot and my heart turned off.

The first few hours passed without incident. Then we began work on a song entitled "My True Soul." Axel and I had cowritten the lyrics, and the song had a bridge with a vocal line and a guitar line repeating like a call and answer. As we listened to it, though, quite suddenly Chino put his hands over his eyes trying not to laugh. He waved a hand though, as if to say, *Ignore me.*

A few moments later, Samson's eyes widened and he burst out laughing, too.

Johns looked around. "Something wrong?"

Samson gestured for him to go back. "Play the bridge again."

Johns started the song again from an earlier point and Axel's voice, soaring with heavy reverb, sang, "A soul, a soul, a soul!" This time it caused the two of them to laugh uncontrollably.

"Oh my God," Ford said, and put his head down on the conference room table, also laughing.

Axel and I looked at each other and then he put a hand to his forehead. "*Oh my God* is right. It sounds like I'm singing 'asshole, asshole.'"

"It doesn't *really*," Chino said, eyes still crinkled from laughter, "but once you hear it, you can't unhear it, and the more you repeat it the more hilarious it gets."

I could see why they were laughing even though I couldn't feel any mirth myself at that moment. I couldn't feel much of anything. It was as if I were in a tank, underwater, while they were all on the surface, and I could only see and hear them from far away. Later we took a conference call from Marcus about the video they planned us to shoot when we got back to LA. I barely absorbed the details. We'd all be going back to California, but I was at the bottom of a well where I couldn't feel anything.

CHAPTER SEVENTEEN

NO STRINGS

GWEN

My call was for three in the afternoon at a private address north of the city. I would have almost thought it was sketchy to be showing up at a residential house except for the production trailers in the circular driveway. The house had a modernist architectural look to it. I went up to the front door but a short woman with her dark straight hair cut in a pageboy waved to me from the nearest trailer.

"Gwen?" She was waving a tablet and she had a walkie-talkie on her hip.

"Sorry," I said, hurrying up to her. "All I had was the address."

"No worries. I'm Nancy Cho, the assistant director. Miles is still with the band at the soundstage, so we're a little behind schedule, but we can get you started with wardrobe and I'll fill you in while you're in the makeup chair, okay?"

"Sounds great!" And it did. Here I'd been bracing myself for Miles Redlace to start insulting me the minute I walked in, and he wasn't even here. There was this nice woman with an air of competence about her instead.

She introduced me to the wardrobe person and they discussed the scenes, deciding we should film some scenes with me in a bathrobe first. Not only that, but these would be scenes of me putting on makeup, so that meant the makeup artist would have to make me look like I wasn't wearing makeup.

While I was in the chair and the makeup person was layering up translucent powder on my face, Nancy told me more about the video. "So the concept is you're a trophy wife to an older, rich man, and this young rock star sweeps you off your feet and rescues you from a life without passion."

"Okay."

"So there will be some story scenes, intercut with some band performance footage and also some artistic lip synch shots where the singer is saying the words while trailing a knife up and down your back. Since the title of the song is 'Razor Sharp.'"

"Do the young wife and the rock star run away at the end?"

"I'm not sure if there will be an actual shot of the escape or if it will merely be implied," Nancy said. "Why?"

"The video is supposed to get people to like the band and the song, right? People might be kind of down on the idea that they're, you know, cheating. Committing adultery."

"Hmm, I hadn't thought of that. Here, have a look at the plot notes while I take this phone call." She handed me her tablet and I read through the synopsis and scene-by-scene plan while the makeup artist worked on my eyebrows.

When Nancy came back, I handed her the tablet. "I'm sure it's going to be great, but it's so obvious a man wrote this."

She chuckled. "Is it?"

"Maybe it's just that my sister is on this whole campaign about how media for women should actually be aimed at women, so we talk about this stuff all the freakin' time, but this video is really aimed at the guys in the audience, and I think most of the fans of The Rough are women who might be turned off by this whole thing."

"You think? But it's a romance where she gets her happy ending; she runs off with the hot guy."

"Yes, but really it's about the two men fighting and the woman is just the prize. And that's emphasized by the fact that the lip synch segments call for a naked woman's back and hips to be visible. It's like soft-core porno for guys."

"Hmm. Well, I suppose we could have the singer shirtless, too? For the sake of equality. If their other videos are any indication, Axel has no problem being nearly naked."

Oh, right, of course it would be Axel playing the part of the young guy. I had somehow been picturing Mal. Of course I had. I wondered if Mal was even going to be present for this part of the filming.

"This isn't about you being unwilling to do those segments, is it?" Nancy asked tentatively. "I can assure you no actual nudity is required. But if it's really a problem we can get a body double."

"No, no, not a problem. I'm just, you know, overthinking everything as usual." What was I doing, criticizing the script? "I know I'm just the talent. I have a tendency to think out loud. The thing is, I know the band a little—you might already know that—and I think they might be uncomfortable portraying one of them as a cheater. I mean, I know they have a 'bad boy' image and all, but this is a little beyond that."

"No worries," Nancy assured me with a smile. "I'll make sure their manager is good with this image-wise or we'll make some changes. Now let's get you into the master bedroom and film some B-roll of you putting your lipstick and jewelry on like you're getting ready to go out for a fancy evening."

We spent the next hour with me primping in front of a mirror while they filmed extreme close-ups of my face, lips, lashes, ears, all while I was supposed to express depths of hidden sadness.

It was a lot easier to do than you'd think. Guess why.

* * *

MAL

I could not have told you what I ate in the time between returning to Los Angeles and the video shoot. I could make some guesses, but I could not have told you what it tasted like. It was like all my senses had shut down. Like without Gwen in my world, there was no reason to open my eyes, or to smell, taste, or touch. The condo seemed very empty. My life seemed very empty. I wasn't even feeling the pain of having lost her so much at that point as . . . dead. I'd gone from a vampire or werewolf who needs too much to a monster that didn't need anything at all, a zombie who didn't even hunger for brains.

In a way, perhaps this was what I was trying to achieve all along. I no longer hungered. I no longer felt the Need. Greed did not own me. I wondered if this was how people who sold all their possessions and became monks felt.

I wondered if I should quit the band. If I was really going to make a completely clean break with any kind of kink, it seemed it might be inevitable. I did not have the energy to contemplate it much, though. Right then, trying to think more than a day or two ahead was beyond me.

The first day of video shooting began as it often did, with the prettifying of our faces and hair—a necessary evil given the lights used for filming—and then us mock-playing through the song on a soundstage that had been made up with risers and lights and fog machines. Typical stuff. I had heard this director was supposed to be some kind of conceptual genius, but I lacked the will to question the motions we went through.

It meant hearing "Razor Sharp" a few hundred times that day, sometimes only a few lines over and over as they strove to get the shot they wanted, with Axel's hair flipping just so in the wind machine or my fingers sliding up the neck of the guitar.

My entire life has been a race
To not become the thing I hate

I wrote that. At the time I'd used the word *race* rather than *fight* because it sounded better with *hate*. But now, hearing it over and over, I couldn't help but think, had I paused to consider that in this race, if I slowed down, I might be caught by the shadow pursuing me? I'd been referring to the way my parents and their ilk had allowed greed to warp their values. All the times I'd told myself I did something for the sake of the band's success, had I merely been fooling myself into thinking I wasn't like my parents because being a successful rock musician wasn't something they would have supported? Yet success meant I'd created a large amount of wealth for the record company, and not an insignificant amount for myself and my bandmates.

Some of whom put the money to good use. Axel had bought a house for his mother, for example. We all gave to charity, me more than the others. Was that really enough to assuage my guilty worry that I was turning out exactly as I'd feared?

No, I told myself, *that's the only good thing to come out of the Gwen situation. You are finally learning to resist and eliminate the Need. The Need is just another form of greed, inappropriately transferred from material possessions to possession of a woman's body.*

These were the thoughts that occupied my mind while we filmed. So it was somewhat startling to see the script that Redlace handed around to us while we were in the shuttle bus taking us and the crew from the soundstage to the next location for filming.

Redlace was a tall man who looked to be in his mid-thirties but slightly balding. He ran a hand through his dark hair as he stood in the aisle of the shuttle bus to address us and only succeeded in making a tuft of it stick up oddly.

"As you'll see, I've taken the song and interpreted it as a plea for heart and passion to win out over material possession and appearances. Roderick Grisham will be playing the part of the rich husband and a young ingenue whom I think you are familiar with will be playing the part of the trophy wife—Gwen Hamilton." He punctuated this announcement with a wink in my direction.

I blinked and shot a look at Christina, who was sitting next to the director at the front of the bus. She gave me an innocent look in return.

A truly innocent look. After all, Christina knew nothing of the Montreal meltdown between me and Gwen. So I couldn't really blame her. I'd been planning to simply tell her *no* the next time she tried to fix us up for publicity. It hadn't occurred to me there would be another opportunity to cross paths with Gwen in a professional realm.

Everyone was quiet for a while, reading the script. Axel was cast as the hero of the piece, meeting the heroine at a posh function in a Cinderella moment, her losing her shoe. Did Redlace really think invoking a clichéd old fairy tale was cutting edge? Besides, the overall message didn't seem all that radical to me. Old rich guy loses trophy wife to sexier, younger rich guy...? Not exactly a rousing moral.

I reminded myself I didn't care.

They brought us to a multilevel house on a hill, white-stuccoed with flat roofs and huge plate-glass windows, making me wonder if Redlace was planning a stone-throwing scene as well. We were shepherded into a rec room down near the garage on the house's lowest level that had been converted into a temporary production office and staff lounge. An instantly recognizable man was sitting on a sectional sofa there, sipping a cup of tea.

"It's my pleasure to introduce you to Roderick Grisham," the director said.

"We've met," I said. "Mr. Grisham, nice to see you again. I was quite impressed by your turn in *Midnight*."

"Oh, I would have much rather played the monster, you know, but they want someone young and devastatingly good-looking for those roles these days and alas I'm no longer young," he said wryly, making me chuckle. "Still, such an honor to work with Ariadne Wood. I was like a schoolboy on Christmas when they told us she was due to visit the set. She's quite reclusive, you know, so I'd never had the pleasure. Such a gracious woman, one of England's best. The only reason she hasn't received every literary accolade we offer is that so little value is placed on fantasy. Imagine that! We penalize writers for taking full use of their imagination. We want them to be imaginative, but only a small bit. The establishment is so terribly small-minded."

A female voice from behind me added, "I would bet if she hadn't been a woman she might have had an easier time of it, too."

"Oh, quite right, quite right, Gwen," Grisham harrumphed, taking her hand and tucking it into his arm. "Kenneally, have you met this charming young lady yet? May I present Ms. Gwen Hamilton, who will be my costar on this production."

The moment I had heard her voice, my heart had turned to a lump of stone. I could barely swallow, and I turned stiffly toward her.

Gwen offered me her hand as if she were a stranger, and I

kissed it as if she were one, even though she said, "Yes. Mal and I know one another."

"Ah, but of course!" Grisham said suddenly, tapping his forehead with his fingers. "You introduced me to her, didn't you, Kenneally? At the *Midnight* premiere. No wonder you two are giving me such sideways looks."

Yes, yes, let him think that was what he was picking up on, not that I was paralyzed by her presence. *Gwen.*

"Okay, folks, have a seat," said an Asian woman who hurried into the room. "We'd like to get some of these exterior shots done before we lose the light." As everyone seated themselves around the sectional sofa and on the armchairs by a nearby wall-mounted flatscreen, she gave way to Redlace himself.

"All right, you've all seen the script, but it's been brought to my attention that, ah, there are a couple of elements we might want to tweak to keep in line with band image. I may be a total diva about some things but honestly, people, Basic is paying me a fuckton of money to do this and I'm not exactly bucking for an Oscar with it. So let me hear you: Is the adultery theme going to alienate your fan base or the American public at large?"

"Adultery is not 'on brand,'" Christina piped up.

"I didn't think you guys had to worry about looking squeaky clean, but yeah, I don't want you to just look like a bunch of worthless fuckboys either." He gave a nod in Christina's direction and took a long swallow from the aluminum thermos he was carrying before he went on. "Frankly, I wrote this script while sitting on the crapper a couple of weeks ago and then I forgot about it. I'm, shall we say, not attached to anything in it. Our main constraint is we've only got two and a half more days of shooting on the schedule and we've already booked locations and wardrobe, obviously. So any changes we make can't be too radical. You get me?"

No one said anything for a few seconds, though a few people glanced at each other. Gwen raised her hand. "Mr. Redlace?"

"Oh my God, call me Miles or I'll have flashbacks to that time I was a substitute teacher and let me tell you it wasn't pretty."

Gwen nodded and smiled. "Miles, okay." She wasn't the slightest bit intimidated by him being a Hollywood big shot, and that was good. She was merely polite. "How about instead of being the trophy wife, she's the guy's daughter, and he's a widower who's overprotected her all her life?"

Redlace raised his eyebrow and opened his mouth as if he were about to object, held the pose for a moment, and then said, "Go on."

"When we were filming the getting ready scenes upstairs, I saw the props people had created—family photos that are all over her dresser. So I thought the past history of the family could be shown in the photos."

Redlace turned to the woman next to him. "Nancy? Oh, by the way, everyone, this is Nancy Cho, my right hand. My right brain, sometimes."

"Hi," she said, and barreled right into answering the question. "Yeah, we can totally do that. Easy. I had another thought, too, Miles."

"Go on."

"I'm not totally happy with the way we've got the cameos for all the band members planned. I know the original idea was to have them appearing as gardeners, deliverymen, and so on. It feels corny and like it might detract from the drama of the house scenes. My thought was—and feel free to shoot me down guys if you find this offensive—to make this banquet thing we're shooting tomorrow into a wedding, and you guys be the wedding band."

The director was nodding his head. "Good, good, I like it. Very organic."

"We can totally ham it up as the wedding band," Axel said.

I cleared my throat and said, "My objection is that the story merely transfers the woman as trophy property from one rich man to another. Not exactly uplifting or radical."

"Gwen said almost the same thing." Nancy snapped her fingers. "That's why it's brilliant! Now it'll be one of the musicians in the band who gets her, right?"

"Yes, yes!" Miles enthused. "Much better from a promo standpoint and also great job striking a blow for the artistic underclass. But is it still... cheating?"

"Not if she's his *daughter*," Gwen reminded him. "In fact, that could be why they elope. The musician should propose to her, and after the father refuses, they elope."

Grisham spoke up gleefully. "Oh, yes, that is so much better, because now I can play the heartbroken widower whose own emotional scars have caused him to utterly ruin his daughter's life to this point. Such pathos."

The director was nodding his head vigorously. "I like it, I like it. That's way more dramatic than the crap I came up with. You're right, gives you a lot more to work with. The reason the father can't go along with the proposal, it's not just class snobbery; it's that being widowed left him so twisted and broken he can't bear the thought of the daughter—who is the spitting image of her mother—leaving him!"

No one spoke for a few moments, and I wondered if that meant the meeting was over, but apparently Miles was not yet done and those who had worked with him before sensed this.

"It still could use a little edge." Miles stood there, thinking, while everyone watched him. Then he upended the coffee down his throat and slammed the thermos down on the coffee table. "Yes! I have it! Tell me if this is too much—it's going to be a huge challenge for the two actors involved. But after the proposal, right? She goes to her father to say, *Daddy, look at my ring. I said yes,* and he goes berserk and tries to force himself on her. Father-daughter insanity-driven incest. Doesn't get much more challenging than that."

"Um...," Christina said. "Um... about the band's image—"

"Oh, oh, oh, of course, but what I forgot to say is that our hero of course breaks in and stops it before it can happen," Miles said. "Then they run away with totally clear consciences because, come on, *ew*. Right? Am I right?"

Christina nodded. "Okay. That works! That totally works."

He turned to Grisham and Gwen. "I know Roddy can handle the challenge, but, Gwen, this might be a tad bit more than you signed up for."

"Bring it on," Gwen said, her chin in the air. "I like a challenge."

"Okay, great, let's get to—"

Axel raised his hand like a schoolboy and even said in a parody of a whiny schoolboy voice, "Um, Mr. Redlace? I have one more question."

"Ha-ha, sure. What is it?"

"Well, it's more of a suggestion. I'm thinking it should really be Mal who does the scenes with Gwen, while I do the lip synch scenes with the knife. See, then I sort of represent the force of desire metatextually, while Mal can just, you know, be badass. He's the one with the badass look, after all."

Nancy waved her hands excitedly. "He can break in by smashing a window with an electric guitar! That would be the most stunning visual!"

"He's the one connected with Gwen in the press," Christina pointed out. "That would be perfect."

I groaned inwardly. Perfect. Yes. Ugh. Well, it would be acting, not real, so I supposed I could put up with anything for two days. It did sound like I was going to get to smash a gigantic window.

"Great! Get the band into the wardrobe trailer to get outfitted and the camera crew should meet me and Roddy in the upstairs bedroom to tackle some establishing shots," Redlace said. "Nobody wander off. When you're off, stay in this room. Feel free to watch the TV. We won't be using the ambient sound from these shots, after all."

Off to the wardrobe trailer I went, feeling Gwen's eyes following me until I was out of sight.

* * *

GWEN

The second day of shooting, we arrived at the ballroom of a local hotel where I'd actually attended society functions in the past. Set dressers were adding extra red velvet drapes and chandeliers, though, because apparently it didn't look posh enough. A few dozen bored extras in formal wear sat around banquet tables checking their phones. The band was in matching tuxes with black velvet lapels.

I had brought a few pairs of my own dress shoes, not trusting that they were going to have something that would fit me well and that I could walk in a ball gown. This turned out to be wise when a full hour of the filming was me walking past the stage where the band was playing and making eye contact with Mal.

Yes, for a full hour, my job was to take these same fifteen or twenty steps over and over and look Mal full in the eyes. They did it from many different angles, with the cameras on the stage, on a dolly beside me, with a handheld close to my face, from over Mal's shoulder, from behind me toward him, and so on. "Seems silly, I know," Miles said, "but this is the *aha* moment, the love at first sight that makes the whole thing go. So it's got to be this hugely significant *zap* of connection."

We got set, me with one arm draped through Roderick's and did that first take.

"Cut, cut, cut!" Miles hurried up to us. "Gwen, when I said 'zap,' I didn't mean like you were trying to fry him with laser beams from your eyes."

"Oh, sorry! I was...just trying to get the angle right!" I blushed a little. I guess I had let a little too much of my upset with Mal show through. I also couldn't get used to how short his hair was—long for a regular guy but short for Mal.

"Remember, you're an overprotected ingenue who looks up and sees...sees..." Miles gestured with his ever-present coffee caddy in his hand, trying to find the right word.

"An angel?" I suggested.

He nodded. "Your salvation from the trap of your life. Yes. And Mal, you've got to return that look like you've never seen a woman so beautiful, like you practically want to just walk off the stage and follow her because you've fallen in love on the spot. Look at her like you're holding yourself back from saying 'I love you' right then and there."

So, twenty, thirty, maybe forty times I did that walk, sometimes with a tiny flutter in my lashes as I looked up, sometimes without, and Mal looked right down into my eyes like he adored me more than anything.

After the hand-held camera work, when they were readying the dolly, I saw him sit on the edge of the riser and try to dab his eyes surreptitiously on his velvet-cuffed sleeve.

Roderick saw it, too, and pulled the handkerchief from his pocket. "Here you are."

"It's nothing," Mal said, waving the cloth aside.

"Dear boy, it is most certainly not nothing. If it were, I would be out of a job."

I had turned my back to them, pretending to be watching the cameraman adjust something, but my ears strained to hear.

"Let me give you a bit of advice," Roderick said. "The secret to being a good actor is to own those emotions."

"I'm not an actor," Mal insisted.

"Today you are," Roderick said sharply, as if affronted that Mal might undertake his duties with less than one-hundred percent commitment. "People think our job is to pretend. They're wrong. Our job is to be real. Even if only in the moment. You have to believe what you say and you have to feel what you feel. What emotion provoked this reaction? Yearning? It looked like yearning."

"Yes," Mal said simply.

"You're doing fine." The elder actor patted him on the shoulder and then the camera was ready and we went back to it.

The next scene was a ballroom dance scene. I congratulated myself again for bringing shoes that fit.

"Let's establish Dad's inappropriate feelings toward his daughter here," Miles said. "Gwen, your attention should keep trying to go to the band onstage, while you go through this increasingly awkward dance. At the end we'll have you pull away somewhat suddenly, and then, Roderick, you'll stumble and fall drunkenly. Gwen, you'll hurry over to help him."

Well, that at least was a reaction I was familiar with. My own father had gotten falling down drunk a lot when I was younger, though he'd been sober for a couple of months now. Well, unless he fell off the wagon in St. Maarten. I resolved to call him tonight when I got home.

"You'll excuse me for touching you in entirely inappropriate ways, my dear," Roderick said. "But when he says 'action,' I am about to become a dirty old man."

For my part, it wouldn't have been so long ago I would have been simply thrilled to ballroom dance with Roderick Grisham, who starred in many of the BBC shows I loved so much. But my role here wasn't to be impressed by this lauded A-list actor. It was to play a girl getting more and more creeped out by her father.

Like he had told Mal, you have to make it real, but I couldn't think about my own father here. Instead I thought about how I felt, how confused and horrified but not quite sure if it was really happening, when Mal had taken me into that restroom with those waiters.

And so it went. As we turned and moved, I swiveled my head to keep looking toward Mal, whose expression went from dark to darker as the filming went on. At one point Miles even commented, "You look like you're ready to leap off the stage and beat him off her with that guitar. Excellent. Keep it up."

The final shots we needed at the ballroom site were by the bathrooms. They let the extras go, since this would be mostly me and Mal alone, with just a few people going in and out of the restroom entrances: Ford and Nancy.

The script called for us to meet by chance by the entrance. I couldn't help but remember running into him at that record company event—the event that led directly to this one because I'd introduced my agent to his band's manager.

"Make awkward small talk. Doesn't matter what you actually say as long as you look haltingly tentative," Miles said from beside the camera.

"Um, hello," Mal said, looking very convincingly unsure of himself.

"Hi."

He cleared his throat. "Nice, um, nice party, isn't it?"

"Yes, rather." I glanced behind me as Nancy entered the women's room. "This, um, reminds me of that time you accused me of stalking you."

"Me too. Small world, isn't it?" He cringed like he knew he was bombing badly, which of course was perfect for his character.

Ford exited the men's room and Mal stepped closer to me, one arm curving protectively between me and the "stranger" before he realized what he was doing, and dropped it suddenly.

"Great, great!" Miles enthused. "Do it again."

* * *

MAL

Fate is doing this to torture me. This was my thought as I spent hour after hour having to moon at Gwen, talk to Gwen, surreptitiously pass Gwen's banquet table to leave a cut flower by her plate, under director's orders to surreptitiously brush her bare shoulder as I went.

Torture. A true test of my resolve to leave kink and therefore Gwen behind.

Seeing her now and knowing I could no longer run my fingers through her hair anytime I wished made my fingers ache. Knowing I could not steal a kiss when the camera was off made my jaw clench. To have her so near but to know we were a million miles apart in our heads made me want to reach out and shake some sense into her... or maybe just reach out. Maybe I needed to get myself into therapy to cure myself of these urges.

No. I just needed to be stronger, that was all. It was time to grow up and quit living in a childish fantasy world. Difficult to do when they were requiring me to play an elaborate game of "let's pretend" in front of the camera. So be it. It wouldn't be the first time I did something unusual or difficult for the sake of the band. I found myself somewhat entranced watching Roderick Grisham ply the acting craft. He was so convincing, so thoroughly anguished, needy, broken, angered, jealous even though all they were doing was dancing, or walking, or whatever tiny segment of action the cameras were capturing. Then the camera would go off and he was instantly Roddy Grisham again.

I finally remarked on it during a break. "I'm still astonished how you do that."

"Do what, my boy?"

"Go from good to evil and vice versa in the blink of an eye."

He chuckled. "You don't seem the type to believe in simplistic manifestations of moral absolutes."

He caught me off guard. "Well, not as such—"

"There's no secret, really. We all have the ability to be hero or villain, to evoke sympathy or revulsion. It's all in knowing the audience. It is all context." He shrugged. "After all, what is a soldier but a hero to his homeland and a villain to his enemy? I would have thought someone with your stage name would embrace the complexity of the human need for violence."

His voice and accent were remarkably similar to an old headmaster of mine, but I respected Grisham far more. "Say that again," I heard myself say, as I tried to wrap my head around his words.

"That I expect you would grasp the subtleties of the human need for violence?"

"What do you mean, 'human need for violence'?"

"I mean we are not a domesticated enough animal not to fight one another. Without some urges to violence, we have no way to defend ourselves, and both the hero and the villain depend upon the same capacity for it. Is that not obvious to you?"

"I suppose I had not thought about it in quite those terms," I admitted.

"The capacity to harm is the capacity to defend," Grisham said.

I knew he was talking about it in the context of defending the nation from invasion, but I could not help but hear the words echo as I thought about the conundrum I had presented Axel with, my urge to cause pain followed by my urge to soothe and protect.

They gathered us around a banquet table when the filming at that location was finished, to go over the schedule. I stared at the paper they handed me instead of at Gwen, who was still in her ball gown but had switched her shoes to Nike trainers.

"Next up," Nancy said, "Crew A, to the house with Miles and Roddy. Crew B, to the soundstage for one last pickup of audience at concert. Gwen, you weren't originally in that, but we want to get some of you in there, too. You guys will finish it pretty quickly and then join us at the house."

"No, no," Miles said, "the lip synch sequences, soundstage. Did someone forget?"

Nancy gave him an annoyed look. "I thought you said you wanted to do it by the swimming pool instead."

"Oh, right. Yes, apparently a total imbecile did forget: *me*. Whatever. How about you remind me of tomorrow's call order, too, before I fuck that up royally, too."

Nancy pulled out another stack of papers and handed one to him and then distributed the rest around. "You can't fuck up location tomorrow because it's all at the house. Full crew at four a.m., we'll do all the shots that require the largest number of people, including the stunts, let them go by lunch; Roddy, Gwen, and Mal in the afternoon, and then we'll grab the last Gwen and Mal shots before we wrap."

I could see why such a detailed schedule was necessary. Instead of filming the scenes in the order they would appear sequentially, the shooting schedule was determined by other logistical necessities.

I looked back at the call sheet for the rest of today and realized once I handed my tux to wardrobe I was free to go. The wardrobe assistant was waiting at the coat closet nearest the ballroom where she had all the hangers she could ever need. Our regular clothes were there.

Axel and I went back there to get out of our costumes. "Did Christina tell you what came in the mail?" he asked as he picked up his folded clothes.

"No, was she supposed to?" I put the jacket on the designated hanger.

"Wedding invitation. Well, strictly speaking a save-the-date card, and a letter asking for advice on where in LA to hold the reception."

I looked at him. "Whose wedding?"

He pulled his shirt over his head. "Layla's. She invited all five of us."

"Really." So that was why she had been trying to get in touch? "Who's the lucky fellow?"

Axel smirked at me but not because he was kidding. "Her girlfriend. Hey, are you going to come hang around during the lip synch sequences?"

I pulled my jeans on, zipping them carefully. "I don't relish hearing 'Razor Sharp' five hundred times today, thank you."

"You don't want to make sure I don't do anything untoward toward Gwen?" he joked.

Before I quite realized it, I had pushed him against the wall, my hand on his chest. "Don't you dare."

"You're mighty possessive for someone who drove her away."

"I'm not possessive. I care deeply about her well-being."

"All I'm going to be doing is, like, artfully dragging a flogger over her shoulders and swirling a knife around. Really."

I backed away from him, pulling my jacket on, unable to even comment on what he was about to do. I could picture it perfectly in my mind like a starving man fantasizing about a steak. I felt the yearning I thought I'd quenched but that had been rekindled and gradually stoked all day long now roaring like a bonfire. I hurried away from him without meeting his eyes. "See you in the morning."

I went directly home. My condo had a small yard, more of a garden, really, between a tall cedar fence and even taller hedges. There was a flagstone patio and a barbecue grill I had never used.

It would do.

I scoured the house for every Ariadne Wood book I could find. I hadn't taken much with me when I'd left England, but a few of her paperbacks and one dog-eared, highlighted, and underlined copy of *On a Midnight Far* had been among the things I had.

I tore the paperbacks into several pieces each, my shoulder muscles straining until the spines gave way, then dumped them into the bowl of the grill, doused them with whiskey, and lit them. It took a few tries to get it going, but then the flames leaped up, consuming more, faster.

I took a swallow straight from the whiskey bottle before I thought maybe I should quit drinking, too. Fine. I upended it into the flames, sending them upward.

I shed my jacket, let it fall to the stone behind me, and reached toward the fire. The same trick I used to do with a candle and the tip of my finger all those years ago I could do with the tongues of flame and my entire hand. My arm.

The odor of singed hair made my eyes water. And the pain told me I was alive, whether I deserved to be or not.

CHAPTER EIGHTEEN

MY TRUE SOUL

GWEN

The third day of shooting started early, so early the sun wasn't up yet, because they wanted to film some night scenes with the exterior of the house. I was starting to see why Miles was never without a cup of coffee in his hand. The wardrobe person checked her notes and took out a box with ten diamond engagement rings in it. "Let's find one that fits."

That wasn't the most intriguing element of my wardrobe for that day, though. That would be the breast shield the color of my skin that she molded to my chest. On top of that I wore a shirt that had been mostly torn open. The idea was that they could film the shirt all torn open like that without any of my actual skin being exposed, though it would look like it in the finished shot.

Wardrobe also dressed a stuntman to look like Mal, in a dark wig, black leather jacket, and jeans. They filmed him trying and failing to beat down the front door. The guy threw himself at the door pretty hard, too, hard enough that I worried he might actually succeed in breaking it. But it didn't, which set up the whole plot point about smashing the window.

The crew had installed a special plate of glass between the back patio and the sitting room, and they had a prop guitar painted to look like Mal's. The stunt coordinator was an older guy with a curly gray ponytail, round glasses, and a baseball cap. He handed the fake guitar to Mal. "We only get one take on this, so we're going to film you swinging and hitting the glass several times and it won't break but we'll get lots of footage of the swing that way."

"It's not breakaway glass?" Mal asked. "I thought they made these out of sugar for movies."

"Oh, they do, for props like bottles, but for a window that we need to film you through, it has to be crystal clear. This is tempered glass like a car windshield. When we film the smash, there's a popper at the bottom that'll do the actual breaking of the glass." He pointed out something on the floor that I couldn't see. "The pieces mostly fall straight down and you won't get too much spray into the room, but Gwen, Rod, you'll want to turn your faces away. Well, you'll turn away reflexively, I bet, but just in case. The pieces will be mostly little pebbles but you still don't want to get one in your eye or your mouth."

We walked through the sequence a few times, with Roddy and I positioned so that he had grabbed me from behind as I tried to flee and Mal swinging the guitar in slow motion. They'd already filmed a fight sequence with a stuntwoman before I got there and now they checked the position to make sure we matched up.

And then we did it. They filmed Mal several times running up to the glass and then finally the big smash. The noise was sudden and terrifying: the popper sounded like a gunshot, and Mal came flying into the room, hair wild, brandishing the guitar.

The crew broke out into applause and then immediately set about cleaning up the broken glass.

Roddy helped me to stand up straight. "Are you quite all right, my dear?"

My eyes were glued on Mal, who was standing there, breathing hard. A props person took the fake guitar away.

"Just a little startled," I said, putting my hand over my heart and forcing myself to look at Roddy and breathe, but all I could see in my mind was Mal, wearing his fury like a cape, like that time he'd played the Linder Mage. "I'll be fine in a minute."

When I looked back, Mal had vanished. I felt his absence like a sudden chill, like the fire had gone out.

Nancy came up to us. "Whew! Nothing like a little excitement at six in the morning. Might as well have you two do some close-ups of the struggle while we've still got some darkness in the bedroom."

They ended up having to shade over the bedroom windows from outside because the sun was coming up too fast, but I guess that worked.

The hardest part about filming the fight scenes is my body kept thinking roughhousing and Roddy tearing my shirt open was foreplay, so I had a few flushes of arousal. Fortunately they were easy to hide, and I had technical aspects of the action to focus on, like one segment of close-up where they filmed him trying to pry the engagement ring off my finger, I kept my hand balled in a fist and then was supposed to punch him in the eye with the ring.

I took the ring off to do the actual contact to Roddy's face, of course. They'd show a separate shot of my fist with the ring, then of the punch, and you wouldn't be able to tell the ring was missing from the shot.

Yes, it felt weird walking around wearing a super-classic diamond engagement ring. The fake stone was fairly huge so it would show up well on camera. I found myself staring at it during the lunch break down in the rec room. Had Mal been serious when he'd said we should stay together but not do BDSM anymore? Could I have traded one for the other?

No, it never would have worked. I would have always felt a part of me was being crushed. If he was truly going vanilla, I had to get over him.

Nancy came and sat beside me. "Nice rock, eh? A real one that size would've tripled our entire props budget."

"Yeah, I bet it would. So, tell me something. Why does Miles have a reputation for being such an asshole? He seems fine to me."

"Miles is a demanding man and when he feels strongly about things, he's not afraid to express himself," Nancy said between bites of chicken salad on a plastic fork. "But he hasn't had anything to fight over or anyone to fight with here. If anything, he was thinking, 'ugh, these rock stars are going to be lazy party animals.' But, no, they've been total troupers. Especially Mal."

I hid a smile. "You'd be the first person ever to say Mal's easy to work with."

Nancy chuckled. "Is he normally not so . . . cooperative?"

"I guess it's the same thing. When he feels really strongly about something, he can be impossible."

"Demanding men can be impossible, but when they're at their best, they're unstoppable," Nancy said, and then licked the last bit of chicken salad off her plate. "Okay, right back to it for me."

They filmed a few sequences with Mal and Roddy struggling with each other. Then we had to do various shots of us running up the street away from the house, hand in hand, escaping.

The first time I put my hand into Mal's, it felt like touching a live wire, like the current that ran through us magnetized us together. His eyes met mine and neither of us looked away until we realized the director was trying to get our attention.

What are you thinking, Mal? Are you having second thoughts about what you said?

He didn't let go of my hand for several minutes, even when we weren't filming, even when we were walking back to take our places.

Miles waved us over toward the gate at the street level. "How about a few with Gwen inside the gate, Mal on the outside. Gwen reaching a hand through the bars, Mal looking at her with angsty yearning in his eyes. Oooh, yes, *nailed it.*"

Then he had us both on the same side of the gate. "Now how about some angst-ridden gazing into one another's eyes. Mal, put your arm around her, two lovebirds about to fly from this cage. That's it."

Being pressed this close to him but having to pretend to be professional, when part of me wanted to just kiss him, or slap him maybe, or shake him until he saw sense, or cry on his shoulder, was difficult. Then again, having the appropriately distressed face of a woman being ripped apart inside, that I could do.

Mal looked equally distressed by my distress. I thought maybe he was just getting the hang of acting, until in a quiet moment he bent his head toward me. "Are you all right?"

"Of course I'm not all right," I whispered. "Heartbreaker."

"Gwen—"

"Okay, good," Miles shouted. "Last bit in this segment, Mal, you playing the guitar solo here in the middle of the street. Where's that guitar? The real one, not the prop. I know he's miming but come on, people." While the crew was busy with Mal, I went back to the rec room to wait. Roddy was there sipping water from a bottle. I got one myself and sat down with him.

"You all right, my dear? You look a bit emotionally taxed."

"You could say that," I said with a sigh.

"Let me guess. Things with our hero are not as smooth as they could be?"

The understatement startled me into laughing. "Hardly anyone knows but we broke up less than a week ago."

"Oh my. I hadn't realized it was quite that severe. He clearly dotes on you."

"Yeah, he loves me so much he told me I should leave him for my own good."

Roddy raised an eyebrow. "More honor than sense?" He patted my hand. "You poor dear." His cell phone rang and he waved me an apology as he answered it and hurried to the far side of the room to speak with whoever it was. His agent, perhaps.

Everyone else was outside or in the trailer, so I wandered upstairs and was surprised by the sound of a camera shutter clicking.

"That's beautiful," said a man with a very large camera held up to his face. He had another camera hanging from his neck. "Put your hands on your hips? Give me a coy smile?"

I did it without thinking and then looked around. None of the rest of the crew was in sight. He lowered the camera and I recognized him: Beau Lavern. I had a sudden sinking feeling—this was the same guy who had been overbearing at that record release party, too. "Excuse me, are you supposed to be here?"

"Just doing my job, ma'am," he said.

Maybe they hired photographers to document the project? I thought.

"If you could just sit here in the light, we could get a few nice shots. You look so pretty when you smile."

"Um, I don't think my character is supposed to look happy and smiley," I said, even as I sat down on the couch where he was pointing. "If you want to do smiley portrait shots, I could go put on the intact version of this shirt."

He already had a camera to his eye, this one digital, emitting a soft *beep* each time he pressed the button. "Oh no, this is fine, just fine. In fact . . ." He went to one knee in front of me, reached out and opened the shirt, exposing the bustier-shaped breast form that covered me. Before I could react—the thought that I was going to move away from him, complain, get him kicked off the set, had barely formed—he let out a whiny, "Oh for crying out loud, they're not even real."

I shifted away on the couch and pulled the tattered shirt closed. "Of course they're not. Excuse me, but you're being very—"

"Gwen, Gwen, I'm sorry," he said, putting the camera down and taking one of my hands before I could snatch it away. He was still on his knees and he held my hand in both of his. His fingers were sweaty and puffy. "I didn't mean to upset you. I'm just trying to capture the moment."

"Okay, well, I have work to do here—"

"I've wanted to tell you this for a long time. A very long time. But the time was never right. I think the right moment is finally here, though. Gwen Hamilton, I love you. No one in the world loves you more than I do."

Oh my God, help, I thought, but I couldn't bring myself to scream it. I was too paralyzed to scream.

"It's so hard to get close to you. I'm so glad we're finally alone."

I forced my mouth to move. "Mr. Lavern, I appreciate your admiration, but—"

"Don't go cold on me, Gwen. Not now. Not after everything I've done for you."

What the hell is he talking about?

"That spread in *EW*? All me. They wouldn't have even bothered with a picture of you if I hadn't pushed them to run it. Come on, you owe me at least a kiss for that. Show your appreciation." He leaned forward like he was going to push his mouth against mine.

"No!" I leaned back, trying to get my foot between my body and his, but all that happened was I got it caught on a camera strap.

"Don't be like this, Gwen, don't be difficult—"

"Difficult!" I tried to push him away with my free hand and that only made things worse. He launched himself onto me, his legs straddling my hips and trapping me against the couch while he tried to grab my free hand.

I tried to punch him in the eye with the engagement ring but I gashed him in the forehead instead.

"Bitch!" He trapped my hand in the crook of his elbow and I took a deep breath to scream.

That was when Mal hit him in the head with the guitar.

He was knocked off me onto the floor, and I scrambled over the back of the couch.

Amazingly, the guy wasn't unconscious. He staggered up, blood trickling from his forehead, and then rushed me like a tackle in football, his arms outstretched. I fled straight through the hole where the window was missing, and he chased me.

I didn't think he'd be able to run faster than me, but he brought me down only a few steps onto the manicured grass. I struggled to get away, twisting in his grasp, but I only succeeded in ending up on my back with him on top. I froze and stopped struggling when I realized he was holding a knife to my cheek.

"I didn't want to have to do this the hard way," he said.

"Neither did I," said Mal, who held a straight razor to Lavern's throat. He loomed behind him like a dark angel, the hand with the razor steady.

"Don't be stupid," Lavern said. "Just back away and I won't hurt her. I just want her to listen to me."

I could see Mal's face just beyond my assailant's. His eyes were narrow and his teeth set. "No. You will drop the knife or I will slit your throat."

"Are you kidding? I could scar her face. She'll never work again."

"The beauty of hers that moves me is deeper than her skin," Mal said.

"You're bluffing."

"I'm going to count to three." Mal's eyes met mine and I knew he was saying that for me. Whatever was about to happen was going to happen on three. "One."

"I just want to talk to her."

"Two."

"Come on, man!"

"Three!"

I twisted desperately away from the knife and heard Lavern scream. I scooted away on the grass and looked back to see Mal holding him by the hair. A couple more members of the crew moved in to help, Nancy and Roddy hurrying to help me up, Nancy asking me, "What happened? What happened?" Miles was ranting about security and how we really shouldn't have needed any on a location like this. One of the tech crew had zip-tied Lavern's hands behind his back and he was bellowing for his lawyer. Nancy rushed away to take a phone call.

Then I was standing alone and saw Mal was off to the side of the knot of people around the hollering madman.

Mal was looking at the shiny, clean straight razor in his hand, turning it back and forth as if he regretted it was actually unbloodied.

Then he saw me looking and closed it, slipped it away, and came to squeeze my hand. "Are you all right?"

I nodded, but my senses were still spinning and my heart wouldn't slow down. "You . . . you didn't cut him."

"Oldest mindfuck in the book," he said, patting the pocket where he'd tucked the razor. "Pretend to cut them with the dull side."

"You knew he'd let go of me to try to protect himself."

Mal nodded but did not smile.

"I really thought you were going to slit his throat," I said. "You really sold it."

"It's like Rod said. When you act, you don't 'pretend.' You feel your real emotions. I wanted that man dead for touching you, and I wanted to be the one to do it." He let go of my hand and pulled back.

"But you didn't." I desperately wanted him to hold me, to give me something solid to lean against, to put his arms around me. "Because you know where the actual line is. You know how to dance all the way to the edge without crossing it."

"I'm no hero," he said.

"You're *my* hero, and that's what matters." I felt my knees going weak.

"We'll see if the police agree," he said as the sound of a siren heralded their approach.

* * *

MAL

The police were brusque and thorough, separating us to take initial statements, then insisting we proceed to the police station for more of the same. By the time they were done with me, Gwen had long since been taken home. It seemed that ultimately they were not going to be charging me with assault, even though I gathered Beau Lavern dearly wanted them to. It appeared that he lived in a fantasy world where Gwen was his prize, his due, his one true love, even though they'd barely spoken in the past.

I heard that night from Axel—who'd heard via Ricki—that someone had been sending Gwen threatening e-mails, and it appeared to be the same man. A genuine stalker.

Then came a message from Nancy Cho asking if it was possible to meet them to do the last scene they needed to complete the video. Of course I agreed immediately.

After all, Gwen would be there.

"Mal, you still there?" Axel's voice came through the phone.

"Yes. Sorry, just answering a text." I was sitting on my back patio, looking at the charred ashes in the bottom of the grill. "Ax, tell me something."

"Sure, what?"

"You've known me longer than anyone."

"Yeah."

"Would you say I have trouble telling fantasy from reality?"

"No, why?"

"Because sometimes I imagine that she loves me."

"If we're talking about Gwen, she *does* love you. If you've got a delusion, man, it's that you don't deserve it."

For some reason his words felt like they seeped directly into my chest, like what had happened today had cracked my armor so much that what he said was finally getting through. "I'm an idiot."

"Yes, you are, but that doesn't mean you don't deserve love."

"I'm an irascible perfectionist who alienates the people I should be cultivating."

"Let me and Christina do the cultivating, Mal. You just do you."

"I seriously contemplated quitting everything a few days ago. Not just kink. Booze, the band—"

"Wait a second, I may have to take back what I said about you having a grip on reality."

"It was just the black dog nipping at my heels," I assured him. "Though perhaps I still prefer not being able to tell if negative thoughts are valid and, oh, thinking all positive thoughts are automatically valid."

"In other words, you may be depressed but at least you're not a wacko stalker who thinks you're the true reason behind people's fame?"

"Yes." Maybe it took seeing someone who was truly crazy to appreciate the measure of my own sanity. I gathered some sticks from under the evergreen bushes and put them into the grill. I lit them with a long match and they caught quickly. "Do you remember the night we got our tattoos?"

"Do I? How could I forget it? You could say it's permanently marked."

"Ha." I stared into the flames. He and I and Chino had gone to a tattoo parlor in Boston after one of the shows we'd played there, to an artist Axel knew from his days on the street. We'd been planning them for a while. Blackwork Celtic-style dragons. The artist took us into her shop at midnight and we didn't leave until morning, because it took all night to finish all three of us. Chino's went up the side of his leg, its tail around his ankle. Axel's wound around his right arm, onto his chest, and held his nipple delicately between his teeth. Mine was on my back, the wings across my shoulders.

The artist did mine last, and by the time she had started I had been slightly delirious from sleep deprivation.

"I had a vision that night," I said. The flames crackled and danced.

"What kind of a vision?"

"That I was stretching my wings, trying to fly, but I was too weighted down by the gold and jewels encrusting me. I had to shake them off before I could take off."

"Oh, there's no symbolism there at all. None."

"Hush. When I could finally fly, I went to the top of a mountain and shook the foundations of a temple until a beautiful woman came out and offered herself to me."

"And?"

"And I couldn't very well actually consummate penetration with her, being not her size. So I commanded the saddle maker there to make a saddle for her with an ivory phallus affixed to it."

"Huh."

"Thus did she give herself to me, and me to her at the same time, achieving a balance of power that should not have been possible between a dragon and a human."

"You were high on endorphins."

"Yes, I was." I threw a few more sticks into the flames and listened to them crackle. "But I think I finally know what the vision means."

"What does it mean?"

"It means I've been an utter fool. But at least I see that now."

* * *

GWEN

I dragged myself into the kitchen feeling like I had been run over by a truck. I guess being slammed to the ground by a bona fide stalker had some aftereffects even though medically I checked out fine. I wondered how Mal was doing. Had I imagined the connection between us when our eyes had met over the shoulder of my attacker? I didn't think I had.

"Wow, I didn't think you'd be up until at least noon," Ricki said from the breakfast table where she was sipping from a huge coffee mug while checking the morning papers on her tablet. "You had a rough day yesterday."

"I've got a call," I said, pulling the almond milk out of the fridge and pouring it into a bowl. "By which I mean an actor thing, not a phone call."

"I know what a call is," Ricki said with a gentle smile.

I got a spoon and sat down at the table. "We need to film one more scene that didn't get finished yesterday."

"There's more coffee in the carafe," she pointed out.

I nodded and got myself a mug and sat back down. It wasn't that early in the morning; I was just muzzy and out of it. "Anything leak to the news yet?"

"I saw a small thing about the 'incident' but nothing much. When they get wind of the e-mail thing, it might blow up a bit, but right now I'm not predicting anything bad for your career from the press."

"Good." I took a sip of the coffee.

"Gwen, are you sure you should go to a film shoot today?"

"Why, do I seem nervous?"

"You're distracted enough that you forgot to add cereal to your bowl."

I looked down into the bowl of almond milk. "Oh, I'm going low carb," I said casually, and picked up the bowl and drank it.

Then busted out laughing, which startled Ricki into laughing, too. She put her hand over her eyes. "You really had me going there for a second!"

Ha. So maybe I could act after all.

"Still," she said when we had settled down again, "I'd feel better if Riggs or Reeve drove you."

"Ricki, what are the chances I have *another* stalker? Zero. They have the guy in custody and he won't be making bail." I sipped a little more coffee. "Though maybe having Riggs take me wouldn't be a bad idea. Just because I'm tired. I didn't sleep well."

"I would imagine," Ricki said.

"Oh, nothing like that. It wasn't like I had nightmares reliving the attack or something. I just lay awake thinking about Mal. I don't know what's going on with him."

Ricki made a sympathetic face. "Is *anything* going on with Mal? The last thing you told me was it was over."

"I don't know. He goes to extremes. When I left Montreal, it was like the world had ended. But the past couple of days it's like I can see the wheels are turning in his head. We've had a couple of... moments. I mean, maybe it's wishful thinking on my part? I feel like he's regretting what he said in Montreal. Then he *did* rescue me..."

My sister looked at me over the top of her immense coffee mug. "Do you want him back?"

"I do," I said with a sigh. "If he'll come to his senses."

"Does he still want to quit kink?"

"I don't know. I mean, I know he's got some issues to work through. But seriously, Mal quitting kink would be like a lion going vegan."

"I guess the real question is would you be better off waiting for him to deal with his issues on his own or being with him when he does?"

I looked into my own coffee. "I'd much rather be with him while he figures it out, because then maybe I'll be part of the solution instead of the problem. I don't know if he's ready to hear that, though."

"Well, I hope he comes to his senses." Ricki got up from the table and stretched. "If he doesn't, you want to go for consolation sushi tonight?"

"Hmm, I don't know."

"You can have sashimi. That's low carb," she said with a wink as she headed toward the home office.

I smiled. My sister would be there to support me whether or not Mal flipped his lid and came up with another excuse why we shouldn't be together.

* * *

They had decided to do the shoot at a coffee shop the crew was able to commandeer after the morning rush had died down. There was one trailer parked outside. Riggs walked me all the way to the door of it. I told him I'd text when we were done, but it could be hours. That was just how these things went. Three and a half days of filming to make a three-minute video.

I didn't see Mal anywhere but maybe he wasn't there yet. I went to the wardrobe assistant first and she turned me around and around.

"I think we should stick with what you're wearing, Gwen. I mean, no offense, but you picked something really sweet and almost demure to wear today."

I was wearing a white cardigan sweater with the top button closed, beige capris, and espadrilles. "Cute but boring was what I was going for," I confessed.

"You're channeling your character is what it is," she said with a warm smile. "Go to makeup."

Makeup was all of two feet away, in the same section of trailer, which made me chuckle. The makeup artist was someone different from the previous day but she looked at reference shots and fixed my makeup and hair.

Still no sign of Mal, which was just as well since I hadn't figured out what I was going to say to him yet. *Hey, thanks for rescuing me, um, wanna hang out?* Yeah, no. Swoon and cry, *My hero!* and fall into his arms? Not likely.

Nancy came into the trailer, her radio at her hip and an earpiece in her ear. "We're going to start with some shots of you on the sidewalk, looking in the window, trying to see if he's here, pacing up and down, waiting for your rendezvous."

They had a few different cameras running, to get different angles, plus Miles swept in with a handheld a couple of times while I paced up and down with a hopeful yet slightly apprehensive look on my face.

Not pretending. Wondering if he was going to show up. Knowing that giving my heart to someone was such a huge deal. The entire future seemed wide open and yet I felt I'd never get through it if he refused to be there with me. *Mal, why? It'll work between us; I know it will. You just have to give it a chance: give yourself the chance to be your best self, too.*

"Okay," I heard Miles call to me from behind the cameras, "now you're going to look to the left and see him coming and your face should light up with delight. Okay? Action."

I looked to the left and there was Mal. He was dressed like a musician, which was to say like himself, wearing the black leather jacket with the dragon on the back, black jeans, and black boots. He had something small and black in his hand. A ring box. His hair was loose in the wind.

He walked slowly up to me, a contemplative expression on his face. A small smile showed in the tightening of one cheek. "They said I can say whatever I want since they're not using the audio."

"Right, of course," I said, then bit my lip. How was I supposed to play this? Miles wasn't saying anything. "So. How are you?"

"I'm well, and you?"

"Damn. You're always going to be better at the small talk game than me."

"My finishing school was more demanding than yours," he said, and a genuine smile appeared for a moment. Then he grew serious. "Here's what I really want to say, though."

He dropped to one knee, held up the ring box, and cracked it open.

My hands flew to my mouth in surprise. A *much* nicer-looking ring than the prop I'd worn yesterday was sparkling at me, the diamond glittering in the sun flanked by two small emeralds. *Is it real?* I mouthed.

He gave an infinitesimal nod.

Tears welled in my eyes. "No, really, is it real?"

"As real as I can be," he said. "I want you to be mine. In every possible way."

"The real me?"

"The real you. Every part of you. The part of you that calls to the beast in me, and the part that calls to my noble side." He was looking up at me and I felt keenly how strange it was for him to be the one on his knees. He swallowed. "And the part of you that brings those two sides of me together. I can't do that without you, Gwen. You are literally what has made me whole."

And you're what made me whole, I thought, but I couldn't speak past the lump forming in my throat.

"You know I'm quick to anger and slow to learn. I'm far from perfect."

Mal, you're perfect for me!

"But you make me want to be. My best self. The self I've discovered through my bond with you. It's going to take time. Maybe that's why I want you forever. Gwen Hamilton," he said firmly, his eyes shining almost as bright as the ring. "Will you marry me?"

Everything I'd been holding in burst out in a flurry of "Yes, yes, yes!" I practically knocked him over I kissed him so hard, until he steadied me and stood, never taking his mouth from mine, until his hands were locked in the small of my back, bending me as the kiss deepened.

"Cut!" Miles yelled. We didn't stop but the crew took that as their cue to break into applause.

EPILOGUE

The first time Mal and I were seen together in public after the engagement was about two months later on the red carpet at the American Music Awards, where The Rough was up for the Favorite Band, Duo, or Group award. The video for "Razor Sharp" had been released that week, and the tale of our engagement on set had become a huge news story.

Which meant that the photographers wanted to go nuts over my dress, and they wanted to see my hand. Not that you can really get good pictures of an engagement ring from ten feet away, but I couldn't go up close with every single one of them.

Mal didn't want to let go of me long enough for me to be photographed alone, but the handlers insisted this was how it was done and he relented, looming next to the backdrop waiting to claim me into his arms again. We took many photos together as well, and I placed my hand on his dark lapel to show off the ring best. I even heard a photographer shout "thank you!" when I did that.

The reporters were just as curious. "Is that 'the ring'?" the sideline reporter for *Entertainment Tonight* asked.

I showed it to her with a grin. "Yes, it's the real ring. It's a shame in the video you actually don't get much of a look at it."

She looked up at Mal and realized his earring had a matching silver-set emerald and diamond. "Classic and classy. So what was it like being proposed to on set?"

"A total surprise," I said.

"What gave you the idea to do it?" she asked Mal.

"We were going through a rocky patch in our relationship," he said smoothly. "I'd let misunderstandings between us get in the way of the truth. I'd stupidly suggested we take a step back. Proposing seemed the most definitive way to commit to taking a step forward, together."

I held in a laugh. I think she'd meant him to answer how he got the idea to do it live on camera, but I loved the answer he gave. "He got all the cast and crew in on the plot to surprise me," I added. "Got my ring size from the costume designer and everything."

"Sneaky!" she said. "I approve."

The next reporter was from one of the viral Internet sites I'd met at a WOMedia press event a few weeks before. She was filming me from her phone, and she also asked the "what was it like" question.

I gave the same answer. "A total surprise."

She turned the phone toward Mal. "What would you have done if she'd said no?"

"Reevaluated my worldview and life choices," he said seriously. That was Mal for you. He would answer any question truthfully and honestly but never in the way you expect.

At last we were past the media gauntlet and moving into the theater. Mal kept his hand at the small of my back. We ran into my agent on our way through the lobby.

"Simon, you remember Mal? Simon Gabriel, Mal Kenneally."

They shook hands. "I must say thank you for the tremendous

attention my client is receiving as a result of not only the video but also the stunt," Simon said. "Many people would have been reluctant to have something so personal exposed this way."

"I did not intend the proposal as a stunt," Mal said, "but I'm pleased it has had positive repercussions."

"Goodness, yes. My phone has been ringing off the hook since the story broke. Gwen, let's meet later this week, hmm? We have a lot of offers to sift through." He patted Mal on the shoulder. "Best wishes to you both."

As he walked away, Mal murmured to me, "Besides, there's so very much more to our personal lives we keep to ourselves." His hand slid over the sleek fabric of my gown and along my tailbone, where the edge of the chastity belt could be felt. "How are you holding up?"

"This thing is going to keep me wet for the entire evening," I whispered into his ear before I kissed him on the cheek.

"Good," Mal said, and kissed me on the hand before leading me toward our seats.

Maddie Rofel loves her job at the exclusive Governor's Club dungeon, but she's made it her business never to get involved with a guest—until now. Chino, charismatic drummer for a rock band, is new to the scene but catches on fast. Now Maddie intends to learn all his secrets—no matter how close to the edge her quest takes them both . . .

A preview of *Hard Rhythm* follows.

CHAPTER ONE

Chino Garcia strutted into the dungeon like the cock of the walk. Or as my dad used to call it, the walk of the cock. "A bad boy like that just wants to stick it somewhere warm," he had warned me.

When I was younger I hadn't heeded that warning. Bad boys were my catnip, the thing that made me roll on my back and yowl. I had plenty of fun, and so did they. But in my years in Hollywood I got jaded to the tattoos and the macho saunter.

Chino crossed the social room to greet Sakura and Ricki, and I saw Sakura look him up and down, perhaps trying to figure out if that cocky attitude translated to dom or sub. I was curious mainly because I hadn't figured him out myself, not because I was interested. In the months since Axel's bandmates had joined, I still hadn't seen Chino play. Oh sure, he joined in happily enough when it was Ricki's birthday and Axel made her crawl through "the paddy-whack machine" like a kindergartner, or that time with the circle jerk. But just because he was sexually adventurous, it didn't reveal whether he was a sadist or a masochist, a top or a bottom, a dom or a sub.

He slipped his leather jacket off to show he was wearing nothing but tattoos underneath. I felt as if a cool breeze had just blown across my own bare shoulders, goose bumps rising and my fingers itching to touch his ink all of a sudden.

Stop it, I told myself. *He annoys the fuck out of you, and you're better off steering clear of him.* I didn't appreciate how Chino seemed to turn everything into a joke. But I found myself adjusting my corset as my nipples hardened against the supple leather when he threw back his head and laughed at something Sakura said. I stared at the long line of his neck, leading down a buff, well-inked chest. Playing drums kept him in ridiculously perfect shape.

My hormones must have been peaking or something. I made myself tear my eyes away from him and went to do a rounds check of the rooms, to see which were in use and whether any of them needed a resupply of condoms or lube. It was still early in the evening, and though Kresley Palmer had strapped his wife over the new padded spanking bench in the Inquisition Room, everyone else was still socializing and warming up.

When I came back, Gwen was showing the new studded paddles to the group. "Can't wait to find out what these feel like!" she was saying. "But I have to wait until Mal gets back."

Chino picked one up and swung it in slow motion like a tennis forehand. He made eyes at me. "Hey, Madison, aren't you the one to usually show off new things around here?"

"You bet I am," I snapped, holding out my hand for the paddle in challenge. "I'd love to see how many you can take before you beg for mercy."

He twirled it by the leather loop on the handle instead of handing it over. "Is that right? Who do you think could take more, you or me?"

Sakura's eyes lit up and she came between us. "If you wanted a fair test, I could paddle you both..."

Chino's eyes were locked on mine, though. "Naw. I think the only way it'd be fair is if we take turns beating each other. You think you can take ten at a time, Maddie? Twenty?"

"Twenty per set, no bondage, hands on the wall, drop hands and you lose," I said, staring right back at him. Oh, I was so on fire to put him in his place, to make him lose that smirk.

"Agreed," he said. "Should we flip a coin to see who goes first?"

I clucked my tongue. "*Tsk*, no. You can beat me first to make sure this contest isn't over too quickly."

He raised an eyebrow as if to say *touché*, and Sakura chuckled, looking back and forth between us. It was she who said, "And what does the winner get from the loser, hmm?"

"Fifteen minutes in private to do whatever we want," Chino said.

"Does the Rotorvator work on men, too?" I asked.

"Definitely," Gwen said.

"Then I know what my fifteen minutes of entertainment will be," I said with a wicked grin. "Sakura, will you judge the contest?"

"Surely," she said with a wicked grin of her own.

Chino gave a little bow in my direction and then gestured toward the empty area of wall across from the Catherine wheel. "If you'll assume the position, please."

I took my skirt off to reveal my thong underneath and placed my hands on the wall. There was no way I was going to lose this contest. Gwen had nicknamed me "Iron Butt" after the first time she'd tested new hardwood paddles on me. I was sure Chino was either going to be all bravado and turn it into a joke or he was going to turn out to be a secret sub, who was going to love being paddled... in which case I might technically lose the contest, but in the big picture I will have won. Fantasies of him looking up at me from his knees, with his ink-black hair plastered to his neck by a passionate sweat, entertained me while I waited for him to start.

What was taking him so long anyway? I glanced back. He was gathering a crowd of spectators.

And he'd stripped down to nothing. My jaw dropped. The real thing was even better than I had imagined. His entire body was lean, hard muscle, not the chunky bulk of a weight-lifting nut but the powerful form of a man who actually used his muscles for something. He'd even stripped off his leather pants, revealing the dragon tattoo on his leg that matched Mal's and Axel's, but I found my eyes drawn to the graceful curve of his cock—already hard, just from anticipation of paddling me? If so, there went my theory that he was a closet subbie.

"You ready?" he said.

"Waiting for you," I sneered.

"Oh ho, so that's how it's gonna be." He tucked the paddle under his arm and ran a hand over my bare buttock, as if feeling out where exactly to hit. "I'll count."

Twenty strokes isn't that many if the beating gets spread around. After all, that's only ten on each butt cheek usually, and with a butt as round as mine the target was pretty wide. And at first he seemed determined to spread the redness all over. He'd barely gotten one good swat in on each part of my bottom before it was time to switch.

He handed me the paddle with a little bow and took my place on the wall. I imitated him, rubbing my hand over the peach fuzz of his buttocks before I took to swinging the paddle. Unlike me, he had hard, tight buns, easy to catch both in one swung. I swung upward slightly, catching the tenderest part of the buttocks—the underside—with each swat. He gritted his teeth, and by the time I neared twenty he was grunting on each blow.

His turn again. "Remember, Madison," he said as he ran his hand over the striking zone, "all you have to do to make the pain stop is put your hands down."

"*Tsk.* Not likely."

"As you wish." He stepped back and swung.

This time he hit much harder and it was me who grunted. Apparently he'd gone easy on me for the first round, but now the gloves were off. He was putting a full swing on each blow and leaving the paddle against my skin so the studs would dig in. Still, I'd suffered worse. This wasn't that bad...

Until he got to eleven and I felt my palms prickle with sweat against the wall. What was going on? All of a sudden there wasn't enough oxygen in the room, but as I sucked in breath after breath the feeling only got worse instead of better.

I felt his hand on my shoulder, solid and warm. The blows had stopped and his voice was calm in my ear. "You all right?"

"Of course, I'm all right." I blinked. Wasn't I? I let out a breath. It was just a little adrenaline rush, I told myself. No big deal.

He sounded bemused. "Because it's your turn."

"Oh." I stood straight, my heart still pounding, but my head high. "I lost count."

I was determined not to lose the contest, but somewhere inside me a battle was raging, a battle to keep my heart. A battle I'd already lost, I just didn't know it yet.

ACKNOWLEDGMENTS

Even though writing is a solitary pursuit, making books is not. These words wouldn't be reaching you right now without the love and encouragement of my agent Lori Perkins, the support of my twenty-five-year partner in life and love corwin, and the talents of the team at Forever, Megha Parekh, Madeleine Colavita, Marissa Sangiacomo, Elizabeth Turner, Jodi Rosoff, Michelle Cashman, and the rest of the gang. I also had the advice and encouragement of writer Melanie Fletcher, who took the early manuscript out for a test drive, and beta-readers Beth Bernobich and Don Luis. And thanks to Jessica and Chas at Rock Star Literary who wrestled with promo and publicity for me so I had time to actually write the book.

Thanks to Girl Scout Cookie for the fire play lesson and various folks from the Geeky Kink Event for helping me with, ahem, "research" on role-playing fantasy scenes: you know who you are. And to everyone carrying the BDSM community torch at the New England Leather Alliance and the Fetish Fair Fleamarket,

Jack, Percy, Iya, Leah, Amanda, Kerry, Danny, Rob, Dyanne, Maggie, and others. Also, CandiAnne at NLA: International—you folks continue to rock the world with awesomeness and education.

I also would like to thank the late Tanith Lee for inspiring fantasies for decades.

Last, thanks to the baristas at Simon's Coffee Shop, where most of this book was written, and the guys at Bourbon Coffee on Mass. Ave where most of the rewrites were done: both shops play awesome music for writing a book like this and they keep the tea flowing.

ABOUT THE AUTHOR

Cecilia Tan writes about her many passions, from erotic fantasy to baseball. Not only is she an author, but she has also edited more than fifty erotic anthologies and founded her own publishing house, Circlet Press. Her short fiction has appeared in numerous magazines and her nonfiction on baseball has been in *Baseball Ink*, *Gotham Baseball* magazine, *Yankees* magazine, *Yankees Annual*, and elsewhere. Cecilia currently resides in Cambridge, Massachusetts, with her lifelong partner and three cats.

You can learn more at:
CeciliaTan.com
Twitter @ceciliatan
Facebook.com/thececiliatan